MW00324991

HALL OF BONES

The Brotherhood of the Eagle Book 1

Tim Hardie

TJH Publications UK

Copyright © 2020 Tim Hardie

All rights reserved

The characters and events portrayed in this book are fictitious. Any similarity to real persons, living or dead, is coincidental and not intended by the author.

No part of this book may be reproduced, or stored in a retrieval system, or transmitted in any form or by any means, electronic, mechanical, photocopying, recording, or otherwise, without express written permission of the publisher.

ISBN 978-1-8381824-1-0

Cover design by Anne Hudson

For my daughters, Emma and Megan

MAP OF LASKAR

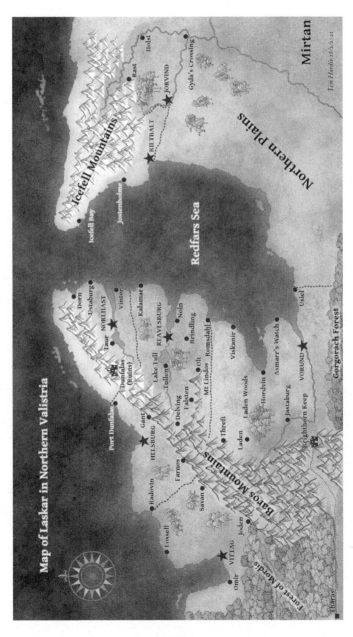

MAP OF ALASKA

PROLOGUE

The chain above me creaks in the wind, rattling as it twists this way and that. I must have slept a little since being forced into the cage. Now the cold has woken me. It's dark, with dawn still some time away. I close my eyes, trying to find rest, although my ravaged body offers me no respite from my wounds. I know that when sleep comes it will be long and black, for my time in Amuran is almost done. Tears course unbidden down my cracked and raw face, as I find myself imagining Desta's arms around me one last time. Would that I could return to the time when I was a child, when life was more carefree. Yet Dinas marks the endless flow of the river of time and its current ceaselessly travels one way, bringing us all to Navan at the end of our allotted span. I have wondered many times in recent days what I will find when Navan greets me at the Halls of the Dead. How will my life be judged? Better than my death, I hope; one only reserved for traitors and kinslayers.

There is a scratching against the bars of the cage, accompanied by the flapping of wings as the crows squabble over the best perch from which to peck at my body. The constant agony is so much part of my identity I'm unaware of the sharp pain as their beaks worry at my ragged and torn flesh. Soon it will be over, I tell myself. Soon. Please. It's odd to think that for so many years I was happy here as I grew up in my father's care. Ulfkell's Keep was my family home and I try to remember those times, long before the Great Hall ran red with blood.

1

CHAPTER 1

"You're lying."

"No, I'm not, Rothgar. Halfhand's even tougher than old Etta. Look," my elder brother Jorik boasted, lifting his white linen shirt to show me his back. Sure enough there were bruises there, already purpling. I stared at the welts, a mixture of awe and envy gnawing the pit of my stomach. "We used real axes, I'm telling you," he continued grimly as he put his clothes back in place. "You'll have to grow some muscles if you're going to survive your first lesson with the weapons master."

"Then why did he hit you on the back? Were you running away?"

"Why you ..."

Jorik was right; I was far smaller but also quicker and nimbler, dodging his grasp and darting off, running past the feasting table of the Great Hall. Jorik was after me in a second, easily gaining with his longer legs. I looked back, laughing, and ran straight into something solid, sending me crashing to the ground. Kolfinnar Marlson, chief of the Reavesburg Clan, regarded me from a great height as Jorik skidded to a halt behind me.

"My boys," he cried warmly as if this scene were nothing out of the ordinary, which was true enough. "Dust yourselves off and take your places at the table. We play host to Gautarr and his son this evening." My father was a powerful physical presence, despite being well into his forties. Barrel-chested and broad-shouldered he was a head taller than most of the men of Reavesburg. Even at fourteen it was obvious Jorik had inherited our father's physique. I took after Mother's slenderer frame. I had high hopes that after a few more feasts I would soon catch up.

We took our places near the head of the feasting table. The seats to the left and right of my father were reserved for those of significant rank, though I noted that my little sister, Nuna, with her golden locks and winning white-toothed smile, soon inveigled herself onto my father's lap. With the death of our mother, Father had a special place in his heart for his seven-year-old daughter. My mother died bringing her into this world and Father cherished Nuna all the more because of that, rather than dwelling on bitterness. Everyone loved Nuna. She had a way of brightening a room with her presence. As the honoured guest and one of Father's jarls, Gautarr Falrufson of Romsdahl sat in the place of honour at my father's right hand side. A few years older than his host, even the massive grizzled warrior was not immune to Nuna's charms, a broad smile spreading across his face as she fed him sweetmeats from her plate. Gautarr's son, Ragnar, a serious young dark-haired man, seemed less enthused, regarding everyone at the table with a suspicious frown. Gautarr's men at Romsdahl defended the southern border of our lands against the Vorund Clan and were held in high regard by our people.

It was a grand occasion and I noted that even Etta, my aged tutor and Father's counsellor, had been persuaded out of her chambers to attend. Olfridor Halfhand clapped Jorik on the back, congratulating him on his latest lesson, oblivious to how this made him wince. As the evening wore on I'm sure my father and Gautarr discussed some significant matters of state. I paid little attention as I crammed my face with fresh bread, boiled pork, salted cheese, smoked fish and pastries. By the end I was too full to move, convinced that by morning I would have grown an inch taller. I was sleepy too, although I had no intention of retiring. Not until Darri, the resident bard of Ulfkell's Keep, had performed for us.

Darri entered the Great Hall with a flourish, settling the noisy crowd with a haunting melody on his lyre. As his audience stilled, he took his usual place by the fire and began with a song about Reave. Always a popular subject, the young bard soon had us all singing along as he recounted the great journey of the clans to escape the ravages of war and find a new life in the harsh lands of the north. Some of the older warriors wept, including Olfridor, as he took us on that long and tragic journey with Reave. It was hard to believe my father now sat in the same chair Reave once occupied one hundred and fifty years ago. In moments, however, Darri altered the sombre and reflective mood, striking up some rousing chords on his lyre before leading the guests in a series of riotous drinking songs. Jorik told me some of them were about *ladies* and should never, ever be repeated in front of Nuna (who had long since been taken, protesting loudly, to her bed). I nodded solemnly, although at ten I had only the vaguest idea what they meant.

All too soon Finnvidor's gentle hand was resting on my shoulder. The commander of Reavesburg's warriors and jarl of Ulfkell's Keep, Finnvidor Einarrson was of an age with my father. Whilst his chief had broadened with the years Finnvidor remained lean and fit and no one could match him with a sword. He was reputed to be a fearsome warrior, although his quiet calm authority drew the respect of his men.

"Come, young master. It's time you were abed." Finnvidor must have seen me get ready to protest as he carefully steered me from the hall. "Your mother would never have permitted you to stay awake until this hour, Rothgar, I can assure you of that."

By all accounts my mother had doted on me and my brother. As she died when I was three years old I had only the haziest of memories of her, so Jorik used to tell me how she would play with us and recounted the songs she used to sing. My earliest memory was her funeral, my father's face a stone mask as he stood before her pyre. Just seven years old, Jorik was crying freely beside me as he held my hand. I remember watching as the flames took hold whilst my father spoke of her lovingly to the assembled throng of mourners, representing every important family of the Reavesburg Clan. He seemed assured that, when the time of judgement came, the Creator would weigh her life and consider her to be worthy; since she was my mother and I was only three I knew my father must be right. I imagined the sparks rising from the pyre were fragments of her soul, bound for Navan's Halls. As dusk crept across the sky each one was carried upwards into the heavens by the wind in a gently ascending whirlpool, dancing before my eyes until their red glow vanished. And still Jorik cried at my side, tightly clutching my hand, as if fearful I too would otherwise vanish.

"You're quiet, young man," Finnvidor observed as we wended our way slowly through the dark corridors of the keep, the sounds of drunken revelry fading behind us into the night.

"I was thinking of my mother," I said simply.

"Alaine was a beautiful woman." Finnvidor's voice in the darkness sounded as sad as I felt. "Your sister is the image of her, you know."

"So people say," I replied, suddenly keen to change the subject. Finnvidor was a warrior and I didn't want him to see me cry; I was the chief's son and it was my duty to be strong. Finnvidor sensed my discomfort, saying no more, leaving me to my thoughts as he escorted me in silence the remaining way to my chambers.

CHAPTER 2

The loss of my mother meant I treasured the time I spent with my father all the more. As I grew older, I realised it must have been difficult for him to look after three children as well as rule his kingdom. However, even when he was away or occupied with affairs of state, there was always someone in the keep entrusted with our care. Finnvidor was never far away, the jarl's sword sworn to protect Kolfinnar's children as much as it was to guard the clan chief himself. Old Etta schooled the three of us, so that we each learned our letters, numbers and history. Whilst Nuna's maids, Amma and Katla, helped teach her the finer points of being a lady of noble birth, it was Olfridor Halfhand, my father's weapons master, who taught Jorik the arts of war. Halfhand took on potential warriors from the age of ten, and only then if he thought them ready. Having reached my tenth birthday in the spring of the year 202, I fully expected to receive my summons to the training circle. As the weeks wore on and spring gave way to summer no call came and I began to wonder why I remained forgotten.

"Olfridor knows your age and desire to prove yourself," my father reassured me when I confronted him on the subject one evening. "He's seen you fight with wooden swords against Bram and Haarl up and down the length of the Great Hall often enough. It was *my* suggestion he take you and Brunn Fourwinds' son together, when young Bram turns ten this summer. There's also another lad he's agreed to take on at my request, so it makes good sense for the three of you to begin your training together." My disappointment must have shown in my face, for my father put his strong arm gently round my shoulder and hugged me. "Your time will come soon enough.

When you're covered head to toe in bruises and every muscle in your body aches, you'll wish you were still playing with those wooden swords, trust me. Listen, the weather's set fair and if that's the case tomorrow morning let's take *Marl's Pride* out to sea. I've seen far too much of the inside of these walls lately."

Hardly able to sleep with excitement that night, I woke early and rushed to the window, where I was greeted by the morning sun glittering off the flat waters of the Redfars Sea. Father kept his promise and Brunn Fourwinds, captain of *Marl's Pride*, welcomed us warmly on board. His crew scurried around him, making the ship ready. The great longship of fifty oars had been built by my father for one purpose – to strike fear and wage war on our rival clans. As its sail, emblazoned with the eagle of the Reavesburg Clan, unfurled and caught the wind we seemed to fly over the waves with each beat of the oars. We headed east down the widening estuary of the River Jelt, Reavesburg's wooden walls and the stone towers of Ulfkell's Keep rapidly receding from view.

"You've lived up to your name this morning, Brunn," Father remarked.

"Aye, Culdaff favours us, and no mistake," said Brunn, a wide white-toothed, amiable grin splitting his beard. The laws of Reave clearly stated the Laskan Clans turn their backs on the gods, following their failure that led to the War of the Avatars. However, sailors like Brunn still offered up their traditional prayers to Culdaff, avatar of the air and winds, and Nanquido, avatar of the waters and the seas. "So, what'll it be? The north coast to Kalamar or south to Romsdahl?"

"Neither," my father laughed. "Let's take her out into the open water and show the boy real seamanship." Brunn nodded and gave the order. By late morning we had left the mouth of the River Jelt behind us and struck out east for the open sea.

I still think fondly of the first time my father took me out to sea as a boy. I would only have been four, still mourning my mother, and I think my father's need to escape Reavesburg was as great as my own that day. The weather was nowhere near as favourable as on this voyage, so the wild iron grey waters of the Redfars Sea had seemed to me like the very edge of the world. As *Marl's Pride* rose and fell with each great foam-flecked wave it wasn't long before I retched back my breakfast, leaning weakly over the side. Today I ran freely about the deck, my friend Bram alongside me, both of us as at home on the water as on dry land. Brunn Fourwinds bellowed orders and his crew swiftly ran to obey his commands. My father looked on with satisfaction as the shore receded behind us and soon we were surrounded by the Redfars Sea, with only a few noisy gulls wheeling about high in the sky for company.

"Which way lies Riltbalt, Son?" my father asked as he clapped a hand on my shoulder. The question was an easy one and I grinned as I pointed east across the blue sea, imagining a distant coast I had never seen where the rival Riltbalt Clan's territory lay. I could see from the look Brunn exchanged with his son Bram that I was right. My father nodded in approval. "So you'll have no trouble telling me where Vorund lies."

"South," I laughed, though I felt a little uneasy. The Vorund Clan were our fiercest enemies, their chief Asmarr ordering frequent raids on our shores. "Father, you don't mean to set sail that far south, do you?" Seeing my worried expression, my father smiled.

"No, Son. One day, when Halfhand tells me you're ready, you'll make that voyage as all men who lay claim to being a warrior of the Reavesburg Clan must do. If we had the time, I'd sail us north to show you the Icefell Mountains that lie on the edge of the Redfars Sea, marking the beginning of the Endless Ocean itself. They say that only the Rannoch Mountains stand taller. And in time you'll stand on the Northern Plains. The people there are so wedded to their horses they don't trust the sea. The grasslands where they live stretch as far as the eye can see, in every direction, with not a tree in sight until you reach the cursed Gorgorach Forest. When I landed there with my own father, I could hardly believe such a place existed."

"And the Baros Mountains and Lake Tull," I said, imagining them all. "Etta has shown me the ancient maps, with the Norlhast Clan lands bordering ours to the north and Vorund and the Northern Plains to the south. And to the west, beyond the Baros Mountains you find the Helsburg and Vittag Clans, who are our allies and trading partners." I smiled, pleased to have a chance to show off what I had learned.

My brow furrowed as a thought struck me. "Father, why are they called the Northern Plains if they lie to the south?"

My father and Brunn laughed aloud. "Because that map of Etta's was drawn by a southerner," Brunn explained. "And the folk round those parts still call themselves the Northern Plainsmen, so the name has stuck, whether it seems a sensible one or not to people like us. You've got to remember that in Laskar pretty much *everything* lies to the south."

"I'm ten now, Father, and soon I'll be a man. Jorik has been to Kalamar and Romsdahl already, whereas I've scarce set foot beyond Reavesburg. I'm old enough, and I should see the lands you rule. And those beyond, as you said."

"Aye, the world is larger than many folk realise, and you'll see more of it in time, Rothgar, I promise. It only seems like yesterday that your mother was holding you to her breast. Things change so quickly." My father became lost for a moment, his eyes gazing far out to sea. "Brunn," he barked suddenly. "Is this really as fast as this damned ship can go?"

**

It was close on nightfall when *Marl's Pride* slid silently into the docks. I was surprised to find a crowd waiting there to greet us. I spotted Jorik and Finnvidor amongst them and knew something had happened. It was obvious that my father sensed it too.

"Finnvidor," he called. "I hardly expected a guard of honour on my return."

"There's news from the south," the jarl replied as Fourwinds' crew hurried to tie *Marl's Pride* to her moorings.

"What's Gautarr demanding *now* that warrants a delegation at this time of night?"

"No. I mean news from the Vorund Clan. This would be better discussed in the keep, chief."

My father shrugged. "If this is as important as you make out, Einarrson, it'll be the gossip of the whole of Reavesburg soon enough. I'd rather hear sooner, so tell me what you know."

"Chief Asmarr is dead," Finnvidor replied flatly. "He's been murdered, and by all accounts it was his youngest son who cut his throat. The Vorund Clan has a new chief and he has blood on his hands."

***

I followed in my father's wake, almost forgotten in the press of men surrounding him. When he reached his chambers in Ulfkell's Keep only Finnvidor, Olfridor, Jorik and Etta were allowed inside. As Finnvidor moved to close the door his grey eyes met mine as I looked up hopefully.

Father beckoned me inside. "Let him stay. As I said, it will be common gossip by morning anyway. Best he hears it first hand from those who know what they're talking about."

"To be frank, we know little enough," Etta remarked. When I had first met her, Etta was already rumoured to be in her ninetieth year. Age had bent her back, so that she walked with a stick, and her face was a papery mass of whiskers and wrinkles. Her long grey hair was always unkempt, although today she had loosely tied it back into a ponytail. My father valued her insight and experience and Etta was never far from his side when he needed counsel.

"What *do* we know?" my father asked.

"That Asmarr, the most powerful chief of the Laskan clans, lies dead. And in his place, his fourth son, Adalrikr, now rules the clan, having slain his own father and his three elder brothers."

"Adalrikr's little more than a boy," Olfridor added. One of my father's oldest and closest friends, he was a great bear of a man. At fifty-two he was almost a decade older than my father but remained a powerful physical presence. After losing two fingers in a battle with the Vorund Clan, Olfridor had decided the leadership of Reavesburg's warriors should be passed to a younger man. Many expected he would be named jarl of Ulfkell's Keep – instead that honour went to Finnvidor Einarrson. Halfhand had contented himself with training the next generation of warriors, leaving the politics and the command of the men in the keep to Finnvidor. Still, the death of a clan chief was significant news, enough to rouse even Olfridor's interest.

"Aren't these good tidings?" he asked. "We've suffered at Asmarr's hand for many years, so I'll not shed a tear on his account. The young lad in his place offers little threat to us, surely?"

Etta scowled and shook her head. "He's no longer a boy, Olfridor. Adalrikr is twenty-two and a grown man. In any case, any *lad* that murders his father and his own kin who were expected to succeed Asmarr concerns me. They all died on one night, which tells me this was planned well in advance. Adalrikr could not have acted alone in this, so he must have allies within the clan, certainly enough to raise him to power."

"I'll confess I know little of this youngest son," Finnvidor admitted. "He's no more than a name to me. Any raids against our shores have been led by the eldest sons, so our paths have never crossed."

"So, do we face a new enemy, or is our old foe about to turn on itself?" asked my father.

"Until Adalrikr shows his hand, we can only guess," Etta said. "It depends on how secure his grip on power is. There's clearly been no appointment by a clan moot. Adalrikr declared himself chief before his father's body was cold, so who knows how the other noble families in Vorund will view that."

"If those who oppose his rule fear their throats will also be opened with a knife, then I doubt there will be many calls for a clan moot," Finnvidor muttered sourly. "We need to know more about what's happening inside Vorund Fastness itself."

Etta gave Finnvidor a shrewd look. "My spy has already risked much to release the bird that brought these tidings to me. I can ask no more of them."

"So, what do we do?" Jorik asked. He looked so young in this company yet one day he would be expected to succeed my father as clan chief, if he were deemed worthy by the Reavesburg Clan's own clan moot.

"We wait," my father answered. "Let's see whether this new bear has claws and designs on our lands. Those who seize power through treachery are often betrayed themselves. Adalrikr's time as chief may last little longer than the current season."

"If Tyrfingr Blackeyes' men have sided with him, he may last longer than that," said Olfridor. Tyrfingr's reputation was as black as his name, and for the past three years his ships were the ones landing most frequently on our shores under the banner of Vorund's bear. Blackeyes had been one of Asmarr's most feared warriors. Had he fallen with his chief or joined forces with those who wielded the knife?

"The message I received was brief, so the fate of Tyrfingr Blackeyes remains to be seen," Etta replied. "You're right, there's little we can do now other than see how this young man fares as he leads his clan. All the same, the manner of his rise to power is ... troubling. Finnvidor, you would do well to send more men to our watch towers. Birds and riders must be sent out as well, to bring this news to Kalamar and Romsdahl without delay. Johan and Gautarr will both want to know of this."

My father crossed his arms and nodded at Finnvidor. "Do as she says. If this Adalrikr wishes to test our strength he'll not find us wanting or unprepared."

***

"Rothgar. At my time of life I count every breath a blessing. Can you explain to me why I should waste a single one of them with you if you fail to pay attention to your studies?"

Whilst I enjoyed a lofty position within my clan, Etta showed me no favour. I began my formal lessons with her when I was five and she had been tutoring my brother Jorik for two years before that. Today I was inattentive, wishing I was sparring with Halfhand in the training grounds, as my brother was this morning. In Etta's presence, that was a dangerous approach.

"Look at this," Etta continued, waving the piece of slate before me. Laskan runes took up little more than half a line. "Don't think my eyes are so weak I can't tell you've not done your work. We've been here for nearly an hour and this is all you have to show for it."

I set to work at once. I learned quickly that disobedience earned a sharp crack on the ear and her acid tongue was to be feared. Even my father seemed afraid of Etta and his jarls all treated her with trepidation. Although one of her beetle black eyes had developed a milky film she could still read well enough with her good eye and if I made even the smallest of errors in my writing she was swift to correct them. I concentrated hard on forming each letter and word perfectly and the remaining hour of our lesson soon passed.

"You've a steady hand," Etta remarked after she inspected my work, wiping the slate clean. It was a sure sign she had found no mistakes requiring her admonishment and I couldn't help suppress a grin. "When you apply your mind to a task, Rothgar, you do it well. Just remember that there's more to a man than a strong sword arm. Your time with Halfhand will come soon enough, and I've no doubt you'll throw yourself into it whole-heartedly. However, you should exercise your mind as well as your body. A clan chief who rules only with the sword sleeps wakefully and their life is short, as Adalrikr Asmarrson the Kinslayer is soon to discover. If you understand your people's hearts, possess wisdom and learn from the knowledge of your forefathers your life will be a long one."

"You speak as if I'll be clan chief one day, Etta. I won't. That honour falls to my brother, not me." I had blurted out the words without thinking. Etta looked at me shrewdly, her eyes narrowed and almost lost in the crows' feet that surrounded them. Then she smiled, a rare event, revealing the few remaining teeth in her mouth.

"Trust a child to speak to their mind, plain and simple. Yes, you're right; everyone expects Jorik to become clan chief and he has acquitted himself well in preparing for that task. Hroar's line is strong, clearly, even to the fourth generation. Yet do you think your father rules alone? Without the support of his jarls and the other noble families, our laws – the same laws that Adalrikr has flouted so brazenly – allow him to be swept aside if a challenge is made and he does not secure the votes needed at the clan moot. A chief must be strong and have the confidence of his people. Your father needs Johan to the north and Gautarr to the south to stand with him if he is to exercise his rule. Should your brother seek the clan's blessing when his time comes, you must help him. A clan chief needs his jarls. A jarl with a strong sword arm is valuable, true enough. Possessing a sharp mind is worth far more. Your father loves Olfridor like a brother, yet he chose Finnvidor as his jarl. Think on that awhile, young man."

The idea that one day I might be jarl of Ulfkell's Keep in Finnvidor's place, serving my brother as chief, was hard to imagine. Our father seemed so strong, he would surely live for many long years and his people loved him. No one would dare challenge him by calling a clan moot, I reasoned. No one else could ever take his place. "I still prefer the sword to the slate, Etta. Darri never sings great ballads about the men who knew all their letters."

"Boys," Etta laughed. "Kolfinnar has no idea of the task he has given me, trying to hammer some sense into your wild head. Go. Find something to occupy yourself with, before I change my mind and ask you to recite the histories of the seven chiefs that ruled Reavesburg before your father." That prospect didn't appeal, so I ran from the room as fast as I could, with Etta's cackling laugh echoing behind me.

CHAPTER 3

The town of Reavesburg was built predominantly of wood, although more recently quarried stone from the mountains had been used for some newer buildings, as good timber was becoming scarce. Etta told me that when her grandmother was a young girl, Clan Chief Reave first brought his people to this land, naming the town he founded on the banks of the River Jelt after him. On first hearing that story I found it hard to imagine someone Etta knew personally had lived through such events. This was during the first decades of the Fallen Age, after the old kingdoms from the Age of Glory had been swept away and the War of the Avatars was still recent enough for it to be in living memory. Etta told me it was the Creator himself who finally ended the great battle between the avatar Morvanos who, with his followers, had sought to take control of Amuran, and Vellandir and his allies who opposed him. Their seven-year war brought Amuran to the brink of destruction, and so the Creator banished them all to the Void in order to bring the conflict to an end. Only those who had chosen not to fight on either side were spared; Nanquido, ruler of the waves, Culdaff, bringer of the winds, Bruar, who gave fire its spark, Rannoch, shaper of the earth, Dinas, keeper of time and Navan, guardian of the Halls of the Dead.

The end of the War did not bring peace, for whilst the warring avatars had been banished their armies remained. The ancient land of Valistria was plunged into a civil war that raged for generations. Reave had shown there was another way, teaching that never again should people place their faith in the wisdom and guidance of the gods. Reave believed that our destiny lay in our own hands and it was our responsibility to shape our lives. Turning his back on the avatars and the old conflicts he travelled with a handful of followers into the barren and deserted lands of Laskar in search of a new life, seeking to escape the civil war that still gripped Valistria. From that small group of people Reave led into the north grew the clan that now bore his name. It was hard to believe one man could found a whole nation and bring people hope in the future once more.

As a boy I would often sit at the dockside with my friends, Bram and Haarl, and watch the trading vessels and warships busily come and go with the tides at Reavesburg docks, dreaming of excitement and adventure. Looking at the great wooden walls surrounding our town, I tried to imagine a time when this land had been untouched. Reave had chosen his location well. The narrow bay afforded good shelter from the fierce storms that could strike without warning on the Redfars Sea, whilst the River Jelt provided plentiful fresh drinking water. Most importantly, the Baros Mountains sheltered the land to the west from the cold winter winds that would howl out of the Endless Ocean. Our crops rarely failed, compared with the more exposed lands of the Vittag or Helsburg clans. With reliable and plentiful harvests our numbers swelled with each passing year.

On a hot summer's afternoon Bram peeped out from behind the barrels on the dockside, craning round for a better view. Ducking back down, he looked at me questioningly. We were both ten years old and knew the responsibilities of manhood would soon be upon us. Until that day came, though, we continued to act as all boys will, seeking out trouble. Our other close friend, Haarl, was no longer our constant companion. Two years older, he had already begun his warrior training and spent most of his time with Finnvidor's guards. Bram's skinny build was similar to mine, whilst his sandy-coloured hair and freckled face were the image of his father, Brunn Fourwinds.

"What did you see?" I hissed.

"He's there, with the other warriors on the docks. Johan Jokellsward and those with him look like they're getting ready to disembark."

I risked a look myself. There was Haarl, his back to us, standing in line at the very end of the guard of honour my father had arranged for Johan's visit. Though his frame was broadening, his chainmail armour was still far too large. I sniggered as he self-consciously pushed his helmet back to prevent it from obscuring his vision.

Glancing at the group of visitors I recognised Johan Jokellsward immediately. Tall and rangy, his long red hair and whiskers were shot through with grey. On his back he carried Jokell's great two-handed sword, the bane of the Norlhast Clan, our enemies to the north led by Karas Greystorm. Amongst his guards I spied Rugga, the Rock of Kalamar, carrying his huge warhammer and young Petr Hamarrson, whose ancient sword was etched with dragon runes, rumoured to have been forged during the War of the Avatars. Kaun Quicksteel was also there, his sharp eyes on the lookout for danger. I had met Johan often enough and knew many of his warriors, since the jarl of Kalamar was a frequent visitor of Ulfkell's Keep. On this occasion, however, he was also accompanied by three people I assumed must be his family. There was a woman, a boy about my age and an older girl. No doubt I would discover the purpose of their visit later – for now there was more important work to be done.

We sprang from our concealed position and let fly with our catapults. Our aim was true, both pebbles striking Haarl's oversized helmet with a clang. It rolled clean off his head as he stumbled forwards, landing with a dull clank on the boards of the jetty, right in front of Johan Jokellsward as his strode towards Reavesburg's gates. Kaun's blade flew from its scabbard in a blur as he interposed himself in front of Johan while Rugga threw back his head and laughed loudly.

"Sheath that blade, Quicksteel," he cried. "You'll have those lads pissing their breeches. It was a jape, nothing more.

And damned fine aim, it has to be said." Rugga's massive frame even made Halfhand appear small in comparison. Despite appearances the Rock of Kalamar had a good heart, always laughing and slow to anger, despite his fearsome appearance. I liked Kaun less well. The younger man had a sour streak and never seemed to enjoy life, though his skill with a blade marked him out as one of the finest warriors of Kalamar. He sheathed his sword with a sullen look, clearly finding the whole affair much less amusing than Rugga.

Haarl, meanwhile, had turned crimson as he fumbled to retrieve his equipment, whilst Finnvidor fixed us with a fearsome glare. Bram and I ducked back into hiding but not before the red-headed boy accompanying Johan had looked straight at us. I swear he winked before Bram seized my shirt and pulled me back behind the barrels, as Johan's and Rugga's laughter rang out across the dockside.

***

"You two!" bellowed Haarl. I put on my most innocent expression as Bram and I turned to meet our furious friend striding towards us across the courtyard outside the Great Hall. Escaping this one looked unlikely, especially with Bram next to me biting his lip to prevent a fit of the giggles. Haarl was a good foot taller than either of us and he looked very angry. On the rare occasions when we resolved our quarrels with fisticuffs, Bram and I always came off worse, even when we fought Haarl together. Up close he looked uncomfortable in his over-large chainmail, his still scarlet face covered with sweat. I noticed Finnvidor standing on the other side of the courtyard, keeping an eye on proceedings as he organised the arrangements for Johan's entourage. Sensibly, he was giving Haarl the chance to sort out his grievance rather than intervening. Haarl pointed a shaking finger in our direction and when he spoke his tone was a great deal quieter than I had expected, though it still carried.

"Think you're clever, the pair of you? Making me look an idiot in front of Finnvidor and everyone? You may be

Kolfinnar's son, Rothgar, but you sure as hell don't behave like it. The warriors in the guardhouse, they'll feast off that one for weeks. It's bad enough I'm the youngest one there without you two making my life a misery all the time."

"Haarl, I'm really sorry," I said, my own face blushing as people nearby turned to look at the altercation. I would have felt better if Haarl had punched me; instead he turned and stomped away from us without another word.

"Uh oh," muttered Bram as Finnvidor approached. He regarded the pair of us sternly, his hand resting on the hilt of his sword. I eyed it warily before glancing up again as he spoke.

"It looks like the pair of you have far too much time on your hands. Your fathers both agree as well, so tomorrow morning you're to report to the weapons master at dawn to begin your training." Bram and I exchanged a look of glee, hardly able to believe our good luck. Finnvidor continued to stare at us with his cold, grey eyes and that moment of joy died as I realised there was a sting in the tail.

"Haarl's right. If you two were his real friends you'd give him a chance to become a man, rather than the butt of your jokes. Clan chief's son or not, I don't care. Haarl is my responsibility now, so leave him be if you want your lessons with Halfhand to continue. Otherwise, we'll find you some other jobs, perhaps helping the thralls spreading manure in the fields." Looking at Finnvidor I had no doubt he was serious. The two of us fled from his sight before he could change his mind.

***

"Fire in the skies." The words insistently broke into my dreaming, pulling me back into the waking world with a start. It was pitch black in my room, dawn still a long way off. I threw back the covers, seeking out my clothes in the darkness. Outside, I could hear a horn sounding dimly in the distance and the rush of booted feet in the corridor beyond my door.

Jorik was now fourteen and we no longer shared the room we had as young boys. My brother was increasingly concerned with the affairs of men, so we saw each other much less frequently. I padded out into the corridor alone. I could hear the sounds of men gathering in the courtyard and ran downstairs to find out more.

Outside, I was greeted by a great hubbub as horses were saddled and men armed. I saw a dishevelled Haarl amongst them, handing out shields and helmets to his older counterparts. Though it was night it was not completely dark; glancing upwards I saw the beacon fire at the top of the tower was lit. I felt a stab of panic. Were we under attack? More men rushed past me, led by Djuri, one of Finnvidor's more promising warriors, and I strained to listen to what was being said.

"... Finnvidor's told us the southern beacons have been lit ..."

"... Must be the Vorund Clan ..."

"... Time for 'em to pay, once and for all ..."

"... They've saddled Kolfinnar's own horse ..."

My ears pricked up at the last remark. Sure enough, I could see my father mounting his horse in the centre of the throng, flanked by Finnvidor and Olfridor. Jorik was there too, and I could tell he was asking to accompany our father. He shook his head, the decision obviously final, and Jorik nodded as Father clapped him firmly on the shoulders. My brother trudged wearily back towards the tower, his eyes widening as he caught sight of me. My father stood up in his saddle, his voice booming out, silencing the assembly at once.

"The southern beacons have been lit, alerting us that enemies have landed in Noln. The hand of the Vorund Clan seems most likely. Whoever our enemy might be we'll show them that a cowardly attack in the middle of the night does not find the Reavesburg Clan unprotected and unprepared. We ride out now on the southern road to meet them. Let us ride swiftly, and make them pay dearly for daring to set foot on our soil."

The warriors roared in response and with a shout of

command Finnvidor led them out of Ulfkell's Keep, loudly calling for the keep gates to be opened. Father and Olfridor rode out side by side on swift coursers, and I saw Johan Jokellsward towards the rear of the column with his own men, riding borrowed horses from our stables. Despite being a guest, this call to arms imposed a duty on all able-bodied men in Reavesburg. I felt a swell of pride as I watched them leave, longing to be old enough to ride with them. It was obvious my brother felt the same way.

"When will they get back?" I asked. Jorik, always proud to show off how much Father trusted him with military tactics, had already told me how the beacons worked. The construction of the watch towers had been devised by the second clan chief, Sigborn Reaveson the Dragonslayer, over one hundred years ago. Each side of the tower top that housed the beacon contained stout panels, which could be lowered or raised on chains. The purpose of this was to direct the warning to the nearest beacon, ensuring help was sent from the closest stronghold. It was also possible, by raising and lowering the beacon's panels, to send further information by means of a prearranged code. As the message had been sent to Reavesburg itself the attack was clearly nearby, making this a bold move by our enemies.

"From what I hear the tower at Noln was lit first," Jorik replied grimly. "It'll take the best part of an hour to reach there on horseback, so there's no telling what they'll find. It may already be over."

"So you may not have missed much," I said consolingly.

"Where's Daddy?" The voice behind us made us both jump. I spun round to see Nuna standing there, sleepy-eyed. Her long blonde hair reached halfway down her back and was the envy of many a woman in Reavesburg. Disturbed from her slumbers, I saw that in its tangled state those tresses could be a curse as well as a blessing.

Jorik crouched down in front of our sister. "There's some trouble in the south, so Father's gone to sort it out. He'll be back tomorrow."

Nuna's eyes were wide. "It must be big trouble if they've lit the beacon. I hate it when I hear stories of those raiders. I've heard people say that they take children off with them and make them work for them as thralls, even if they were born as karls or nobles. Is that true, do you think? I'd hate to be a thrall."

"Well," began Jorik. "Raiders do sometimes take captives as slaves as well as goods and cattle but that could never happen to you in Ulfkell's Keep. Even if it did, Father would sail right across the Redfars Sea and back to bring you safely home."

Nuna smiled, satisfied with Jorik's answer. "I'm tired," she announced, holding out her hand. Jorik nodded to me and I led her back to her chamber. I glanced back once to see Jorik standing there, anxiously looking at the closed gates of Ulfkell's Keep.

***

After handing Nuna back to Amma, I returned to my own room. I lay on the bed, finding sleep impossible. I wondered what Father and his warriors would find at Noln. If the raiders were still ashore there was no doubt Father would lead the attack to drive them away. I knew fighting at night on horseback against an unknown enemy would be hazardous. That night I imagined what life would be like if I lost my father: it was a troubling thought.

"Can't sleep either?" Jorik asked, looking at me standing there in the doorway to his chambers. He put a brawny arm around my shoulders. "Come on inside."

Jorik's room was one of the largest in the north tower, furnished with all the trappings befitting a young prince. He had lit a fire in the hearth and from the way it was stacked it was clear he planned to wait up all night until there was news. I threw myself down into a chair by the fire and Jorik sat opposite me, looking into the flames.

"I'm worried about Father," I blurted out.

"Me too. We've never had raids this close to Reavesburg before." Jorik clasped his hands together, deep in thought. Finally, he broke into a rather unconvincing smile. "Father's the clan chief and a great warrior. With Finnvidor, Johan and Olfridor by his side, he's bound to be safe."

"What if he's not? What'll happen to us? What about Nuna?"

"Rothgar, listen to me. If the worst happens then nothing bad will happen to you. I may be young but I'm a man now. If it comes to that I'm ready to be clan chief and make my father proud. We'll have Johan's support and soon those ties will be even stronger; I'll not let any harm come to you or Nuna."

Listening to Jorik say those things disturbed me. While I had grown up knowing the mantle of clan chief would one day be passed on to him I always imagined my father living to a ripe old age, like my grandfather, dying peacefully in a far off future. Now it dawned on me that all this could happen tonight. A sick feeling gnawed the pit of my stomach. I saw my brother in a different light, prepared to act as everyone expected. The nagging doubt I had in the back of my mind was whether someone so young could really be expected to act as the clan's leader and protector. Rivals for the title could challenge Jorik to single combat if they wanted to assert their own claim, even if the clan moot voted in my brother's favour. If Jorik were defeated I wondered what would happen to me. I leant my head back in the chair and squeezed my tired eyes shut, trying to bring more pleasant thoughts to mind.

"… Let me fetch you something to eat and drink …" Jorik was saying. By the time his servant came he found me fast asleep, tightly curled up in front of the fire.

**

I started awake for a second time as Jorik shook my shoulder. The room was filled with light; it was now early morning.

"They're back." Jorik announced. Although he looked haggard and exhausted, he ran from the room with renewed energy. I hurtled after him, still half-asleep and stiff from lying in the chair. I expected to find my father in the courtyard but he was nowhere to be seen. Instead, people were hurrying through the gates of Ulfkell's Keep into Reavesburg itself. Jorik and I joined the throng, unnoticed, and were swept along with the tide of people pressing towards the market square. As we grew nearer I could hear the rise and fall of a man's voice, addressing the crowd. Although I was still too far away to discern the words, my heart leapt as I recognised the tone of my father. In a superstitious moment I offered up a prayer to Dinuvillan, long-banished avatar of good fortune, that the news was favourable.

With a great deal of pushing, elbowing and squirming, we forced our way toward the front of the crowd. Finnvidor stood there impassively, silently challenging anyone to set foot across an invisible line that separated the warriors from the people of Reavesburg. My father sat behind him, still on horseback. Flanking him were about twenty of Reavesburg's finest fighters, alongside Johan and his own men. My breath caught in my chest as I saw that each held aloft a spear upon which was planted the head of one of our foes. As the crowd began cheering I knew we had been victorious. At that moment Father's eyes met mine and he said something to Finnvidor, who easily parted the crowd to bring us over to him.

"My boys. Looks like we know young Adalrikr's colours, true enough. The ships were flying his banner when we came upon them. The young bear's still a cub, though, if he thinks he can send his longships to raid at my own doorstep. Some of his ships made it to the water but there's two more that won't. Reckon we'll send those back down to his shoreline in good time with Reavesburg crew at the oars."

"You're alright, then," I said, the heady feeling of relief washing over me. My remark caught him by surprise, a frown creasing his forehead.

"Alright? Of course I'm alright. Do you think me too old to swing a sword these days when raiders attack outside my own keep?" Jumping down from his horse he grasped me and my brother in a bone-crushing hug. "Not yet, anyway. I sent a fair few of the Vorund Clan's warriors to Navan's Halls last night. Adalrikr's not going to make that mistake again. What do you say, Johan – shall we return the favour and set Vorund's lands to the torch?"

"Aye," shouted Rugga. "Let them taste our steel." A great cry went up at those words, with warriors and karls alike shouting for justice and vengeance. Johan remained unmoved, however, his craggy face calm and thoughtful as he replied.

"His arrogance won't go unpunished. Still, such matters are best discussed in private, rather than the market square. I always find a horn of ale helps me to plan my battles."

"And I always find I have a thirst after one," added Olfridor, drawing a huge cheer from the warriors.

"To Ulfkell's Keep," my father called. "Mount the heads of our enemies on the walls for all to see. They'll serve as a warning to this proud young chief next time he thinks to threaten my lands." With that he mounted his courser, pulling me up into the saddle with one strong arm, so that I rode back with him to the sound of adulation and acclaim all the way to the gates of Ulfkell's Keep.

CHAPTER 4

The Great Hall had not seen such a celebration in my lifetime as ale flowed and an endless supply of food was brought up from the kitchens. All the talk concerned the Vorund Clan's ships landing on our shores, their unmistakable banner depicting a bear on its hind legs. The trading port of Noln had taken some damage and casualties before our warriors caught the raiders unawares. The deeds of Kolfinnar in routing the attack had provided Darri with the inspiration to compose a new ballad. He was drunkenly trying out some new verses in front of Katla, who seemed to find the whole performance hilarious. By the evening, Father, Olfridor and Johan were all deep in their cups, huddled together conspiratorially as they shared some lewd joke. Jorik was hovering on the fringes, trying to look as if he belonged there.

I chewed on my last piece of warm roasted beef, fat dripping down my hands into my trencher. I was trying to spot Bram amongst the noisy crowd when the red-haired boy from Johan's party plopped himself down on the bench next to me.

"Bandor Johansson," he announced above the raucous din, the first time I'd met Johan's son. He stuck out a hand and took my greasy fingers in his. "You're Rothgar Kolfinnarson, aren't you? I met your brother when he came to Kalamar Castle. You look just like him."

"That's me," I nodded.

"That was some strike with those catapults," he chuckled.

"I'm not sure Haarl's forgiven me for that one yet."

Bandor leant closer to me, straining to hear and I motioned for him to follow me into the quieter courtyard outside. Even here, there were bands of revellers singing songs or reliving the battle from the previous night. We wended our way amongst them, glad to escape the smoke and heat of the feasting hall.

"When my father described Ulfkell's Keep to me I never imagined it would be so huge," Bandor said, genuine awe in his voice. "I can't believe I'll be living here."

I shot the boy a quizzical look and he looked back at me, surprised.

"Didn't your father tell you? I'm to be schooled by Halfhand himself this summer. It's some sort of debt he owes my father, I think."

"No, he didn't mention it," I replied slowly, realising this was the other boy my father had mentioned would be joining us. "That means we'll be in training together. I was supposed to start this morning but ..." I gestured to the people in the courtyard.

"Father says Halfhand's still the most skilful warrior in Reavesburg," Bandor continued. "Our fighters are some of the best, so that's high praise from him. He says it's only right that as brothers we learn to fight side by side."

"Your brother's here too? I thought you only had a sister."

Bandor looked at me blankly for a moment. "I don't have a brother," he laughed. "I'm talking about you. We'll be as good as brothers after the wedding."

"What wedding?" I asked, feeling stupid and glad that the darkening evening hid my flushed face. Bandor's jaw dropped before he quickly recovered himself.

"My sister, Reesha, and your brother Jorik are to be betrothed. The reason my father's here is to settle the terms of her dowry over this coming week. You really didn't know?"

I realised what Jorik had been talking about last night. What other reason would Johan have had for bringing his whole family to Ulfkell's Keep? It had probably been the talk of the keep for weeks and I hadn't noticed, too busy plotting with

Bram where to hide so I'd have the best vantage point for my catapult. I had planned to show off my home to Bandor and he knew more about what went on here than I did. I felt childish and a fool. To his credit, Bandor sensed this and tried to make amends.

"He was probably going to tell you today, before the raid. Father only told me when we left on the boat."

"I expect so," I replied sullenly, scuffing my feet along the ground.

***

The following morning I was rudely awoken by someone pounding at my door. I staggered to my feet in the darkness, wondering which servant would dare to rouse me in such a manner. My anger disappeared when my father strode into my chamber and I remembered my deferred dawn lesson with Halfhand. I dragged myself into my clothes, rubbing sleep from my eyes as the first dim rays of the sun began to creep across the sky. Despite the hour my father looked as if he had been up for hours and showed no ill effects from last night's revelry. Perhaps he hadn't slept at all.

"Now remember, Son, Halfhand will show you no special treatment because you're my boy," my father began for the third time as I trotted by his side, trying to keep pace with his long strides. "If anything, he'll be harder on you, just as he was with Jorik, to show the others there's no favouritism. It's just a pity ..." He threw out his hands, struggling to find the right words as he regarded my skinny frame. "Well, you're still growing and if I think you're ready, you're ready."

"Is Jorik going to marry Reesha?" I asked. Whatever response my father had been looking for, he was unprepared for that question.

"Of course he is," he spluttered. "Why do you think she's here? To take in the sea air? Didn't you know?"

"Bandor told me," I answered. Father looked thoughtful for a moment.

"Well, you know now. I thought I'd told you ... maybe

it was Jorik ... Anyway, this is the *last* thing you should be thinking of today. Halfhand won't hold back, Son. You need your mind on the task in hand. Your turn for marriage will come soon enough, when I've found you the right girl." I felt slightly queasy as my father continued to march towards the training ground. Whether from nerves or horror at the offhand way in which my father seemed to think I would be married off I was unable to tell.

Since his appointment as weapons master every aspiring warrior sought to learn from Olfridor. Johan's son was being granted a great honour to be Olfridor's pupil, and I realised it was Father's way of further cementing my family's ties with Johan. I just wished he'd consulted his own family more widely. Still, he was right, now was not the time to lose my wits. Many before me had broken an arm or a jaw in their first session with Halfhand. Or worse.

Bram was already waiting there with Bandor when I arrived with my father and he offered me a weak smile. I was oddly pleased to see that both boys looked as nervous as I felt. My heart sank when I saw Jorik standing nearby with Johan. Kaun Quicksteel and Brunn Fourwinds were also gathered to watch the proceedings, the captain of *Marl's Pride* beaming as he looked on proudly at his son. Though I knew they were only there to encourage us, I wished my first lesson wasn't going to be conducted in front of such a large audience.

Olfridor broke into a wide smile as I approached, his broken teeth stained black and brown from the foul Berian tobacco he favoured. "Sit down, Rothgar. You two, join him there." The three of us sat together on a wooden bench whilst Olfridor circled us, regarding us intently.

"You came here today as boys," he rumbled. "It's my job to turn you into men." Olfridor stuck out his maimed hand, its three remaining digits spread out before us. "Three things you need to remember here, which is just as well or I'd have to use my other hand. First, you might be a prince or beggar when you're outside this training ground, but when you're here with me *my word is law.* Just do as I say when I say it. I don't expect to have to remind any of you lads of that *ever again.* Second, you're all here to learn, so listen well and watch carefully. The folks that get hurt here are the ones that don't pay attention; they think they know best. You'll get no sympathy from me if you're one of them – maybe just a few smashed teeth to remember *that* particular lesson." Olfridor chuckled at his own joke.

"Last of all, no one so much as *touches* any of the weapons here or uses them unless I tell them they're ready. We start with wooden swords today. While you may think that's the stuff of boys you'll be thanking me by the end of this morning that's all we used. Now, you," Olfridor pointed at Bram, who almost fell off the bench in fright. "Let's see what you've got."

The morning passed by in a blur of frenetic activity and I forgot my father and brother were watching with my first sword swing. As the sun rose I was soon drenched in sweat and my arm ached from the effort of holding the heavy wooden sword. Even so, when Halfhand dismissed us I longed for more.

"You'll not say that when you wake up tomorrow morning," Halfhand assured me. "You'll be as stiff as a board, trust me. You did well, though. I think you surprised your old man today."

I walked back through the courtyard with Bram and Bandor, head held high as I savoured Olfridor's praise. Ravenous, we headed straight for the kitchens, much to the consternation of the cook when she saw three muddy and sweaty boys pilfering one of her freshly baked loaves. We ran before we were apprehended and I led the others to one of my favourite hiding-places – a small passageway hidden under the main staircase that wound its way up the north tower. As we shared out the warm bread it was as if the three of us had been friends for years as we relived the exploits of the morning, recounting every move and boasting of the bruises Olfridor had dealt us. That day will remain with me always.

***

During the following week, life in the keep revolved around the negotiations for Jorik and Reesha's betrothal and Bandor became my constant companion. As well as our training with Halfhand he joined me in my schooling with Etta. Bandor thought being taught by a ninety-five year old would give him license to run amok, despite my dire warnings. The old crone soon corrected that erroneous assumption. As I grew older, I had begun to appreciate just how remarkable a woman Etta was. She still moved with surprising speed and her knowledge of the history of our people was unsurpassed. When the time came for her to pass on to Navan's Halls, our clan would lose a part of itself. I had seen Darri speaking with Etta frequently in the evenings in recent years, ensuring that the oral traditions and tales stored in her mind were passed on to the next generation.

Bandor's revelation about Jorik's impending marriage had jolted something deep inside me. Games with Bram were all well and good but I wanted to know more about what was happening within the keep. The north tower's secret passages and spy holes had been perfect for playing hide-and-seek with Jorik and Nuna. Now their true purpose appealed to me for the first time. Despite having only known Bandor for five days, one evening I suggested we explore one of them. I knew Father and Johan were in discussions in one of the private chambers, and I wanted to prove to Bandor I was the master of my own home. I'm ashamed to say that the danger of revealing such secrets to a relative stranger never occurred to me. As far as I was concerned, Bandor was as good as my brother and in our burgeoning friendship we held nothing back from each other.

Designed to provide a means of escape should the north tower be taken, the secret passageways within it were an innovation of Ulfkell, Sigborn's son. The narrow cobwebbed corridors were illuminated by small gaps in the stonework, which allowed a fraction of the light from the main parts of the tower to filter into this shadowy domain. We dared not risk our own light for fear of revealing ourselves, so we crept on blindly, feeling with our hands and feet, eyes straining to pierce the gloom. Soon I could hear muffled voices ahead and knew we had reached our goal. Leading Bandor by the arm I found the set of spyholes cut into the wall which looked out onto the chamber where my father, Finnvidor and Johan were sitting, deep in conversation. I was unsurprised to see Etta was with them too.

"You neglect Gautarr and his lands at your peril," Etta was saying to my father. "I agree that cementing your family ties with Johan strengthens your position. What I'm saying is you need to offer the same gesture to Gautarr, if you want to avoid causing offence."

"Gautarr complains too much," protested my father, though he looked thoughtful as he mulled over Etta's words. Clearly Johan agreed with her.

"You would too, Kolfinnar, if your lands and warriors were the bulwark between the Reavesburg Clan and the raiders from Vorund."

"Didn't we ride out side by side to battle less than a week ago to fight them and drive them from our shores?" my father exploded, slamming his palm on the wooden table. I jumped in fright at his temper, despite being separated by almost a foot of worked stone, and lost my footing. I held my breath for a moment as Bandor helped to steady me, worried the noise had revealed our presence. However, the voices in the chamber continued as before.

"No one is denying that," Finnvidor replied. "All Etta is saying is Ulfkell's Keep and its surrounding lands are far more secure than your northern and southern borders."

Johan nodded in agreement. "I'm honoured our families will be joined together. I welcome Jorik and Reesha's marriage and I pray to Lamornna they produce an heir to secure your line. Surely though Kolfinnar, you must see it from Gautarr's perspective? If you don't show his family the same degree of respect you risk rousing his old ambitions to become chief. Don't forget I supported your claim when Marl died. When the time comes for Jorik to lead his people he'll need that support again, and more importantly Gautarr will need to stand with him. Slight him now and you'll hand Gautarr or his son Ragnar the perfect excuse to rise up against your own son and challenge him."

"Einarrson and Jokellsward both speak wisely," Etta agreed, regarding my father intently with her single good eye. "You would do well to listen to them."

My father nodded, the redness in his cheeks fading as he took a breath. He stood, stretching his arms as his back cracked audibly, before walking to the window of the chamber.

"My father warned me once that you're less in control of your life as a chief than you might imagine. He was right. I've placed a great deal on Jorik's shoulders as my first born son. It's time for Rothgar to take up his responsibilities. Who do you propose?"

"Gautarr's line is hardly awash with eligible young maidens," Etta replied. "As you know, Ragnar is his only surviving natural child. There is his niece, though, Freydja Egilldottir, who is a year younger than Rothgar. That would be a suitable match. She is not as close a blood relative as would be ideal but Gautarr will not complain. He's brought up Freydja and her older brother since they were orphaned and regards them as his own, though he naturally favours Ragnar. He would certainly consider his family's treatment as being equal to Jokellsward's, if you were to propose such a pairing."

My father listened as Etta spoke, his head bowed. It struck me that I had never before seen him so weary and full of worry. "I hear the wisdom of your advice. Perhaps the girl will not take after her uncle. I'd like to think of Rothgar enjoying a happy marriage."

"It matters little if he likes her or not," snapped Etta. "Stop being so sentimental. A happy marriage doesn't stop a dagger between your shoulder blades. If Gautarr moves to seize your title he'll not stop at killing Jorik. As the next in line, Rothgar would also have to die. Don't pretend you don't know this; to secure Jorik's rule, Rothgar and Nuna must both play their part ..."

I could listen no more. Turning, I ran back through the passageway, careless of whether anyone heard me. Bandor struggled to keep up as I darted left and right, anxious to be as far away as possible from my father, Johan and Etta. Until then, I had so wanted to be a man. I thought that came with holding a sword and proving my worth to Olfridor Halfhand. Now I knew it meant my father marrying me off to a girl I had never even met to placate a rival. I hurried to my chamber without a word to Bandor, lest he saw the tears stinging the corners of my eyes.

CHAPTER 5

Following the announcement of Jorik and Reesha's betrothal, Johan and his wife Damona left Reavesburg with their daughter amid great fanfare and excitement. The two were to be wed in the spring of the following year. Jorik seemed pleased, though I doubted he had much say in the matter. With her bright red hair and cheerful smile, Reesha seemed pleasant enough, though I could muster little enthusiasm or interest in the girl. For the sake of Bandor I kept my own counsel.

Bandor remained at Ulfkell's Keep with me to complete his training with Halfhand. We didn't speak of what we overheard in the passageway and I tried hard to forget the conversation had even taken place. It was a futile effort, of course; seeing Etta every day hardly helped. It may have been my imagination but whenever our eyes met, she seemed to regard me in a different light. I wondered more than once whether she had heard the sound of running feet behind the walls and knew her conference with my father had been spied upon.

I expected my father to tell me of his plans for my betrothal to Freydja. However, as the days slowly passed and turned into weeks it appeared that any such discussion would not be forthcoming. It occurred to me that Gautarr would have to be consulted and there was always the chance, however remote, that he would not approve of the match. Perhaps my father had changed his mind. Arranged marriages amongst the nobility were commonplace and I knew this well. I had just never considered how this would affect me when my own turn came. What rankled was the lack of control I had over my own life, which soon became a festering sore in my mind. Whilst I wanted to challenge my father over his plans, doing so would mean admitting I had been spying on him. That would not be well-received, so instead I took to avoiding my father wherever possible. Somewhat unfairly, I gave Jorik the same treatment and, looking back, I feel guilty about my behaviour. I can see now that, whatever I was feeling, Jorik was probably experiencing similar emotions and would probably have valued the company of his younger brother. Instead, I gave him nothing – too wrapped up in my own imagined torments. A boy of ten can be selfish indeed.

Soon, however, talk in Reavesburg did not centre on Jorik's wedding. The year 202 saw further raids by the Vorund Clan up and down our coast; the improved summer weather allowing Adalrikr Asmarrson's ships to strike out further across the Redfars Sea. News came from Romsdahl in the south that Gautarr Falrufson was hard pressed to hold the invaders back and Tyrfingr Blackeyes' black-sailed ship was seen harrying our shores. When Father sent more men from Reavesburg to Romsdahl, the attacks came closer to home, taking advantage of our reduced patrols. To make matters worse, Johan's warriors were forced to repel raiding parties from the Norlhast Clan, led by their jarl Sigurd Albriktson, who could see the Reavesburg Clan's warriors were spread more thinly than ever. People said Reavesburg had never experienced such relentless raiding in living memory, and with each foray into our territory, a little more of my father's authority was lost.

Such things made me concentrate on my weapons skill with Halfhand. Whilst Bram favoured the axe and hammer my lighter frame better suited the sword. I soon began to impress with my natural speed and before long had progressed from wooden weapons to a blunted steel sword. The extra weight took some getting used to but with each month I grew stronger. Soon I could spar with Bram and Bandor and the other older boys being trained by Halfhand as their equal and, occasionally, their better. After a while Haarl would join us for some lessons, giving Olfridor another measure as to how we were progressing against the skills of those already in Finnvidor's ranks. Haarl took satisfaction in giving me a fair few bruises for my trouble, for which I could hardly blame him. After that, Bram and I were careful not to tease Haarl any more.

Throughout the summer months we watched as many of our trading ships were sunk by our enemies. Nor did the Vorund Clan spare the vessels of Helsburg and Vittag, depriving us of vital supplies and diminishing our coffers as trade began to decline. The people of Reavesburg were never happier to welcome winter, which brought with it the familiar howling winds and fierce storms from the Endless Ocean. As the treacherous seas finally drove our enemies back to their ports, we were allowed some respite. It was agreed between Johan and my father that Bandor would stay at Ulfkell's Keep that winter. Whilst I was pleased my friend would remain with me, deep inside I knew it meant my father didn't think it safe for his friend's son to travel north.

So that year the Reavesburg Clan enjoyed the harsh wintertime season, despite its chill, for the peace it brought to our land. As Bandor, Bram, Haarl and I warmed ourselves in front of the roaring fire in the Great Hall, Darri kept us all entertained with his stories. Sensing the mood of the people, he recounted tales of other times when our clan had been hard pressed. The story of Hroar Helstromson, sixth clan chief of Reavesburg, reminded us of how we had prevailed against Vorund in the past, though it cost Hroar his life. Even Olfridor had tears in his eyes by the time Darri finished singing. For my part, I felt we were living through another such time that, one day, would resonate through the songs the bards sang to future generations.

***

Spring brought both fear and joy in equal measure. As the seas calmed, Adalrikr sent forth Tyrfingr Blackeyes and his ships once more to plague our shores. Brunn Fourwinds patrolled the coast as our fleet sought to drive off the invaders before they could land. Despite those efforts all too often the watch tower beacons would be lit, calling for aid. When the attacks were near Reavesburg Father would lead his warriors with Finnvidor and Djuri to repel them. Further out across the clan lands the news remained grim, with livestock seized, crops burned and people enslaved or slain by our foes. My father seemed greyer and more careworn as he received these tidings.

The one thing that seemed to draw the people of Reavesburg together was Jorik and Reesha's forthcoming wedding. Jorik appeared to be genuinely looking forward to taking the final step towards manhood, and Bandor's pride in his sister was evident in everything he said. I was careful to keep my own thoughts to myself, now I fully understood the implications of an arranged marriage for my own life. My father had still not raised the subject of Freydja with me. Perhaps the arrangements for Jorik's wedding were enough for him at the moment: I certainly had no intention of broaching the matter.

*****

I woke to find the air thick with sea mist on the morning of my brother's wedding. My finest clothes had been laid out for me to wear and I dressed hastily to escape the early spring morning chill. The keep hummed with excitement as I wandered, unnoticed, into the kitchens in search of breakfast. Servants seemed to occupy each square foot of every room, busily rushing about like bees in a hive, anxious to complete their errands and move on to the next. Johan and Gautarr would both be in attendance for the ceremony, in keeping with Jorik's status as a future chief. My father was sparing no expense as their host on such an auspicious occasion.

Other than to look my best I had no formal role on the day itself. Not wishing to incur my father's wrath by ruining my outfit, I sought out Bandor and the two of us whiled away the morning playing dice and kings in the hall. Bandor had been heartened by seeing his family again after their months of separation and was in good spirits. It dawned on me that today we would indeed become brothers as our families united. I could wish for no better friend or brother-in-law, and I began to catch the mood of the day for the first time.

By some miracle the two of us managed to stay out of trouble until it was time to make our way to the grove. There had been some debate about whether to hold the ceremony within the safety of Ulfkell's Keep but my father would not hear of it, and Finnvidor soon dropped the point. Long before Reavesburg had been fortified our people had married in the sacred grove, which lay on the edge of the woods outside the town. I could see why Finnvidor was anxious, as the spot was exposed and not easily defended from raiders. My father's response was as blunt as a blow from a warhammer. Kolfinnar Marlson was not going to hide away in fear and conduct the marriage of his son in secret. As our procession left Reavesburg and began to wend its way up the hill towards the forest, I could see his point. Kolfinnar's finest warriors were accompanied by those of Johan and Gautarr, each keen to show the strength of their own families. Rugga the Rock stood there proudly alongside Petr Hamarrson and Kaun Quicksteel. Gautarr was flanked by great warriors from his own household, such as tall Audwin Strongshield and Domarr the Oak. As the noon sun glinted off polished armour and the steel of the weapons borne by our warriors my heart swelled with pride. It would take a bold raider from Vorund to attack such a force, even on a calm spring day.

Jorik looked composed as he stood on the spot where our father had pledged himself to our mother, Alaine, all those years ago. Now fifteen, Jorik was standing before his people as a man rather than a boy. He was only an inch or so shorter than our father and two or three more summers would see him pass that mark. Father's pride in his eldest son was obvious, and I was surprised to feel my breath catch in my chest as I looked at them both. The crowd of onlookers parted as Reesha was led towards her intended by Johan Jokellsward. Her garlanded red hair framed a youthful face, for she was only my elder by a year. Yet she walked with all the grace and poise of a woman twice her age. A little part of me fell under her spell that day, and I could see from Jorik's visage I was not the only one. I had expected my father to preside over the ceremony however as Jorik and Reesha took their places before him it was Etta who moved forward. The crowd watched her silently as she reached out and joined the couple's hands together within her gnarled fist. When she spoke there was no quaver in her voice to betray her advancing years.

"For more than one hundred and sixty years our people have come to this place, so that a man and a woman may pledge themselves to one another before witnesses. By that pledge they bind their two families together as close as any bond of blood. They become a family in their own right and, if Lamornna is pleased, then in the fullness of time they shall bring forth children to secure the future of the Reavesburg Clan. Are you both ready to swear oaths to each other in this sacred place, before this assembly?" Both Jorik and Reesha nodded and Etta broke into one of her rare gap-toothed smiles.

"Good. Jorik, do you swear to pledge yourself to Reesha as her husband and to take her into your home as your wife?"

Jorik looked uncomfortable as all eyes turned on him. He smiled at Reesha and, squeezing her hand, he steadied his nerves and answered clearly, "I do," to a general murmuring of approval from the crowd.

"Reesha. Do you swear to pledge yourself to Jorik as his wife and unite yourself with his family?"

"I do," Reesha replied confidently and a ripple of applause could be heard, as well as a stifled sob from her mother, Damona.

"Then go forth from this place with our blessings as husband and wife and begin your new life together," cried Etta.

A great roar erupted from the crowd as Jorik leant close to kiss his bride. Only Gautarr and his family showed a certain lack of enthusiasm for the occasion, clapping only briefly and with restraint. The fierce warrior turned his gaze upon me and my innards froze. My father and Johan embraced warmly and Bandor put his arm round my shoulders.

"Bandor! You're my brother now." A small form darted through the throng, golden hair trailing in her wake as Nuna collided with my friend, almost bowling him over. He laughed good-naturedly, as my sister disentangled herself from him and turned her impish face in my direction.

"Uh oh. If I were you, Rothgar, I'd find my way back to the keep as quick as you can. Run, before they catch you." She dashed off faster than I could blink. As I tried to pick out Nuna's retreating form in the crowd I heard a man say my name and turned to find Gautarr Falrufson standing next to me.

"Rothgar," he rumbled with a cold smile. He folded his enormous bare arms as he looked down on me, his son, Ragnar, tall and dark-haired, at his side. At twenty Ragnar was already married with a young son and would one day assume the leadership of Gautarr's household at Romsdahl. Behind them were a boy and girl. The boy was perhaps a year or two older than me. Despite the difference in their years, his resemblance to Ragnar was striking and I knew this was Gautarr's nephew, Throm. From the boy's suspicious stare I guessed the pretty dark-haired young girl at his side must be Freydja, his sister.

Ragnar looked me up and down appraisingly. "Well, Father, I have to say I would have hoped for more from Kolfinnar's second son. Jorik already has the makings of a fine warrior. As for you Rothgar, well, I've seen more muscle on a knotted rope."

"Halfhand says Rothgar's faster with a sword than anyone his age that he's ever trained," Bandor spoke up boldly in my defence. Ragnar deigned to glance in Bandor's direction and my friend met his gaze steadily. A condescending smile played on the young man's lips as he replied.

"If Halfhand were still so fast, he wouldn't carry that name. I doubt he can say much else to the boy's father in the circumstances. It seems his offer is a poor second compared to the favour he has just bestowed on Jokellsward's family."

"Kolfinnar wants me to marry *him*!" cried Freydja in dismay. Her eyes looked daggers at me, displeasure distorting her attractive features. "Uncle, say this isn't so. He's not even *clean*." Despite myself, I found my hand moving across my face, wiping imaginary dirt away from my nose and mouth. I wanted to put these people in their place with some witty remark. No words came and instead I stood there stupidly, anger burning in my chest and a crimson tide rising up my neck and face.

"This is hardly the place to discuss such matters." Etta suddenly materialised in our midst. I took some satisfaction in seeing Gautarr take a step backwards before recovering himself.

"Freydja's opinion matters to me, old crone," the great warrior replied, though he kept his voice low. "I've brought her up as my own. I'll not have her married off cheaply to some whelp who looks like the runt of the litter. As for a dowry, well, Kolfinnar can think again. If this is his idea of a match he should be offering better terms to me." With that remark Gautarr strode away, Ragnar, Throm and Freydja following in his wake. Etta turned to me, a kindly expression on her face. I became aware that my mouth was hanging open and, with some effort, managed to shut it.

"I'm sorry, Rothgar. Gautarr's idea of politics is so crude, it's breathtaking sometimes. I'm sorry you had to learn all this in such an ill-considered way."

"I knew already," I said unthinkingly. Etta's eyebrows narrowed at that remark, though she didn't press me for the source of my information.

"That makes things easier, I suppose. Do you know what that was?"

"Gautarr and his family are still learning how to pay someone a compliment?" It was a weak jest, drawing a small chuckle from Etta nonetheless.

"No. Gautarr is raising the stakes in the negotiations for your marriage to Freydja. By slighting you he hopes to improve the terms. Perhaps a smaller dowry will be paid to your father. It may be that he seeks a place for her at Ulfkell's Keep, or for your father to agree to build a new castle for you both to live in. I know Gautarr wants to improve his defences on the southern border with Vorund and he needs to find a way to raise the coin for that venture."

"I'd have to leave Ulfkell's Keep?" I cried, aghast. "This is my home. Why should I leave?"

"No," Etta replied. "This is your home now. In time it will be Jorik's home – as first born son when he claims the title of chief. Your duty is to secure his borders and protect his rule; the price of strengthening this alliance might be making your home in the south, as part of your pledge to Gautarr's family."

"You can't force me to marry her," I argued. "She's vile, and in any case she hates me." Etta chuckled again, seeming to enjoy a joke I found wholly unfunny.

"The touch of Meras can be swift, striking at the heart of a man so that for him there is only one woman in the whole world. That is the love Darri sings of in his great ballads. It makes for a good story. However, Meras can also do her work more slowly and enduring love can grow between two people, even without that first spark. That is the form of love upon which the ruling families of this clan have built their power and their alliances. Don't let the rudeness of a ten-year-old girl colour your views about her; her uncle gave her little choice except to say those things, otherwise she would have undermined his authority."

"What do you know of love?" I spat back. "You're so old and shrivelled even the clan's grandfathers wouldn't want you." It was the most stupid and daring thing I had ever said to Etta and I waited for a blow from her bony hand. It didn't come and, to my shame, Etta only looked back at me with compassion.

"Trust me boy, I've known what it is to fall in love and

understand the cost of losing that love too. I've led a full life, I can assure you; too full at times, perhaps. I'm not laughing at your predicament, believe me. Just remember that when your father met Alaine he said much the same thing as you did about Freydja. Yet when she died I've never seen a man so beside himself with grief. Perhaps it's wrong to place the burdens of a man on the shoulders of a young boy but that's the position you've been born into. Your father wants this marriage, and you'll do your duty when the time comes if you love him and want to do right by your brother. Think on those words a while before saying the first thing that comes into your head. You're brighter than that." I stared, dumbfounded, as Etta patted me on the shoulder and melted away into the gaggle of wedding guests, who were beginning to make their way back towards the keep. I fell into step with them, my mood black.

"I mean it. I'm never going to marry that girl."

Bandor nodded in agreement at my remark. "Don't worry, Rothgar. That's not going to happen. She'd sooner kill you first."

CHAPTER 6

Recalling Bandor's jest from all those years ago brought a smile to my cracked lips as I hung, shivering, in the darkness. I chuckled weakly at the memory, instantly regretting it as spasms of pain wracked my body. Death was coming and I welcomed the prospect. How ironic – meeting my fate within sight of Ulfkell's Keep. I'd resented Father's plans for my future because I never wanted to leave this place; now it seemed I would be granted my wish. My only regret was this wasn't the death I wanted. A warrior's choice would always be to die in battle for the glory of his clan, deeds that would inspire men like Darri to write songs that would resonate in the Great Hall for generations to come. There would be no songs about Rothgar the Traitor. 'Kinslayer', they had called me, the words wounding more deeply than the wicked work of my torturers. Had I fallen in my first battle, my people's memory of me would have been so different.

Rarely is a man given the choice as to when and how his time on Amuran should end; my father deserved better than his fate. For a time Reavesburg was blessed as, after three years of marriage, Jorik and Reesha celebrated the birth of their firstborn son. They honoured our father by naming the boy Kolfinnar and I swear there has never been a prouder grandfather in Reavesburg. As he grew and took his first steps, I saw more than a little of my younger self in my nephew. At the age of two Kolfinnar the Younger, as we took to calling him, found my toy wooden swords and was soon terrorising Ulfkell's Keep. Although I was now sixteen and a grown man in my own right, I indulged him as enthusiastically as my fellow warriors, fighting duels up and down the length of the

Great Hall.

It was always my father who my nephew *really* wanted to engage in deadly battle. That particular spring afternoon remains etched on my mind. Jorik and I both laughed, whilst Father fought fiercely with his grandson. I winced as the boy cracked him hard on the shins, causing his grandfather to yelp in genuine pain. A moment later young Kolfinnar landed the fatal blow to Father's unprotected chest. He sank to his knees, clutching at his imagined injury whilst the boy celebrated.

"I win. I win. Again, Grandfather, again."

"I think that's enough, Kolfinnar," called Jorik as he walked to his rescue. I smiled as I watched Father drop his wooden sword on the floor from nerveless fingers, thinking he was a better actor than me. My heart lurched as I saw his body spasm, face contorted in agony as he slipped to the floor before gasping and lying there, unmoving.

***

The rest of that day is a blur. I recall servants bustling into the Great Hall, Reesha sweeping a wailing Kolfinnar up in her arms as she soothed her son, Jorik shouting and weeping as he tried to rouse our father. My first clear memory is sitting at my father's bedside with Jorik three days later. Etta was tending him and I had harboured a small hope her skills could revive our chief. Etta was swift to correct me.

"There is nothing I can do for him," she informed us both, her voice unsteady. "This malady has broken his body." She took his hand in her bony fingers, holding him tight. "He cannot move his right side and his speech has been lost. In truth, it would have been better if he'd been struck down dead. This is no life, yet it is the one Myshall has decreed should be his for the remainder of his years. My boys, I am so sorry. You must both be strong now, for Kolfinnar Marlson is no longer the man he once was."

Etta spoke rightly, since my father bore a new name for the last months of his life. 'Kolfinnar the Crippled', they called him. It was a cruel and undeserved title for such an active and brave man, aged just forty-nine.

***

As the news of my father's fate spread, visitors from the various clans came to Ulfkell's Keep like vultures. Bothvatr Dalkrson, chief of the Helsburg Clan, arrived with a large retinue who enjoyed the hospitality of our hall for several days longer than was seemly. The leader of the Vittag Clan, Ingioy the White Widow, paid a much briefer visit. She was accompanied by her daughter Valka, a famous shieldmaiden and warrior from the west, who had been her mother's jarl for several years. Ingioy seemed genuinely moved at my father's plight, talking softly to him for a time as Finnvidor looked on. The lips of our visitors uttered fine words, paying our father every respect, whilst their eyes spoke differently. As they offered their continued support, they looked at the broken body of our father lying on a bier by the fire, propped up on cushions, the better to see his visitors. They took stock of Jorik; the twenty-year-old man who was now, in all but name, Reavesburg clan chief. They regarded his wiry sixteen-year-old brother, still completing his training under Olfridor Halfhand. In short, they decided to drive up their prices.

A succession of town elders also visited during this time. Sandar Tindirson came from the western lands to pay his respects, although I couldn't remember anything the young man said after he left. Old Hrodi Whitebeard attended from Olt with his quarrelling son Radholf and irritating grandson Alfarr. I recall Lundvarr from Noln wept when he saw the state of my father.

Ragnar represented Gautarr's family. The mutual stubbornness of Father and Gautarr over the years had stalled any serious plans concerning my wedding. Ragnar was reassessing whether the match remained beneficial for his family. Much would depend on how Jorik led our people in the coming months. Gautarr's absence from our halls was considered a slight not just to Kolfinnar but Jorik too, as clan chief elect.

The only people we were glad to see during that grim time were Johan and Bandor. Johan was grief-stricken, whilst my father was embarrassed at his friend seeing him in this condition. My father's mental faculties remained sharp but his drooping mouth and weak tongue could no longer form those familiar words of command. The only means he had for making himself understood was by writing, using clumsy and unformed letters with his stronger left hand. Even this tired him greatly and often he would simply sleep by the fire, sometimes accompanied by his grandson who sat there wondering what he had done to his grandpa. On the evening of Johan Jokellsward's arrival the four of us gathered round the fire of the Great Hall, discussing the future in hushed tones, whilst my father slept fitfully nearby.

"These are dangerous times for us all," observed Johan as Jorik described Ragnar's recent visit to Ulfkell's Keep. "The fact Gautarr didn't come shows his hand. He'll listen to Ragnar's report before deciding whether to support Kolfinnar as chief or Jorik as his successor. It's a great pity the close ties that exist between our two families weren't forged with his as well." Johan shot me a dark look as he made this remark – I had not done my duty in eagerly marrying Freydja.

"Do you think Gautarr will make a claim for the title of clan chief himself?" asked Jorik.

"Perhaps. However, Gautarr is no longer a young man. He can't fight your father in this condition and claim the title in the usual way by trial of arms. If he forces the issue *you* would need to fight, in order to prove your right to the title. Gautarr won't relish the prospect of taking on a man more than thirty years younger, especially one who's been trained by Halfhand. Even though you may not have seen battle first hand you've skill enough to test Gautarr's mettle. If there's to be a challenge it may be his son, Ragnar, who issues it. That would be a much more serious contest and, I'm afraid to say, one where I would fear for you, Jorik. Ragnar is a deadly warrior."

"The title of clan chief is my birth right; let them come and try and take it," snarled Jorik.

"Gautarr will not act yet," countered Johan, resting his hand on Jorik's shoulder. "Kolfinnar is well-respected and liked by the people, despite our troubles. Gautarr will wait to see how you deal with things in his place. Trade negotiations with Vittag and Helsburg have already proved difficult. Next we can expect renewed attacks from Norlhast, Riltbalt and Vorund. If things go badly for you Gautarr will have a stronger case for his family assuming control. He'll probably offer you the choice of standing aside, so a more experienced man can assume the leadership of our people. Rest assured, if you agree it won't be long before you're found with a dagger in your back. Better to confront your foes face to face, than be beguiled by such trickery."

Jorik sighed. "Hardly comforting words, though your advice is welcome, Johan. My son will be glad to see his other grandfather as well. He's not been himself since ... Well, you've always known how to cheer him up."

Johan smiled at the mention of his first grandchild. "Life goes on, my boy, that's true enough. These aren't easy times, so we have to take comfort where we can. Reesha will support you, as will I."

Bandor and I walked back towards my chambers that night in silence. Bandor had remained at Ulfkell's Keep for the past six years as Kolfinnar's ward, training hard with Olfridor. He was now an accomplished fighter, skilled with sword, axe and bow and a close match with me. Together with Bram the three of us were fast friends, sharing everything together – yet I was unable to find the words to express my feelings. In one moment my life had become more complicated than I would have thought possible. I think Bandor understood this better than I did. He hugged me as we parted outside the door to his room, and I choked back tears as I clasped my brother-in-law tightly. Some were for the plight of my father and, to my shame, some were born out of self-pity for my own situation.

Candles had been lit in my chamber and a warm fire crackled in the grate to ward off the cold. As I began to undress, I heard my door open and close quietly behind me. I turned to see Desta framed in the doorway, a mischievous smile on her face. She moved gracefully towards me, her long dark hair untied and falling about her face in a manner that she knew I found attractive. With each step she undid another button on her servant's shift, stirring feelings in me I had forgotten existed. I let my shirt fall to the floor as Desta put her arms about me and drew my face towards her own.

"I've missed you," she whispered as she kissed me, running her hands through my hair. "I've wanted to speak to you and comfort you since your father fell ill but there's never been chance. Why have you not come to my chambers?"

"Father is ill," I replied curtly. "He's never going to recover. Things are different now."

"What are you saying?" Desta looked hurt, tears welling in her hazel eyes. I realised she was reappraising the distance I'd kept from her in recent weeks, wondering if I had cast her aside. With a pang, I saw how I had neglected Desta, not giving my lover of the past year a moment's thought since my father collapsed three weeks ago. Guiltily I hugged her tightly and returned her kisses, seeking to comfort her and be comforted myself.

"I'm sorry. I've ignored you, Desta. I didn't mean to, only things have been so difficult since Father fell ill. I've had to support Jorik; they're going to look on him to lead us now and he'll need my help."

"I understand, Rothgar, I do. Everyone's saying Kolfinnar is crippled and Jorik must take up his duties as chief."

"Some won't be happy with that – Gautarr's family for one. It looks like I'll really have to marry his niece Freydja to help stave off a challenge to Jorik's title." As I spoke the words I instantly regretted them. Too wrapped up in what my father's illness meant for me, I'd forgotten their impact on Desta. As a servant in Ulfkell's Keep her status was too lowly for marriage ever to be a serious consideration, a fact we both understood. As long as I didn't consider the future I always felt happy with Desta, so I cursed my careless words as they threatened to ruin one of those precious moments. Desta took a step back and regarded me intently with a hard stare.

"And when, *exactly*, did you intend to tell me about this? Did you plan to let me know before I began to prepare the food at your wedding feast?"

"Desta, please, I've been betrothed to Freydja since I was ten years old. I don't like it and to be frank neither does she. You know this as well as I do." Desperate to win back favour, I was pleased as her expression softened. I ploughed on with my speech, hoping to repair the damage and keep the one thing in life I treasured intact. "Nothing is certain. Gautarr has never fully supported our match and negotiations on the terms have dragged on for six years, so there's no reason to think anything will be resolved soon. For now, at least, I'm still free. You know it's you that I want to be with, if only things were different."

Emboldened by the fact Desta didn't slap me, I reached out and slid my arm around her waist, drawing her close to me once more.

"I'm sorry, Rothgar. I just wish we could be together."

"So do I," I whispered, undoing the last remaining buttons of her dress so that it gathered on the floor around her. That night we both forgot our troubles, ignoring the harsh realities of our circumstances, wilfully pushing them aside as we took comfort in one another.

***

The emissary from the Vorund Clan arrived at noon the following day, which caught us unawares. Desta was one of the servants who brought our meal to us in the Great Hall and Bandor noticed my admiring glance as she poured my ale. I'd not told him of my feelings for her, although he must have had his suspicions. I was spared from answering any awkward questions by a commotion at the entrance to the hall, where a group of people had gathered. I saw Olfridor purposefully striding towards the head of the table. He spoke quietly to Jorik, his face dark with anger.

"The Vorund Clan have sent someone to pay respects to Kolfinnar. Finnvidor has taken their arms. Even so, you need to tread carefully with this one, young master. Tyrfingr Blackeyes himself is here – an evil bastard and no mistake."

Blackeyes; the name was grimly familiar to us all and his presence did not bode well. Jorik swallowed as he composed himself, whilst Olfridor took up a position to his left, his hand on the handle of his axe. I watched as a small man walked towards us, escorted by several of our best warriors, including Finnvidor, whose long hair was now streaked with grey. The Vorund symbol of the bear was emblazoned in fine enamel on Blackeyes' steel breastplate. I swallowed as he drew closer and saw our visitor was well named, for Tyrfingr's eyes were black pools. There was no white, pupil or iris, just two great black fathomless orbs. Though our warriors towered over this visitor, I felt a pang of fear and couldn't help myself as I looked away, unable to bear his gaze.

Tyrfingr held out his hands, palms open, signifying that he came in peace and unarmed. His dark hair was lank, hanging in long curtains on either side of a sallow face. Tyrfingr Blackeyes was the man responsible for leading many of the raids on our shores. His hands were covered in the blood of my people, making his journey to Ulfkell's Keep such an audacious tactic. Was Adalrikr *mocking* us by sending such a brutal man to pay Kolfinnar his respects? My father was asleep by the fire, watched over by Johan and Bandor. They looked at Blackeyes with undisguised hatred as, unperturbed, he approached Jorik, bowing low under Finnvidor's watchful gaze.

"Hail, Jorik, clan chief elect of the Reavesburg Clan. My name is Tyrfingr Blackeyes and I have been sent here to speak on behalf of Adalrikr Asmarrson, chief of the Vorund Clan. Kolfinnar Marlson was a mighty warrior and in his twilight years it is right that we offer our respects to so worthy an adversary." Tyrfingr's voice was not what I had expected. It was the cultured voice of a noble that filled our halls, not the uncouth speech of someone low-born. His words carried effortlessly and I could see Blackeyes had the rapt attention of everyone as he spoke, including Desta who had quite forgotten her duties. My father stirred in his sleep, unaware of the presence of a bitter enemy in his own Great Hall.

"So thoughtful," answered my brother. "Only Adalrikr would have considered it appropriate to send a murderer of our people into our very midst to offer his, no doubt, heartfelt condolences in this time of trouble for our family."

"Very droll. I am here for a reason. Since your father is still sound asleep, I will entrust the message to you, young as you are. Adalrikr offers you terms that you should consider carefully, boy, before you reject them out of hand. His generous offer is this. If you swear yourself to be subject to Adalrikr Asmarrson's rule, and cede your territory to our clan, then your family will be allowed to live. In addition –"

Jorik was on his feet in an instant, cutting Blackeyes off in mid-flow as he roared in anger. "How *dare* you set foot in my home and then speak to me in such a manner. Perhaps my reply should be to send back your head to Adalrikr."

"You have never shed blood," Blackeyes observed, with a sour look. "Your father protected you, fighting his own battles whilst you were safe behind the thick walls of your keep. Do not threaten me, boy, when I come to your miserable town unarmed. I am here as Adalrikr's ambassador. If you do not recognise that, then place a sword in my hands if you wish to deal me death with honour."

"Do it," snarled Olfridor. "Give him a blade and I'll carve him up good, Jorik. We don't have to listen to scum like him." Halfhand's words provoked a murmur of assent, which rippled down the hall. Jorik held up his hand and silence fell at once.

"You placed little regard on granting my people an honourable death when you were raiding our lands."

"They were not warriors," replied Blackeyes, as if that excused everything. "I am duty bound to tell you Adalrikr's terms, no matter how unwelcome they may be to you. In return for your loyalty, you will also pay tribute each spring, sending us a tenth of your produce, goods and coin. In addition, Adalrikr demands you send six men and six women with the tribute. They shall all be between the ages of eighteen and twenty-four, fit, healthy and wholesome to look upon, to serve as Adalrikr's personal thralls." As Blackeyes set out these further terms discontented grumblings filled the Great Hall and Olfridor Halfhand could take no more.

"Enough!" he roared, silencing everyone. Blackeyes didn't flinch, merely bowing his head as if Halfhand had politely asked to be given a moment to make a point during an interesting debate between two scholars. "You've got a pair, Tyrfingr, and no mistake, to come to Ulfkell's Keep alone demanding our surrender. Do you take us all for cowards? I'll sooner die than bend the knee to Adalrikr – the lad killed his own father."

"Asmarr was weak," retorted Blackeyes, his composure suddenly less controlled. "I would have driven in the knife myself, had Adalrikr asked me too. Now I serve a master with vision, who will rise above the petty squabbles of our competing families and clans. One day you will all pay homage and call him king of Laskar, if you're still alive."

"Get out," cried Jorik. "Go while you still can. Tell Adalrikr his terms are unacceptable and insulting. He should watch his own borders before laying claim to Reavesburg lands."

Tyrfingr Blackeyes paused for a moment and I waited for him to say something more. Only then did I notice that his gaze was no longer on my brother. Etta's stooped form stood half shrouded in the shadows of the hall, leaning on her stick. Adalrikr's emissary was watching her with an odd expression on his face. Was it surprise or fear? It was gone before I could make up my mind, and he turned back to look at my brother.

"Foolish boy. They were generous terms. You'll regret your hasty words, though perhaps not for long." Blackeyes swept from the Great Hall, Finnvidor and his men falling in step to escort him outside the gates of Reavesburg.

CHAPTER 7

The challenge laid down by the Vorund Clan could not go unanswered by Jorik, not after the insults of Tyrfingr Blackeyes. At sixteen and of noble blood, I was deemed too young to be sent into war: the Reavesburg Clan couldn't afford to lose both my father's heirs in a single battle. I burned to prove myself worthy as a man and a warrior but Jorik and the elders of our clan were adamant. There were other ways I could serve my brother at this time, and I knew the duty I was expected to perform. The question was whether Gautarr still wanted the match.

Reavesburg warriors are usually blooded in their first raids against the weaker clans or the Northern Plainsmen. Jorik faced the unenviable challenge of an engagement with Vorund. Ulfkell's Keep was soon in uproar and Jorik sought me out amidst the chaos, making me promise to care for Reesha and his son if he didn't return.

"It won't come to that," I said, trying to keep the worry out of my own voice.

"You know it might. Much as I hate to admit it, Blackeyes was right. I've still to be blooded and if I expect our people to follow me I have to lead this attack, otherwise I'll never be worthy to sit on Reave's Chair. I need to know that if anything happens to me, you'll care for Reesha and Kolfinnar. If the worst happens you'll have to lead our people ..."

Jorik broke off, clasping me tightly. Only our grandfather, Marl, had ruled our clan at a younger age than Jorik. If the title passed to me at my tender years Gautarr or Ragnar were sure to challenge for the leadership. If my brother died at the hands of the Vorund Clan it would be a death sentence for me as well. The stakes had never been higher as Finnvidor prepared our warships for a raid into Vorund Clan territory and their northerly settlements near Viskanir.

I wandered through the keep, somewhat at a loss, since I had no real role in the plans for the attack. My thoughts were so far away my heart almost stopped when Etta spoke. It was rumoured she had now passed her hundredth year, though of course there were none still alive who could vouch for that fact. Regardless, her ability to creep up on me unawares seemed undiminished.

"Poor Rothgar, you look so lost. Trust me, your time will come soon enough. Always with young noble men they dream of proving themselves in battle. Remember that path can be a short one."

I was bad-tempered and in no mood for Etta's wisdom. "And what would you know of war and the ways of men, old woman?"

"What, *precisely*, do you know of it, stripling?" Etta retorted. My face reddened as the truth of her words struck home. Was Jorik any better prepared for what lay before him?

"I've lived under the rule of *five* clan chiefs," Etta continued, prodding me with her stick to drive her point home. "You don't understand war just by knowing how to hold a sword in your hand. Knowing your foes and why you set out to war is far more important than wielding an axe or a blade."

"Are you saying Jorik shouldn't set forth on this raid?"

"No, I'm not. Jorik has no choice other than to strike at Adalrikr's forces. If he hesitates he will appear weak, and our rival clans will raid us. He'll also invite Gautarr to challenge for the leadership of our clan if he lets Blackeyes' taunts go unanswered. No, Jorik must go to war and prove himself worthy of the name Kolfinnarson. What's just as important is that you must also prove yourself worthy too."

I thought I knew what Etta was referring to and my disappointment at being left behind in Reavesburg caused me to rail at her words. "Marriage. Is that all you think I'm good for? Why have I spent all these years learning swordsmanship with Halfhand if the only thing I'm supposed to do is marry some bad-tempered –"

"Please spare me the lecture. You're young – I pray that's the only reason you're so self-pitying. Listen to what I'm saying and stop thinking about yourself for a moment." My mouth dropped open at Etta's rebuke and the old crone was unrelenting as she continued her reprimand.

"Do you think that Blackeyes or Adalrikr are unskilled in the art of war? They have forced Jorik's hand and he must attack them. Knowing this, if you were Adalrikr what would you do?"

I paused as I digested Etta's words and her one good eye regarded me intently, making me squirm under her scrutiny. I forced myself to relax, applying myself to this question as I would to any other lesson of my aged tutor; the answer struck me forcibly.

"Adalrikr will wait until Jorik sets sail with our strongest warriors. Then, when Reavesburg is relatively unprotected, he will strike at us, showing Jorik to be impetuous and a poor leader. He's set a trap for us, one which we have no choice except to walk into."

"Exactly," Etta hissed. "Clearly I haven't been wasting my time with you after all. So, why do you skulk about Ulfkell's Keep with the air of someone who has been wronged and unjustly ignored? You want to be a warrior? This is your chance to prove your worth."

"I'm sorry, Etta, I spoke out of turn before. I can see why my father relies on your counsel." I began to spring back down the stairs with a renewed sense of purpose, intent on seeking out Olfridor. Yet before I had gone more than ten paces, Etta spoke to me again, bringing me to a halt with little more than a whisper.

"What about Desta?" My stomach churned at those words. We had been so discreet. Was there *nothing* Etta didn't know? It was pointless to feign ignorance.

"I'm not yet married, Etta. Are you going to tell me I'm the first man to have bedded another woman before his wedding day?"

"Of course not. Nor will you be the first noble to sire a bastard by a servant girl. You have been with her a *year*, Rothgar. It takes less time than that to bring forth a child into this world. Who do you think it is that gives Desta the herbs to keep her womb barren?" I stared at Etta, unable to admit I had never given such things a moment's thought. She seemed to read my mind as she continued relentlessly.

"Those herbs are not completely effective. Sooner or later Desta will find herself with child if you continue down this path. A child from the line of Kolfinnar in these times will be a target for your enemies, as will the child's mother. If I know of your nightly trysts with Desta, then there's a risk others already do within the keep. Has Desta held her tongue? No, don't look at me like that – can you know that for *certain*? Not everyone in this keep is loyal to you. I have my spies in every clan and you should be in no doubt other chiefs have their own whisperers, right here in this keep. So, if you care for her at all, set her aside, as you should have done when your father first fell ill."

"Thank you for your advice," I replied stiffly.

Etta looked at me for a time, and when she spoke again her tone was gentler. "Rothgar, listen to me. I only want the best for you, believe me. I'm trying to spare both of you from the misery that can only follow from pursuing this path. You and Desta are not destined to be together, whatever your feelings are for her now. Some things cannot be, and no amount of wishing otherwise can change that fact."

"Thank you for your advice," I repeated, turning and descending the stairs once more, desperate to escape from Etta's presence as if Tyrfingr Blackeyes himself was pursuing me. She said nothing else as I fled, although I felt her burning gaze was on me until, breathing unsteadily and with shaking hands, I firmly closed the door to my chamber.

***

As our forces rode towards the coastal town of Noln that morning the smell of smoke was noticeable, even at this distance. I glanced across at Olfridor Halfhand, his lined face set determinedly as he surveyed the scene. He was one of the few warriors with any real experience of battle in my company. Most were young men still completing their weapons training, such as Bram and Bandor. At eighteen Haarl was one of the oldest of the warriors under my command.

After Etta's warning, I had spoken to Olfridor, confiding in him my concerns about the risk of a counterattack from Vorund. To his credit, he had listened carefully to the words of Kolfinnar's inexperienced younger son.

"You spoken to your brother about this?"

I shook my head. "Jorik's placed me in command of the defence of Ulfkell's Keep whilst Finnvidor's away. We can't know for certain that there'll even be an attack, it's just a possible tactic Etta thinks the Vorund Clan might use."

Olfridor looked thoughtful, scratching his greying beard. "In my experience Etta has an uncanny knack of guessing these things right. I agree with you, though; there's no need to start any rumours that'll cause panic and Jorik's got enough on his mind right now. Viskanir will be a tough fight and I don't want him taking too few men with him so that our own strike at Adalrikr fails. No, we need to keep this one quiet. Just leave things to me."

Jorik set sail amid great fanfare, waving confidently to the crowd gathered on the docks as he stood on the deck of *Marl's Pride*, Brunn Fourwinds shouting out various orders to his crew. He looked so like our father I had to take several deep breaths to hold back tears, wishing bitterly he could have seen this sight for himself. Johan Jokellsward's own longship, *Hammerhead*, was already sailing down the River Jelt towards the sea. The docks heaved with activity as Finnvidor supervised loading the last of the supplies onto his own vessel.

Six ships in total were setting out for Viskanir, a fearsome war party designed to send Adalrikr a clear message.

Reesha was not there to see off her husband, unable to contain her sobbing as Jorik made ready in Ulfkell's Keep. I helped buckle him into his chainmail armour myself before handing him his sword. My brother was ready for battle but his face looked strained as he tried to comfort Reesha.

"I'll be back in just six days, Reesha. Five if the winds favour us and there's none better than Brunn at reading those."

Reesha turned her tear-streaked face to Jorik, nursing Kolfinnar on her lap. "Just take care. I'll be praying to Dinuvillan for you."

"*Take care?*" grumbled Jorik afterwards as we hurried towards the docks, Finnvidor shouting at people to get out of the way as an honour guard formed around us in the courtyard. "I'm sailing into a battle. What exactly does she expect me to do?"

"Just come back alive," I answered.

Jorik smiled at that. "A good plan. Tell Reesha not to worry, I'll see her and Kolfinnar in just six days; you have my word on that."

Despite Jorik's confident words, the knot of worry that had settled in my stomach since my conversation with Etta tightened another notch as I watched *Marl's Pride* cast off, the oarsmen taking the strain and manoeuvring her out into the river.

"God's, I wish I was going with them," muttered Bram, standing next to me on the dockside.

"Me too. It's good to have you with me here, all the same," I replied, clapping him on the back. "Our time will come soon enough."

A good part of me hoped I was wrong as Olfridor and Haarl quietly made preparations to ensure the small garrison left stationed in Reavesburg was ready to respond quickly to any attack. It was only two days later that the beacons were lit, just as Etta had predicted. Noln had been the scene of

Father's last great victory over the Vorund Clan six years ago. On reflection it was an obvious move, designed to challenge Jorik's authority on the very doorstep of his own hall and prove he was not the man our father was. As we rounded a bend in the road a cry went up from my men as we saw a thick cloud of smoke hanging over Noln, a dark stain spreading across the clear blue sky. I spurred my horse forwards, fearing we were too late and our enemies had already escaped.

As we swiftly closed the distance I spied three ships beached on the bay at Noln, the image of the bear emblazoned on their sails. I swallowed as I saw the black sails on one ship clearly displaying Tyrfingr Blackeyes' white bear sigil. Noln's wooden gates were standing wide open, the Vorund raiders marshalling their captives as they dragged various items of booty towards their ships. I wondered whether they still had anyone on watch now their dawn raid was almost complete and, if so, how attentive they were being to their duties.

"Keep quiet," I called out to those riding alongside me, some fifty men (or, in some cases, boys). I tried to instil a note of command into my voice I didn't truly feel, even as Olfridor nodded at me in agreement. "No war cry. Let's catch them unawares." As one our cavalry force broke into a gallop and in moments battle was joined.

I had expected to feel fear and there was certainly a sense of that as I drew my sword at the head of our charge. More than that I felt excitement and, unexpectedly, resignation and indifference to my fate. Any Laskan warrior is raised to believe death in battle is the most honourable way to reach Navan's Halls. This was something I'd been trained to do since I was ten years old. My sword felt part of me, perfectly fitting the grip of my hand. The tangled web of politics and intrigue at Ulfkell's Keep was forgotten in the dizzying rush and excitement of war. I was about to become a man in the eyes of my people and if I fell today, I knew my father would be proud.

It was clear as we reached the beach that Noln's

defenders had already been defeated. Vorund's warriors were busy trying to separate men and women who had been captured as thralls from screaming relatives, desperate to bargain for their freedom or else saying tearful farewells to their loved ones. In the tumult taking place in front of their ships, we were upon the raiders before they even realised they were under attack. I shifted my weight, swung my sword and was surprised at its sharpness as it cut through the neck of the armoured man dragging a husband and wife apart. She screamed in fright as he dropped to the ground, dead before he hit the sand. We broke upon our foes silently, the momentum of our charge driving us deep into their midst, as sword and axe hacked down upon our enemies.

I brought my courser around, regrouping with Olfridor and Bram as the Vorund Clan scattered before us. Attacking unarmed men, women and children was one thing but these raiders were unprepared to engage a mounted company of warriors, even though they outnumbered us two to one. There was panic in their ranks as our foes dropped the goods they were carrying and abandoned their captives in a desperate bid to reach their ships. I looked up to see the crews of all three vessels desperately pushing their longships back out into the sea. Olfridor, Bram and I spurred our horses forwards in an attempt to interfere with their escape and cut off Vorund's retreating warriors, targeting Blackeyes' black-sailed ship. I swung my sword again and one of the Vorund Clan's fighters fell into the shallow sea, his blood tainting the water red. War seemed ridiculously easy in those giddy moments, and I wondered why the Vorund Clan was so feared. None of my foes was brave enough to raise their weapon against me.

I didn't see the arrow, instead feeling its impact as my horse shuddered and shrieked in fright and pain. My courser stumbled on the wet sand and went down, dragging me with her. A wave hit my face and I was underwater, my leg pinned beneath the weight of the thrashing animal. I struggled to hold onto my sword, fighting to free myself from the saddle.

I forced my head above the waves, spitting out salt water and straining to free my leg as my horse gurgled, her struggling already fading as she bled to death from the arrow in her neck. In the distance behind me I could hear cries of alarm from both Bram and Olfridor. Another wave knocked into me as I slid my leg out from the saddle and found my feet in an ungainly fashion. I looked up at the retreating black-sailed ship, now deep enough into the water for its crew to deploy their oars and pull for safety and the open sea. At the stern stood Tyrfingr Blackeyes, drawing back his bow once more. He released the arrow and I saw it approach me as a dark blur. The feathers of the shaft grazed my neck as the arrow skimmed above my right shoulder. I fell, warm blood flowing freely from my neck as I landed in the stinging salt water once more. I flailed helplessly for a moment, before strong arms bore me upwards and I gratefully took in great shuddering breaths of air.

"Look out," yelled Olfridor. Having dismounted to haul me to my feet, my weapon's master ran to meet the first warrior bearing down upon us. I watched dumbly as he brought his axe round in a wide arc, burying it in his skull. In one swift motion he checked his stride and jerked the weapon free before bringing it up to parry the blow of the next warrior. With the benefit of surprise, a mounted warrior is no match for an opponent on foot across open ground. Now, with no such advantage and faced with men who knew they must reach the safety of their ships if they were to stand any chance of returning home, my position was far weaker. The only thing in my favour was that every oar stroke of their ship left these men further behind on the shore. They would not tarry in their bid to escape – neither would they allow me to stand in their way.

More than a dozen men were splashing through the waters towards me. I brought up my blade and swung wildly at the first man, connecting with nothing more solid than air. He charged past me into the deeper waters, calling out franticly to his comrades on the ship not to leave him behind. I paid him no more attention as the next man bore down on me, his bearded face snarling beneath a fine steel helmet. He swiped at me with his axe and I parried the blow with my sword, marvelling at how perfectly balanced my weapon was. I slid the blade down the shaft of the warrior's axe, taking grim satisfaction in his shocked cry as I sliced away the fingers of his right hand. The man gasped in agony as he dropped to his knees, before I silenced him with a further blow to the head.

Suddenly I was alone. The surviving warriors were past me, climbing aboard their ship. I could see Blackeyes regarding me balefully, unable to loose another arrow amid the confusion as the last of his men scrambled aboard. The ship's oars struck the water and propelled it out into the Redfars Sea as Olfridor joined me, gasping, at my side.

"You alright?" he shouted. I grinned stupidly up at him, feeling a swell of pride as he clapped me on the shoulder. I looked out at the three retreating ships and my heart jumped as our own longships came into view, young Ulf's vessel leading the way. Cries of dismay rose up from the Vorund Clan's vessels as three of our own bore down on them. Archers stationed aboard my ships let loose a volley of arrows into the nearest raiding craft. I could hear shouts and screams and watched as the beat of their oars become unsteady, slowing the raider's ship enough for our own to close upon it. Grappling hooks flew out, biting deep into both wood and flesh, as the Vorund craft was dragged towards Ulf's ship. In moments our warriors leapt across into the enemy vessel, swiftly bringing it under their control. The remaining two Vorund Clan ships, including the one occupied by Tyrfingr Blackeyes, had by now caught the wind and were making swift progress southwards. My own ships gave chase but regardless of the outcome one captured longship from the Vorund Clan was already a fine prize.

I turned back to watch as those unfortunate members of the Vorund Clan who had been left behind were killed by my men; we would not be taking any thralls back to Reavesburg today. I saw Bram riding slowly towards me and hailed him, glad to see my friend had acquitted himself with honour. A smile broke upon his ashen face as he approached me, before he slid from the saddle of his horse into the sea. Olfridor and I reached him in moments, pulling him out from the cold water and dragging him back onto the sandy beach. I glanced down and my stomach turned over as I saw the black-feathered shaft of an arrow buried deep into his thigh: blood was gushing from the wound. My hand flew to my grazed neck and I turned back to my own dead horse, my gaze resting on an identical black-fletched arrow that lay buried in the poor beast.

"Rothgar," Bram gasped. "I took two of them with me. Father should be proud."

"You'll no doubt add to that tally," I replied, intent on staunching the relentless flow of blood, as Olfridor began tearing strips of cloth to make a bandage. Bram's face was white and he shivered as he laughed at my words. I told myself it was the effects of the water.

"I'm cold, Rothgar. I need to rest ... Find a warm fire ..."

With Olfridor's help, I carried Bram up from the beach into the ravaged town of Noln. I barely saw the distressed townsfolk on the shore, weeping over lost loved ones or the destruction of their possessions and livelihood. Noln itself was alight in several places, people rushing about with buckets as they tried to douse the blaze. We ignored them all and reached a quieter spot near an undamaged inn. I pounded on the door and demanded admittance, barging inside when there was no answer. Together, Olfridor and I dragged Bram into the deserted bar, setting him down as gently as we could.

"We need to find some dry clothes and get that shaft out of him," I barked at Olfridor. I had no idea how to go about such a thing. Halfhand had seen more battles than I could count and he would know what to do.

"Rothgar, listen to me, son. It's too late. There's nothing we can do for the lad, now. I'm sorry."

I looked down to see Bram's glassy, sightless eyes staring back at me. I placed my arms around his still warm body, feeling as if someone had stabbed my guts.

Olfridor laid a hand gently on my shoulder. "It's never the same as it is in the songs, son. I'm sorry."

Dazed and confused, I released my hold on my friend and stumbled from the silent inn, Olfridor half-carrying my weight.

CHAPTER 8

Vorund's dead were claimed by the bloody surf as the afternoon's high tide crashed onto the beach. Stripped clean of anything useful, the bodies of our enemy were washed back into the sea, never to plague our shores again. Yet we all knew that sooner or later more ships would appear on the horizon, bearing the banner of the black bear on their sails. We had to pay our respects for our own dead, tend to the wounded and rebuild Noln's defences.

Against Blackeyes' disorganised warriors our small mounted force had suffered few casualties: just four dead, including Bram, and another eight with relatively minor injuries. Haarl sported a ragged cut across his eyebrows with a mixture of discomfort and pride. Now battle was over I became aware of the pain in my left leg, caused when I was trapped under my horse. I was relieved nothing was broken. I didn't want to bear the same name as my father.

The townsfolk of Noln had suffered far worse, with more than thirty of their people slain. At least we arrived in time to prevent Blackeyes from boarding with his captives, sparing them the humiliation of life as thralls. Even so, it would take time to repair the damage to the gates of the town and a number of its buildings would have to be demolished. I saw Lundvarr, Noln's noble-born town elder, wringing his hands as he surveyed the scene. His normally fine clothes were ragged and his dark curly hair unkempt. People now pressed around him, clamouring for his attention. I limped forwards, squaring my shoulders to hide my tiredness and grief. Lundvarr's wild eyes fixed on me with a desperate gleam, stark white against his soot-blackened face. He stepped forward, grasping my hand in both of his as he fell to his knees.

"Jorik Kolfinnarson, we are forever in your family's debt. Truly, you are your father's son. Twice now, the family of the eighth clan chief has ridden to our aid in my time as elder." I cleared my throat, wondering how best to respond. I decided to be straightforward, even though the man's unfortunate mistake rankled.

"It's my duty to defend my people, Lundvarr. Yet you accord me an honour that is not mine to accept. I am Rothgar Kolfinnarson, Kolfinnar's younger son. Even now my brother Jorik is at sea, intent on raiding the Vorund Clan's shores and avenging the losses they have inflicted upon us. My duty is to keep watch over Reavesburg whilst he is gone." As Lundvarr comprehended the full meaning of my words, his eyes grew impossibly wider with fear.

"My lord. Of course, please, a thousand apologies. How could I have mistaken you? Indeed, I have met you and your brother before – clearly you are both your father's sons. The likeness you both share with him is most marked. Of course, your brother is a far taller and broader man than yourself and I should have realised ..." Lundvarr gave an odd strangled cry and ran his hands through his hair. I reminded myself I had come to help these people as Lundvarr babbled on. "... that is to say that ... er ... though lighter of frame your ... your speed and skill with a sword is legendary. Ahem ... Yes indeed, word of it has spread even as far as here. Now I can say I've seen with my own eyes how you slew ten men as your warriors broke Blackeyes upon the beach. A deed fit for great Darri himself to put to song ..."

"Three," I corrected, hauling Lundvarr to his feet before the spectacle became even more embarrassing. "I killed three of Blackeyes' warriors this morning, though I wish it had been more. Had we come sooner, we might have prevented the breach of your walls and perhaps Tyrfingr Blackeyes would be in chains."

"Their fire arrows caused the greatest harm," Lundvarr

replied, his voice shaking as he wondered whether or not he had given offence. "The fires caused such panic and confusion it was difficult for us to man the walls effectively. They scaled them where our defences were thin and overwhelmed the men at the gates. Once they were open there was little we could do."

I nodded towards the town square, where the captured weapons and armour of more than forty slain Vorund warriors had been piled, recovered by my men from the beach before they were lost to the tide. The spoils of war were mine by right.

"Keep it all. You can use it to re-equip your own fighting men. Sell whatever you don't require to help pay for the repairs you need to make to Noln."

"Rothgar Kolfinnarson," Lundvarr gushed. "You're a generous man indeed. How can we ever repay you?"

"The captured ship is payment enough. She's a fine vessel for me to bring back to Reavesburg and I'm sure her loss will grieve Tyrfingr Blackeyes greatly. I'll take some satisfaction in that."

Lundvarr clasped my hands one last time and took his leave. I watched as he called the townsfolk together and they swiftly laid hands on the heap of plunder. Haarl glanced up questioningly, though at a nod from me he didn't interfere; within moments the pile of arms and armour had vanished. I turned away to find Bandor approaching me, his face sombre.

"That was certainly an act of kindness. Your father carried back everything seized from the Vorund Clan when he rode out to defend Noln."

"I'm not my father. The better defended Noln is the more able they'll be to repel any invaders. Watch towers or no, the warriors of Ulfkell's Keep can't ride out to stop every raid on our shores. Today, I'll take the ship. That'll be a sight for Jorik when he returns."

"Aye, that it will," chuckled Bandor. The familiarity of his laughter was comforting, if somewhat at odds with his blood-spattered face. "Listen, Olfridor's asking for you. You're needed at the pyre."

***

I looked down on Bram's face one last time. My boyhood friend looked serene, lying next to his three fellow warriors, all of them dressed in armour and clutching their swords or axes. Their glorious deaths assured that they would carry their weapons proudly into Navan's Halls. Noln's fallen townsfolk were honoured to share the pyre with my warriors. My men had worked throughout the day to build the enormous woodpile. When one of the townsfolk foolishly complained within earshot of Olfridor that we wasted wood needed to rebuild Noln, I thought the old warrior would have his head. At his scowl the man fled, to mutters of derision from the warriors gathered there. Our people had given their lives for their clan and, in return, we were duty bound to attend to their remains with the greatest respect.

As I stepped forward to light the pyre I suddenly recalled the day of my mother's funeral. The formal words my father had used returned to me easily, as if I had learned them by rote in one of Etta's lessons that morning. I thought of Tyrfingr's arrow missing by a hair's breadth, absently running my fingers over the raw cut on the side of my neck.

"It's the fate of all mankind to follow the flow of the river of time. The river whose current only travels endlessly in one direction, bringing us all to Navan when our allotted span is up. May Navan welcome those who have fallen today warmly into the Halls of the Dead, as they proudly join their ancestors. We all know the Creator will judge us by our deeds when Dinas' watch finally comes to an end, and we pray he will judge as worthy those we put to rest today. And so we commit their souls to Navan's care, until the time of judgement."

Those old words found new meaning as a wall of sound thundered from my warriors, each one beating their weapons on their shields and roaring battle cries. My shaking hand thrust the burning torch deep into the pyre and I held my breath for a moment, only exhaling as the flames caught and smoke began to waft up around the bodies in front of me.

In minutes, the whole pyre was ablaze, glowing redly in the gathering gloom as the sun began to set. As I stood there, Halfhand clapped me firmly on the shoulders, sending pain shooting through my injured leg.

"Well spoken," he said quietly, looking deep into the fire. "You've a way with words, like your father. You shouldered a man's burden today. I'm proud of you and your father will be too, when he hears what happened today."

I nodded, guilty tears coursing down my cheeks, unchecked. "I think the arrow that took Bram's life was meant for me. It was Tyrfingr Blackeyes who let it fly. Another inch and I'd be lying on that pyre."

"That's often the way of it," Olfridor replied. "When I was young, I thought nothing and no one could bring me down in a straight fight. Took me years to figure blind luck plays its part. You don't see many warriors reach my age. Truth is, I've only seen this many winters because I put aside my axe eighteen years ago, after I earned my current name. Being called 'Halfhand' isn't something I'm proud of. Knew even back then I was getting slow and Finnvidor was ready to take my place. But being an old warrior's not an easy path, either, and Kolfinnar knew that well enough, which is why he asked me to train his young lads to be fighters. I knew it was an honour, and all, though it's not the same. What I'm trying to say is I was glad to ride out at your side, like old times. I was ready to die today, as were all these warriors following you, Bram included, because you're Kolfinnar's kin. You've proved you're your father's son today, and I reckon the Vorund Clan might think twice before they cross swords with us again."

I understood what Olfridor was telling me. Given the choice, my father would have chosen death at the hands of the Vorund Clan when he rode out to repel the attack on Noln, had he known that six years later he would see out the rest of his days bed-ridden. Even so, as the fire took hold and thick smoke billowed into the darkening sky, I couldn't help feeling that Bram deserved more than sixteen years before his life was cut short.

***

We rode out from Noln as heroes the following morning. My leg had stiffened in the night and burned like fire in the saddle. I set my face and ignored it, waving to the townsfolk as they cheered my company of warriors. We rode back towards Reavesburg with our heads held high, enjoying the crowd's adulation. It struck me forcibly I was now a man in the eyes of my people. If Jorik could find similar fortune then, perhaps, our line would be assured after all.

I wished Bram were riding at my side. I could see his freckled face as clearly as if he stood before me, and smiled remembering the times we had filched food from under Cook's nose in the kitchens of Ulfkell's Keep. Bram, too, had earned his place as a warrior yesterday. It was some comfort but I still averted my gaze as we rode out past the smouldering funeral pyre.

"How's the leg?" Bandor asked, riding next to me, his expression thoughtful. He had been close to Bram too.

"I'll live. Look at you – not a scratch."

"I wonder if that's how Father will see it."

"Well, he wanted Halfhand to school you in the arts of war."

"I'm not sure riding out with him to fight Tyrfingr Blackeyes himself was what he had in mind."

We laughed aloud at that, imagining Johan's face when he learned his only son had followed me into to battle against the Vorund Clan's most feared warrior at just sixteen. As for my father, well, surely now he would see me in a new light.

***

Reavesburg was deathly quiet in the dawn light as our small force wended its way down the road. I saw Olfridor's face tighten as he looked ahead and I did the same, half expecting to see a column of smoke rising from Ulfkell's Keep. I felt tense, imagining a cunning double-bluff by Blackeyes, striking whilst I had left my home undefended. Reavesburg seemed peaceful enough, yet as we rode through the docks I was struck by the absence of any activity. Normally, the fishermen would be landing last night's catch whilst merchants argued about whose goods should be unloaded first, all under the watchful eye of Finnvidor's men. The silence was unnerving, and the rest of my men began to murmur in hushed tones. I glanced at the keep and spied a black flag flying from the North Tower. Spurring my horse forward, ignoring the cries of alarm from Olfridor and Bandor, I rode hard for the gates. Two warriors were standing there, heads bowed.

"Open the gates," I bellowed. They obeyed me without hesitation and I charged through the deserted streets of the town, skidding to a halt in the courtyard of Ulfkell's Keep where Desta called out to me. I paid her no heed as I hastily dismounted, ignoring the discomfort in my leg, and pushed open the doors to the Great Hall. Inside, the room was empty, save for a small blonde figure by the fire. She was crying. I limped the length of the hall to where Nuna lay sprawled over the still body of our father. He seemed to be at peace, although I could find none myself as I looked down at my sobbing sister. In that moment I felt utterly alone.

CHAPTER 9

Reesha's beautiful face was drawn tight with worry as she hugged me. Amma was busy entertaining young Kolfinnar, whilst Reesha took my hands and led me to a seat in her chambers. Nuna, now a young woman in her own right, had become Reesha's constant companion and joined us. My sister had, mercifully, ceased her crying. She had yet to utter a single word since my arrival that morning, her normally stunning blonde locks hanging dishevelled about her tear-stained face. Reesha was more forthcoming, explaining how Father had been taken ill with laboured breathing shortly after my departure for Noln. Etta had tended to him without delay, but his heart gave out as he slept in the Great Hall. I sat there grimly, absorbing the news. While Reesha had been fond of my father, I knew the real reason for this audience and she came to the point soon enough.

"Rothgar, what are we to do?" she asked. "Jorik's away at sea with the best part of our strength, and he may never return. What's to become of us?" I looked at my sister-in-law, trying to muster confidence I didn't feel. Becoming a man, blooded in battle, counted for little now.

"I can remember talking to Jorik and having the same worries when Father last rode out to fight the Vorund Clan," I answered. "You've nothing to fear, Reesha."

"The difference is Kolfinnar returned alive. Now he's dead." I jumped out of my seat in fright, whirling round to find Etta had been in the room all the time.

"Is that meant to be comforting?" I gasped, heart hammering. "Are you saying Jorik isn't coming back?"

"No one can say for certain what your brother's fate will

be at the hands of Adalrikr's forces. The point is that even if he does come back he's not Kolfinnar Marlson, and neither are you. I prayed Kolfinnar would live longer, to allow more time for you two boys to grow. It wasn't to be and now both of you are more vulnerable than ever. You have to think with your wits, Rothgar, and make plans for what's to come, because as soon as your father's funeral is over Gautarr will call for a clan moot. The elders of the clan will have to decide whether to put their faith in you and your brother, or turn to someone else to lead them."

"They'll follow me," I insisted. "I saw that yesterday. If Jorik fares as well in battle too then we'll have the support of our people."

"Perhaps," Etta mused. "Gautarr has no skill for politics but don't forget he's led his people against the Vorund Clan more times than you can count. Both he and Ragnar can claim more experience on the battlefield than you or your brother. The question is whether the people look to your family out of loyalty, seek a great warrior in Gautarr or agree a compromise."

"Meaning?"

"Johan Jokellsward, of course. Remember, if the people choose another leader your only course is to assert your right to the title in trial by combat. Are you, or Jorik for that matter, willing to kill Gautarr or Johan to preserve your father's line?"

Reesha bridled at that remark. "Etta. How dare you. You're talking about my father and Kolfinnar's grandfather. I can assure you that he has no designs on being chief."

"Your father may feel he has no choice, if Kolfinnar's sons are unable to muster enough support. Better take control and secure Bandor's succession than Gautarr, who, let's be frank, will have you and your son done away with should he rise to power." At these words Amma gave a small cry, whisking Kolfinnar out of the room to play in another part of the keep. I wondered how much the boy had understood of the conversation so far.

"I'm sorry, Reesha," Etta continued, her voice softer.

"Some truths are harsh and hard to hear. That doesn't make them any the less true. It's important you listen to me. I was Kolfinnar's advisor for almost twenty years, and played the same role for Marl before that. You need to think and not just act if you're to see yourselves through to the other side of this crisis."

"And you think you're best placed to advise us?" I asked.

"Yes, my boy. Yes, I most certainly do," replied Etta, grinning at me.

***

The water in the tub was hot, its warmth working its way deep into my aching muscles. Desta wet my hair and began to wash it with firm, gentle strokes. It was not uncommon for servants to perform such tasks for the nobles they attended and, naturally, I favoured Desta in such matters. My back and shoulders were stiff, whilst my backside was feeling the effects of the ride. I stretched out my leg, sporting a colourful display of black and purple bruises, and sighed deeply as I found myself mulling over Etta's words in the peace and quiet of my chamber. Jorik had been groomed to lead our people from the moment of his birth. The role, at least for now, had passed to me and, whilst I felt unready for the burden, there was no one else to take it. Etta spoke wisely but I realised I knew little about the woman herself. She had been one of my father's closest advisors over the years. With him gone, I had to decide whether I could trust the old woman. As a boy I had only ever looked on her as my aged tutor. Now, as I thought more carefully, I understood how my father must have relied upon her wealth of experience to help guide his rule. As Desta took a cake of soap and began to wash away the dirt of road and battle, I reflected I would be a fool to spurn her offer of assistance.

"Do you need anything further, my lord?" Desta asked, her voice quiet.

"I'll rest here a while longer, Desta, that's all. And please, in my chambers I would prefer it if you called me Rothgar." She was silent for a long time and I began to wonder if she were going to answer at all.

"You're chief now. At least until such time as your brother returns from sea. I wasn't sure whether you still wanted anything more of me." I turned in the water so that I faced her, staying the movement of her wet soapy hands with mine.

"Desta, yesterday I saw one of my best friends die in battle before my eyes and today I lost my father. And all anyone has said to me concerns the future of the Reavesburg Clan, not my loss. Believe me, I need you now more than ever." She smiled, her young face lighting up. In that moment I truly meant what I said, heedless of the danger I placed her in as I drew her lips towards mine.

**

I rose quietly, leaving Desta undisturbed in my bed as I padded across the floor to the window of my chamber. Carefully opening the wooden shutters, I peered outside. It was a clear night and I could see the wooden docks down by the sea, standing out stark white in the light of the full moon. The captured Vorund ship had been moored there earlier that afternoon, after Ulf's vessels brought her back from Noln. I watched as she gently bobbed up and down on the waves, the calm motion at odds with the violence of the previous day. I realised my father would never know me as a man. He would never hear of my deeds during the battle at Noln, when I drove off Tyrfingr Blackeyes himself. I stood there for a long time, looking up into the glittering stars in the night sky, while tears coursed silently and unchecked down my face.

**

My composure was restored the following day; it was expected of me and I tried to conduct all my duties in a manner that would make my father proud. The beacons on the watch towers had been lit the previous night, conveying the message up and down the coast to Kalamar and Romsdahl that Kolfinnar Marlson was dead. Haarl had also despatched riders inland to bring them the grim news, whilst merchant vessels carried the tidings back to Ingioy and Bothvatr. A clan moot was customary, when the leaders of the six most influential families in the Reavesburg Clan would meet to discuss the succession. On some occasions, the election of the new chief was a formality. This time, I knew the clan gathering could pose many difficulties.

I set those concerns to one side, however, as I dealt with the more immediate task of my father's funeral. It felt comforting to have something practical to arrange, giving my day a sense of purpose; and in Jorik's absence I was glad of the distraction. The pyre of Noln was still fresh in my mind, and such an end would have been fitting for my father. However, since he was our chief I felt he was due a greater honour, and my eyes fixed on the captured ship from Vorund. The only plunder from my victory, signifying the rite of passage from boyhood to manhood, seemed the proper tribute for a son to offer his late father. The ship was readied, stacked with wood and oil by Olfridor, Ulf, Bandor and Haarl, garlanded with flowers by Reesha, Amma, Katla and Nuna. I dressed my father in his armour myself, noting with sorrow how this dwarfed his wasted frame. As he was laid aboard the ship, I placed his sword at his side, whispered my goodbyes and walked back to the crowd of onlookers gathered on the dockside.

Slowly the funeral ship was towed out towards the open sea, before its unfurled sail, now bearing the Reavesburg emblem of the eagle, caught the breeze and it began to pick up speed of its own accord. Olfridor passed me the bow and I drew back the string and waited as he lit the arrow; I was never keen on archery and knew it would be an ill omen to miss my target. Taking careful aim, I loosed the shaft and watched it arc gracefully over the water. There was a dull thud as it found its mark, drawing appreciative noises from the crowd of mourners and a clap on the back from Halfhand. In minutes, the entire ship was ablaze.

I was unable to take my eyes off the sight of the burning

vessel. Nearby, Darri struck up a song of mourning, recalling the great deeds of all the clan chiefs of Reavesburg. He expertly weaved the events of my father's own life into the familiar song, as if those verses had always formed part of the original composition. I was struck that, in years to come, this was how my father would be remembered. Tears stung my eyes once more and I was grateful for the presence of Olfridor and Bandor as they silently shared my grief with me.

"You alright?" asked Halfhand, his hand on my shoulder.

"Not really, Olfridor. Now it falls to me to keep my father's kingdom together, and it's a heavy burden."

"Us," Bandor remarked. "It falls to all of us. We'll stand by you at the clan moot."

"That we will," Olfridor agreed. "But bollocks to all that. For now, we forget about the worries tomorrow brings. We'll go back to the Great Hall and we'll drink to your father's memory. This is his day, so let's drown our sorrows and remember him as the great man he was. To be frank, Darri's song's so dull he's giving me a headache." As Olfridor steered me away, I looked back one final time at the blazing Vorund craft, watching as Father's soul was carried to Navan's Halls. Could I live up to his memory and achievements?

***

Three hours later my main achievement was to remain upright in the Great Hall. The remnants of a fine feast in my father's honour lay scattered across the long table or else amongst the reeds on the floor. Ale flowed freely, and servants, thralls and my young warriors alike all drank to the name and memory of Kolfinnar Marlson. Olfridor, however, had saved something special. The old warrior had acquired a taste for a number of habits from the kingdom of Beria, which lay far to the west beyond the Baros Mountains and the clan lands of Vittag. Puffing on his pipe, he produced a bottle of Tharas whisky, which he generously shared with me, Bandor and Haarl.

"You've all deserved a cup or two of this ... No, don't

drink it too fast," he cried as Haarl tipped back his head and downed his measure in one, before turning bright red and choking noisily. Olfridor slapped him hard on the back and Haarl promptly disappeared under our table with a grunt. I waited for him to clamber back into his seat, laughing when his rumbling snores confirmed I'd literally drunk my friend under the table. At least I could take my drink. Looking down at the table, I wondered which of the three swirling earthenware cups was mine. I reached out and, seeing three hands, found myself at a loss to know which of them belonged to me. Olfridor noticed my confusion and pressed the cup into my hand.

"Drink up. Only do it *slowly*."

"Slowly," echoed Bandor, as expensive whisky dribbled down his chin. "*Slowly*."

"Damn it, Bandor. Do you know how much that stuff costs? Good job I make allowances for those I school, ain't it?"

"Sorry. Just having some trouble ... er ... finding my mouth, Olfridor. War wound, I reckon. I took a blow to the head back at Noln, you know."

"War wound, my arse. You're drunk, and that's no surprise – you young lads can't match a man of my experience. They don't teach those noble born anything these days, such as appreciating a fine Berian whisky."

"*Slowly*," I repeated, somewhat behind the others in this conversation. I brought the cup to my mouth and took a sip, enjoying the fiery taste. A warm glow suffused my body, and I felt less worn down by life. Kolfinnar the Younger was still awake, tearing round the Great Hall with a gaggle of children, drawing much amusement from everyone watching. I could remember, not so long ago, when that child would have been me. What would my nephew have to worry about when he was my age, I wondered?

"To old friends," toasted Halfhand. "Kolfinnar, you were like a brother to me. I'll miss you sorely."

"To my father," I added and all three of us drank to that.

"Slowly, Bandor, slowly," Olfridor muttered as my friend downed his measure before burping loudly.

"Oops," he said, his head dropping and falling onto the table with a soft clunk. I looked down at Bandor, with his tangle of red hair, hand clasped tightly round his empty cup and laughed out loud. For some reason, though, I was crying. Olfridor enveloped me in a bear-like hug, cracking my ribs in his powerful grip.

"Come on, son. Time to get out of here."

Outside in the courtyard it was quieter, the cool air jolting me awake. I took a few deep breaths, trying to steady myself. Tharas whisky was clearly to be treated with caution. Staring into the darkness I was surprised to see Nuna watching me, sitting on a bench by the wall of the keep. Olfridor saw her too.

"Looks like she's in need of some company. You'd better go and see how she's doing." I nodded and walked, with only the barest hint of weaving, towards my sister. She looked up and hastily dried her eyes.

"Don't worry," I said as I sat down heavily, gripping the arm of the bench to steady myself. "No one will mind if you shed a few tears over Father. He was a great man."

"You're drunk," Nuna observed, a playful note in her voice. "Father would be *so* proud."

"Huh. I've tried to live up to his expectations and, when I finally became a man, he misses it."

Nuna put her arm around my shoulder. "Well I'm proud of you. Really," she added, looking at my sceptical face. "You've surprised a lot of people in the past few days, you know. Everyone always talks about Jorik, remarking on how much he's like Father and how one day he'll lead us all to victory against Adalrikr. Now, though, people are talking like that about you."

"Living in the shadow of men like our father and brother isn't easy, you know."

Nuna chuckled, fixing me with a piercing stare. "You

think you're the only one to share that experience? Try being a woman in Ulfkell's Keep. With Father gone, everything is going to change."

"That doesn't follow," I replied, somewhat hurt at Nuna's lack of faith in my ability to hold our family together.

"Jorik and Etta have already been scheming. They've plans for me, just as they have for you. Now Father's dead everything will have to happen so much sooner, and I'm not sure I'm ready."

"What do you mean?" I asked, baffled. Anger rose up in me, as I realised that once again I was late discovering the latest political manoeuvrings in Ulfkell's Keep.

Nuna regarded me sadly. "You think that witch, Etta, only spent her time dreaming up your marriage plans? If Freydja Egilldottir is your idea of a nightmare, then you need to think again. I'd rather be in your shoes, Brother, that's for sure."

"Look," I said, a little drunkenly. "I'm in charge now, while Jorik's gone. If you want me to sort something out for you, you only have to say."

Nuna laughed loudly. "Of course. Now you're in charge Reavesburg women will have the right to speak at a clan moot and choose their own husbands. It's kind of you to say so, Rothgar, and I know you mean well. The trouble is, if you'd been keener marrying Freydja or if Father had taken a firmer hand with Gautarr, we'd have a united clan behind us. Now, with the growing threat from Vorund, we have to unite in other ways."

"Nuna, what do you mean? Have I caused you trouble of some kind?" I reached out, taking my sister's hand in mine, squeezing it tightly.

"Oh Rothgar, don't worry about it; what's done is done. In your position, I'd have thought exactly the same. Forget what I said, and for tonight just walk with me awhile. I want to remember Father and all the times we spent here, growing up together. That's if you can stand up straight, of course. Olfridor Halfhand's not exactly a temperate man; I'm surprised you're still conscious."

"I can take my drink," I boasted. "You should see Bandor and Haarl, though."

Together, we walked arm in arm through the courtyard, past the stables where Father once placed me on the back of his own horse, giving me my first riding lesson. We entered Ulfkell's Keep again, unnoticed, and wound our way to the kitchens. The servants were busy clearing up now the feast was over. Cook saw us and let us take up a corner to ourselves. Within minutes, she had produced one of our favourite childhood treats. Nuna's eyes lit up as Cook served up a plate of pancakes with bilberry jam.

"Thought you'd both like that," she whispered before heading back to organise the throng of servants scurrying about the kitchens, all anxious to be done with their tasks so that they could head off to bed. I smiled, sinking my teeth into a pancake with relish. Nuna did the same, and I found myself thinking that for some people in Ulfkell's Keep I would always be the boy tearing round the Great Hall, wooden sword in hand.

CHAPTER 10

Darri's voice resounded throughout the Great Hall as he announced the arrival of the sixth and final ruling family at the clan moot. Kolfinnar Marlson had been dead a week and to all intents and purposes he was already forgotten. All the talk in Ulfkell's Keep concerned Jorik's continued absence, each passing day he was overdue a growing weight settling on my shoulders.

"Sandar Tindirson of Lake Tull," Darri proclaimed. A handsome young man in his early twenties with long blond hair, Sandar would normally have been the youngest speaker at the clan moot. This year, though, both Bandor and I found ourselves speaking on behalf of our respective families: two young men in their teens. I wondered once more whether we could carry the day and thought back on my discussions with Etta.

"Sandar will be no problem," the old woman assured me yesterday, as we met to prepare for the moot. "Reavesburg stands guard at the mouth of the River Jelt which leads to Lake Tull. Their people have been loyal to us for generations. This moot turns on Lundvarr."

I nodded, seeing the obvious logic there. Gautarr would declare for his own family's right to claim the title. Old Hrodi Myndillson of Olt would side with him, as their people always did, for much the same reason that those of Lake Tull favoured the ruling family of Reavesburg. Bandor's support on behalf of the people of Kalamar could be counted on. I felt less sure of Noln and the loyalty of Lundvarr as their town elder. However, I had personally liberated their people from enslavement by Tyrfingr Blackeyes; surely that meant something. If so, that made it four families to two, and only a foolish man would challenge the natural heir to the title with just two families supporting him.

"Lundvarr is a fickle one," Etta said, peering at me with her good eye. "He's a merchant rather than a warrior, and they think differently. His first concern will be whether your family can maintain the trade links with Vittag and Helsburg that his town has always enjoyed."

"Gautarr can hardly offer him that," I countered. "He's only seeking war with Vorund, which Lundvarr knows is bad for business."

"A weak chief is bad for business too. Look how Bothvatr and Ingioy have already raised their prices for timber, coal and iron ore. Perhaps Lundvarr will think Gautarr's strength might help right the balance."

I threw up my hands in frustration. "I saved the man's life. What more would you have me do?"

"Nothing. There's nothing more you can do; not now, with so little time. This is what I meant when I said I wished your father had lived longer. Even though he was a shadow of the man he was, people still owed him a sense of loyalty. I was hoping you and Jorik would have time to build on that legacy and forge strong bonds of your own. Instead, Rathlin has claimed him, and the time of reckoning is upon you."

"Hardly comforting," I remarked.

"Rothgar, it's down to you, I'm afraid. You need to carry four votes out of six at the clan moot. Anything less and Gautarr will challenge you. He may do so anyway, there's no telling really. Gautarr has never forgotten he let the chance of ruling the Reavesburg Clan slip away when your father came to power. I fear he may hold a grudge against you just because of that."

"So he'll probably try and kill me regardless," I retorted. "That's a cheering thought."

Etta cackled mirthlessly. "Since when did you ask me to give you words of cheer, boy? You have Desta to do that.

I speak it as I see it. Just remember, Gautarr isn't invincible and the other families have no true love for him, not even Old Hrodi."

As I sat in the Great Hall, reflecting on Etta's words, I glanced at the faces lined before me. The long trestle table had been moved aside, allowing rows of benches to be placed in a circle comprising six segments – one for each of the ruling families. They were all taking their places now Tindirson had arrived. Further benches had been set beyond the circle, allowing more junior nobles, warriors, karls, merchants and farmers to watch the proceedings.

Sandar Tindirson had arrived with a few of his townsfolk and servants in tow. Lundvarr took his seat in the next row. He was a different man from the last time I had seen him, his dark curly hair now washed and clean, fine clothes reflecting his prosperous trading links with our allies west of the mountains. I smiled and Lundvarr glanced away nervously, mopping a sheen of sweat from his brow with the back of his hand. My spirits fell a little.

Bandor had taken up the section of benches to my right, sitting alone. Johan was still away at war with my brother and the senior members of his household, who would normally have assembled for this meeting. It mattered little; each family only had one vote and Bandor's was the only one which counted. I knew I could rely on my friend, although he looked as nervous as I felt, his face drawn and grey in the dim light of the hall.

Hrodi took an age to shuffle into the circle, leaning heavily on the arm of his son Radholf. Despite his age, he still possessed a full head of white hair and a long beard and whiskers, also stark white, of which he was enormously proud. I found myself holding my breath as I watched him bend his stiff back inch by inch, as Radholf, who was already well into middle-age, gradually eased him down onto the front bench. Only once Hrodi was seated comfortably did Gautarr deign to join the circle. Although I was flanked by Olfridor,

Ulf and Haarl, our numbers were still depleted in comparison to Gautarr's retinue. Half-a-dozen of his best warriors took up the benches behind Gautarr, including Domarr, Audwin and Haki, whilst his son Ragnar and young nephew, Throm, sat either side of him. Every member of the group was wearing full armour, although Gautarr's arms were bare, showing his bulging muscles. His battle axe lay between his feet, his palms resting easily on its shaft. Unlike Lundvarr, Gautarr fixed me with a firm stare and did not break it. If I had been in any doubt before, it was now clear for all to see that Gautarr Falrufson was staking his claim to lead the Reavesburg Clan.

Once Gautarr was ready Darri's voice rolled out in the vast space of the Great Hall, calling for order. The chatter of the crowd ceased almost instantly, a few people hurrying to find their places as the clan moot began. My stomach roiled and I had to clamp my mouth shut for a moment, fearing I would retch.

Olfridor gently laid a hand on my shoulder. "Easy, lad, we're all here for you. The fear of something's worse than the doing of it. Come on, now. They're waiting." I nodded and rose to my feet, clasping my hands behind my back so no one could see them shaking. This was far worse than riding out to battle – indeed, it was probably more dangerous. I cleared my throat, took a breath and addressed the circle.

"Elders of the Reavesburg Clan, welcome to Ulfkell's Keep. This is a sombre occasion, for my father has passed on to Navan's Halls. His family has led the Reavesburg Clan for nearly seventy years, since my great-grandfather, Hroar Helstromson, took power as the sixth clan chief. The line of Hroar has led our people well during that time. We have prospered through the wisdom of their rule and relied on their protection when our lands have been under threat. Now the time has come to choose who will lead our clan following my father's death."

"A pretty little speech from the boy," called out Gautarr. "Where's the meat of it, though? Fine words won't keep

Adalrikr's forces at bay." His men laughed loudly at the joke as Darri rose from his seat.

"Enough. This is a clan moot and you'll respect its rules. Each family will have their turn to speak – *without* interruption." Gautarr gave a smirk and cast a sidelong glance at Ragnar and Throm, his lack of respect for the proceedings obvious. Still, he kept his tongue as I pressed on.

"My brother, Jorik, is Kolfinnar's rightful heir as chief. I speak and act on his behalf today, whilst he is away fighting the Vorund Clan. Our laws require the new chief is confirmed by vote at a clan moot. Any who feel they are better placed to lead our people have the right to speak now and make their case before those assembled here."

I sat down. Darri rose and looked around the five families, taking his time before speaking. "Rothgar Kolfinnarson has asserted his brother's right to the title. Now, each of you must declare your allegiance to Jorik Kolfinnarson or declare your own intent to lead our people."

"Now I must speak," Gautarr said, rising from his bench. "Why is it that this boy stands before us today? Where's his brother? Where's Bandor's father? They've been gone ten days and were supposed to be back in five." He paused, letting his words sink in with the crowd. "I've grim news, my friends. Before I sailed here from Romsdahl with my men, there were tidings from my spies in Vorund. They reported that a small fleet of Reavesburg ships had launched a raid on Viskanir, only to founder on the treacherous sandbanks in bad weather as they tried to land. My spies say all the ships concerned were wrecked and no one made it ashore."

"You hard-hearted bastard, Gautarr," snarled Olfridor. "You've been here as a guest under our roof all day and you wait until *now* to break that news to us?" At a look from Darri, Olfridor fell silent. I glanced over at Bandor, sitting with his head in his hands as he absorbed the news of the death of his father.

"This is about the future of our people, Halfhand,"

roared Gautarr. "Better everyone hears it the once when they're all together and can be told the truth. Better that, than learn the news through rumours, each one telling a different tale till no one can know what's really happened. Fact is, Jorik's failed. He had a strong heart, I grant him that. He did the right thing to stand up to Adalrikr, but his failure means we're in a worse plight than ever. Let's speak frankly here. The Reavesburg Clan needs more than a boy and an old cripple to lead them. Johan Jokellsward might have been an option, if Jorik hadn't led him to his death at sea. Now, there's only one choice. Adalrikr's going to come looking for revenge and to enforce Tyrfingr Blackeyes' demands, especially now we've challenged his power. You need a warrior at a time like this and I'm the man to lead as chief, not that green boy over there trying to hold on to his father's memory." Gautarr surveyed the circle slowly, gauging the effect of his words. Everyone was huddled together, talking in urgent whispers.

"It can't be," breathed Haarl next to me.

"Steady," rumbled Olfridor. "Keep your heads. There's something not right here, I know it."

I shook my head. "If Jorik's dead this changes everything." The hall fell silent again as Hrodi Whitebeard managed to rise to his feet to speak.

"This is terrible news," he wheezed, his voice barely more than a whisper. "Truly terrible. Kolfinnar was a great man and we owe him and his sons a debt of loyalty. However, in times like this, you have to make the right decision for your people. The people of Olt vote to support Gautarr Falrufson's claim." Gautarr's men cheered, despite Darri's glare, as Old Hrodi lowered himself down unsteadily onto his bench.

Bandor was next to speak. "The people of Kalamar vote for the claim of Jorik ..." his voice trailed off nervously and Gautarr did not bother to stifle a snort of laughter. Bandor looked on the verge of tears as he fought to compose himself, speaking in a cracked voice as he struggled to continue. "The people of Kalamar vote for *Rothgar* Kolfinnarson. I've fought side by side with him and the blood of his father runs true in his veins." Silence greeted this statement and I knew it was all over, even before Sandar and Lundvarr had spoken. Bandor sank back on his seat as if he had been delivered a body blow.

"The people of Lake Tull declare their support for Gautarr Falrufson," young Sandar proclaimed. This brought more cheering from Gautarr's camp, although the noise seemed to come from a long way off. Lundvarr was on his feet, wringing his hands together nervously.

"Rothgar ... you were brave and generous when you came to Noln's aid ... if only ... well, I mean to say ..."

"Get on with it," cried Ragnar.

"Well. Yes. I'm sorry Rothgar but Noln votes for Gautarr Falrufson. I can see no other way forward ..." The rest of his apology was drowned by the din, as Gautarr celebrated with his warriors. Anger boiled up inside me, sweeping away my nerves. They were acting as if Gautarr were chief already, laughing and joking after gleefully delivering the news of the deaths of my brother, Bandor's father and the loss of the finest warriors of Ulfkell's Keep. I was on my feet, a red mist clouding my vision, swallowing the Great Hall, until all I could see was Gautarr, slapping Ragnar's back, his grizzled beard split by a wide grin. Slowly, the sound in the hall faded and sensing something was amiss, Gautarr turned and saw me watching him.

"Surely not?" he laughed. "Forget it, lad, it's over. Four votes to two in my favour, and those for you cast by mere boys with more pimples than years between them."

"If Jorik is dead, then by rights I'm Kolfinnar's heir. If the clan moot does not vote in my favour then I have the right to assert my claim by trial of combat." Gautarr spluttered at these words, as an anxious murmur rippled through the crowd. He regarded me long and hard, hefting up his great axe in one hand, letting me sense the weight of it. It was a weapon that had seen much use, its shaft covered in scratches and notches, though the blade itself was clean and sharp, a cruel piece of steel gleaming in the hall's firelight.

"Walk away, lad. You've got to know when you're beaten. I won't shirk from killing you if that's want you want, so think about it. Even if you get lucky and bring me down, do you really think the clan will follow a sixteen-year-old? We're at *war*. Who's going to lead them into battle? You think they'd rather follow you than me?"

"I'd sooner die facing my enemy than with a knife in my back, Gautarr. You think I'm fool enough to believe you'll let me live if I stand aside?" Gautarr's face broke into a wicked grin. He didn't bother to contradict my statement.

"You're your father's son, alright, and no mistake. Pity he died when he did. A few more years on both you and me and I might have thought differently. That's life for you – no one ever said it was fair. Trial by combat, then, lad. I'll make it quick, don't you worry."

CHAPTER 11

The courtyard of Ulfkell's Keep was deathly silent, although there was a great crowd of onlookers gathered around the large circle chalked on the ground to mark out the boundary for the contest. There were no rowdy shouts of encouragement as I stepped forward. Somewhere, someone was sobbing. Looking up I spied Desta, her long dark hair soaked through by the rain, plastering it to her head. Etta stood by her, a bony hand resting on Desta's shoulder, her face almost hidden beneath a dark hood. I swallowed. This was not a crowd looking forward to a fight: they were mourners at my funeral. Well, at least I had a good turnout.

The rain would be a problem. The heavy downpour had appeared from nowhere, rolling in from the sea and soaking everything. The cobbles of the courtyard were slick and treacherous underfoot, the water already washing away the hastily-drawn lines of the combat circle. I rolled my shoulders as I felt the annoying rain dripping down my collar and into my chainmail armour. I would soon have more pressing concerns as Gautarr strode into the circle to a subdued cheer. Beaded droplets of water gathered on the banded steel armour he wore and speckled his grey beard. Ragnar handed him his helmet and he pushed it firmly onto his head.

"Come on, boy. No one wants to stand around in this weather longer than they have to." He looked at the onlookers, expecting some response from his joke. Other than Audwin laughing half-heartedly there was some faint coughing in the crowd and Desta's muffled sobs. Gautarr might have won the vote at the clan moot but out here, surrounded by the people of Reavesburg, it was clear he had little support. Despite being their favourite it was also obvious no one thought I stood a chance.

"Just remember what I taught you," muttered Olfridor quietly as he handed me my helmet. "Gautarr's blows will be powerful but a sword is faster. Use your speed to your advantage and there might well be a twist in this tale, son." I nodded, the raindrops pattering dully on the surface of my helm as I stepped into the circle.

Gautarr took a few steps forwards, until we were close to one another in the middle of the ring. Here, the grey curtain of rain hid the onlookers from sight, as if the two of us were alone in the courtyard. Ragnar's stifled shout of support for his father registered on the limit of my hearing, as if he'd been calling from the docks rather than a few feet away. I realised it mattered little if hundreds watched me die. All my focus was drawn towards the powerfully-built man before me. Gautarr's body was packed with hard muscle. He'd been fighting the Vorund Clan before I was born, and if age had taken some of his speed he'd lost none of his strength or experience. The hot anger I felt in the Great Hall had long since melted away, replaced by an odd sense of detachment. Only one of us would leave this circle alive. I concentrated on the task in hand, embracing the risk of death just as I had on the beach in Noln. Olfridor Halfhand had trained me to be a warrior: death was just an occupational hazard, after all. Gautarr's expression changed as he looked down on me, the big man a head taller. He had expected to see cowardice and fear in his opponent; now all he saw was determination.

"You meet your fate well, boy," he said. "I've got to respect you for that. There's no dishonour in walking away from a fight you can't win."

"Alright. You can walk away if you want, old man. I won't hold it against you."

Gautarr chuckled. "I gave you every chance, lad." He raised his axe, planted his feet and moved forwards, swinging the heavy weapon round with both hands in a wide arc.

I watched the axe whistling towards my head, cutting through the rain and leaving a trail of spray behind it. The whole move seemed to take an absurdly long time, easily allowing me to step out of harm's way. Raising my shield, I swung my own sword, cutting at Gautarr's side before he could recover from his stroke. The man grunted with effort as he changed the direction of his attack, parrying my blow and replying with one of his own. I blocked with my shield, feeling the impact of the blow as it numbed my forearm and sent a jolt of pain up into my shoulder. Gautarr pressed on, hammering at my defences, forcing me back, step by step.

My sword darted out, hissing through the rain, missing Gautarr's body by a hair's breadth. Gautarr's eyes went wide, stark white orbs in the shadow of his helmet. I cut back again, forcing the older warrior to duck to one side as my blade whistled past his head. It gave me a chance to go on the attack but Gautarr blocked my next strike with the shaft of his great axe. I tried to slide my sword down its length to shear away Gautarr's fingers, remembering how effective that move had been at Noln. Gautarr was wise to the trick, pulling away sharply. I staggered forwards, carried on by my own momentum and cursed as my legs were swept from under me by the axe shaft. I heard a sharp communal intake of breath from the hidden crowd as I rolled with the blow, metal scraping harshly on the slick cobbles. I found my feet and whirled round to face Gautarr as he bore down on me once more.

I felt a sharp pain stab from my ankle, running up the length of my left leg and into my hip – the fight was aggravating my injury from Noln. I clenched my teeth and pushed it from my mind as I met Gautarr head on and we clashed in a flurry of blows. Suddenly my sword locked with the head of Gautarr's axe. We stared for a moment, the older man's face fixed with a fierce grin, as we tested each other's strength. My wrist began to ache as I clung on grimly. I had a knife tucked into my belt – little use against this brute of a man if I allowed him to disarm me. Without warning I stepped in closer, slamming my shield into the warrior, sending him reeling backwards. I was aware of a distant throbbing in my leg as I slashed my freed sword left and right, watching as Gautarr lazily parried each blow. Then I lurched to one side as my left foot skidded on the wet ground, crying out involuntarily with the pain.

"Now that's unfortunate," hissed Gautarr, taking a step back to allow a pause in the fight. "It's not always the last battle that kills you. An injury picked up another time can come back to bite you, if your body's not strong enough. That's the difference between seasoned wood and a sapling, I guess." I breathed in deeply and watched Gautarr's chest heaving. The man was taking this opportunity to draw breath, riling me as he tried to gather his own strength.

"How poetic," I snarled, springing forward, aware even as I did so that I was now having to favour my right leg. I raised my sword and brought it crashing down. Gautarr was faster than I expected, and I cut through clean air, my blade jarring in my hand as it sent up sparks from the damp courtyard stones. Gautarr jabbed at me with the butt of his axe, the point of the shaft finding its way through my defences and cracking me in my ribs as I struggled to recover my position. I pushed the pain aside as I swept my sword round, trying to retake the initiative.

Gautarr was a canny opponent. He allowed me to press forward, blocking my blows and forcing me to come on towards him. The effort was taking its toll and I realised I was now limping with each step, my breathing ragged, ribs burning with pain. Suddenly the pattern changed, Gautarr whirling his great axe about his head and hammering my shield and sword with heavy blows, too fast for me to even think of a counter-attack. I gasped, my mind racing, as I tried to move back quickly enough to take myself out of the warrior's range. I needed time to think and catch my breath – Gautarr allowed me no such luxury.

I took another step and without warning my weakened

leg gave way under me, sending me crashing down hard onto my back on the stones, winded and gasping for air. The force of the impact jarred my sword from my hand and I watched, despairing, as it clattered out of reach and Gautarr loomed above me. My hand scrabbled for the knife in my belt but my foe was unrelenting, blows hammering down on my shield and causing me to cry out in fury as I realised the inevitability of my fate. Finally, Gautarr hooked the head of his axe onto the rim of my shield and with a great shout he pulled hard, splitting the straps holding it in place. He sent my shield bouncing off into the crowd and followed through with a kick to my stomach, breaking the knife I clutched desperately in my hand, leaving me sprawled, face down, on the wet cobbles. All the air was gone from my body. I could no more find the strength to raise myself than pick up Ulfkell's Keep, so I waited for the final blow that would end the contest.

My breathing was shallow as my stomach burned with pain. Why was Gautarr taking his time? Another breath, and then another. Was he waiting for me to recover? Was he waiting for me to raise myself up to face death like a man, rather than sprawled out on the ground? My bleary eyes focused on the large raindrops that continued to pelt from the sky. They hissed on the dark stone in front of my face, each one coolly splashing me with droplets of water, mingling redly with blood that was flowing from a cut in my mouth. Slowly I became aware of another sound – an excited chatter from the crowd of onlookers. Still Gautarr's fatal strike didn't land. With a great effort I steadied my breathing and pushed myself up from the floor. As I raised my head, I saw three indistinct figures had forced their way into the combat circle. It was as if the rain had coalesced, forming dense watery shadows. Gautarr was regarding them darkly, his breathing laboured, and I watched one of the three figures walk towards me.

"Easy, lad. Are you alright?" Johan Jokellsward's face swam into view. Olfridor's firm hands helped me up, with Johan's arm round my shoulders protecting my burning leg.

I glanced at the other two new arrivals. My brother, Jorik, smouldered with undisguised rage and his resemblance to our father at that moment was undeniable. Finnvidor flanked him, carrying something in a small damp sack, his grey eyes hard and emotionless in stark contrast to my brother.

"By the gods," Gautarr breathed. "We'd heard dire news you'd run aground and been shipwrecked. Turns out those tidings were false, eh?" He tried to keep his voice light and friendly, convincing no one. As he spoke Ragnar and Throm had quietly stepped forwards into the circle, hands resting easily on the hilt of their weapons. Domarr, Haki and Audwin's shadowy forms loomed just behind them.

"Strange," Finnvidor replied calmly. "We suffered no such mishap. We gave the Vorund Clan something to think about, alright. Their crops and flocks north of Viskanir aren't so plentiful now. A fair few of their warriors won't be raising a sword against us again, either." There were some cries and shouts of approval from those gathered at that news. I smiled to myself, knowing Jorik had done well. If only he'd returned sooner perhaps this whole matter could have been avoided.

"No," Finnvidor continued. "We had good fortune until the return leg. Just as we passed Romsdahl we were unlucky enough to find ourselves faced with a fleet of Riltbalt ships. They came right at us at night, sank one of our ships and killed a few of our men too. It was a bloody business."

"Looks like I owe you, then, Finnvidor," Gautarr observed, still trying to keep the tone of the conversation pleasant. "Looks like you spared my home from a raid. I guess it was always going to happen, that the other clans would try to test us, knowing we were so heavily engaged fighting Adalrikr."

"They flew Riltbalt's banner of the hammer and star, alright. Fought hard, too. It was just blind luck we heard them coming in the dark and that gave us a chance to get ready. If they'd caught us unawares, I reckon we'd have been finished." Finnvidor turned his attention towards Throm, obviously to the surprise of the young man.

"I remember your father, Egill. Fought with him, side by side, against the Vorund Clan in the battle that killed him. Kolfinnar had sent me down with a company to lend support to Gautarr and Egill on our southern borders. Egill was a good man, Throm, and I was glad to have known him. You form strong bonds with the men you fight alongside, so I remember all Egill's company well, including brave Igull. It saddens me he had to die a traitor's death on your uncle's orders, leading an attack against his own clan, sailing under a false banner."

With that, Finnvidor tossed the bag over to Gautarr's feet. It landed with a wet thud, spilling its contents on the ground. There was a shocked cry from the crowd as the head of a bearded man rolled out and came to rest against Gautarr's booted feet. Its face wore an oddly peaceful expression, mouth slightly open, eyes closed. Gautarr's reaction was more interesting, for there was no doubt he recognised the dead man before him. Ragnar kept his composure but Throm took a step back muttering something and turned to Gautarr with an appalled look.

"You treacherous bastard," exploded Olfridor, his hand moving towards the axe hanging from his belt. "Let's see how –"

"This isn't your fight, Halfhand," Johan retorted. "Leave it."

Jorik's axe swept through the air and Gautarr only just reacted in time to block it. For a moment I thought Ragnar would lead his men into the fray. A shout from Gautarr stopped him in his tracks; this was the real battle for the leadership of the Reavesburg Clan.

While Gautarr may have been tired from his exertions in fighting me just minutes before, I honestly doubt there would have been any other outcome to this contest had the two men faced each other fresh. I had never seen Jorik wield a weapon in anger before and now I could see why Olfridor was so proud of his pupil. A grown man in his prime, Jorik was blindingly fast and delivered his blows with skill and power, constantly forcing Gautarr onto the defensive. His rage was focussed and channelled into striking down his father's jarl. Moments later there was a cracking sound and the dull crash of metal on metal as he landed a blow to Gautarr's chest. Gautarr went down on one knee, his two-handed axe falling away, leaving him prone. Jorik landed a crunching blow to the side of Gautarr's head with the flat of his axe, ripping the chinstrap off his helmet and sending it flying from his head. The big man gasped, falling on his back as Jorik's booted foot connected with his face with a sickening crunch. A spray of blood flew up and I watched a tooth spinning away in a white blur, landing with a faint crack on the cobbles. Ragnar and Throm stood there, rooted to the spot, waiting for the fatal blow to fall, just as I had only a few short minutes ago. Jorik lifted his axe and stopped, looking down onto Gautarr's broken face. His breath escaped noisily through his nose and mouth amid bubbles of blood.

"You're a snake, Gautarr," Jorik spat. "You like to pretend you're the great warrior while everyone knows you'd sooner get someone else to do your dirty work for you. Igull deserved better than that."

"Enough words," Gautarr rasped. "Get on with it. You know what you have to do."

"I've seen the black flag flying, so I know I'm chief now. Didn't think I return to this sort of homecoming, though. Thing is, I've seen too many good men of the Reavesburg Clan die at each others' hands already, thanks to you. If I kill you that means there'll be a blood feud between my family and Ragnar. Tyrfingr Blackeyes would just love that, wouldn't he? Watching us kill each other off, before he comes back in the finish the job.

"It pains me to say it, but in these times I need men like you. I'll give you a choice. Swear loyalty to me and my family and I'll let you live. If you can't ally yourself to me, then I'll kill you as the traitor you are, and my men will make sure Ragnar,

Throm and the rest of your company never leave Ulfkell's Keep alive. That keeps things nice and simple, doesn't it? What's it to be?"

Gautarr's bloody face grimaced in pain and disgrace as he looked back at Jorik. I heard Finnvidor slide his sword from its sheath, saw Olfridor grasp his axe in his hand. Johan, Djuri, Rugga, Kaun and Brunn all stepped silently into the ring. Ragnar nodded to his men, hands hovering over the hilts of their weapons, everyone waiting to see which way this whole sorry mess would turn out. I tottered dizzily on my feet, wondering where my sword was and whether I would be any use in the coming fight even if I could find it. Slowly Gautarr eased himself into a sitting position, staring up at Jorik the whole time with undisguised hatred, rivers of dark blood running down from his nose and mouth onto his dented armour. He hawked and spat several times, then knelt and prostrated himself before my brother. The crowd gave an audible gasp, whilst Ragnar turned away, unable to bring himself to watch the humiliating scene.

"By the gods lad, you're your father's son, no mistake. For the sake of my son, I'm your man now, heart and soul. I swear it on the spirit of my father and on the lives of my grandchildren. Let us live and I promise you'll never regret showing us mercy."

"We'll see," muttered Jorik. "And it's not lad, old man. It's chief."

CHAPTER 12

"Must you go?" Desta's voice was insistent, and I honestly thought twice about whether to attend the meeting with my brother that morning. Ignoring the first order of the new chief of Reavesburg struck me as being an unwise move. I reluctantly threw back the blankets of my bed and heaved myself into a sitting position. My body protested, following the pummelling I'd taken at Gautarr's hands.

"Yes, my love. I'm sorry. Duty calls, even at this ungodly hour."

"Surely Jorik can do without you today," Desta wheedled, wrapping her arms tightly round my chest. I gasped in pain and her grip relaxed as she giggled at my discomfort. "You see. You can hardly move. You should be resting in bed, not rushing back off to duty. Jorik should give you time to recover from your exertions."

"I'll not get any rest with you," I replied, playfully slapping her hands away as I hobbled out of bed and began to gather up my clothes. "My brother's the chief now. Winning the fight with Gautarr was important, but it doesn't secure his rule. We've still much to do."

"I still can't believe Jorik let that monster live. He nearly killed you, and tried to kill Jorik too."

"Jorik made the right decision. It will be worth it to see Gautarr and his men leave Reavesburg in disgrace. He'll never command the respect he enjoyed previously with our clan."

"Can he really be trusted?" Desta's dark brown eyes looked up at me, wide with worry. I fought against the urge to take her in my arms and comfort her. I sighed, knowing I couldn't afford to miss my first meeting with Jorik since his return by allowing myself to be led back to my bed. Instead, I tried to arrange my face into a convincing smile, all the while fumbling with my breeches.

"No. What's more important is Jorik's shown he's the stronger man and, for now, that's enough. The other members of the clan moot have all fallen into line, even Hrodi Myndillson. Without their support, Gautarr would be foolish to challenge Jorik's rule. That threat has passed, at least for now."

Did I really believe those words? As I limped up the stairs of the North Tower to Jorik's chambers I had to admit to some scepticism. Nevertheless, we'd come through this crisis, for which I was thankful. When I arrived, Olfridor Halfhand was standing guard at the door and Reesha was just leaving, Kolfinnar clutching her hand. The boy looked at me, wide-eyed, and I wondered exactly how much he had seen of yesterday's events as Reesha embraced me.

"Rothgar. You look terrible. Should you really be up and about today?"

"I'm fine," I laughed, trying not to wince at the pain this brought to my ribs. Reesha squeezed me tightly once more, making me gasp, before taking Kolfinnar's small hand and leading him away. I nodded at Olfridor as I walked into my brother's chambers.

It was no surprise to see Etta in attendance, once more privately directing the affairs of my family. Jorik was sitting next to her at an ornate table by the window, looking tired and careworn, Finnvidor Einarrson sitting opposite. My brother looked older than his twenty years. Johan stood by the window, arms folded, long greying red hair hanging down over his shoulders, framing his craggy features. Bandor stood next to his father, called to offer the clan chief counsel for the first time.

"There they go," Johan remarked, scowling. I hobbled over to the window and peered out. Down below I could see Gautarr and his men walking through the main gates of the keep, heading back towards their ship moored in the docks. Gautarr strode at their front, his bruised and bloody head held high, apparently entirely unrepentant. "I wonder if we'll live to regret that decision?"

"There was no right decision," Etta declared. "Kill Gautarr and Ragnar would have been sworn to seek revenge. Go further and slay Gautarr's whole family, and who would stand as the bulwark in the south between our clan and Vorund? If Romsdahl were to fall into Adalrikr's hands, that would be a disaster. This way, Gautarr owes Jorik his life and, perhaps, his loyalty."

"The so-called *loyalty* of a man who plotted to murder him? You'll forgive me, Etta, if I set little store on those empty words. We've released someone every bit as dangerous as Adalrikr Asmarrson –"

"Good or ill, the decision has been made." Jorik's stark statement cut off Johan mid-sentence and led to an uneasy silence. Jorik placed his head in his hands, running them through his hair, as he gathered his thoughts before speaking again. "My father's dead and my rule hangs by a thread. I'm forced to rely on the mutual interest I share with my enemy to keep an even worse adversary from seizing our lands. Do I need to justify every choice I make to you, Johan Jokellsward? Does my jarl have so little respect for my rule?"

"No, Jorik, you know ..." Jorik glowered and Johan paused for a moment before continuing. "No, *Chief*. I'm your man just as I was your father's. My grandson is your heir, so can you really doubt my devotion?" Johan's words seemed to satisfy Jorik, who gave a curt nod. At his gesture we all gathered to sit around the table, Bandor's eyes wide after having witnessed Jorik's firm treatment of his father. I sank gratefully into my seat and stretched out my aching leg, still sore from the climb up the tower.

"While we stand divided before Adalrikr, it's only matter of time before he crushes us," observed Finnvidor. "We need everyone to rally to your cause, Chief, or all is lost."

Jorik nodded, musing on his jarl's words. "Perhaps an alliance with Gautarr's family would have cooled his ambitions to become chief. It matters little, for that opportunity is gone. Gautarr will never agree to the match between his niece and Rothgar now, his pride won't allow it. No, Gautarr will now see any marriage between his family and Rothgar as an admission of weakness." My pride was a little stung at that remark, as Jorik continued. "Still, Finnvidor's right – an alliance is required if we are to survive. I can see no alternative to Etta's plan." I glanced over at Etta, whose expression was inscrutable.

Johan's views on the subject were obvious as he sprang to his feet. "What? I thought I made my views clear on the voyage that there's no way I'll allow *that* to happen. If you think –"

"If you turn your back on me, Johan, you as good as send me, my wife and son to our graves. Your daughter. Your grandson. Think on that before you challenge me again." Jorik was also on his feet, his finger pointing inches away from Johan's face. The older man looked up at Jorik, breathing hard. I began to wonder if Jokellsward was about take matters further. Instead he stalked back to his chair, sitting down heavily opposite Jorik. The two glared at each other, and the uncomfortable silence in the room stretched on, until Johan finally spoke.

"When my father died, I can remember how lonely I felt, knowing the leadership of my house at Kalamar now rested on my shoulders. Believe me when I say I understand how you feel. I can only try to imagine how much harder it must be for you with the added burden of being our chief. I'll follow you, just as I did your father. The people will too, especially after they saw Gautarr bested yesterday." Johan paused and I could tell he was mustering his courage to challenge his new clan chief once more. "Jorik, what you propose is an alliance with one of our rival clans. I've lost many good men and fast friends in battle against Norlhast. The ordinary folk of Kalamar will remember all too well suffering at their hands, and they'll find it hard to accept that their former enemy is suddenly a friend. Gautarr might be a backstabbing traitor but he's one of our own. Our clan would sooner trust him than Karas Greystorm, hard though that might be for you to hear."

"And would they prefer Adalrikr Asmarrson sitting on Reave's Chair in the Great Hall, with the people of Reavesburg under his heel? You saw how well-armed their warriors are, even in the outlying settlements. The raiding this year has been endless and now word reaches us of a large fleet being constructed in Vorund itself. Time is running out and if the clans remain divided Adalrikr will defeat us, one by one."

"The clans of Reavesburg and Romsdahl were once separate, many years ago," added Etta. "It was Sigborn Dragonslayer who united them and he did so peacefully, rather than with the sword."

Jorik nodded in agreement. "And if you remember that particular history lesson, Sigborn took that decision when we were under threat in the south from the Vorund Clan."

"Yes, he took that decision and little good it did him when he lay dying following a battle against the Norlhast Clan," Johan responded.

Jorik breathed out steadily, composing himself. "The history between our two clans means there's only one person who can broker this deal. Johan, I want you to go to Karas and entreat him to listen to my offer. Rothgar will accompany you, as soon as he's fit to travel. As for Bandor, well, after seven years there's little more Halfhand can teach him. I understand he proved himself in battle at Noln, fighting alongside my brother. Now it's time for him to return home to Kalamar."

"Jorik," I interrupted. "What is it you're proposing exactly? What do you want me to do?"

"Forge an alliance," Etta replied, her piercing beetle-black eye looking into mine. "Karas Greystorm is hard-pressed. He suffers, too, at the hands of Adalrikr and he has had precious few victories against his foe, unlike us. His greatest fear is that Johan will launch an attack whilst he is weakened. The time is right to offer him an alternative to that fate."

"You'll speak for me on this matter," added Jorik. "Karas will suspect a trick of some kind. When you offer him Nuna's hand in marriage and the substantial dowry that goes with her he'll know how serious my intentions are. It will give Greystorm peace with his nearest neighbour and the finances he needs to begin to rebuild. In return, all hostilities between our two clans will cease and, when I call for aid, Norlhast will send its warriors to fight alongside ours in the campaign against Vorund."

I sat there for a moment, digesting the full meaning of Jorik's words. Karas Greystorm was some twenty years Nuna's senior and, if the rumours were true, more than a little touched by madness. I wondered if my sister had been consulted when Etta hatched her latest plan.

"And if Karas doesn't agree to this?" I asked.

Jorik's reply was uncompromising. "Then Johan's forces are to crush him utterly. I cannot afford to have an enemy at my back as I fight Adalrikr and seek to quell dissent amongst my own people. It's time to show our enemies our true mettle. Greystorm should be left in no doubt about the choices that lie before him."

"A bold plan to achieve our aims," added Finnvidor. "Adalrikr means our destruction and we have to increase our strength if our way of life is to prevail. As Etta says, this is not without precedent."

Johan shook his head as he listened to Jorik and Finnvidor's words. "I tell you, the people of Kalamar will never accept this alliance, even if Karas agrees to your terms. They've suffered at Karas' hands and Bekan before him –"

Johan's latest protest was ended abruptly as Jorik stood and slammed both palms on the table, the noise reverberating around the room. The muscles in his shoulders bulged and his stance was so reminiscent of our father that, for a moment, I forgot it was Jorik who was asserting his authority over his father-in-law.

"Then you will lead by example, Johan Jokellsward. You will extend the hand of friendship to your former foe, and your son will speak in support of your actions in Kalamar. Where my brother leads, you will follow. If this isn't acceptable I fear the friendship between our two houses will end with this disagreement. Do you want me as your enemy, Johan, or are you still my jarl?"

I swallowed as I watched this exchange. Jorik, always the dutiful son, now had a hard, steely glint in his eyes. Jorik clearly enjoyed power and he wasn't afraid to use it. He was the chief, our father forgotten as Jorik assumed the role he'd been preparing to play all his life.

"No," Johan bit off the word. "You're the chief, I'm your jarl. We'll set sail for Norlhast as soon as Rothgar has healed from his wounds."

"A week then," Jorik replied, without asking me if I considered this to be sufficient time to recover. "You're dismissed. Not you, Rothgar," he added as we all made to leave. I sank back down into my seat as Johan stalked from the chamber, red-faced, Bandor in tow looking worried. Finnvidor held open the door as Etta shuffled towards it more slowly, her knowing smile showing that everything had unfolded according to her chosen design. The door closed quietly behind her, leaving me alone with my brother.

"I wanted to thank you," Jorik began. "Tyrfingr played us well. The raid on Noln placed you in a difficult position and you dealt with it better than I could have imagined, for one so young. Then to face the death of our father and have to stand up to that snake, Gautarr, in combat. I chose a bad time to leave Ulfkell's Keep."

"I knew you'd come back," I answered with more confidence than I'd felt at the time. "I could hardly have stood aside to let Falrufson take control. His rule would have been a disaster."

"He's a brutal man. You need to understand that, for us,

staying in power now means we have to be every bit as tough. There are some hard decisions to be made and you've seen Johan isn't happy taking orders from a man almost twenty years his junior. He'll be wondering now whether he's made the right choice following Kolfinnar's son, no matter how far back his friendship went with our father. With that in mind, I have to ask something more from you, Brother."

"Ask it."

"Watch Johan and ensure he conducts the negotiations exactly as I have commanded. If he doesn't, I'll need you to act, even if that sets you against Bandor. Do you understand what I'm telling you?" I nodded, my mouth dry as a wave of nausea rose up inside me. Jorik smile lacked warmth.

"This is power, Rothgar. Do you think I enjoy the thought of giving Nuna away in marriage to our enemy? The time for old grudges is past. They won't help us now with the threat we face. Karas is wealthy and he'll care well for young Nuna, I'm sure. The dowry will ensure that she lives in comfort."

"Just one thing I have to know," I asked. "This plan. Whose idea was it? Yours or Etta's?"

"We first spoke of this after Tyrfingr Blackeyes came calling. Etta has served as an advisor to the Reavesburg Clan's rulers since the time of our grandfather. I know Father trusted her with his life and I'd be a fool to ignore her advice. However, the decision is mine, not hers."

I mulled over these words as I limped away from Jorik's chambers under Olfridor's watchful gaze. Etta had always said my role would be to support my brother's rule. Now he was the ninth clan chief of Reavesburg, and the time had come to play my part. I began to wonder exactly what the price of my loyalty would be.

CHAPTER 13

The oars struck the water with a steady rhythm, pulling Johan's ship, *Hammerhead*, swiftly away from Reavesburg's docks. I watched my home recede into the distance, drawing my cloak tightly around my body to keep out the morning chill of late spring. Mist hung above the water, thick enough to hide the banks of the estuary into which the River Jelt flowed. Alongside us, the other two ships in Johan's small force were little more than dark shapes on the water, the beat of their oars keeping time with our larger vessel. I glanced over at Bandor, sitting opposite me with his hands to an oar, pulling with all his might. It was a task I would have shared were I not recovering from my injuries, which were healing slowly. I wondered whether Bandor was looking forward to returning to his childhood home. Bandor had lived at Ulfkell's Keep for the last seven years and there had been some tearful goodbyes on the quayside, as we bade our farewells to Nuna, Reesha and young Kolfinnar. I thought of my own parting with Desta that morning with a pang of regret. Since learning of my imminent departure, Desta had divided her time between nursing my wounds and making love to me with hitherto unexpected passion and enthusiasm. Although I was unsure this was the best way for me to recover, I didn't protest too much.

"Enough," I finally gasped that morning. "Honestly, woman, didn't last night satisfy you? You'll be the death of me." Desta giggled as she rolled off my sweating body and stretched out languidly by my side. I took a moment to enjoy the sight of her naked form, knowing it would be the last time for a while that I would be in such an enviable position.

"What are you thinking?" she asked playfully, wrapping

herself up in the blankets, much to my disappointment.

"Only that I'll miss you whilst I'm away."

Desta snorted. "Oh, I'm sure. The noble ladies of Kalamar are scarcely likely to turn your head whilst you're gone. After all, how can they compare to a common servant girl at Ulfkell's Keep?" She looked at me, her pretty face framed in a tangle of dark curls, the blanket wrapped around her doing nothing to hide the wonderful curves of her body. I leaned forward to kiss her, ignoring a twinge in my sore ribs.

"I'll hardly be the most popular man there, if you must know. I'm brokering an alliance with the Norlhast Clan, remember? I'm more likely to feel a dagger in my guts than a kiss on my lips."

"Don't," snapped Desta. "Don't even joke about such things, please. I'll worry about you every night you're away. Don't make it any worse."

"I'm sorry," I laughed. "It won't come to that, I'm sure." Unless, of course, Johan failed to carry out Jorik's orders, in which case my hand would be the one wielding the knife. I pushed the thought aside. Such things did not belong here, not with the time I spent with Desta. I forced levity into my voice that I didn't feel and regretfully left the warmth of my bed.

"Time and tide wait for no one, not even the brother of the chief," I remarked. "I'll be back, trust me. Until then, you'll just have to live off the glowing memory of your time with me … Watch out." One of my boots narrowly missed my ear and Desta laughed again.

"Why did I fall in love with someone with such a big head? Go on then, get ready but please promise me you'll take care. No one's safe, not in these times, and I won't rest easy till you're safely back at Ulfkell's Keep."

I realised Bandor was watching me as I broke out into a broad smile, enjoying the memory of this morning. Thinking I was smiling at him, he grinned back as he heaved at the oar once more. Reavesburg had now vanished, swallowed up in the mist. Soon we would be on the open sea, following the coast round to the north towards Kalamar Castle, Johan Jokellsward's fortress on the border with Norlhast. After a brief stop there, we would continue our voyage into Norlhast waters, flying under a flag of parley. I sorely hoped the Norlhast Clan would respect that, otherwise our mission would be short-lived indeed.

***

"More wine?" I shook my head at Johan's wife as I politely declined.

"No, thank you, Damona. I've never had much of a head for Berian delicacies."

"Except for the whisky they distil at Tharas?" grinned Bandor.

Damona spun around to face her son. "And what, exactly, do *you* know of such things, young man?" Johan chuckled, tearing into a warm loaf of bread with enthusiasm. Bandor's family sat at the head of their table, surrounded in the dim firelight of their feasting hall by dozens of Johan's fighting men and their wives. The role of the guard of honour that met me on my arrival at Kalamar, led by Rugga the Rock and Kaun Quicksteel, seemed to extend to partaking in their leader's hospitality towards his guest.

"I think the weapons master at Ulfkell's Keep has broadened the subjects upon which he teaches his pupils," observed Johan between bites.

"Really?" Damona arched her eyebrows. "You never learned such things from him in your time?"

"You weren't trained by Halfhand too, were you?" I exclaimed.

"I wish I were that young," Johan laughed. "No, back then Olfridor went by a different name. Olfridor Falrufson was the leader of Marl's warriors when I first met him and I was only eighteen when we fought together. Let's just say that when the fighting was done, Olfridor was never shy concerning the various benefits of Berian whisky. I was there in the battle three years later that maimed him. Your father was newly appointed as chief and many thought he should cut his ties with Olfridor after that, especially after what had happened with Gautarr the previous year. That was the thing about your father, though – always loyal to those who were loyal to him. It's a lesson Jorik should take to heart. Your brother needs to trust those around him, though I admit it's a hard thing to do when people like Gautarr are hatching plots –"

"Olfridor Falrufson?" I interrupted. "Are you telling me Olfridor is Gautarr's *brother*?"

"You didn't know?"

"Why would I? He's been weapons master since before I was born and he's never mentioned it once."

Johan looked thoughtfully at me, setting down his goblet. He paused for a long time before speaking again.

"Egill was always the steady hand in that family. He had the respect of his two younger brothers, Olfridor and Gautarr, and he led the house of Romsdahl well after the death of their father, Falruf. Like his father he was a warrior and, as is often the way of such things, he fell in battle against the Vorund Clan, leaving behind two children, Throm and Freydja. Gautarr was beside himself with grief and he blamed your father, Kolfinnar, for Egill's death. It rankled him that back then Olfridor fought alongside Marl and then later Kolfinnar, though of course he did it with Egill's agreement. He said Kolfinnar had left the people of Romsdahl to fend for themselves, that he never gave any support to his southern border and didn't care who died to protect him."

"That's a lie!" I exploded.

Johan held up a hand, bidding me to hear him out. "I know it is. Grief can do strange things to a man. People say Gautarr was never the same after the death of his daughter Svena, and of course he lost his eldest son Hroarr to a storm in the Redfars Sea as well. Anyway, Gautarr had already talked a few years earlier about staking a claim to be chief when old Marl died, although Egill would have none of it. Didn't stop Gautarr making his case at the clan moot but none of the families would back him, not with Egill openly supporting Kolfinnar. Now with Egill dead, Gautarr was ready for making a challenge all over again, only this time Olfridor opposed him. Thing was, Olfridor was Halfhand by then. A maimed man can't lead his people and Gautarr had taken over as head of the House of Romsdahl in his stead. That's why Kolfinnar took Olfridor as weapons master in Ulfkell's Keep, to give him a purpose in life and make sure he wasn't under the heel of Gautarr.

"Anyhow, once Olfridor publicly spoke out against Gautarr's claim at the next clan moot, that was it between them. Gautarr didn't manage to get one of the other houses to support him, not even Hrodi Whitebeard, and he never forgave Olfridor for the humiliation. So, think now about how much more this latest defeat will have hurt him. That's why I don't agree with Jorik, and I'll admit that freely to you here in my own house. Gautarr's never going to give up designs on being chief whilst there's breath left in his body. Your brother missed a chance to end it all." Johan let out a long sigh and sat back in his chair, watching me. "Didn't your father tell you *any* of this?"

"No. He wasn't much for telling us about anything," I admitted, provoking a chuckle from my host. So Olfridor and Gautarr were brothers. How could I not have known such a thing? It seemed that those who kept secrets in Ulfkell's Keep never chose to admit me to their inner circle. Now Johan's animosity towards Gautarr made much more sense and I wondered if Jorik was any better informed than I was. If not, whose judgement and experience was the greater? Johan or Jorik? Or was I asking the wrong question? Etta knew more than any of them. I resolved to keep my mind open in the future; either my brother didn't know every detail of our history or else he chose not to share everything with me. I found it hard to decide which of the two was worse.

"I agree with my husband," added Damona. "Look at those bruises on your face. Bandor always speaks so highly of you in his letters, Rothgar. The thought of that brute of a man ... that he so nearly killed you ..." She shuddered and fell silent. I was touched by her concern and smiled awkwardly, uncertain what to say. At nearly forty Damona was still a very attractive woman, her long blonde hair only just beginning to show the first signs of grey. The laughter lines around her eyes were in keeping with her friendly demeanour, as she made every effort to make me feel welcome at Kalamar Castle.

"Well, we should all be grateful Rothgar had the heart to stand up against Gautarr," Johan declared loudly, to murmurs of approval up and down the feasting hall. "You've earned the right to eat and drink with warriors, young man. With you at his side, Jorik need have no fear."

***

Kalamar Castle had been home to Johan's adoptive family for three generations, a gift from Hroar Helstromson to his loyal followers after seizing the land from the Norlhast Clan. Its grey stone towers looked out protectively over the small coastal town of Kalamar, which marked the northernmost extent of the Reavesburg Clan's territory. As the sun set behind us, Bandor and I looked out from the highest tower over the town spread out before us. Beyond lay the harbour, the waters of the Redfars Sea oily and dark in the fading light. The possession of Kalamar remained a source of contention with the Norlhast Clan, who still claimed the land was theirs. More than sixty years of occupation by our people told a different tale, our enemies too weak to reclaim what Hroar won in battle. Now, all that was about to change; our enemies would soon be our friends and Karas Greystorm was my future brother-in-law.

"I never thanked you," I began, searching for the right words. Bandor looked at me quizzically.

"Thanked me for what? You were the one fighting toe to toe against Gautarr."

"And you were the only one who spoke up for me at the clan moot. The *only* one, and that took some guts. Before we go our separate ways I wanted to let you know I'll never forget you supported me. We've fought together and stood side by side as allies and I'll miss you when I return to Reavesburg." Bandor was quiet for a long time, resting his hand lightly on my shoulder. I cleared my throat, forcing out the rest of the words before I lost the courage to speak them.

"Bandor, listen. Jorik's counting on your father to prove to Karas that the time has come to set aside our differences. I know that's going to be hard for him, so I need to know I can count on his support."

"And you want me to make sure he gives it?" There was an odd note in Bandor's voice, although in the growing darkness it was impossible to read his expression.

"Jorik's the new chief. Your father's playing a dangerous game, openly telling me he disagrees with Jorik's decisions. He's got to stop seeing Jorik as the young son of his friend. He's clan chief now and Jorik's questioning everyone's loyalty, even mine. I just don't want your father taking this a step too far and crossing the line with my brother."

"It's clear which side you're on." The bitter tone was unmistakable now, and my insides turned to ice.

"We're all on the same side, fighting Adalrikr and supporting Jorik's rule. All I'm asking is you discuss this with your father. A lot has changed in such a short space of time ..." The words died in my mouth as Bandor turned away.

"You're right, things have changed. Perhaps it's best I'm staying in Kalamar."

"Don't be like that, please. You need to understand I'm not my brother and any influence I have with Jorik has its limits. I'm trying to help you and your father here."

Bandor turned and walked away from me, only pausing as he reached the door to the stairs. "I'll think about what you say. Just don't ask me to choose between your brother and my father." He left without another word, leaving me alone with my thoughts.

CHAPTER 14

I looked for a chance to mend things with Bandor before my departure from Kalamar. Unfortunately, he seemed determined to avoid me and the opportunity never arose. I only saw him again as the *Hammerhead* set sail that morning, standing on the docks alongside his mother with his arm protectively around her waist, her face taut with worry. Bandor wore a sombre expression, only acknowledging me coolly as he raised his hand in farewell. A hollow feeling settled in my chest as I reflected on the awkward way we had parted. My fingers curled tightly around the gunwale as I fought to master my anger, furious that both Bandor and his father were either unable or too stubborn to see I was trying to help them. As the figures on the docks retreated into the distance, I turned my attention northwards. Our vessel seemed impossibly small as it cut its way through the choppy waters, little more than a cork bobbing over the white-crested waves. Amid the immensity of the Redfars Sea I felt trapped and insignificant, unable to escape the situation the ship was now propelling me towards.

I realised my position was similar to Nuna's, and guilt washed over me as I thought of my role in arranging her marriage to Karas. Before leaving Ulfkell's Keep, I had sought her out with a heavy heart to say my goodbyes. I found her talking with Katla and Amma, sitting on the same bench in the courtyard where we had spoken after Father's funeral. Her golden hair hung down her back in two long plaits, as was the fashion amongst the ladies in Reavesburg that year. The effect was striking, particularly when she smiled at my approach. I found myself taken a little aback, for the first time seeing her as a young woman. I swallowed, my thoughts swirling about in my mind like leaves on the wind.

"I thought I might find you here," I began. Amma and Katla politely excused themselves, realising this was a private conversation. Nuna looked up at me, hands clasped tightly together on her lap.

"I've just seen Johan leave the tower," she replied. "He had a face like a thundercloud. What could possibly have put him in such a bad temper?" Nuna raised an eyebrow at me, regarding me with a piercing stare.

I blurted out the words without thinking. "Jorik's told me about how you're to be wed to Karas Greystorm. You hinted as much the night of Father's funeral. I didn't know what Jorik intended at the time, though, I swear it."

Nuna took my hand. "It's always been the fate of the women in the chief's household to have their marriages arranged for political ends. I've never expected anything different."

"Being married to one of our enemies? Can you really say that's what you want? By all accounts Karas is ... an unusual character ..."

"Careful," Nuna interjected. "That's Johan speaking. Part of me doesn't like the thought of marrying a man that much older than myself, I'll admit. Another part of me is proud I'll play a role in bringing about peace between our two clans. Who knows, unifying the clans may force Adalrikr to think again about threatening our people. I can't wield a sword and ride out into battle like you. I've reflected on this for some time, and this is something I *can* do for our people. Can you understand that?"

I sighed. I couldn't fault her logic, though I thought I heard Etta's words weaving their way into Nuna's speech.

"I still feel responsible," I said finally. "I admire you for what you're prepared to do but all this stems from the divisions within our own clan. I could have done something to rectify that myself, a long time ago."

"What, you think if you'd already married Freydja Egilldottir none of this would be happening? Rothgar, life is never that simple. Adalrikr would still be a threat. Believe me, Etta has had this particular scheme in mind for some time. Anyway, do you really think you caused the divisions that bedevil our clan? No, they've been created by one man's determination to wrest power from our family. Gautarr has deliberately delayed the negotiations around your marriage. And it was Gautarr's actions in setting himself up against Jorik's rule and duelling with you that have now made marriage between you and Freydja impossible. Gautarr has always put his own interests above those of the Reavesburg Clan. I'll not be so weak."

Nuna's words were meant to encourage me, yet the encounter did nothing to lift my spirits. It dawned on me how selfish I'd been whilst growing up in Ulfkell's Keep. Nuna had a much wider perspective on such matters, despite her tender years.

"Jorik's asked me to negotiate with Karas on his behalf. The terms are stark. He can either agree to ally himself with our clan and marry you, or it's war. It could be an uncomfortable meeting."

Nuna looked troubled for a moment. "Then you must do your best to sue for peace and make Greystorm see reason. If we find ourselves at war on two fronts I fear Jorik will have overreached himself. The challenge Gautarr set down seems to have driven him to prove himself to be twice the man our father was. This plan can't fail, Rothgar, for all our sakes."

Wrapped in my thoughts on the deck of the ship I became aware I was no longer alone. Johan was beside me, watching the water speeding by now the sail had caught the wind. The *Hammerhead's* sail was pure white rather than the traditional tan or red commonly used, our clan emblem of an eagle replaced by an image of an open hand, indicating we came in peace. Drawing myself back to the present I nodded, silently acknowledging his presence. The warrior's craggy face broke into a thin smile, the wind whipping his long red hair back behind him like a pennant. He spoke in a quiet voice, ensuring his words didn't carry to the crew nearby.

"I know something took place between you and Bandor before we left. I can tell things aren't right. Standing here brooding over it won't make any difference, but perhaps I can help by speaking to him when we return?"

I shook my head. "Thank you, but no. It was a misunderstanding, that's all, and it'll soon be mended. I'll make sure we speak after we return from our meeting with Karas." Johan nodded and didn't press the subject further, turning instead to more immediate concerns.

"Since Jorik has packed us both off on this trip for good or ill, we should make sure no mistakes are made. How much do you actually know about Karas Greystorm? I'm guessing Etta has mentioned him during your studies?"

"She has," I replied. "Karas leads a weakened clan at the moment. His last few raids against our defences have all been unsuccessful and he's also come under increased attack from Vorund in recent years. Back in the time of their previous chief, Bekan, the Norlhast Clan was stronger and I know your father was hard pressed at times to hold him at bay."

"True enough," muttered Johan. "Those were dark days indeed. Did you know my father lost his three natural sons at the hands of Bekan?"

"Bandor told me," I said. The story was that Jokell had taken Johan in after finding him abandoned as a baby, left out to die on the moors. The young foundling had ultimately risen to lead the House of Kalamar after the deaths of Jokell's three sons.

"Karas Greystorm is not strong following his recent defeats," I continued. "Etta also told me he suffered tragedy in his own life. Katrin, his first wife, died in childbirth and when Norlhast was struck by the blood plague three years ago it claimed Karas' second wife, Thora, and both their daughters. Karas also caught the disease and many thought he would die.

I've heard the illness left him scarred and greyed his hair. His people now call him Greystorm to reflect that change and the difficulties he has weathered in life. They say that he looks much older than his thirty-five years."

Johan pursed his lips and nodded. "You've been paying more attention than Etta would have us believe. You're right that Karas is not the man he once was, mentally or physically, placing him under threat from within his own clan. Sigurd Albriktson is his jarl and many talk of him as Karas' natural successor. Karas also has shamans at his court. Has Etta spoken to you about them?"

"A little. Etta says that a true shaman has the ability to communicate with the banished avatars who ruled this world before the Fallen Age. Father never had much time for them in Ulfkell's Keep. He always said that the tribes settled in the lands of Laskar to make a new start following the War of the Avatars, not to remain beholden to them."

Johan nodded. "After the death of his family, Karas fell into a deep despair. The stories I have been told are that he looked to the shamans for news of his wife and daughters in the afterlife. Navan is an avatar, after all, and he holds the keys to the Halls of the Dead. So shamans flocked to his court, both true and false. I swear that some of the battles Karas fought against us were founded on omens and portents from these charlatans, which is why the Norlhast Clan has suffered such a sharp decline in their fortunes in war. Nowadays a trio of women have his favour at court, although little is known of them. Any tidings concerning them merely refer to a 'coven' at Norlhast. They are the ones who hold true power in Karas' court, so we must be careful not to anger them."

"Some people say Karas lost his mind following his family's death. Do you believe that?"

"They might well be right. I've crossed swords with Sigurd but I've never met Karas in person. Who knows what we will find when we arrive? I imagine you must have some concerns about your sister becoming his bride?" Johan's statement hung there between us, as he looked straight out to sea. So, we came to it at last, the real reason for this quiet conversation. I tried to answer carefully, though I could feel my face flushing red as I did so.

"Nuna's prepared to do what's required to bring about peace. Are you, Johan?"

"This isn't about peace at all. It's about Jorik's determination to go to war with Adalrikr and gathering the forces he requires by any means necessary. Your father would never have agreed to this course of action."

"My father's dead," I said in a low voice. "Jorik has given his orders and we're to obey our new chief." Johan uttered a vile oath and spat into the sea. I had always enjoyed a good relationship with him up till now, thinking of him as a benevolent uncle and the father of my best friend. Now Johan looked at me with contempt.

"Boy, you've no idea what you're talking about. Do you honestly think I'll be any more welcome in Karas' presence than Tyrfingr Blackeyes was when he set foot in Ulfkell's Keep? Many of my own people will want to kill me for brokering any deal with their nearest enemy. We've suffered at their hands too many times simply to forget all that has happened in the past. Jorik asks too much of me this time." Johan's brows furrowed as his gaze bore into me. "I've thought about this moment. It would be all too easy for your voyage to end here by my dagger, long before we reach Norlhast. You'd never see land again and I could report to Jorik that Greystorm rejected our terms out of hand, killed you and we're now at war with his clan. My men would back up my story." I stood there, still as a rock, though my heart hammered in my chest. I thought of reaching for my sword, despite knowing I could never fight the entire crew of the ship single-handed.

"Your brother is hardly thinking of your welfare, is he?" Johan continued. "He's young and inexperienced and Etta holds too much sway over him. That's putting you in danger on this voyage and the Reavesburg Clan on course for war.

Raiding is one thing; it's been a way of life for our people for generations. Jorik has greater ambitions. He wants to bring down the Vorund Clan and unseat Adalrikr from power; he told me as much on our last voyage together. Even united with the Norlhast, Vittag and Helsburg Clans he'll never succeed." I stood there on the swaying deck of the ship, listening to Johan's words. I recalled my earlier conversation with Nuna back at home and heard echoes of her own concerns in what Johan was now saying.

"So, where does that leave us?" I finally asked. "My brother is chief, and I owe him my allegiance as well as my life. Do you stand with him, or does our mission end right here at sea?" I tried to make my wavering voice sound brave. Johan scowled, making no move towards the great two-handed sword hanging from his back.

"Jorik's married my daughter and sired my only grandchild. You're part of my family now and I could no more raise my hand against you than I could against that small boy. For the sake of my family and in memory of your father, who was the greatest friend I ever had, I'll stand by you and Jorik."

"Thank you," I replied, unclenching my hand from the hilt of my sword, my fingers numb from gripping it so hard. "I know how much this is costing you, Johan."

"No. You really don't. No matter, the decision is made, as Jorik would say. I've told you what I think and you're no more able to turn this ship aside from its course than I am. We're bound together now. All I'd say is don't breathe a word of any of this to the crew – that's my concern, after all this is over. Only you and I will be setting foot ashore, and we don't know how negotiations with Karas will go. No sense in telling people what they don't need to know."

I nodded in agreement, relieved the discussion was over. I admired Johan's direct approach, and he had offered me another perspective on recent events. I wondered how my father had maintained his nineteen-year rule with such an iron grip. In a matter of weeks Jorik was already mired in all manner of difficulties. I also thought ruefully about the need to keep our mission secret and how indiscreet I'd been with Desta. A sense of disquiet settled upon me as our ship headed northwards, towards Norlhast and our audience with Karas Greystorm.

CHAPTER 15

The threatening crowd surrounded us on all sides, filling the air with noise, as Kalfr Albriktson bellowed loudly for people to make room. His cries went unheeded and every step was a struggle. I found myself shoved roughly, losing my footing, and only Johan's firm hand prevented me from falling.

"I've got you. Come on, it's not much further now."

The press of the crowd crushed the air from my lungs and I was unable to reply: merely focusing on placing one foot in front of the other was proving to be enough of an effort. A grey bearded man loomed into view, his face inches from my own. He spat straight at me, so close I could feel his hot breath and taste the tang of his sweat. Angered, I lashed out as we were carried apart and continued to fight our way through the throng. I grimly wiped my face clean amid the jeers and mocking calls.

"You killed my brother, Jokellsward! You'll never leave Norlhast alive."

"... Kolfinnar's son, I tell you ... Look, right there ..."

"... hanging's too good for scum like them ... urgh!" The last speaker fell silent as Kalfr's fist smashed into his mouth, sending him reeling back into the noisy mob.

"Out of the way, damn it, or so help me I'll run the next man through who blocks our path!" roared Kalfr, hand on the hilt of his sword, challenging anyone to cross him. "They're here under flag of parley and my protection. Clear the way. Now!"

Kalfr was a short stocky man with blond hair and a thin scar running from his cheek to his lip on his left side. When he smiled on greeting us at the docks I noticed he was missing a good few teeth. Unfortunately, what he was not lacking was company, as a sizeable crowd had already gathered by the time we landed.

Johan had decided it was too risky to dock the *Hammerhead* at Norlhast, since it was our only means of escape. The two of us rowed out in a small boat towards the docks, whilst the crew of our ship watched our progress from a safe distance under their parley flag. As we drew close, I saw the crowd gathered there and drew a deep breath to steady my nerves. When we landed I realised Johan knew the thickset warrior who led the welcoming party.

"Kalfr," he called out. "Sigurd Albriktson's younger brother," he said in a lower tone to me by way of explanation. "We come on a matter of importance, seeking an audience with Karas Greystorm. You'll see from the sails of my ship that we've come in peace."

"Johan Jokellsward," Kalfr's eyes widened with recognition. "You've some balls, landing here after what you did at Vintor." The warrior drew back his hair, revealing only half an ear on his left side, part of the injury that scarred his face. "You left me there for dead – well it's time for some payback, I'd say."

"Shut your hole and listen to me, Kalfr," Johan snapped. "Kill me and you'll have the Reavesburg Clan hammering on the doors of your keep within a week, baying for blood. Karas will want to hear us out, I promise you. After that, he can decide what happens next."

"Huh, I guess he will. Who's the frightened rabbit you've got with you?"

"I'm Rothgar Kolfinnarson," I replied, trying to sound is if I was used to such encounters and faced far worse in my time. "I'm the brother of Jorik, chief of the Reavesburg Clan, and I'm here to speak on his behalf."

Kalfr chuckled, making an odd wheezy sound. "Oh, this just gets better and better. Well, you've come for an audience with our chief and that's just what you'll get. I wouldn't want to miss this."

Kalfr helped us from the boat, disarmed us and escorted us towards Karas' keep with some of his warriors. As for Norlhast, I was able to see little of the town as we were soon surrounded, once word spread about who had landed in the white-sailed ship.

We were jostled and shoved by the rabble, and the din was deafening. Kalfr virtually beat a path through those before him and Johan and I struggled to keep up with his pace. Insults were hurled at us from every direction, and I had to steel myself to avoid turning tail and running for the safety of the boat. I reminded myself that the mob would tear me to pieces without Kalfr's protection. Forcing myself to walk still deeper into Norlhast required every scrap of courage I could muster. Johan looked grim as he ploughed on beside me, watching his feet rather than meeting the eyes of the citizens of the town. Most of the jeering was directed at him, and I doubted my brother could have contrived to send a more unpopular envoy to Norlhast. His tactics looked more and more like a gamble, and I began to wonder whether Johan had been right all along.

The crowd parted to reveal a small wooden door. Armed guards stood on either side of a completely unremarkable building. A course of white dry stones, some two feet high, formed the foundations upon which had been set a wall of turf. This rose in a shallow slope to form a low roof, a wisp of smoke drifting up from a vent at the very centre. It was a far meaner dwelling than the wooden houses found in even the poorer districts of Reavesburg, and I looked at Johan in confusion. He appeared equally baffled.

"Why are we stopping here?" I asked Kalfr, fearing some trick.

"You wanted to see our chief, didn't you?" the warrior asked, once again giving us a wheezy chuckle.

"He lives here?" Johan gasped. "Why doesn't he live in your keep?"

"You'll have to ask him," Kalfr replied, grinning an unpleasant smile. With that he gestured for the guards to make way and pushed the pair of us through the doorway.

Inside the air was dark and smoky and the airless atmosphere was not helped by the fact Kalfr shut the door firmly behind us. At least it deadened the noise of the crowd outside. It took my eyes a little time to adjust, since the only light emanated from a long fire running the length of the simple dwelling, consisting of a single room. At the far end a grey-haired man sat on a tall wooden chair, his feet resting on a footstool. On his right stood a short thickset warrior, wearing chainmail armour, with his hand on the hilt of his sword. The resemblance of this man to Kalfr meant this must be Sigurd Albriktson, his elder brother and jarl of Norlhast Keep. Around the long fire pit squatted three cloaked women – presumably the 'coven' Johan had referred to. Their hoods were drawn up, hiding their faces in the gloom. Slowly, the grey-haired man raised his head, as if he had been woken from a deep sleep.

"Is that Kalfr?" he croaked, his voice rasping and thin.

"It is, Chief." Kalfr's voice boomed in comparison, filling the tiny space with noise as if we were standing inside a drum. "We have visitors. Johan Jokellsward and Rothgar Kolfinnarson, from the Reavesburg Clan." At this announcement Sigurd took a step towards us, drawing his blade in a swift, easy motion. The three women crouching round the fire moved as one, looking up and staring at us from within the depths of their hooded faces.

"They're unarmed," Kalfr reassured his brother, as he led us towards Karas. Sigurd nodded, keeping his weapon drawn. Despite Sigurd's concern, the news that enemies were standing in his own home did not rouse any reaction in the Norlhast chief.

As we drew closer, Karas' appearance took me by surprise. Even after his seizure, my father had retained a healthier aspect than the man sitting before us. Karas Greystorm was well-named. Life appeared to have ravaged him, gouging deep ageing lines into the pock-marked face of a man still in his middle thirties. His grey hair was thin, long and matted, hanging loose about his shoulders in unflattering rats' tails, his chin sporting a ragged and uneven beard. I looked into his weak watery blue eyes and wondered if he saw me at all, his gaze distant and unfocused. Karas' frame was skinny and he barely filled his fine though dusty clothes. His face and the skeletal hands protruding from the sleeves of his robe were an unhealthy stark white: thick blue veins clearly visible under the translucent skin, despite the red glow of the fire. With his lack of movement, it was easy to imagine I was having an audience with a life-size porcelain marionette. I swallowed and looked to Johan for inspiration as to how to address the Norlhast chief. It was obvious from his face that he was equally taken aback by Karas' lack of vitality. A long silence settled over the scene until, to my surprise, it was broken by Karas.

"Eh? What did you say, Kalfr? Why have you disturbed me?"

Kalfr cleared his throat and began his introductions again. "Chief, the Reavesburg Clan have sent two emissaries, sailing under a flag of parley."

"Parley, you say? Then these men are … are who? Who did you say? Why … why is the flag of parley necessary?"

Karas looked uncertain as Sigurd stepped up close to the chair and whispered something into Karas' ear. As he listened, Greystorm turned to us again, and this time a flicker of recognition illuminated his eyes.

"Johan Jokellsward. I remember you now. Butcher of Vintor. Occupier of Kalamar, your seat stolen from us by Hroar Helstromson. Yes … I remember, I remember everything you have done to us."

"He's your enemy," one of the three cloaked women cried, startling me so violently I almost stepped into the fire pit. "He's not welcome here. He and his young friend should not have come. Kill them."

"Yes …." Karas paused, regarding us both dispassionately, the embers of the fire briefly stoked in his spirit already fading away. "Yes, we should kill them … I think that would be best."

"Wait," Johan shouted in alarm. "Karas Greystorm, we are here on a matter of great importance. You must allow us to speak before acting so rashly."

"Am I being rash?" Karas asked Sigurd. The coven spoke in unison before he could answer.

"Kill them."

"Kill them now, before they poison you with their lies."

"Yes, don't listen to their false words. Act now and swiftly to end their lives, before they lead you astray."

The coven were silenced as Sigurd's voice rang with a note of command so absent from his own chief. "These men are warriors of their clan. They've walked into our midst unarmed seeking an audience with our chief. Enemy or no, they have the right to speak. This is our way and you would do well to respect our traditions."

At his words the women skulked back into the shadows of the room, muttering under their breath while stopping short of openly contradicting the jarl.

"Of course, Sigurd, you're right," Karas agreed. "They have the right to speak … Unless you think …." Karas' voice trailed away and Sigurd glowered in the direction of the women, who made no further objection. Johan seized the opportunity before Greystorm changed his mind again.

"Karas Greystorm, news will no doubt have reached you of the recent death of Kolfinnar Marlson, the Reavesburg chief. His son, Jorik, has now assumed that title and though young, he has already proved himself in battle against the Vorund Clan, our mutual enemy. Jorik Kolfinnarson seeks to broker an alliance with your people and put an end to the skirmishes along his northern border. This will enable him to bring his forces to bear in the south and drive back the Vorund Clan. Both our peoples have suffered from their raiding in recent years and now it's clear they grow stronger still. Tyrfingr Blackeyes is a dark name we both know. He has already demanded tribute from the Reavesburg Clan, and I am sure you have received similar threats. Adalrikr Asmarrson's ambitions are growing, and the time has come to unite if we are to thwart his aims."

"Lies," hissed one of the women from the darkness, beyond the light of the fire. My frayed nerves were already stretched to breaking point and the whisperings of the coven sparked my anger.

"Silence. Let us speak," I rebuked them, surprising myself with my boldness. It even caught Karas' attention.

"Who is this young man? You should learn some manners, boy. These ladies are my trusted advisors. They offer me comfort ... in my time of grief ..." Tears welled up in those pale blue eyes. I caught Sigurd's expression – an odd mixture of pity for his chief and disgust for the female shamans who held sway in Karas' court. It was obvious the Norlhast Clan was deeply divided, and perhaps weaker than any of us had previously thought. It crossed my mind that as allies they might be able to offer us far less than Jorik hoped.

"This is Rothgar Kolfinnarson," Kalfr supplied. "He's Kolfinnar's younger son."

"I'm here to speak on behalf of my brother, as a sign of good faith as to the sincerity of our offer. I would urge you to consider it most carefully."

Sigurd raised an eyebrow. "An alliance, you say? Jorik's ambitions are vast indeed if he seeks to rival the Vorund Clan for power. However, my people have long memories and Johan Jokellsward is well-known to us. Some might say his name is more hated than Tyrfingr Blackeyes in these parts. You expect us to believe the words of this man? To believe he now comes offering the hand of friendship and seeking peace for us all? And if Jorik is victorious in his war against Vorund, what then? With his power so increased, what is to stop him from turning his attention back on Norlhast and commanding Jokellsward to lay waste our lands once again?"

"Jorik is willing to offer the hand of my sister, Nuna, in marriage to Karas Greystorm. By this act our clans will be united and our families joined in wedlock," I replied evenly. "These are not empty words to secure a temporary truce. Jorik believes we must unite against the threat from Vorund, if we are to survive at all. We need allies in our nearest neighbours."

"They are false." The sibilant whisperings of Karas' shamans made the hair on the back of my neck stand on end. Yet this time their words went unheeded; my revelation had caught both Karas and Sigurd by surprise and I had their full attention.

"I'm here to vouch for the truth of what Rothgar says," added Johan. "My father battled over the same ground with Bekan that you and I have contested in our time. Much blood has been spilt on both sides. My own house will need to be persuaded that times have changed but, just as I have led them to war, so it's my responsibility to lead them as we set aside our differences."

"And if I refuse this generous offer?" Karas asked.

Johan cleared his throat and spoke clearly so none could mistake his answer. "Jorik cannot afford an enemy at his back if he's to fight Adalrikr. His command is that I return to Kalamar, muster my forces and lay waste to Norlhast and your lands, enslave your people and use them as thralls in the vanguard of our army to fight against the Vorund Clan. He believes the threat posed by Adalrikr Asmarrson is so great that anyone not allied to us in seeking his destruction is as good as fighting for him. I assure you this is a battle neither of us need but refusal of our terms will lead to conflict. These are dangerous times, Karas Greystorm, and the time for action has now come."

"Boldly spoken," Sigurd Albriktson acknowledged. "My forces are more than able to defend themselves, Jokellsward. Come and lay siege to Norlhast Keep if you wish. You will find a warm welcome awaits you here."

"And yet ..." Greystorm groped for words. He became lost in thought for so long I began to wonder if he'd forgotten the point he wished to make. "And yet ... as Jokellsward says, this is not a fight that suits either clan. Jorik will not want a dagger in his back as he takes on Adalrikr, so he must deal with the threat we pose, once and for all. His scheme is bold ... and it has merit. Yes ... I see some advantage in this." As he spoke, Karas seemed to shed some of the torpor that mired his spirit. His eyes flickered and came back to life, if only for a moment. Sigurd's face was dark and troubled as he exchanged a look with his brother. The trio of women were far more vocal in their objections, springing forward, their voices shrill with anger and alarm.

"No, my lord, don't listen to them."

"You cannot trust the words of Jokellsward. He has been a scourge of our people for years."

"This is a trap. Pay their words no heed."

Karas Greystorm looked at the three women mildly, saying nothing until they ceased their protests. He simply sat there, regarding us with a blank expression. Slowly he turned to Sigurd.

"Old friend, lend me your arm. We should continue these discussions back at the keep. If you ... if you could help me ... to stand ... yes, thank you. It has been a while ... too long since I was last there."

"Gladly, walk with me," Sigurd said, shooting a look at the shamans that sent them shuffling back into the shadows once more. "Kalfr, have the guards disperse the crowd outside. You two," he added, gesturing to me and Johan. "You'll join us as well."

"Yes," added Karas, standing unsteadily. "Please, join us. It's so long since I've had guests to entertain. Far too long."

CHAPTER 16

Etta's wrinkled face cracked into a rare smile as she and Jorik listened carefully to my report following my return from Norlhast. Etta made me describe every detail, equally interested in my account of the events on the voyage as the outcome of our negotiations with Karas Greystorm. I felt a great sense of satisfaction as I spoke – everything had gone far better than I dared hope.

Karas was hospitable and Sigurd took great care to ensure only he and his brother attended to us. He clearly feared for our safety if we were left in the sole care of other guards or servants from the Norlhast Clan. Karas was incredibly frail; walking at the pace of his tottering steps up to the gates of Norlhast Keep was one of the longest journeys of my life. The denizens of the town did not push and jostle us this time, keeping a respectful distance as they watched their fragile chief make his slow way through the streets. I had time to observe the town in more detail, noting how every house was constructed in the same way as the one we had visited. Trees were sparse this far north and it was obvious Karas' clan used what timber they had for their prized whaling ships, rather than their homes. Norlhast Keep dominated the small town, rising up in its centre like a vast mountain of weathered white stone – although it was a far smaller structure than the keep in Reavesburg. Norlhast's fortress was a square tower, rising four storeys high. At each corner four smaller towers had been added, providing an excellent vantage point to watch the surrounding land and the river mouth that led out to the sea.

Inside, we were offered comfortable quarters, although

everything was dusty or damp from long disuse. Johan and I discussed this, wondering whether Karas had forsaken the keep after the death of his family. However, the opportunity to delicately raise the subject never arose.

Although physically weak, Karas Greystorm roused himself in our presence and proved to be more astute both politically and tactically than I first supposed. Norlhast had suffered badly from heavy raiding by Vorund in recent years, and it soon became clear Karas feared they would eventually be overwhelmed by their enemy. He clearly saw Jorik's offer of an alliance as the only means by which his people would be able to survive. He was far more amenable to the idea than Johan or I had expected, making the task of the negotiations much more straightforward. Afterwards, on our return journey, Johan remarked it had been like debating with a drowning man whether or not he wanted us to throw him a rope.

Naturally, the subject of Nuna was discussed; Karas making clear he did not expect to be married to some *'lumpen and unwholesome old maid'*. Looking at Norlhast's decrepit chief I thought he was applying a degree of double-standards. Fortunately, Johan was better prepared for this topic of conversation, ably describing Nuna in glowing terms. The matter of her dowry was soon settled and a temporary truce of all hostilities between the Reavesburg and Norlhast Clans was agreed. There was only one condition, upon which Karas was adamant.

"And that condition was what, exactly?" Jorik enquired.

"Karas wants to meet Nuna before agreeing the match. Furthermore, he demands proof she is ready and able to bear children. That struck me forcibly when we were there – Karas is haunted by the loss of his daughters. He found it almost impossible to refuse the opportunity, when we offered him the chance to wed again and provide an heir to secure his line."

"Strange," observed Etta. "If such things were so important to him, why not marry a young maiden from his own clan? He's been widowed for three years."

"Honestly, I believe when we arrived and put forward our offer, that was the first time he even considered the possibility. Sigurd hinted Karas has been mad with grief following his loss and his own illness."

"It's surprising Sigurd hasn't made a move for power himself," Jorik remarked.

"I agree. He's the obvious choice to take the place of a weak chief; yet instead Sigurd is content to act as jarl and support Karas. The two of them are close." Etta closed her eyes, storing away that useful fact for future reference.

"And that was his only condition, once the dowry was settled?" asked Jorik. I nodded in agreement.

"Not an unreasonable request," said Etta. "Nuna has not yet started her monthly cycle. Karas will want to know she is able to bear him children, although following his illness whether he can give her any is another matter. This may well mean a delay to the marriage, although we can hardly object now Karas has agreed to a truce."

Her remark left me feeling uncomfortable. I hardly felt proud about my part in conducting the terms of Nuna's marriage to such a weak and feeble man, so the idea I might also be consigning her to childlessness did not sit easily. I recalled Nuna's words and her resolve, assuring me she was willing to make sacrifices for the sake of our clan. I wondered how long it would last, alone with Karas in his gloomy keep, far from family and friends. If Jorik shared such concerns he kept them well hidden.

Etta and Jorik were also anxious to know how the outcome of the negotiations was received in Kalamar. I explained how Johan delivered the news to his people with great skill. Both Bandor and I spoke up in support of the proposed unification of the two clans – an intimidating prospect in the feasting hall where the audience consisted entirely of Johan's toughest, hardened veterans. The desire for victory against Vorund was eventually enough to override their natural dislike of their traditional enemy in the north.

When Rugga spoke in favour of the union, I knew the day was won even as Kaun scowled darkly over the proceedings. Ultimately, Johan secured their support, preventing a dangerous divide opening up within the Kalamar household. My only regret was that Bandor remained aloof. What little conversation we had was strained and formal, and he was cold as we parted ways on my return to Reavesburg. I hoped time would mend the rift between us, so I chose not to share the matter with Jorik and Etta, thinking it of little consequence now Johan Jokellsward had shown such loyalty to our cause.

"Nuna should visit Norlhast before the summer is out," Etta counselled, as our meeting drew to a close. "We must build upon the goodwill fostered by this first meeting, whilst it's fresh in the minds of all concerned. Of course, she will require a chaperone: someone Karas has grown to trust." Her good eye gleamed as she fixed me with a meaningful stare.

"You mean me?"

"There's little more you can learn from Olfridor," Jorik said. "You've proven yourself able in the art of diplomacy, Rothgar. I can think of no one I would rather send to protect our sister. She will require a female servant to attend her as well. I was thinking of sending Amma or Katla but Kolfinnar is so devoted to them these days, Reesha assures me he'll wail night and day if they're gone. Nuna is friendly with Desta, and Reesha speaks very highly of her." Caught off-guard, I glanced towards Etta, unsure whether she would counsel Jorik against this particular idea. She raised an eyebrow at me, saying nothing, so the matter was decided. I left Jorik's chambers, unsure whether or not this was a good thing.

***

Jorik wasted no time announcing Nuna's betrothal to Karas Greystorm and the news was received with a variety of reactions. Openly, everyone supported Jorik's proposal for peace in the north. However, snatches of conversation I overheard between some of the warriors when they thought they were unobserved told a different story. There was disquiet amongst them as they struggled to adjust to the fact their former enemies were now allies. Many doubted Karas would keep his word, although few saw him as a potential threat compared with the Vorund Clan. Hearing this view expressed in Ulfkell's Keep, Jorik's personal stronghold, made me re-evaluate what I had witnessed in Kalamar, where hatred of the Norlhast Clan ran deep. I realised I had been naïve, taking the statements of Johan's warriors at face value. Johan Jokellsward still had work to do in Kalamar. I also wondered if there was more to Bandor's sudden return home than I had first imagined.

My return to Ulfkell's Keep enabled me to resume my clandestine romance with Desta. Whilst I hadn't forgotten Etta's warning, I convinced myself things had changed. I told myself that, now my engagement to Freydja had foundered, I was free to see whoever I wanted. The truth was I loved this young woman; I was unable to contemplate a life that did not include her, so I ignored the fact Jorik would never allow us to marry. Neither of us spoke of this openly, though we both knew the truth; otherwise, there would have been no need to keep our relationship a secret.

More difficult was my reunion with Nuna. I owed her an honest account of my meeting with Karas Greystorm, although I tried to present Norlhast's chief in the best possible light. Nuna listened attentively as I explained she would be meeting him in person in the next few weeks. I was impressed at how she maintained her bearing, accepting everything with equanimity and a resolve to serve her family well. Nevertheless, in a quiet moment I asked Reesha to watch over Nuna. My sister-in-law seemed genuinely touched at my concern and promised she would offer any support she could. My conscience salved, I went about my business in the keep and began preparing for the return journey to Norlhast.

Those plans were interrupted when the Vorund Clan struck our shores once again in strength, Finnvidor leading our men and driving the invaders back. No sooner had he returned than news soon reached us that Gautarr's warriors at Romsdahl had also repelled a force of some size. Although Ragnar had been wounded during the encounter, we suffered relatively few casualties. Jorik made a point of despatching a messenger to thank Gautarr for standing firm once more. The lack of any response from Gautarr was troubling, although not altogether unexpected.

More disturbing were the reports that whilst we were engaged with Adalrikr's forces other raiding parties were striking at Riltbalt and Norlhast territories. Several Helsburg and Vittag merchant ships also failed to reach their destinations. It became clear Adalrikr was showing his rival clans his power, demonstrating he was able to send his forces against all of us, if he wished. Outwardly, Jorik maintained a calm and determined demeanour at his court as the scale of Adalrikr's recent raiding became clear. In my audiences with him and Etta in his private chambers it was another matter – it was clear his confidence was badly shaken.

"Rothgar, I want you to set sail with Nuna tomorrow at the first tide. We've delayed too long on our promise to Karas."

"It's hardly the best weather to be taking to the seas," I countered, surprised by this sudden turn of events. "We can't afford to lose our ship and place Nuna in danger –"

"Bad weather means no raiding. I'd rather trust Brunn Fourwinds to bring you both through a summer storm than run the gauntlet of Vorund's ships. You'll sail in *Marl's Pride*."

"The visit itself will need to be a surprise," added Etta, her shrewd face watching mine intently. "Make your final preparations as quietly as you can. I'll speak to Nuna and Desta and ensure they're both ready to travel. Remember there are many people in our camp and Karas' who would much prefer this marriage never took place. Proceed with caution, Rothgar, and be careful whom you trust."

"I've already asked Olfridor to accompany me," I told them. "He's no diplomat and has some history with Norlhast himself. However, there's no one I'd rather have as Nuna's bodyguard. It also shows to our new allies things have changed."

Etta smiled. "A good choice. Building bridges between old enemies is the right tactic. Just remember Halfhand may also prove to be a tempting target – make sure you don't place him in harm's way."

"For a mission such as this I can make do without my weapons master for a little while," Jorik agreed. He rose from his seat and clapped me on both shoulders. It was a rare familiar gesture from my brother these days. It struck me that since he'd become chief we'd grown more distant.

I clasped his hands in mine, fondly recalling easier times. "I'll make sure I bring him and Nuna back safely."

"You'd better, Brother, and tread carefully yourself, too. Tyrfingr Blackeyes has been quiet of late, and that makes me uneasy."

CHAPTER 17

"Is that the best you can do?" Kalfr laughed and spurred his horse forwards, the gelding's hooves digging deep into the dirt, sending clods flying in his wake. I was forced to duck and urged my own steed forwards, anxious to prove to the Norlhast warrior I was no coward. Kalfr Albriktson was an able horseman, and he easily outpaced me as we crossed the open moorlands that lay to the north of Norlhast. In the distance, the northernmost peaks of the Baros Mountains dominated the skyline; their iron grey sides topped with snow Kalfr said never melted, even in mid-summer. As I struggled to remain firmly seated in my saddle, Kalfr eventually took pity on me, slowing his horse to a steady trot and allowing me to ride up alongside. The warrior broke into a grin, made somewhat lopsided by his old scar, and I smiled back, acknowledging I'd been bested by my host on this occasion.

"You ride well," I managed to gasp as I caught my breath.

The stocky warrior rubbed his horse's neck fondly. "Our clan symbol may be the whale, but give me a horse over a ship any time. I've spent too many days on the Redfars Sea, feeling too hungry, cold or wet for comfort. Sigurd's always blathering on about the 'freedom of the trackless sea.' It's out here, just me alone with Swift, that's when I truly feel free."

"A good name," I acknowledged. "After our journey here, I'll confess seafaring holds less appeal than it once did."

That was an understatement: the voyage from Reavesburg to Norlhast had been horrendous. A driving northern wind hampered our progress for much of the journey, battering us with fearsome swells and unpleasant squalls. Three days out the weather turned into a full-blown storm, severely testing Brunn's crew as they fought to keep our vessel afloat and two men were lost to the Redfars Sea. My fear for the safety of Nuna and Desta didn't abate until, with relief, we entered the mouth of the River Taur and I gave the order to hoist the sail made specially on Karas Greystorm's instructions.

Our flag of parley now showed the emblem of both the eagle and the whale on its bright white canvas, the bird soaring over the water jet issuing from the blowhole of the great beast of the sea. It was another tangible sign times were changing and new alliances being forged, although I was still cautious and left Brunn in charge of *Marl's Pride* in the River Taur, rowing ashore in a small boat with just Nuna, Desta and Olfridor. Despite being barely able to sit up during the terrible voyage, Nuna displayed her courage, alighting on the dockside looking remarkably fresh. Only the trembling of her hand as I steadied her betrayed a combination of exhaustion and nerves. Karas did not greet her in person, since the exact day of our arrival had not been fixed. However, Sigurd Albriktson had clearly been alerted to our appearance, and he led a guard of honour that escorted the four of us to Norlhast Keep.

Karas Greystorm had taken up residence at his old keep once more. His hall was echoing and cold, lacking the life and vitality found in Ulfkell's Keep or Johan's feasting hall in Kalamar Castle. Karas sat in the same chair I'd seen in the turf house in Norlhast, his posture slack. The trio of hooded women skulked in the shadows – the coven still wielding their influence.

The sound of Sigurd's boots broke the heavy silence as he led the way towards Karas. I glanced at Nuna, walking arm in arm with Desta, her head held proud and high. Olfridor brought up the rear of our party, his eyes watchful as he scanned the shadows of the hall for any signs of danger. In recognition of the truce between our two clans, Sigurd had not disarmed us on our arrival. My sword hung in its scabbard and the touch of the cool metal of its wire hilt was reassuring, as was the presence of my weapons master at my back. I had been afraid when I first landed at Norlhast. On my second visit, though, I felt worse; the stakes were higher and one mistake could lead to ruin. As Sigurd stopped a few paces from Karas I squared my shoulders, pushing such thoughts aside as I prepared to address Nuna's suitor.

"Rothgar Kolfinnarson has returned," Sigurd announced, his voice resounding loudly and breaking the silence in the empty chamber. "He wishes to introduce you to his sister, Nuna Kolfinnardottir." Karas' blue eyes widened as he heard those words. There was a shuffling sound, as his ever-present coven stood and sidled closer to inspect these new arrivals.

"Nuna," Karas breathed the name rather than spoke it aloud. "Forgive me if I do not stand to greet you. Time has not been kind to me, as you can see. Please, young lady, step forward so I may see you more clearly."

I gave Nuna a reassuring nod as she unclasped herself from Desta and walked up towards the raised dais on which Karas was sitting. Her voice rang out confidently as she addressed him.

"Karas Greystorm, chief of the Norlhast Clan, my brother, Jorik, has proposed to seal his pact with you by offering my hand in marriage. As you requested, I have made the long journey to Norlhast, so we may meet and become better acquainted."

"You are so young ... My eldest daughter, Gretta, was but a little younger than you when she died. What year were you born, young lady?"

"The one-hundred and ninety-fifth year of the Fallen Age, my lord. I am thirteen years of age." Nuna's simple words struck Karas like a body blow. He drew in a long, ragged breath as he steadied himself before replying.

"The same *year* as poor Gretta ... Can it really be that she would now have been old enough ... old enough to be making plans for her own betrothal? It cannot be ..." Karas seemed to withdraw into himself and an awkward silence filled the room.

One of the three members of the coven stepped forward and drew back her hood. In keeping with Darri's stories, I expected she would be old and wizened. Instead a young woman presented herself to me, tall and attractive with high cheek bones and long dark hair.

"I am Nereth, advisor to Karas Greystorm with my sisters, Lysa and Shula. I'll admit I didn't believe you when you last visited the keep. Yet here you stand, true to your word, presenting your pretty young sister to our chief. I confess, I'm surprised at your boldness."

I bowed low. "Times change, Nereth. The offer of friendship was an honest one and the pact between our clans will enable both our people to prosper."

Nereth tilted her head, so that she looked down on me. "And the offer to annihilate our people, if we did not agree to Jorik Kolfinnarson's most generous offer? Presumably that was *honest* too? You will forgive me if I don't feign joy at your presence here."

Sigurd looked a little strained as Karas continued to sit on his chair during this exchange, eyes focussed on some distant scene only he could see. "As Rothgar has said, times change. Our guests have had a long and difficult journey, Chief. Perhaps they should retire to their quarters for a time, before joining us this evening for food and drink?"

His jarl accepted Karas' silence as assent and took his leave. He guided us back through the keep to the same rooms Johan and I had used as our quarters on our last visit. I was pleased to note someone had taken the trouble to air and clean them on this occasion.

"You must forgive our chief," apologised Sigurd. "The illness and his loss, well, they've all taken their toll on him."

"He seems to carry a great weight of sadness," Nuna observed.

"If you'd met him just a few short years ago," Sigurd shook his head. "You'd have found a different man. I pray you

144

can bring him back again, young lady, for all our sakes."

After Sigurd left us alone, Olfridor and I inspected the chambers. Someone had already brought up our baggage from the boat and Desta swiftly set about unpacking various items that belonged to Nuna. I had deliberately kept my distance from my sister's maid on this trip, though the voyage had afforded us little opportunity for anything else. Now we were here in Norlhast, though, I was determined to ensure that I didn't draw any unnecessary attention to Desta that might put her in danger.

Our chambers comprised a well-furnished reception room large enough for us to entertain a small party of visitors, if such occasion arose. On either side two bedrooms adjoined this room, one of which Desta and Nuna would share. Olfridor and I would use the other. I peered out from the window of the main chamber, looking down onto the mean low houses of Norlhast. The town seemed so small from my vantage point and it felt as if my sister were marrying far beneath her station. I turned to look at her, noting her tired expression now she was no longer in the company of our hosts.

"Desta, leave that for now. Just find my sister something to wear for this evening. Nuna, take the chance to rest in your room. You'll want to feel refreshed when you next meet Karas."

My sister laughed at my advice, looking exhausted. "Do you really think he would notice either way? Honestly, Rothgar, this is … well, this isn't what I expected."

I walked over and took Nuna's hands in mine, trying to offer her words of comfort I scarcely believed myself.

"Nuna, we have to make the best of this. We're here for a while and that'll give you chance to get to know Karas. Sigurd speaks highly of him. I think there's more to Karas Greystorm than meets the eye."

"Perhaps," Nuna replied sceptically. "You're right, though, I need to rest. Come and wake me later, please. I'll need time to prepare for this evening."

I watched as Desta escorted her into the bedroom, firmly closing the door behind them. My stomach churned, as if a dozen eels were snaking around inside me. I swallowed hard, all the while thinking the same question that had plagued me since setting sail from Reavesburg. Were we really doing the right thing marrying Nuna to this man?

"Fish ain't bad," Olfridor remarked, jolting me out of my reverie. The big warrior was sampling some food that had been left on a table.

"I'm surprised you can stomach anything after that voyage."

Olfridor chuckled. "I'm not hungry, son. I'm just making sure our host's hospitality is as welcoming as on your last visit. Wouldn't do for Karas to change his mind and try to do away with you, now would it?" He paused, taking in a deep breath. "Can't believe I've just met their chief. Sigurd's right – he must be a shadow of the man he once was. I've clashed swords with Bekan more than once, when I was fighting up here in the north. If I didn't know it for a fact, I'd never believe Karas beat Bekan in single combat to come to power. Leastways, not the man we've just seen."

***

I reflected on Halfhand's words that evening. Dinner was a subdued affair, with just six of us eating at a table that could easily have seated a score or more warriors. I sat with Nuna and Olfridor opposite Karas, who was joined by Sigurd and Kalfr. For a time little was said, with only the noise of the servants' echoing footsteps filling the hall as they waited on us. As our meal was served by Sigurd's personal serving girl, Ottama, the jarl made polite conversation, grimly outlining how the most recent Vorund raids, led by Adalrikr's jarl Joarr the Hammer, had depleted their crops and livestock. Olfridor's face darkened at the name, explaining his brother, Egill, had died at Joarr's hand many years ago.

"Our alliance will give you an opportunity to have your vengeance," Kalfr remarked.

"Let's hope you're right," said Olfridor.

Sigurd was a taciturn man, occupied with the practicalities of running a kingdom in the effective absence of its true ruler. His younger brother, in contrast, soon began laughing and joking with Olfridor as if the two of them were old friends: an altogether more ebullient character, although I wondered how real his outward friendliness really was. Johan had almost killed Kalfr in battle, leaving those scars on his face. Could the Norlhast warrior really let such a thing rest, rather than seek to settle the score? Johan's words of warning came back to me. *'We've suffered at their hands too many times simply to forget all that has happened in the past.'* Yet if this alliance were to have any chance of success then people like Kalfr would have to do just that.

All the while Karas Greystorm ate little of the food put before him, his eyes often straying to Nuna. At length he set down his goblet and broke his silence in a voice so soft I had to lean forwards to hear him clearly. "Young lady, I fear it has been a long time since these halls were filled with the sounds of song and laughter. I have given no thought as to entertainment during your stay. It's remiss of me to have neglected you in this way. Tomorrow we shall put that right. Tell me, do you ride?"

"A little, my lord," Nuna replied.

"Good. I think you will find my lands in the north have their own beauty and charm. Sigurd, have the horses made ready in the morning. We will ride out onto the moors after we've broken fast. They offer a splendid view of Norlhast and its surrounding lands."

Sigurd looked uneasily at Karas. "Are you intending to join us, Chief?" he asked at last, voicing the very question I was thinking. Karas seemed barely able to remain upright at his table – I couldn't imagine him riding anywhere, let alone outside in the open country.

"I will have difficulty showing young Nuna the extent of my realm if I never leave Norlhast. I have been languishing here too long, Sigurd. It is time to ... to live again. It is almost as if ... as if I have forgotten how." Kalfr and Sigurd exchanged a glance with each other, although Karas himself did not appear to notice.

"As you wish, Chief," Sigurd answered, his face troubled.

**

The morning proved to be a fine one, the sun slowly rising in a cloudless azure sky. In the far north the air was cold and sharp early in the day despite it being mid-summer, so we set off from Norlhast Keep wrapped in fur-lined cloaks. Karas took this a step further, dressing in thick woollens. Sigurd helped him to mount his horse and, once in the saddle, Karas looked comfortable. His blue eyes had a gleam to them that had been missing for most of the short time I'd known him. Sigurd and Kalfr accompanied us, along with six other horsemen from the Norlhast Clan. I rode out with Olfridor and Nuna, who looked a little anxious as the horses began to move forwards. She was a nervous rider but she set her face determinedly, and soon seemed comfortable with the gentle pace Karas was setting. As he exchanged pleasantries with Nuna, I deliberately fell back to allow them some privacy, surveying the picturesque landscape. Karas had not been exaggerating its beauty; the rolling moorland was covered in purple heather and dotted with bright yellow gorse bush flowers. The chatter of birds filled the air and an iridescent dragonfly buzzed past, prompting an excited cry from Nuna. This far north summer was an all too brief season. Soon autumn would return, the last of the crops would be harvested and people would make ready for the return of winter.

Karas Greystorm became more animated in Nuna's presence, pointing out the various features of the terrain and explaining the extent of his domain. At length we paused and, looking back, we could appreciate how far we had climbed. Norlhast was laid out before us at the mouth of the River Taur, the waters snaking like beaten silver, wending their way out into the sea. Karas sighed as he looked upon his lands, a smile upon his face, though he seemed to sit lower in his saddle than when we had left.

"Truly it is *good* to feel the sun on my face and breathe the fresh air once more," he announced. "I fear, though, that my strength is not what it was. Sigurd, please lead the way back if you will."

Kalfr's mount stirred at these words and he whispered calmly to her, stilling her restless steps. "I think Swift would enjoy some more vigorous exercise. Care to ride on?" he asked me. I glanced at Olfridor, who nodded in agreement.

"Go on, son. Nuna'll be fine with me."

Kalfr gave his horse the spurs and we headed towards the peaks of the Baros Mountains. Though it was soon clear Kalfr was the superior rider, I enjoyed the moment of freedom. I gave my horse her head, letting her fly across the moors, exhilarated by her speed and sure-footedness. Once the race was over, we both allowed our horses to rest, circling back towards Norlhast at a more sedate pace.

"Karas seems a changed man since my last visit," I ventured. Kalfr nodded and proved to be as talkative as ever.

"Little by little, he's finding his way back since you arrived. Our chief's been in a dark place these past three years. Sigurd's still fretting that he'll try and do too much. Hah. The way he talks you wouldn't think they were born just a few years apart."

"Karas relies greatly upon your brother."

"Too much, truth be told." Kalfr's honest answer caught me off guard for a moment. "Sigurd never thought Karas would still be in the state he's in, this long after Thora and her children died. After his illness people began calling for Karas to step aside. Sigurd supported him when many expected that as jarl he'd be the next one to lead us. At the time we both thought a few months were what Karas needed – not *years*. Thing is, he and Sigurd go way back together, so once my brother had pledged his cause to Karas there was no honourable way for him to change his mind. That decision cost us, mind. Made us look weak and Adalrikr's messengers soon came knocking, didn't they?"

I remembered Tyrfingr Blackeyes' visit to Ulfkell's Keep. "That can hardly have been an easy conversation," I offered.

"Sigurd spoke for us all, turning them away with nothing to show for their troubles. But with each year the Vorund Clan's attacks grew bolder, striking deeper and closer to Norlhast Keep every time. And all the while Karas sat in that damned chair of his, dreaming of the life he'd lost while his kingdom slowly crumbled around him. My father Albrikt tried to set him straight and make him see sense, only by then Karas was in thrall to that coven of witches. They promised they had the power to speak to his dead wife and children. What with their chanting and their foul smokes, I swear Karas damned well believed them."

"And you don't?"

"They're no charlatans, although we had plenty of those turn up when Karas' desire to speak to the dead became widely known. No, they have some powers, even though they've never had any intention of helping Karas." Kalfr spat onto the ground. "Those three are driven by the power they hold over our chief. They let him believe he's spoken to those death has taken. The dead are gone forever in my view, for what it's worth."

I thought of my father, struck down by illness and dead before I could prove my prowess as a warrior. I believed when I died we would be reunited in Navan's Halls until the time of judgement came. Young as I was, I was shocked by Kalfr's stark views on life.

"Don't you seek to win glory as a warrior, so you can enter Navan's Halls with honour?" I asked.

Kalfr thought for a while before replying. "I want the members of my clan to respect me," he said at length. "When you've seen as many men die as I have, you begin to wonder. A man's life can end so swiftly, without warning. Why did the spear find the man next to me, when I could so easily have been the target? I've seen the smallest wound fester and grow bad, taking the life of the strongest warrior. You're still young, Rothgar. I've a wife and four children now – what's glory in battle worth if I never see them again? These past years I'll confess I've grown fearful for them, because one day the Vorund Clan will come in strength. When that day comes Joarr or Tyrfingr won't be content with raiding our shores. Norlhast Keep will be the prize. If Adalrikr chose, he could send his jarls to seize our lands tomorrow." Kalfr looked at me with a hard, penetrating gaze. "That's why we have to take this chance. You've given Karas hope for the first time in years, and you can see the change in him already. Your brother Jorik is the only chief who's stood up to Adalrikr and defied him, taking the fight to his own shores. That's a man I can follow, if it gives my family a chance to live long in the land they were born in."

When we returned to Norlhast, Kalfr didn't lead us back to the keep. Instead, we rode through the streets until we reached an unassuming dwelling near the centre of the town. As we approached the door burst open and four young children spilled out, all talking at once and waving at Kalfr. Laughing, he dismounted and swept the youngest of them up in his arms, hugging the little boy tightly, whilst the other three children chattered on. A plump harassed-looking woman, whom I assumed must be Kalfr's wife, came to the door and broke into a wide smile.

"Will you eat with us?" asked Kalfr as he disentangled himself from the gaggle of children and tethered Swift to a post outside his house. "While I can't promise the grand surroundings of Norlhast Keep you'll find my table a good deal friendlier."

"I'd be honoured," I replied, sliding down from my saddle.

CHAPTER 18

Each day during our stay Nuna met Karas, accompanied by her chaperone Desta and Olfridor, her watchful bodyguard. I divided my time between those audiences with Karas and checking on the welfare of the crew of *Marl's Pride*, now quartered in one of the four towers of Norlhast Keep. My men needed little supervision whilst they were under Brunn Fourwinds' command. Despite this, Sigurd advised that until things were more settled it was unwise for them to roam freely about the town. Boredom soon set in and I tried to ensure they didn't feel forgotten, sparring with them on occasion and sharing news with Brunn. Meanwhile Karas was a changed man, his renewed vigour more noticeable with each passing day, and I felt confident he would approve of the match with my sister.

"He's very kind," Nuna acknowledged one evening, as we discussed the day's events in our chambers. "He's shown me every courtesy since we arrived and he's growing stronger; it's as if the years are falling away from him. It's just a pity he's still so *grey*."

"His name is Karas *Greystorm*," I retorted, amused by the remark. "What did you honestly expect?"

Nuna looked thoughtful at my light-hearted comment. "I didn't expect the man we met on the first day. He's still broken by grief; aged and shattered by it. Now he's changing, slowly, for the better. The only time he seems old and forgetful is when those three awful women are by his side." The coven. It all came back to those mysterious women.

"You're good for him," I said. "Don't worry about the coven. I'll deal with them."

I spent a much of my days in the company of Kalfr and his family, believing it was important I mixed openly with the Norlhast Clan, despite Sigurd's warnings. The arrangement was also useful, since it was from Kalfr that I learned more details about the coven. Lysa, Nereth and Shula had come to Karas whilst he still lay bedridden and wracked by the disease that had robbed him of his family. They proclaimed they were healers and Albrikt the Wise, Karas' chief counsellor and Kalfr and Sigurd's father, allowed them access to the Norlhast chief. At first Karas did recover and the three young women were allowed to remain at his court. Then Karas began speaking of his desire to reach out and talk to his lost family one last time. Many shamans and other more dubious characters flocked to this call, promising Karas they could make his wish come true. In the end it was to Nereth he turned, for she claimed to be a shaman with the rare gift of speaking to Rathlin, avatar of death. In the society of the Laskan clans, shamans were not as highly regarded as their warrior brethren. This view could be traced back to the founders of the clans, such as Reave and Norl, who led their people into the harsh northlands to escape the endless turmoil and strife, as Morvanos' surviving generals fought amongst themselves for dominance at the end of the War. They sought to return to older ways, when men relied on their own strength and prowess to shape their destiny. Consequently, shamans were distrusted in the north and had been a rare sight at my father's court in Reavesburg. This made Karas Greystorm's request all the more unusual.

"Navan keeps the souls of the dead in his halls," I pointed out to Kalfr that evening whilst we shared a drink in his home, as he told me this story after his wife Luta had taken the children off to bed. "Rathlin brought death into the world, charging Navan with guarding the Halls of the Dead. It's said that none pass through his gates without Navan's consent, so why –?"

Kalfr's answer was abrupt and angry. "Look, lad, it wouldn't have mattered if she'd walked the streets stark naked, saying she was the moon itself. Karas was ready to believe *anything* and those three … Well, they have a way of making him listen. You must have realised that during your time here. My father was Karas' most trusted counsellor and, although he'd welcomed Nereth and her friends to court at first, he strongly argued against this latest nonsense. He was banished from court that very day, after eight years in Greystorm's service. That was when Sigurd and I both began to regret the decision to keep Karas in power. By then it was too late to turn back. We'd sworn an oath to protect and serve him when he ousted Bekan from power. I'd sooner die than be an oath breaker."

"Yet nobody has come forward to challenge Karas in the three years he's been like this?" I asked.

"Where's the honour in unseating a man like Karas from power? Trial by combat? No one could seriously look upon you as a chief if you rose to power by killing a man in that state. No, it would have to be a clan moot and the trouble is Sigurd's pledged his support to Karas. No one wants to oppose him, and to be frank he's effectively led our people since Karas fell sick anyway. So, things have remained as they are, and I suppose they would have been finally settled at a clan moot after Karas died. Now, though, there's the prospect of an heir. Were that to come to pass, things could get interesting."

I took a sip of ale, mulling over Kalfr's words. "You mean the noble Norlhast families who were biding their time, waiting for their sickly chief to pass away, now fear they've lost their chance of seizing power?"

"Exactly. The heir naturally takes the title, so timing is everything now. If Karas dies childless or his heir is too young to assume the responsibilities of leadership, another will be chosen by the clan moot. If Greystorm enjoys a long life and his heir is fit and strong, well, he'll probably carry the day and Karas' line will continue. Power's a fickle thing – hard to get and slippery to hold onto. There are those in Norlhast who'd prefer this marriage never to take place. I've wondered for a long time who Nereth and her coven are really working for in all this. Trust me, if this scheme of your brother's is to work you'll need to deal with them, because from what Sigurd says they're still opposed to the idea."

Sigurd Albriktson was an occasional guest at Kalfr's home. As jarl of Norlhast Keep his elder brother was the leader of the Norlhast warriors. However, in the three years since Sigurd had been responsible for administering Norlhast's affairs the duties of drilling the warriors and training the more promising youngsters had fallen to Kalfr. Watching them practise in the keep's courtyard, I could tell Kalfr was both liked and respected by those in his charge. Sigurd was an altogether different character. Although his skill as a warrior and tactician commanded respect he remained more aloof from his men. Reticent when in company, he was a difficult man to get to know. Kalfr told me his brother had never married, his first loyalty being to the Norlhast Clan and its chief. In many ways he reminded me of Finnvidor Einarrson: both jarls had the same steely determination and were not men you would cross lightly.

I realised it was costing Sigurd and Kalfr to support the proposed marriage between the two clans, now news of Karas' betrothal was well-known. One evening Kalfr had taken me to the largest of the taverns in Norlhast, unsurprisingly called The Whale. The first night we entered, I was met with some hard stares and a few warriors stood up and left without a word, one of them shoving Kalfr as they walked past. *'We've suffered at their hands too many times simply to forget all that has happened in the past.'* Johan Jokellsward's words rang true as much for some members of the Norlhast Clan as it did for the people of Kalamar. Yet others openly showed their support, embracing me and telling me how it was time for peace. Some merchants sought favours from me, seeking access to trade not just with Reavesburg but Vittag and Helsburg too. It was obvious Norlhast's merchants saw our alliance as an opportunity for them to grow in prosperity.

I was pondering all these things as I walked back towards Norlhast Keep, after parting ways with Kalfr outside The Whale that evening. The air had been thick and heavy all day, and now the summer storm it promised arrived with a vengeance. It was well-known that even in the summer months the Redfars Sea could be as placid and still as a mirror, only for the northern winds to bring a storm as fierce as any during the winter season in the space of an hour. Brunn Fourwinds' two drowned sailors could attest to that. Even so, the weather this summer had been particularly unpredictable, violent storms interspersing themselves with bright sunshine. I pulled up the hood of my cloak to keep out the driving wind and rain that battered me every step of the way back to the keep. I was so preoccupied I didn't notice the three figures until I stumbled across them. Three men, dressed in leather armour and each of them armed. One of them put a firm hand on my shoulder and pushed me back, pinning me against the rough stone wall of one of the turf-roofed houses.

"Look who it is," announced the man who had shoved me. "Rothgar Kolfinnarson. The boy who speaks for Reavesburg's chief, eh? You're a long way from home, boy, and all alone." That brought a chuckle from the other two. The speaker's breath carried the strong smell of ale and the taint of decaying teeth, his bearded face inches from my own.

"Get your hands off me," I snarled, breaking his grip on my shoulder as I shoved him away, sending him stumbling backwards. I closed my hand on the hilt of my sword, knowing if I drew steel things would not go well. I was outnumbered, unarmoured and the confined space meant I couldn't make best use of my sword. I was also a little the worse for wear from drink, although the men surrounding me seemed to have suffered more. In the gloom I thought I recognised them as being part of a group who'd angrily walked out of The Whale that night. It seemed they were still nursing their grudge.

"Look at him," mocked the leader. "Walking round Norlhast like he owns the place. You think we don't know your little scheme? All this talk of an alliance is a fancy way of saying Karas is going to bend the knee to Jorik." He spat onto the ground at my feet. "I lost a fair few of my boys to your friend, Johan Jokellsward, over the years. Think that's something I can just put aside, when you come marching in here telling everyone it's time for peace? What do you know? I bet you've never even drawn that sword in anger."

Lightning flashed at that moment, illuminating the scene for an instant in bright white light. The speaker and his companions had drawn daggers, gleaming like fangs before the darkness swallowed them once more. Thunder rolled overhead, deafening me and momentarily drowning out the sound of my hammering heart, pounding in my ears. I didn't want to fight these men; shedding blood in these streets would spell the end of any fledgling alliance. The three of them stepped closer, the leader raising his knife, wet and glistening as the rain fell. I tightened my grip on my sword, loosening it in its scabbard and prepared to fight for my life. Suddenly the leader of the men was lying on his back, sprawled in the mud. His two companions turned to find a stranger in their midst, the point of his longsword hovering inches from the throat of the nearest one. Their own blades appeared inadequate, and both men dropped them onto the ground, each landing with a soft wet thud.

"Pick yourself up and leave now, Vrand," barked Sigurd. Relief washed over me as I heard the jarl's voice, loud even over the noise of the storm. "Go and sober up. I don't want to kill a drunken fool, though I will if you don't drop that knife." Vrand scrambled to his feet, the fire of his anger doused. He threw his weapon down at Sigurd's feet.

"Thought better of you than this, Sigurd," he said, wiping the mud from his face.

"Think whatever you like. Now go." The men left, vanishing into the rain and darkness. Only the daggers lying in the street left any evidence of the encounter, until Sigurd gathered them up and tucked them into his belt. "You alright?"

he asked me gruffly.

I realised I was still holding tight onto my sword and forced myself to let go. "I think so. By the gods, Sigurd, I owe you my life."

"That you do. I've warned Kalfr it's unwise to let you wander about Norlhast unguarded. My brother thought it would help build up trust between our warriors and our guests from Reavesburg. Looks like it was you doing the trusting on your own tonight."

"You have my thanks," I said awkwardly, rain pattering off my cloak. Another lightning flash overhead made me jump, my nerves frayed. I was anxious to be away from this place and find shelter from the storm. "I must get back to the keep," I told Sigurd. "I think I've had my fill of adventures for one night."

"That's true enough," the warrior replied. "As it happens, I was looking for you. Karas has ... There's no delicate way to put this, so I'll say it straight. Karas has had a change of heart about his betrothal to your sister. I want you to speak to him, and I need you to do it now."

CHAPTER 19

"What's happened?" I asked Sigurd as we hurried through the gates of Norlhast Keep. The warrior held up a hand, waiting whilst Styrman, one of the keep's servants, helped us shed our sodden cloaks before retreating soundlessly. When he was sure we were alone, Sigurd spoke to me in a soft undertone as we headed towards the main hall of the keep.

"Who else but the coven. I've tried to keep an eye on those bitches, making sure I'm around whenever they're together with Karas. Trouble is I can't watch him night and day and something's happened to him since his evening meal, I'm sure of it."

"What? Are you saying they've poisoned him?"

"I've had my suspicions for a while that they're adding something to his food. Nothing to put his life at risk, just to make him more ... biddable. I've had the servants in the kitchen changed three times and still they seem to find a way."

"What do you want me to do?" I asked, feeling distinctly unprepared. "Shall I get Brunn and some of his men to help us?"

My suggestion drew an angry retort from the jarl. "No. Gods, no, I don't want your men to see him like this. I've already handpicked some of my own warriors, men I know I can trust. Just help me prise him away from the coven. He may respond to you better as his honoured guest, rather than an old face he knows too well. And if I can somehow throw those three witches into the dungeons under this keep, all the better."

A half-dozen warriors met us at the doors to the main hall. I recognised Brosa amongst them. The young man was friendly with Kalfr and from what I had seen of the drills in the courtyard, he was a skilful warrior. Standing by the doors I could hear girlish giggling from within the hall and for a wild moment imagined Nuna was inside. As the realisation dawned on me of what I might be about to find I steeled myself and nodded to Sigurd. Together we pushed open the heavy oak doors and walked into the hall, flanked by Sigurd's warriors. The scene didn't flatter the Norlhast chief, as I saw Lysa, Nereth and Shula had shed their cloaks and cowls, dressed instead in gossamer silks that clung revealingly to their young bodies, leaving nothing to the imagination. A few of the warriors at my side stopped in their tracks, jaws hanging open at the sight. Sigurd remained completely unaffected and continued to walk down the hall, with me hurrying to keep up.

Apart from Nereth I'd not seen these women without their cowls before, but Kalfr had described them to me. I knew the youngest of the three, Shula, with her long blonde hair was the one perched on Karas' lap. Dark-haired and slender, Nereth was running her hands through Karas' grey locks, whilst Lysa sat at the head of the table, her auburn tresses falling in attractive curls about her head. All three women were beautiful and, confronted by their state of undress, I was profoundly glad Nuna was not here.

Lysa turned, smiling at my discomfort. "Oh, Sigurd, you're so *thoughtless*. Why have you dragged poor Rothgar in here? He's only a boy, after all."

"What in the name Kumil's black heart do you think you're doing?" Sigurd replied through clenched teeth. Lysa giggled and rose in a smooth, sinuous motion. She walked towards the stocky warrior, hips swayed hypnotically from side to side and I blushed as I realised I was able to see through her diaphanous clothing. I began to redden and looked away, abashed, which Lysa found amusing.

"Oh, Sigurd," she purred, a delicate hand stroking the black stubble on his cheek. "If you could only see how *serious* you are. You should join us – I doubt Karas will be able to keep all three of us occupied."

"I don't mind lending a hand," called out one of the warriors, provoking guffaws of laughter from the rest of the men, until they were silenced by a venomous stare from Sigurd. He turned to Lysa, a look of pure loathing on his face.

"Take your hand away from me, witch. The three of you are behaving like whores." He spat out the word and the three women laughed in his face.

"Is that ... Is that Sigurd?" Karas' bleary eyes struggled to focus as he peered around Shula. "What's he doing here, my young ladies?"

"I'm reminding you that you are *betrothed*," Sigurd told his chief.

"Not any more," the women chorused, giggling again.

"We've persuaded your chief it's such a bad idea," Nereth explained. "The Reavesburg Clan is no friend to us."

"And you're no friend to Norlhast," I snapped, finally finding my voice. I was distinctly aware that my face was now a deep shade of scarlet. I couldn't decide who I felt more embarrassed for – myself or the pathetic figure of Karas sitting in his chair, the man I was asking my sister to marry. As that thought struck home, anger began to course through me.

"I risked storms, raiders and the life of my sister to cross the Redfars Sea and bring Nuna to you, at your request. This is how you repay us?" Cold fury settled in the pit my stomach and I marched up to the dais where Karas was sitting. I reached out, roughly dragging Shula off Karas' lap. She stumbled and fell hard onto the ground with a cry.

"What's he saying?" Karas asked. "Who *is* this lad?"

"No one," hissed Nereth. "You should have him executed. Look what he did to Shula."

Karas regarded me blankly, with no hint of recognition in his pale, watery blue eyes. "Yes ... Yes ... Poor Shula. Guards. Kill this man." There was an uneasy murmur as the six warriors exchanged glances, having no appetite to obey their chief's command. My anger mixed with pity as I saw how little regard his men had for their chief.

"Don't you remember Nuna?" I asked Karas. "You courted her all this week and seemed much recovered from your infirmities. What's happened to you?"

"Silence." Nereth's voice was shrill as her eyes bore down on me. "Warriors of Norlhast, your chief gave you an order. Take this wretched boy away and kill him."

"We don't take orders from the likes of you," cried Brosa. The unmistakable ring of steel sounded in the hall as the men drew their weapons, Sigurd looking on with a satisfied air. It was only then that I realised Nuna and Olfridor were standing at the doorway.

"Karas," my sister called softly, eyes wide with surprise.

"You're too late," mocked Lysa. "Your betrothed is with us now, back here he belongs."

"Nuna?" Karas blinked as my sister glided towards him, her carriage proud and erect, ignoring the coven completely. Olfridor's stood in the hall entrance, open-mouthed in shock. Without warning the hall was plunged into darkness. I blinked and gasped, the blackness so intense it seemed to surround me and drive the air from my body. I heard Nuna cry out in fright and fear clutched at my heart.

"No, no, no," Sigurd was shouting. There was a clatter as one of his men stumbled and fell, sword clanging as it struck the stone flags. Elsewhere there was cursing and shouts of confusion from Karas.

"A present from me," hissed Shula's voice from the darkness. I felt movement in the air in front of my face and dropped to my left instinctively. A blade caught my shirt, effortlessly cutting the fabric, though failing to draw blood. I drew my sword, screaming at Olfridor to protect Nuna, although I knew that he was as blinded as I was. In that moment Shula's blade slashed across my chest, a wild strike that left a burning line of agony in its wake. I lunged with my sword, uncertain if I was dealing a blow to friend or foe as my blade struck home, cutting deeply through flesh and bone. A woman cried out, and in the same moment the torches in the hall blazed back into life. Shula swayed in front of me, blood gushing from a wound that had opened her from shoulder to hip. As she died her spell broke, the torchlight illuminating a scene that filled my heart with horror.

Sigurd and one of his men were wrestling with Nereth, two of his warriors already lying dead or dying at their feet. Karas had risen from his seat, his eyes wide and disbelieving. Meanwhile, Lysa had hold of Nuna's long hair, knotting it round her fist as she raised a hideous, curved knife of black metal. I sprang to her defence, wondering where such a weapon could have come from and sensing a strange *otherness* to it that made my blood run cold. Even as I ran forwards, I knew I was too far away to reach my sister – it was all going to end here in tragedy, and I was unable to do anything to stop it happening.

Lysa's head jerked back with a sharp snap of breaking bone as Olfridor Halfhand's axe found its mark. The blow tore off the woman's face in a shower of blood. The knife fell from Lysa's fingers and she crashed to the floor, Nuna's hair still gripped tightly in her other hand, dragging her, weeping, onto the ground.

"It's alright, girl. It's alright," Olfridor said, as he stooped to reach her. "Are you hurt?"

I turned to see Nereth bring her own knife down, cutting off the hand of the unfortunate Norlhast warrior she was fighting with Sigurd. He sank down on his knees screaming at the same time as Sigurd, who had lost his sword in the struggle, landed a solid punch to her face. The force of the impact sent her reeling across the feasting table. Together I advanced with Olfridor, Sigurd and the remaining three warriors, weapons drawn and levelled at Nereth as she groggily struggled to rise.

"Don't kill her," barked Sigurd. "A quick death is too merciful. Bind and gag this whore and take her to the dungeons." Brosa and another of the warriors carried out

Sigurd's orders without hesitation.

Two of the Norlhast warriors lay dead, their blood pooling darkly as it spread over the cold stone floor. The man who had lost his hand had gone deathly pale and silent, staring at the ruin of his arm as his comrade tried to help him. I turned away from the broken bodies of the two witches Olfridor and I had slain, unable to look too closely, and hurried towards Nuna. I breathed deeply to steady my nerves, aware of the pain in my chest. As I took another step the feeling worsened and I glanced down to see my clothes soaked in my own blood, the wound bleeding freely. There was something else, I realised: a numbness spreading from the edges of the cut. My chest tightened and I sank to my knees.

"Rothgar," Nuna called out in alarm. She ran to me, gripping my arm. Her face wavered, swimming in and out of focus. Dimly I heard the warrior tending to his wounded friend cry out in panic as he watched him begin to thrash and writhe in agony.

I was helpless as the ground rushed up to meet me. My head struck hard stone as the wound in my chest burned like fire. I opened my mouth to scream, only for the darkness to swallow me once more.

CHAPTER 20

The planks of the wooden jetty were warmed by the sun, pleasantly radiating heat as I sat with my feet dangling into the water below. The waves beat against the wood with a steady rhythm, comforting and familiar. The walls of Reavesburg rose up behind me, and I found myself wondering what I was doing here. There was something important Jorik had entrusted to me, hovering there on the edge of my memory. I gave up trying to remember, sitting back and enjoying the sun on my face. It struck me the docks were uncharacteristically quiet. As I scanned the waters I realised there wasn't a ship in sight, the wooden quayside deserted; no merchants, no sailors, no children running errands. I swallowed, my mouth dry. I would have given anything for a drink of cool water. The sun, so agreeable a few minutes ago, seemed too large and bright in the clear, cloudless sky. I squinted, looking away; familiar as my surroundings were, this was an uncomfortable spot. I resolved to return to Ulfkell's Keep and rose, walking back along the docks, wiping sweat from my brow.

The planks of the wooden jetty were hot against my bare feet. I sat down, cooling them by dangling them into the water below. The waves beat against the wood with a steady rhythm, comforting and familiar. The walls of Reavesburg rose up behind me, dominating the surrounding area. I frowned, wondering what I was doing here. If I'd been heading back to Ulfkell's Keep, why was I sitting on the jetty? There was something else too. Something important Jorik had entrusted to me, hovering just out of reach at the edge of my memory. I couldn't summon it forth and gave up, leaning back and feeling the hot sun on my face, sweat beading on my forehead.

I was tired, I realised, as well as thirsty. My tongue felt dry, sticking to the roof of my mouth. I needed to find shade and something to drink. No one else was foolish enough to be out here in this heat; no merchants, no sailors, no children running errands. I rose and headed back to Ulfkell's Keep, alarmed as a wave of dizziness washed over me. I'd been out in the sun too long.

The planks of the wooden jetty were burning hot against my bare feet. I cursed as a long splinter broke off, burying itself deep into the sole of my foot. I sat down, biting my lip as I drew out the thin sliver of wood between finger and thumb, tossing it into the water below. The waves beat against the wood with a steady rhythm, comforting and familiar. The walls of Reavesburg rose up behind me, dominating the surrounding area. I frowned, wondering what I was doing here. I'd been heading back to Ulfkell's Keep, so why was I sitting on the end of the jetty once more? There was something else too. Something important Jorik had entrusted to me, hovering just beyond my grasp. Try as I might, I couldn't remember. My strength failed me and I gave up, lying back on the wooden boards. The sun burned fiercely, beating down on my face, as sweat soaked into my shirt.

I lay there for a time, wondering whether I would ever be able to find the energy to return home. The docks were so quiet and empty; no merchants, no sailors; just the one sandy-haired child running an errand of some kind. He skidded breathlessly to a halt beside me. With an effort I propped myself up onto my elbows, turning to get a better look at this new arrival. My mouth was like sand, my lips parched and cracked. I grimaced in pain as I tried to speak, my swollen tongue and broken lips struggling to form the words.

"Yes, lad? Is there … is there something … you want?"

"It's time to go, Rothgar," he answered. I knew I should recognise his voice – even my memory was failing me. Jorik had entrusted something important to me, and now I couldn't even remember what it was.

"That doesn't matter right now," the boy said, as if he had read my thoughts. "All that matters is that you need to leave here, quickly."

"Tried. Tried already. Always end up ... back here."

"Try not to speak. You don't need to. Just listen to me – I don't mean leave the jetty. I mean leave this *place* and return to Norlhast."

"Norlhast?" That made no sense at all. Why would I go to the land of my enemies? Unless it had something to do with whatever Jorik had entrusted to me. If I could just *remember* what that was. Why could I not remember?

"Being in Norlhast makes much more sense than sitting on the dockside in Reavesburg," the boy argued. "Can't you remember? Jorik sent you to protect Nuna and finalise her marriage to Karas Greystorm. The coven didn't like that one bit and they tried to stop it happening. If you don't go back there soon they'll succeed."

Myshall's bane, who was this annoying boy? Despite the heat I was beginning to shiver, so I rolled onto my side, hugging my knees to my chest to try and keep warm. That made little sense, trying to stay warm whilst the sun blazed above me, so hot the timbers of the docks were dry as kindling. Whoever this boy was, he was persistent. He grabbed my shoulders and shook me roughly, pulling me back into a sitting position. My chin drooped onto my chest but the sandy-haired boy took a tight hold of my hair and pulled it back, lifting my heavy head.

"Don't fall asleep." His voice had a note of anxiety, replacing his easy manner. "Not here. Not if you want to return home."

"Am home," I argued, even as part of me doubted what I was saying. There was something wrong. The sun filled half the sky, the blue colours draining away to the very edges of my vision. The bright yellow light danced on the waters of the River Jelt, as it widened on its journey towards the sea, glittering so brightly it hurt my eyes. It was only then that I saw two dark shapes break the surface of the water, disappearing again so quickly I wondered if I had seen them at all.

"They're real," the boy advised me. His face was taut with fear, his skin white beneath the freckles covering the bridge of his nose. I looked back to see the waters break once more, much closer this time. Against the backdrop of the white-hot sun it was impossible to discern any details, as they moved independently of the motion of the waves. Moments later they surfaced again, and I realised two people were walking towards me, emerging on foot from the shallows. They were only black silhouettes in the harsh light, although I could see from their shape and movements that they were women. I felt a tightness in my stomach, though I was unsure why. I wanted nothing to do with these women as I rose on shaking legs, helped by the boy, and turned towards Reavesburg's gates. If I could just reach Ulfkell's Keep, I knew I would be safe.

A young woman barred my path, dressed in gossamer-thin silks. Her resplendent dark hair streamed out behind her, constantly moving as it rippled in the sunshine. It struck me forcibly that I hadn't felt a breath of wind since first setting foot on these wretched docks.

"Rothgar," she purred. "Is this the landscape of your mind? How desperately unimaginative."

"Nereth," I breathed. Memories came flooding back to me, the weight of them forcing me to my knees. The sandy-haired boy sank under my dead weight, though he kept a tight grip on my arm. *Bram.* My childhood friend was here with me. Not as he was when he died in Noln, but as I remembered him when we were still children, running free about the town without a care in the world. I wasn't alone.

Nereth noticed Bram for the first time. "You've brought a friend. No matter, he can't help you. No one can. My sisters are coming." My skin crawled as I understood who it was walking towards me from the sea. Moments later there was a wet thud behind me.

"Don't look back," cried Bram, even as I turned to see Shula clawing her way up the poles of the jetty. Her naked body hung open where my sword had almost split her in two, the hideous wound yawning widely as she struggled to find the purchase she needed to haul herself out of the sea. As I watched with horrified fascination, the ruin of Lysa's sightless face emerged, wet fingers feeling blindly for a firm hand hold. My bare feet slid on the jetty as I tried to push myself away from the monstrous sight, smearing a trail of blood from the wound caused by the splinter.

"Bram ... help ... me," I managed to gasp as I staggered to my feet, backing away from the dead witches. A gap opened in the bloody pulp of Lysa's face, revealing her remaining white teeth and half her jaw in a broken travesty of a smile.

"I've helped you as much as I can," he said sorrowfully. Then Nereth was upon me, my strength no match for hers. Bram was hurled back onto the wooden boards as I was flung into the waiting hands of the two undead members of the coven.

"He's yours, sisters," crowed Nereth. "Take him." Cold hands gripped my legs and body. I clung desperately to the side of the jetty, looking into the eyes of Bram as he crouched, winded, on the floor.

"Help me."

Bram was oddly calm, ignored by Nereth as she looked down on my feeble struggles. "This world isn't real, Rothgar – only they are. They can't hurt you if you can leave this all behind." Then he was gone as I lost my grip, the cold smack of the seawater driving the breath from my body as Lysa and Shula dragged me under the waves.

Whatever Bram said, the water felt real enough. I opened my mouth to scream as the broken bodies of my captors bore me into the depths, away from the bright light at the surface and into the darkness below. Their grip was iron, my efforts to free myself puny and ineffective as I fought to break their hold. I finally gave up struggling as water began to fill my lungs, a sense of calm descending upon me as I embraced the inevitability of my fate. An odd thought occurred to me as I noticed how much deeper the sea was than it had been just moments before when I was on the surface. *'This world isn't real, Rothgar.'* Bram's words echoed in my mind. I had been injured, a poisonous wound left by Shula's blade, yet here my body was whole again. A sun filling half the sky? My dead friend at my side? As I drifted downwards, a smile broke on my face. Nereth had told me herself: *'is this the landscape of your mind?'* It was time to wake up. The water vanished, the hands of Shula and Lysa transforming themselves into blankets wrapped tightly around my body. I thrashed in the bed, provoking a cry of alarm from someone nearby. I heard footsteps approach as I tore at the covers, fighting to free myself from their grasp. My hand connected with someone's jaw, sending them crashing to the floor.

"Rothgar. Please, you need to lie still. You're safe now," Desta was shouting. For one terrified moment I thought I had hurt her. Then I saw Olfridor sprawled on the floor, shaking his head as he tried to get up.

"Safe to say he's awake," he muttered ruefully.

"Lie still, lad," came a deep man's voice I didn't recognise. Strong hands gently pressed on my shoulders, pushing me back onto the soft down of the bed. All the fight went out of me and I became aware of a throbbing pain, running like fire across my chest. Sleep folded me in her arms, taking away the hurt and drawing me back into a mercifully dreamless slumber.

***

"... there, did you see? His eyelids flickered." A woman's voice. Desta. Desta was with me. I felt a flood of relief.

"Is he awake? Rothgar, it's Olfridor. Can you hear me, son?"

"In the name of Ilanasa, give the boy room to breathe. We don't want to smother him." A deep-voiced man. The stranger.

I lay on the bed, trying to stay awake. Nereth had not plagued my dreams again, for which I was thankful. With a massive effort I opened my eyes and although the brightness of the light forced me to screw them tight shut again, Olfridor saw the movement.

"There. He opened his eyes. He's going to live."

"Rothgar." The deep-voiced stranger was talking. "My name is Albrikt, father to Sigurd and Kalfr. You're safe now, young man. Rest easy. No need to rush things; the body takes its own time to heal itself. I know that well enough at my age."

"Where ... am ... I?" The words came haltingly. Gods, I was thirsty. "Water," I croaked. A water skin of some sort with a metal funnel was pressed to my lips. I drank greedily, choking a little, as my dry throat struggled to swallow the cool water.

"You're in your own rooms at Norlhast Keep," answered Albrikt. I opened my eyes, my vision blurred. The speaker was a large, bald, bearded man, his features impossible to discern. "Your friends and family have hardly left your bedside this past week."

I looked around to see Olfridor staring down on me. I saw little other than his black-toothed smile – enough to give me cause to grin. I drank more water from the skin and felt stronger, pushing myself into an upright position with the aid or Olfridor and Albrikt. My vision began to return and I was aware of a pulling on my chest. Looking down, I could see I was wrapped in fresh bandages.

"My lord," Desta said, tears spilling freely down her face. "We thought you'd never come back to us."

"How bad ... How bad is it?" I asked.

"You're fortunate," Albrikt answered. "Every other man who took a wound from the knives wielded by the coven died. We thought for a while you would suffer the same fate. You have some rare strength, young man. The wound has not festered, if that is what you fear, and you have fought whatever venom the blade was laced with."

"Let me see," I ordered. Albrikt nodded and deftly removed the wrappings and the herbs he had used to prevent corruption. Glancing down, I saw a long cut running from just under my left nipple all the way to the bottom of my ribcage on my right hand side. There would be a scar, although the wound had been neatly stitched, skin pale and white rather than red and inflamed. It still hurt, though not as badly as before.

"You have my thanks," I managed to say.

Albrikt's bald head bobbed. "And you have mine. To serve in these halls again is all the reward I seek, Rothgar Kolfinnarson. And that's because of you, so really I must offer you my heartfelt thanks. The coven was poison to Karas Greystorm, both for his body and his mind. I couldn't make him see the truth. You and your beautiful young sister have changed all that."

At that moment the door to my chambers burst open and Nuna charged into the room, all sense of decorum forgotten, unbraided blonde hair loose about her shoulders. "Rothgar, you're awake. I told you to wake me when he opened his eyes," she snapped at Desta and Olfridor. I saw Sigurd and Brunn follow my sister into the room, Karas Greystorm in their wake.

"He's only just recovered," Albrikt explained. "I wanted to ensure your brother's wits were unaffected by his long sleep."

"How long?" I asked.

"A week, my lord," Desta replied.

"On the third day you rallied long enough to give me a right hook to the face," added Olfridor with a smile. "In the circumstances, I'll forgive you for that one."

"Where's Nereth?" I asked, memories flooding back in a jumble. The room fell silent and the smiles on people's faces faltered.

"I'll tell him," Sigurd said. "It's my responsibility."

"There's no need. She's escaped, hasn't she?"

Sigurd bowed his head. "I left my best men watching her, I swear it. Kalfr took up the watch too. She was chained and gagged, though even when she was in her cell there was something ... No one could stand to be down there guarding her door for more than an hour or two before they had to be relieved. Then, on the third day, she vanished. I know she had help, I just know it. The door was still locked when Kalfr opened it to check on her and found she was gone."

"The same day I woke for the first time?"

"Yes, as it happens," Albrikt answered, his brow furrowed as he regarded me curiously.

"Rothgar, I swear on the bones of my father that Nereth will be found," said Karas. "She'll not escape justice, I promise you." I was struck by how much stronger Karas' voice sounded. Even his bearing was more animated, his posture upright. Though his hair remained grey, the lines about his face were smoother, his pallid flesh more colourful and drawn less tightly across his bones. "You've freed me, Rothgar, you and your sister. Nereth and her evil brethren came to me at a time when I was weak, and they preyed on that. Three years they robbed from me, leaving me languishing in the pit of my own grief. I allowed them to gain a terrible hold over me and, to my eternal shame, you saw the depths of depravity they brought me to." To my surprise Karas bent the knee and knelt at my bedside, clasping my hand in both of his. "I can only beg for your forgiveness and ask that you return to Ulfkell's Keep and give a favourable report of me. If your brother will give me your sister's hand then I'll pledge our cause to yours. Together, united, we shall stand against the Vorund Clan. Adalrikr shall rue the day he roused the eagle and the whale. We'll break his ships, burn his lands and drive him back to skulk in his stone towers at Vorund Fastness; this I promise you."

Olfridor, Brunn and Sigurd all added their voice to Karas', cheering his words and clapping each other on the shoulders like brothers. Nuna leant across and put her arms around my shoulders while Desta stole a moment to plant a kiss on my brow. Albrikt beamed benevolently down on the scene, and I wanted to savour the moment that brought our clans together in unison against our enemy. Instead, Nereth's words came to me, like poison tipped arrows.

'He's yours, sisters. Take him.'

CHAPTER 21

"You tell a good story, Rothgar, yet I know there's more to this tale." Etta's single, beady black eye bored deep into my own. I shifted in my seat, distinctly uncomfortable now I was left alone in Jorik's chambers with the old crone. Etta had a way of seeing and knowing things that made me afraid. Were there no secrets this old woman wasn't privy to?

"Etta, you see shadows and conspiracies where none exist," I replied.

Etta's frown hardened at my glib answer. "Don't you *dare* treat me like a fool, boy. I was rooting out shadows and conspiracies while you were still sucking on your mama's teats, so don't lie to me. While Jorik and Finnvidor may have left this room singing your praises I know *something else* happened out there. I'm trying to help you, and I can't do that if you hold back the truth. How else do you think I can advise your hot-headed brother, unless I know more than him? Now talk."

I'd enjoyed my brother's adulation since *Marl's Pride* landed at the docks of Reavesburg. Karas Greystorm had approved of the match with Nuna and, even more importantly in Jorik's eyes, he was now in our debt. The fact it was due to my brush with death was of little consequence to Jorik. Moreover, my dealings with the coven turned me into something of a folk hero in Norlhast. Whereas before Sigurd and Kalfr had risked their reputations to support me, now I was mobbed by followers anxious to curry my favour. Young Brosa spread the tale of how Olfridor Halfhand and I slew two of the witches holding their chief in thrall. The fact Nereth escaped just days later from a locked cell in the dungeons of Norlhast Keep was conveniently forgotten, not sitting well with the miracle of the marked improvement in the health of the Norlhast chief. Some versions of the tale I heard even involved Karas rising from his chair in a rage as the spells were broken and beheading Nereth himself, a story that soon became the accepted truth amongst the common folk.

When I was fit enough to walk the streets of Norlhast, I was grateful to Kalfr and Luta for their hospitality. Kalfr's humble home, filled with his rowdy children and straight-talking wife, was a welcome refuge from the flatterers flocking to Karas' court. My injury delayed our departure, the wound taking the best part of a month to heal sufficiently before I was ready to board ship. Thus it was the beginning of the autumn season when the time finally came for us to depart. By then I was sorry to make my goodbyes to Kalfr and his family. The Norlhast warrior had become a true friend and I knew I would miss his good company and the laughter of his wife and children.

The raiding season was nearly over and Adalrikr's ships had been quiet of late. Nevertheless, Karas took no chances, sending two of his own longships to escort us home, both bearing the unified banners of our two clans on their sails. Much to Brunn Fourwinds' relief Adalrikr's ships were not at sea (or else engaged elsewhere, raiding other shores) and our journey was untroubled by the dire weather that plagued the outward leg of our trip.

We stopped off overnight at Kalamar, as Jorik had asked me to bear the tidings of events in Norlhast to Johan in person. Father's old ally would need to hear the outcome of our mission, so he could deal with his own people accordingly. When we arrived, Johan and Damona greeted us warmly, and his court welcomed the news that Karas and Nuna's betrothal was now agreed.

"I'll confess I doubted it was worth it," Johan told me that evening at a feast in our honour in Kalamar Castle. "My people have been troubled by the news of the alliance, as well you know. Now, though, the sacrifices made begin to show their worth. Peace in the north, and war against our foes in the south. This may yet prove to be your brother's greatest legacy in his short reign as chief."

Damona was more forthcoming. I had seen what was set on the spikes of the castle wall as we entered the harbour at Kalamar. The heads were still fresh enough to attract the crows, busy tearing off strips of flesh and squabbling over the choicest morsels; their cawing filling the evening skies with a deafening clamour. It was the fate of traitors and rebels to be displayed on the walls of the jarls' castle after justice had been meted out.

"Tread carefully," Damona had whispered to me in the dying hours of the feast, when Johan and Olfridor were both lying slumped on the table, long ago having succumbed to an overindulgence of mead and spirits. "Whilst you have won the hearts of many, remember others still stubbornly refuse to accept times have changed." Damona's sweet perfume hung heavily about her, an intoxicating scent, as she told me of Kaun Quicksteel's rebellion.

Johan had not been as open concerning the matter, making light of the incident during the feast. Damona told a different tale and from her I learned Kaun had joined Johan to hunt in the woods with a dozen other warriors. Only on that morning had Rugga chosen to accompany Kalamar's jarl, making the company thirteen strong, including Bandor. Once deep in the woods, with the hunters spread out searching for game, Kaun and five of the men with him fell upon Johan, calling him a traitor. Johan was nearly unhorsed and three of the warriors loyal to him fell at Quicksteel's hand before Rugga arrived, swinging his great hammer with Bandor riding at his side. Together they killed two of the attackers and drove the others off. Kaun was apprehended when the rest of his men took flight. Johan and Kaun had been fast friends for years but that didn't prevent Johan striking off Kaun's head with Jokell's great two-handed sword before a crowd assembled outside the gates of Kalamar Castle, called to witness the jarl's justice.

"At least Kaun didn't succeed," I observed as Damona finished her tale. "And he could only muster a handful of supporters."

Damona looked at me searchingly. "A handful of supporters willing to kill their jarl and his only son. Whilst only a few may have been willing to raise a hand against Johan, many privately agree with what Kaun Quicksteel did. Kaun was a man Johan trusted and loved, so to discover he could stoop to such treachery shook him. If Rugga hadn't chosen to join that hunt, I believe I'd be lighting a pyre for my husband and beloved son, and many more would have been emboldened to flock to Kaun's cause. Jorik's steering a dangerous course, and it's putting my family in peril. Make sure he hears that part of the story and remembers his realm extends beyond the walls of Ulfkell's Keep."

Relieved as I was Johan and Bandor had escaped the attempt on their lives unscathed, my one regret was that Bandor was not at Kalamar when I landed. He had ridden out with hand-picked warriors including Rugga, Svan and Johan's new second Petr Hamarrson to hunt down the last of Kaun's supporters, who had taken refuge in the hills inland. As I prepared to leave on the morning tide, I left a message for my friend with his father, wishing him good hunting and saying he would be missed by me at Ulfkell's Keep.

"I'll pass that on," Johan told me with a smile. "Trust me, by the time you land at Reavesburg there'll be a raven with a message telling you three more heads sit on a spike atop Kalamar Castle."

Johan's words proved to be true, for a letter did indeed await me bearing just such news when I reached home. I recognised Bandor's fine flowing script on the parchment, although there was no warmth in the letter, the first I had received from him since our disagreement earlier in the year. I realised Bandor blamed both me and Jorik for placing his family's life at risk. Jorik brushed the matter off when I told him of the incident.

"If the worst thing Johan has had to deal with is six rebels who are now all missing their heads, then I say we've done well. A common enemy is a great unifying force, Rothgar. I'm giving people a chance to crush Adalrikr once and for all. The clan will support me in this, you'll see."

I had given Jorik, Finnvidor and Etta a full report. Now Etta sat there demanding the whole truth. I had wondered on the voyage back home whether my encounter with Nereth had been forged in the dream world rather than reality. Now I had to face my fears once more, as l told the old crone everything that had happened since I felt the touch of Shula's dagger. Etta closed her eyes, absorbing all the details as I recounted them. It was hard for me to relive that moment of horror on the jetty, and I realised the details were etched into my mind. Unlike a dream, half-remembered by the time I awoke and forgotten by mid-morning, my torment on Reavesburg's docks remained as fresh as ever. Hard as it was to go back to that place, it was a relief to share my story with someone.

Etta took her time before offering her thoughts. "Sigurd is a thrice damned fool for hesitating. He should have killed Nereth when he had the chance in Karas' great hall. Let's hope Greystorm is as good as his word and hunts this foul woman down. I tell you, Rothgar, you have an unfortunate habit of acquiring enemies as you go through life."

"I've never *really* believed Darri's tales about magic and sorcery," I said. "I always thought magic was gone from Amuran after the War, with just the shamans whispering the words of the avatars from beyond the Void. When Shula put us all into darkness … Etta, I'll admit I was afraid. There was something unnatural about those three women and how they enslaved Karas so completely."

"Hah. The northern tribes have turned their back on magic, right enough. While the Laskan clans and the Northern Plainsmen follow the way of the warrior that doesn't mean magic has gone. The avatars brought that knowledge into

Amuran, and their banishment didn't take magic away. Much has been lost as a result of the War, true enough, yet there are still many who practise such arts today. The kingdom of Mirtan, which borders the Northern Plains to the east, is governed by its mages from their capital at Seroch. Their magic is no mere trickery, as some might have you believe. The power those mages wield is real, the jealously guarded secrets of a lost age that the Chapters of Seroch believe they will one day restore. Their new Grand Mage of the Three Chapters, Serena, possesses both the skill and cunning to make Mirtan the most powerful nation in Valistria. I've been watching her progress with great interest. There are also established, though much less powerful, magical orders active in the kingdoms of Beria, Oomrhat and Lagash."

"So, what do you think? When I saw Nereth, was it just a dream or something more?"

Etta cackled, amused by my question. "I wasn't there. Only you can answer that question. What do *you* think?"

As I sat there thinking the answer came to me clearly. "Bram said I was dreaming, but I *know* Nereth and her sisters were real. Somehow, they found a way to enter my dream and I'm certain that if I hadn't managed to wake I wouldn't be sitting here now, telling you this tale."

Etta nodded. "I don't think it is a coincidence Nereth appeared to you the third time you found yourself on the jetty. I think each of those incidents represented a day for you, as you lay injured in your bed. Nereth escaped from her cell on the third day. Once free, she was able to enter your dreams fully, only for you to narrowly escape from her clutches."

"If she has that power, it's strange she's not appeared to me since."

"Perhaps she was only able to do so because you were weak and vulnerable. That doesn't mean it can't happen again, though. I need to understand this more fully, so you can guard against such attacks in the future."

"Kalfr told me Nereth was a seer of Rathlin. If that's true

she must be powerful indeed to also walk in another person's dreams." I shuddered at the memory.

"Kalfr also told you not to believe a word those three uttered, and I think he spoke right. A shaman is not the same as a mage; I think we're dealing with someone trained in the magical arts, not the innate abilities of a shaman. No doubt posing as such gave her credence with Karas, desperate as he was in his grief." Etta grimaced. "As I said, you have a knack of choosing powerful enemies. Tyrfingr Blackeyes, Gautarr Falrufson and now Nereth, not to mention all those in Reavesburg, Kalamar and Norlhast who think of you as a turncoat for brokering Nuna's marriage to Karas. No mean feat during your scant sixteen years."

I blanched at those words. "I'll confess I finally felt safe again, back inside the walls of Ulfkell's Keep. Until now, that is."

"You should certainly lock your doors at night," Etta chortled, seeming to delight in my discomfort. "No, listen, I *want* you to be a little scared; to know that you can count on nothing being certain in life. Fear is a quality your brother sorely lacks. His successes in battle against Adalrikr have given him great confidence, and he thinks Adalrikr is afraid to engage him in the face of his growing power, now the alliance with Norlhast has been sealed. Since you left for Karas Greystorm's court, the raiding that was so relentless before has ceased. Finnvidor thinks perhaps Adalrikr has turned to easier targets, such as Gunnsteinn Haddison's Riltbalt Clan; yet we hear no reports of such things from our spies there."

"And what do you think?"

"Adalrikr is biding his time, trying to get Jorik to drop his guard. We know Adalrikr is not one to shirk from spilling blood to gain power. In battle I think perhaps your brother might have the edge, but there's more than one way to win a war and, above all else, Adalrikr has cunning. Perhaps Nereth and her sisters were his agents, and he was counting on them to foil Jorik's scheme without lifting a sword against either clan. Do you realise if you'd died from your wounds in Norlhast that would have changed everything? Jorik would have been honour-bound to avenge your death and many would have seen it as a betrayal by the Norlhast Clan. The coven were part of Karas' court, so people would think Greystorm himself responsible. We could now be at war again with the Norlhast Clan, all thoughts of marriage and fighting Adalrikr's forces forgotten. Who can say where the truth lies? All I know is Adalrikr has been building up his power since he became chief six years ago and he'll not be idle now, I can assure you. I fear your brother's confidence is misplaced. He'll not hear of it from me. Perhaps he will from you? You're in favour after all your exploits in Norlhast, so maybe you can talk some sense into him."

"It would be better if we had some proof as to what Adalrikr was plotting. There was no hint Nereth and the members of her coven had any links with him, it's just speculation on your part."

"I know," Etta heaved herself stiffly out of her chair, grasping her stick in a gnarled hand. "That's what pains me most, more than this damned aching back and these worn out knees of mine. Your brother's bold and courageous, good qualities to possess. The trouble is I can't make him see that just because Adalrikr's ships have stopped raiding our shores that doesn't mean the Vorund Clan isn't still plotting his downfall. Jorik insulted Adalrikr and openly defied him when Tyrfingr came as his emissary; Adalrikr will *never* let that slight go unpunished. Jorik has none of your guile, Rothgar. He takes his enemies on face to face; look how he dealt with Gautarr, for example. He just can't imagine his enemy won't act in the same way. Adalrikr's too clever for that, I'm afraid."

"Jorik's not just a fighting man," I argued. "He's pursued the Norlhast alliance."

Etta snorted with contempt, giving me a withering look as she shuffled towards the door. "It was *my* scheme, remember? Just speak to him if you can and try and make sure he stays on his guard."

Despite Etta's warnings, it did feel good to be back at Ulfkell's Keep. I passed Ulf and Djuri on the way to my chambers, both warriors greeting me warmly, clapping me on the back. Familiar sights, sounds and people helped put the difficult times at Norlhast behind me. Even so, there was a nagging worry in my mind as it occurred to me we relied far too much on Etta. Finnvidor was steadfast and dependable as my brother's jarl but he lacked imagination, whilst the idea of Gautarr as Jorik's main counsellor was laughable. Johan was shrewd and would offer good advice, yet his stronghold lay far from Reavesburg. Would he be prepared to forsake his own household at Kalamar Castle and join Jorik here at Ulfkell's Keep? With his own people currently plotting against him it seemed doubtful.

So where did that leave us? Dependent on the counsel of a woman who had, by all accounts, seen her hundredth year – although Etta declared she'd long since stopped counting the passing summers. Someone would have to fill her place when she died and it was hard to imagine who that person might be.

I opened the door to my chamber, my head swimming with Etta's sharp words, each as comforting as a knife pressed to my throat. When I saw Desta sitting there, waiting for me on my bed, my heart stopped for a moment. Etta's warning about locking my chambers came to mind, which I doubted was the effect Desta had intended when she planned her surprise.

"Will my lord require anything else this evening before he retires?" Desta asked. I struggled to find my voice, having studiously kept away from her the whole time we were in Norlhast. I reflected that we had been apart for a *long* time, a point was that was obviously not lost on Desta. "You've neglected me all summer," she continued. "You told me this was for my own safety. We're safe now, wouldn't you agree?"

What did old Etta know anyway? "Without question," I replied, closing and locking the door behind me.

CHAPTER 22

I stared down at the jumble of stone, watching as dozens of thralls busily moved like ants below us, some mixing mortar, whilst others laboured laying the first course of stonework. The solid foundations in this part of the wall had already been sunk deep into the earth.

"Whatever Adalrikr's been up to over the summer is no concern of mine," Jorik assured me, as he admired the building work. "I've not been idle with my time. Wooden defences are too vulnerable, so it's time to build our walls in stone. Ulfkell's Keep is strong but when *these* walls are built, the whole town of Reavesburg will be impregnable. It takes vision, and coin for that matter, to undertake such a task, like Ulfkell when he fortified the keep. Now it bears his name and he's remembered by each generation. These walls will bear my name, too, when they're completed." My brother folded his broad muscular arms, looking hugely satisfied with himself. I didn't point out Sigborn Reaveson actually had the vision to construct the keep. It fell to his son, Ulfkell, to complete the work after Sigborn was slain in battle, ironically enough by the Norlhast Clan. The name of Ulfkell's Keep was his only legacy to the clan. Ulfkell died from the blood plague just two years after its completion, leaving no issue to continue Reave's legendary line.

"Don't you think it odd that Vorund's constant raiding ended so suddenly?" I asked, thinking this an ideal opportunity to act on Etta's advice.

"Hah. We've given them too many bloody noses. Gautarr's walls remain strong and Finnvidor's warriors have driven off every raiding party that's dared to put a foot on our shores."

"Not *every* time," I argued. "Haarl told me our warriors arrived too late on more than one occasion to protect the more remote villages. He said many a time Tyrfingr Blackeyes and his cronies had done their evil work and fled before our warriors arrived."

Jorik grunted, looking annoyed. "Well, we can't protect every tiny settlement people choose to build. The risk of raiding has always been there. Maybe Tyrfingr's been put off setting out to sea since these damnable summer storms started. Honestly, Rothgar, the way people like Sandar and Hrodi complain about the damage to their crops or listening to Lundvarr bemoaning lost shipments from the clans west of the mountains, you'd think they'd prefer to be raided."

He's grown comfortable and accustomed to his role, I reflected. In the two months I'd been away I could sense the change in my brother. Now the pressure of the raids from Vorund had ended, Jorik was convinced this was all his own doing. He had markedly grown in confidence as he succeeded in each new endeavour, particularly with the forging of the Norlhast alliance. Whilst I was glad my brother's rule was more secure, part of me worried it would take little for the tide to turn against us once more.

My fear was that Adalrikr planned to strike at us unawares, launching a final raid as autumn turned to winter in order to break our spirits. If he had such plans we would never know, for the winter season of the years 208 to 209 of the Fallen Age was the hardest in living memory. Heavy snows were carried down with the northern winds from the Endless Ocean, bitingly cold. The Redfars Sea was soon filled with giant icebergs, enormous white mountains that defied belief, drifting slowly by on the current as I watched from the warmth of my chambers in the North Tower. Later the Redfars Sea itself froze solid, trapping our fleet in the docks. A few hardy souls ventured onto the ice to cut holes through to the dark waters below in order to fish. They said that the sea had become a vast plain of ice as far as the eye could see in every direction. Some speculated that the ice now stretched from coast to coast, making it possible to walk from Reavesburg to Riltbalt. No one was brave enough to verify the truth of the theory, though, and make the two-hundred mile journey on foot to find out.

Sandar and Hrodi had been right to complain about the loss of their crops to the weather, since the damage caused by the summer storms resulted in a poorer yield at harvest time. With our fishermen unable to set out to sea fish was also in short supply and our stores of food were stretched thin. Though Jorik's table in the Great Hall never wanted, Haarl confided in me that there was hardship in Reavesburg itself. In weather such as this, Haarl's guard duties were curtailed and we had more time to spend together, as we once had as boys, dicing or playing kings on Finnvidor's old scratched wooden board.

And all the time the snows fell, the wind shaping it into great drifts covering the docks, filling the courtyard of the keep and half burying the houses of the town. Work on the defensive wall had to be abandoned, so instead Jorik set his thralls to work clearing the town's streets of snow day and night. Few souls chose to venture out in such cold, preferring to stay warm beside the cooking fire, for those fortunate enough to have something to cook.

With such prolonged inactivity the warriors in the keep soon grew restless. To help pass the time Olfridor had the Great Hall cleared each day, allowing room for the men to spar, which gave me a chance to regain my strength. The long white scar along my chest had healed well thanks to Albrikt's skilful care. Now I was strong enough to test my skills with blunted steel against the likes of Olfridor, Haarl, Djuri and Ulf. The practice earned me a few bruises until I found my speed and stamina beginning to return in the weeks that followed, garnering praise from Olfridor and grudging respect from my fellow warriors.

Darri earned his bread that winter, keeping us all entertained through the interminable days and long dark nights with his stories and songs. People flocked to the Great Hall whenever he took up his seat by the fireside, eager to hear him sing and laugh at his jokes and stories. I can remember them listening with rapt faces on a rare occasion when he recounted one of the tales of the Age of Glory, when the avatars walked openly amongst both men and dragons.

He spoke of the forging of Amuran in the First Days, when the Creator called forth the avatars to aid him in his labours in order to give shape to the world and a home in which life could flourish. How Rannoch formed the rocks and stone, aided by Bruar, who set the great fire at Amuran's core, which still burns to this very day. Darri recounted how Culdaff gathered together the four winds whilst Nanquido poured out the waters to form the oceans, seas and rivers. Yet even in those early times there was conflict between the Avatars, as Altandu placed the sun in the sky to banish the darkness of the night so beloved of Ceren.

"For Ceren found the darkness beautiful and she was determined this should not be lost," Darri told us, as Kolfinnar the Younger sat listening open-mouthed on Reesha's lap. "It was Ceren who deemed that the sun should set at a given time and then rise again. As the sun set and night fell so ended the first true day on Amuran and Altandu wept, believing the darkness to be an unlovely thing. It is said her tears shone with a silver radiance and each that fell became a star, shining high and bright in the dark night. Altandu also set the pale moon in the night sky; to give its light to the creatures that would one day walk upon the surface of Amuran. Ceren was furious at Altandu's meddling and she opposed the moon's creation. Thus, the moon is not fixed in the sky but waxes and wanes. The Creator was grieved at this struggle, for from that time Altandu and Ceren were filled with hatred for one another and were forever in opposition. The Creator knew that in giving the avatars complete freedom there was always the risk of conflict. Yet his design had been for the avatars to create everything with one heart and now that would never come to pass. And so it was that the first seeds were sown in the struggle that would one day lead to the War of the Avatars."

Darri always has a way of making familiar tales sound fresh and new with each retelling. Those stories even drew Etta from her hiding-place, her eyes twinkling as she listened to the bard. Darri's performances were also welcome for another reason; the absence of news. Our ships were landlocked by ice, the roads impassable with the snow. Jorik was anxious for tidings of how Johan fared in Kalamar and what Gautarr was plotting in Romsdahl. As he waited through that long winter no messengers or birds reached Ulfkell's Keep. Reavesburg became our whole world, cut off from the nearby settlements. The only consolation was that Adalrikr was similarly trapped in his own fortress of Vorund Fastness, many miles away.

The weather had some compensations, since I was able to spend more time with my family, playing with young Kolfinnar, reminiscing with Jorik and talking to Nuna. Aside from Desta, it was my sister whose company I most enjoyed that winter. I had fretted for months about her betrothal to Karas and how she would react, remembering my own horror at my father's scheme to marry me to Freydja. Nuna's expectations as a young woman of noble birth were more realistic than my own had ever been. As a maiden of just thirteen she was still young but to me she seemed so much older than her years. I smiled to myself as I remembered her as a girl, racing about the keep with her long blonde hair trailing behind her, always in search of her older brothers. Soon she would leave Ulfkell's Keep for good, to live with Karas in Norlhast, and I realised I would miss her sorely. Nuna laughed when I confessed this to her.

"Etta taught you your letters. We can still write to one another and I'm sure Jorik will send you to Norlhast from time to time."

I shrugged. "Perhaps. There was talk once of me lending my sword arm to Gautarr in an effort to bring him back within the fold. Jorik may choose to pursue that scheme again, in which case you may find it's Olfridor who comes calling."

Nuna laughed out loud. "Olfridor? I love the man dearly, but as smooth-tongued emissary? Why that would be a disaster. No, I suppose Jorik would dispatch Finnvidor instead, who would be a poor replacement for your company. I doubt you'll find yourself in Gautarr's stronghold, though. Now your betrothal with Freydja is over surely Jorik will want to keep you close."

"Perhaps," I mused. "I'm not Jorik's jarl, though."

"Don't forget Finnvidor's almost fifty – he won't hold that title forever. In time, Jorik will need to appoint a younger man to lead his warriors into battle. Everyone expects that to be you, Rothgar, you must know that. Who was it he sent twice to speak to Karas Greystorm? He'll be relying on you more and more in the coming years, trust me. Besides, Karas swears you're the boldest young warrior he's ever met, since you freed him from the spells of the coven."

"Not quick enough to avoid the witch's blade," I replied, rubbing my hand over my chest. Though the injury had healed the memory of that brutal fight, shrouded in darkness, remained painful.

"Quick enough to save my life," Nuna said, squeezing my hand. "Karas is in your debt and so am I. I know in time I'll be happy with him, and we've you to thank for that."

"You've changed your opinion of him, then?" I asked.

Nuna looked thoughtful as she considered her response. "At heart he's a good man. There's many a wife who can't say that of her husband. We've all heard Darri sing the great ballads of star-struck lovers whose destiny it is to be together but that's just in stories. I'll be content with Karas, I think, and he can give me a life of my own in return. Look at Reesha and Jorik. Reesha told me she'd only met Jorik once before they were wedded. Now she has Kolfinnar and she's the lady of Ulfkell's Keep. If I can give Karas an heir, I'll sit at his side as the lady of Norlhast." A faint smile played on the edges of Nuna's mouth and she looked at me shyly, the mask of the lady falling away just for an instant. "I'm truly a woman now, so when the weather calms Jorik will send word to Karas that we can be wed in the spring. The two clans will be joined and I'm proud I can play a part in that."

"I'll still miss you," I answered, surprised at the quaver in my voice. I drew my sister close, suddenly grateful for the ice and snow that held us prisoner at Reavesburg. Yet all too soon the spring thaws came, and as I watched Jorik's ravens fly north bearing their messages to Karas Greystorm, I knew Nuna and I only had a few short weeks left before our lives took their separate paths.

CHAPTER 23

"I *have* to go," Desta insisted, though the look in her eyes suggested she wished otherwise. "Do you have any idea how many wedding guests Jorik has invited? They'll notice if they're not fed, believe me."

As she gathered up her clothes in the dim light radiating from the embers of the fire, I let out a long sigh. "Do you know how much I've missed you this past week, while you've busied yourself with your duties? Bring back the snows of winter, when I had you all to myself."

"Spring always follows winter, Rothgar, just as sure as night follows day. And if Cook doesn't find me readying the fires in the kitchens, you can be just as sure that she'll beat me soundly."

Desta's remark, made in jest, angered me all the same. "The woman I love shouldn't be beaten by the cook," I snapped. "I used to enjoy arranging our meetings in secret but now ... Well, things would be so much easier if we could just be open with people. I've been thinking, Desta, while we've been apart these past few days. I could speak to Jorik about this. I took a blade in Norlhast on his behalf, so if I asked a boon of him ..." I hesitated, unable to make out Desta's expression in the gloom as she hurriedly dressed. My heart was in my mouth and I forced myself to say the words before my courage failed. "I could ask him for anything, Desta. I could ask him for your hand if –"

"Don't," Desta sighed, as she hitched her dress over her shoulders. She walked towards me, gently placing two fingers on my lips as I started to protest. "Please, don't. Don't talk of what can never be. My father Humli is only a freedman, and nothing you say will ever change that fact. The lords of Ulfkell's Keep never marry their servants, they only ..." Her words came to a halt as she wiped her hand across her face. I reached out towards her as Desta leaned in, pressing her lips on mine and kissing me passionately. Then she stood hurriedly and walked swiftly to the door. Her hand was on the latch when my words gave her cause to hesitate.

"Is that really your answer?" My voice betrayed my heartfelt words, so the tone I managed was closer to a whine.

"It's the only answer there can ever be," Desta replied, before gently lifting the latch and vanishing silently into the darkness of the corridor.

I lay on my bed for a time, with only the dim glow of the fire for company. Eventually, force of habit made me get up and walk over to the door. Etta's words had become lodged in my mind, and these days I would find no rest unless the door was securely locked. Even then I was unable to sleep; I felt in turns angry, embarrassed and a fool, until eventually I experienced an unhappy combination of all three. I should never have spoken those words but it was too late to call them back.

I awoke with a start later that morning, feeling tired and weary. I washed in a bowl of cold water, the shock reviving me, before dressing in woollen breeches and donning a fine linen shirt, over which I pulled on a jerkin emblazoned with the Reavesburg eagle. This was a gift Jorik had presented to me for the wedding and as I put on my boots and buckled my sword belt, I reflected that this day marked the culmination of my brother's ambitions. All the noble families of the Reavesburg Clan were present, as with the spring Jorik's riders spread word of the coming marriage throughout our land. Ulfkell's Keep hosted delegations from Kalamar, Romsdahl, Lake Tull, Noln and Olt. Bothvatr and Ingioy both sent their congratulations from the western clans as well as wedding gifts. Karas Greystorm had arrived from Norlhast two days ago, his ship leading three others captained by Albrikt, Sigurd and Brosa.

Only Johan had arrived with as many longships and warriors, one more than Gautarr had brought. I was disappointed that Kalfr was not amongst the Norlhast wedding party, as Karas had left him in charge of Norlhast Keep in his absence. However, I was pleased to see Johan set ashore with both Bandor and Damona at his side. I had decided it was time to mend things with my old friend. Although the opportunity had not yet presented itself, I was determined I would find a way to make peace with Bandor.

Ulfkell's Keep was a hive of activity, servants hurrying along the corridors as the final preparations for the wedding feast were made. I spied Ottama, Sigurd's servant, heading away from the kitchens with a tray of food, no doubt bringing him his breakfast. I smiled and she shyly looked down at her feet as she hurried down the corridor. Somewhere in the kitchens, Desta would be working but I knew better than to try and find her now. Instead I made for the courtyard of the keep, where many of the warriors had already assembled, readying themselves for the march to the sacred grove, where Nuna and Karas would say their vows. They would be guarded by hundreds of warriors from both clans, providing Finnvidor and Sigurd could keep the peace, since many still harboured suspicions concerning their new allies. Both jarls made sure their presence was obvious, talking casually to one another as if they were old friends. I also spied Johan Jokellsward with his men, arms folded and a frown on his face as he surveyed the scene, Damona standing nervously by his side clutching Bandor's arm.

"Rothgar," Sigurd called out when he saw me. "A good morning for a wedding, wouldn't you say? Your brother has done us the honour of allowing my father to preside over the ceremony." This was not news to me. The arrangements for the wedding had been discussed at great length with Jorik during the long winter months in Ulfkell's Keep. As the leader of the stronger clan in this alliance, it was only right that Jorik was the host and summoned his nobles and new friends to Reavesburg. Still, it was important to show respect to the Norlhast Clan as well and Etta had suggested Albrikt perform the service, stepping aside from her traditional role as town elder.

"It will be a finer morning still if we organise this rabble and begin to make our way to the grove," muttered Finnvidor, his grey eyes watching the men milling before him, gathered together in small knots reflecting the clans and houses to which they belonged. The Romsdahl men congregated around Audwin Strongshield, as they waited for Gautarr's family. They were eyed suspiciously by a group of warriors surrounding Brunn and Djuri as they stood restlessly nearby. I could see what Finnvidor meant and why Johan looked so worried; one wrong word, one jest in poor taste and the alliance could founder on the edge of a hot-headed warrior's blade in this very courtyard. There was no sign of Nuna or Karas and I felt a flicker of anxiety.

"I'm surprised you've the nerve to stand there, Strongshield," Djuri called out, egged on by some of the men around him. "Last time you were in this yard our chief was giving Gautarr a beating he's not likely to forget."

"Djuri. That's enough," barked Finnvidor, whilst old Brunn reached over and placed a hand on his young friend's shoulder to restrain him.

Audwin simply smiled at the remark. The tallest man in the courtyard by a head, he towered over his companions, seeming all the larger for the huge black beard he sported, which was plaited into two long strands that almost reached his waist. "Don't worry, Einarrson – Djuri's always been a fat bellows. I reckon if he was pricked by steel that'd let some of the hot air out of him. Another time, perhaps, since that wouldn't be fitting behaviour for guests at a wedding. Gautarr did no more than assert his rights in trial by combat to lead our clan, and well you know it. Jorik proved his right to be the stronger on the day and none can complain about that, now can they?"

He also tried to kill my brother by treachery to avoid ever having to fight him in the first place. I kept my own counsel as Jorik would never forgive me for stoking the fires and risking his plans, especially on this day of all days. I groaned inwardly as Gautarr himself entered the courtyard gates from his encampment outside the town, flanked by more of his warriors including his son, Ragnar, and nephew Throm. Gautarr's lack of tact and desire to settle any argument with his battle-axe was the last thing this situation needed. Fortunately, Albrikt and Karas chose this moment to also make their appearance, quietening the argument that was threatening to boil over in violence.

"Well met, my friends," Albrikt's deep voice boomed out across the courtyard, his manner casual and relaxed, although he must surely have sensed the rising tension of those around him. "A fine spring day for a wedding, lacking only one thing – the bride. Rothgar, where is your pretty young sister hiding herself?" Albrikt had certainly dressed for the occasion, wearing long flowing robes of white and purple. Karas Greystorm's attire was more subdued – an elegant linen shirt, finely-spun woollen breeches and expertly tooled black leather boots and gloves. His matching black cloak was trimmed in fox fur and sported the whale crest of the Norlhast Clan, stylishly sewn in white. The outfit was carefully chosen, helping to conceal his wasted and slender frame in the company of so many warriors.

"You need wait no longer," Nuna's voice rang out in reply and I turned to see her gracefully descending the steps from the North Tower, arm in arm with Jorik in the absence of our father. Reesha and Kolfinnar the Younger walked a step behind them both, the boy looking bemused by the whole affair. Nuna's hair had been expertly arranged, the golden locks held up by pins and cascading attractively about her face. She looked much older than her true years and silence slowly settled across the courtyard, as all the men took note of her.

"My wife to be," Karas declared. "Never before have

you looked so beautiful, Nuna." My sister beamed at the compliment.

"It's time," Jorik called out. "Today two clans will wed and join as one, just as a husband is joined to his wife. I've waited a long time to see this day, and I don't intend to wait any longer."

"I think we all know which clan will be the dutiful wife, don't we?" I heard Audwin Strongshield mutter in an undertone to Gautarr as Jorik helped Nuna to mount her horse in order to protect her pure white gown on the journey to the grove. A few feet away I saw Sigurd regard Audwin darkly as the wedding procession began to wind out through the gate towards the sacred grove.

***

The Great Hall was packed with people that night, all shouting and laughing as the players struck up another tune, struggling to be heard above the raucous din. Nuna's skirts fanned out as Karas whirled her about the hall, her eyes bright and cheeks flushed, whilst onlookers cheered and clapped in time to the music. Nearby Jorik and Reesha danced as well, alongside Johan and Damona and many other noble men and women of both clans. The air was hot and close, filled with the rich smells left over from the earlier wedding feast, and my headed pounded from too much drink. Dancing was definitely not a good idea, so instead I weaved my way to one of the tables set against the wall and sat down heavily on a bench.

"You look somewhat the worse for wear, Rothgar," a young dark-haired woman remarked as she emerged from the throng and walked towards me. I frowned, trying to place her.

"Freydja. Why is it that every time we meet, you always find me less than presentable?" Freydja had grown tall since Jorik's wedding, her long dark hair braided and swept down behind her slender back. She moved gracefully too, in contrast to me slumped on my bench. Whilst Freydja was just a year younger than me she looked much older than her sixteen years.

"It's been a long time since we last saw each other. It isn't every day you see two clans uniting in the face of their enemy." She sat down beside me in a swift, fluid motion. Freydja was all poise and refinement and there seemed to be little of Gautarr in her bearing and appearance; she took after her adoptive mother, Jora, who was also at the feast. It was said that the only person Gautarr truly feared was his slender willow of a wife.

"We seem destined to meet at weddings," I quipped. Freydja laughed, a delicate cultured sound that was pleasing on the ear.

"Although not at our own. I confess that until today I only remembered you as the small, quiet boy with dirt on his nose. I see you've grown into a fine young man as the years have passed."

I grinned and, emboldened by drink, said the first thing that came into my mind. "And you have blossomed into a beautiful woman, Freydja. I'm sure that Romsdahl Castle must seem a dark, cold place without you to grace its halls."

"Poetical and charming," Freydja smiled warmly. "Perhaps you would have been a good choice after all. It's a pity Uncle and Jorik will never see eye to eye after what happened last year. Ragnar told me how bravely you duelled with my uncle, you know. He said you might even have bested him if you hadn't gone into that fight wounded – and that's high praise from Ragnar, though he'd never say it to your face. He's a flinty one, my cousin, although fatherhood has mellowed him a little. Still, I thought you'd like to hear that. I know what it's like to be overlooked. Everyone talks of how Jorik bested my uncle in the trial. I can't help wonder what the outcome would have been if the two of you hadn't fought first? Because events played out as they have, that means my hand will be given to Bandor Johanson."

"Bandor," I exclaimed, caught completely off-guard.

"The axe has to be buried. Father could never stomach marrying me into the family that defeated him in trial by combat in front of all his men. A union with the household of Johan Jokellsward further seals an alliance that strengthens our clan. A storm is coming, Rothgar, and Jorik wants us all standing united to face it together – or should that be Etta? Your brother strikes me as the kind of man who would fight the entire Vorund Clan single-handed if he could. Etta plays a much longer game, doesn't she?"

I'd searched all evening for Bandor, having failed to find a moment to speak to him at the wedding ceremony itself. Now I understood where he had been – Johan would have had the sensitivity to properly introduce his son to his bride to be. No doubt Damona and Jora played their part in the arrangements too, since Jora would never have trusted her blunt husband to handle such a matter. I felt a fleeting moment of annoyance Jorik had not seen fit to share this proposal with me, even though I had known for a long time my marriage with Freydja would never happen. As the adopted daughter of a jarl, she would have to be wed to someone of importance and Bandor was the obvious choice.

"You're lucky, Freydja," I said finally. "Bandor's a good man and he's been a great friend to me over the years. You'll be happy with him, I'm sure."

"It would matter little if he was a one-eyed dwarf with a stutter," Freydja remarked. "One day he'll rule Kalamar Castle in his father's stead and ultimately that's all that matters. Thank you for your kind words, though. I'm sure both Jorik and Bandor will want to talk to you of this, since they still need to formally break our engagement."

"It looks as if I'll have to marry the one-eyed bearded dwarf with a limp Old Hrodi has sired," I joked. "As you say, the fate of our lives can turn on the smallest of things." I looked up to see Bandor standing just a few feet away from us, his face almost as red as his fiery hair. I rose awkwardly and clasped my old friend in a fierce hug.

"You know, then?" he asked, nodding in Freydja's direction.

"I would have said you were welcome to her until tonight. Now, though, I'm not so sure ... I wish you every happiness, Bandor, truly."

"Let's drink to that," Bandor answered, leading me back into the throng of the Great Hall, his arm around my shoulder.

CHAPTER 24

"You're drunk."

"Not *that* drunk," I protested. Desta had a wry smile on her face as she ran her hand delicately over the front of my breeches, although she didn't allow me to step through the doorway.

"So I see. Shouldn't you still be at the festivities? You seemed to be enjoying yourself with Freydja Egilldottir."

"She's betrothed to Bandor now, so there's no need to be so jealous. Anyway, there's few folk left in the Great Hall." Gautarr and his family and followers had left Ulfkell's Keep earlier in the evening, returning to their encampment outside Reavesburg. I saw Jora's hand in that decision, recognising that leaving the Romsdahl household under Jorik's roof would only lead to violence with last year's memories still fresh in people's minds. Jorik had not stinted in his duties as a host, inviting Gautarr to share in the food at his table each day. Having seen Gautarr's pavilion I could vouch for the fact that the Romsdahl household wanted for nothing, their accommodations arguably more spacious and well-appointed than many of the guest chambers in Ulfkell's Keep. When I stole away from the Great Hall it had been slowly emptying, men picking up their friends from the floor where they had fallen in a stupor and leading them back to their chambers. As Bandor left with his mother and father and the servants began to clear away the remains of the feast I noticed Desta wasn't among them. Stealing away to find her in her chambers I was pleased to have guessed correctly about her whereabouts, although I wondered if I had been right about her intentions.

"Perhaps you should retire for the night yourself," Desta

suggested.

"That was my plan. I hoped to be able to retire with you, though. Isn't that why you abandoned your duties this evening?"

Desta laughed. "I've burned my wrist on one of the pots in the kitchens," she explained, drawing back the sleeve of her dress to show me the glistening red welt on her arm. "Cook told me to go and rest, which isn't what you have in mind at all."

"Please," I insisted. "I don't want to leave things between us as they were this morning. I meant what I said."

"I know you did. That's why I shouldn't let you inside." But Desta opened the door to her chambers all the same.

***

Ulfkell's Keep was quiet as I walked to corridors in the dead of night, making my way back towards the Great Hall with a much steadier stride. I saw Ottama scurrying past, face down as always, and reflected that the life of a servant was not one to be envied. Sigurd had the poor girl at his beck and call from dawn to dusk. Desta didn't deserve that life. I strengthened my resolve to find my brother and speak to him about her, whilst he was still in a good mood from the wedding celebrations. With the alliances secure with Norlhast, Kalamar and Romsdahl I was sure Jorik could spare his younger brother. Kalfr had married his childhood sweetheart, so why not I?

"Still standing, Rothgar?" Djuri asked, approaching me from the opposite direction, dressed in chainmail with his hand on his sword. The tall man had not been drinking, having drawn lots along with unlucky Haarl and a handful of other warriors for guard duty on the wedding day. "Brunn Fourwinds wagered we'd find you curled up next to the hearth in the Great Hall by now."

"Looks like Fourwinds lost his bet, then. You're his sober witness."

"That I am," Djuri replied ruefully. "Haarl's convinced

Olfridor rigged the lots somehow. I've never seen the lad look so furious as when he drew out the short straw. When I did the same it soon wiped the smile off my face, though."

I clapped Djuri on the shoulder and left him to continue his patrol. When I returned to the Great Hall, it was almost deserted. Little Kolfinnar was still running around, wrestling playfully with Olfridor near the fire. Karas and Nuna had long since retired to begin married life together and Jorik sat slouched in Reave's Chair at the top of the dais, ale mug in his hand. He raised an eyebrow at my reappearance but if he wondered where I'd been, he chose not to ask. Reesha was sitting next to him in a smaller chair, half-asleep with her arm wrapped around his shoulder. Standing with his arms folded, watching over proceedings with his calm grey eyes, was Finnvidor.

Olfridor released Kolfinnar, who ran back to his father, and turned to look at the jarl. "Honestly, Finnvidor, you need to unbend a little. This here's a wedding feast, not a wake. Don't think I've ever seen you with more than water in your cup."

"My father was all too fond of his drink. It led him to an early grave," Finnvidor replied steadily. "I've no intention of following in his footsteps, Halfhand."

"Course. I knew that. Sorry Finnvidor, no offence meant. Shouldn't have brought it up like that ... Just saying that sometimes you could do with relaxing a little more, that's all." Olfridor broke into a wide smile, his beard framing his tobacco-stained black teeth. "I guess I ain't one to lecture on temperance ..." He frowned and at the same time my heart jumped, as in the corner of my eye I became aware of movement in the shadows at the edges of the room. Finnvidor sensed it too but as his hands closed around the hilt of his sword a dark figure stepped forwards, arm raised, and buried a dagger right up to the handle in the jarl's neck. I watched aghast as he took a tottering step forward, blood gushing from the wound like a fountain as his assailant tore the blade free, opening up a bright red gash across this throat. Finnvidor choked noisily as he sank to his knees, a tide of blood spreading over his jerkin, before falling flat on his face. There was a dull clang as Jorik's tankard hit the floor and I became aware of Kolfinnar's wailing as around twenty dark-cloaked men emerged from the shadows on all sides, blocking both exits from the Great Hall.

"What the …?" gasped Olfridor, springing to his feet, a little the worse for wear with drink as he swept out his axe from his belt. I drew my sword from its scabbard, the noise of the metal ringing eerily. There was a man in front of me, sword in hand and I leapt forwards with a snarl, swinging the blade down towards him, watching him parry and fall back, as I pressed on. Then my legs were swept out from under me and as I sprawled on the floor men grasped my arms, kicking my blade out of my hand. I struggled vainly, feeling a knee pressing into my back, whilst a big, burly arm wrapped itself tightly round my neck. I gasped for breath as I was hauled upright, already dizzy from lack of air.

Olfridor still stood with his back to the fire, swinging his axe wildly to keep our attackers at bay. "Come on," he roared. "Which of you bastards is brave enough to be first? Well, then? Let's see what you've – urgh!" The air thrummed and an arrow struck Olfridor deep in the chest on his right hand side, burying itself right up to the black fletching. He took a step back, eyes wide in surprise.

"I'm sorry, Halfhand. No glory for you today." The voice was familiar. I tried to turn my head in my captor's strong grip to see who was speaking. I heard a bow being stretched back and tried to choke out a warning to my friend. Olfridor heard the noise too and bellowed a challenge as he jumped across one of the feasting tables to charge his foe. He had barely taken a stride, though, before another black-fletched arrow found its mark, knocking him over and sending him crashing back onto the table, scattering food and cups in every direction. Kolfinnar's wailing reached a new pitch and I could hear

Reesha calling for help, her voice suddenly silenced by a blow from one of the men. At the head of the table, two cloaked figures had hold of Jorik's arms, whilst a third held a knife to his throat.

"Someone shut that mewling brat up," snarled the speaker. One of the men stepped forwards, stabbing my helpless nephew swiftly three times with a long knife. Reesha flew at the man with a scream, biting and clawing with wild rage until two others intercepted her, dragging her to the floor. Her head hit the stones underneath the rushes with a sharp crack and all the fight went out of her as Kolfinnar slid, lifeless, to the floor. I could hear Jorik struggling, fearless of the blade at this throat, the men grunting with the effort of holding him back.

"There isn't time to do what I'd like with your wife, Jorik." Tyrfingr Blackeyes finally stepped into view and began walking the length of the hall. He set his bow aside, drawing out a short sword, keenly sharp, edge glinting in the firelight. "I'll have to make do with the fact that she watched her only son die before her eyes."

"Coward," snarled Jorik, a thin trickle of blood running down his neck, as he continued to strain against the men holding him down. "I'll have my vengeance on you for this. Come and fight me, man to man."

Tyrfingr laughed, though the deep wells of his eyes lacked any trace of emotion. "Why? I much prefer it this way. Oh, look, your weapons master is still alive."

I turned, horrified to see Olfridor had lifted his head up from the table, his maimed hand gripped around an arrow protruding from just above his heart. His other hand still held his axe, though it shook with the effort. Blood bubbled up from his lips between his blackened teeth, both arrows robbing him of the breath to hurl any insults at his enemy. Blackeyes regarded him dispassionately, nodding to one of his accomplices, who walked up to the table. The man hefted an axe in one hand, swinging it down almost lazily with sufficient force to split Olfridor Halfhand's skull in half. I wanted to close my eyes, to look away from the scene of horror unfolding in front of me. Now I found myself dragged towards the dais, where my brother was pinned down, as helpless as me.

"Where was I? Oh, yes, I remember. I was saying what I'd like to do to your wife."

Blackeyes dragged Reesha back in front of Jorik, his free hand gripping her long red hair. She was recovering from her fall and I could see the dread in her face, as she looked directly at me. I stared back, helpless. Surely *someone* must hear all this commotion, I thought desperately. This couldn't happen. Not right here, not in the heart of my own home.

Jorik chose that moment to act. His powerful arms shrugged off Blackeyes' warriors as he sprang towards Tyrfingr with a shout. His effort was short-lived as the man with the knife was too quick and stuck the blade into the small of Jorik's back. Gasping in pain, Jorik fell forwards at Tyrfingr's feet and was swiftly surrounded by more men, holding him down once more as they beat him into submission.

"It doesn't do to linger," Blackeyes continued as if nothing had happened. "She's a fine-looking woman but sadly, for both of us, my orders mean we'll never become better acquainted." His short sword whipped through the air and Reesha's terrified scream was silenced as the blade cut through her throat. Blackeyes kept hold of her long hair, allowing her to hang there in front of us. There was a hideous whistling sound as the air left her body and we watched her jerk and writhe. Bile filled my mouth and I retched, much to the disgust of the man still gripping me tightly round my neck. When Reesha was still, Blackeyes dropped her lifeless body to the floor without ceremony. He took hold of Jorik's chin, forcing him to look up, so their eyes met.

"You were too ambitious, Jorik. Adalrikr does not enjoy the thought of rivals. You dare to attack our lands? You dare to forge alliances that publicly challenge the power of the Vorund Clan? After this day, no one shall ever act so foolishly. They will remember this day for a long, long time."

"You murderer. Only a coward kills helpless women and children," retorted Jorik, through a bloody mouth and broken nose.

"You put them at risk. If you'd accepted my terms, your wife and son would still be alive. Now it's too late. Perhaps your successor will have fewer qualms about paying Adalrikr the tribute he demands." Their eyes locked and Tyrfingr waited, watching as drops of Reesha's blood ran down Jorik's face. "Nothing more to say? Don't you want to know who's responsible?"

"What are you talking about?" gasped Jorik.

"Why, who betrayed you? Haven't you wondered who let me and my men into Ulfkell's Keep tonight?" Tyrfingr glanced towards me. "Your younger brother was more ambitious than you realised, Jorik. You'd be surprised what an overlooked man will do to rise to power." Jorik's eyes widened, as Blackeyes' hand moved in a blur, stabbing my brother in the stomach and twisting the blade, enjoying the moment and the pain he was causing. At that point I lost all self-control.

The man holding my neck screamed in pain as I sank my teeth into his arm. His grip loosened and I tore myself free, lashing out fiercely, my fist connecting with the nose of another man, breaking it with a sharp snap. Blackeyes thrust his sword into Jorik once more as I tried to pummel my way towards my brother. Already the element of surprise was fading, men pressing in around me once more. A fist connected hard with my head, dimming my vision, and I staggered to one side. Moments later I was overwhelmed, hands dragging me to the floor, pinning me down, blows delivered from every direction.

"Stop." The response was instantaneous as the assault ceased, though I remained held firmly in place. There was the distant sound of footsteps, coming closer, and shouts of alarm from somewhere within the keep. This was the moment, then, when I faced my own death. Not in battle and glory as it might have been at Noln. Not fighting in the duelling circle for the honour of my family and my clan. No, here was my death; murdered in my own home. Hands released me and without their support I sprawled face down on the floor.

"Pitiful," Tyrfingr remarked. "Can this boy really be the one that routed my forces at Noln? I expected more, somehow. Jorik was a more impressive specimen."

"My lord, time is short. We must go."

"Agreed. Well, then, Rothgar. Know this and remember it well. You have witnessed the fate of those who defy the will of Adalrikr Asmarrson. Believe me when I say he has far more dreadful servants to do his bidding than I. Still, you caused me a great deal of embarrassment before my master and I do not forget such things. I have something special planned for you, young man. Once this is over, you'll wish you'd stayed curled up in your bed in Ulfkell's Keep, rather than riding to the aid of Noln, I assure you."

I swallowed back the vile taste of vomit in my mouth, full of fear, as I closed my eyes and waited for the blade to strike. Time stretched on, and the blow did not fall. Slowly, I opened my eyes and was startled to find I was alone in the Great Hall, left relatively unhurt amid the scene of carnage. I struggled up onto all fours and shakily crawled over to my brother. Jorik lay moaning softly, blood running freely from several deep wounds in his broad body. Even as my hands feebly tried to stem the flow I knew my brother was dying and his soul would soon leave his body to be with Navan.

"Brother, listen to me ..." he rasped, fighting to form each word.

"I'm here, Jorik. Speak to me."

"Is it ... is it true? Did you ... did you really lead Blackeyes here tonight ... to kill my wife ... and ... and to ... murder my child?"

"No," I cried, tears running down my face. "No, Jorik, you must believe me. I would never do that, never." I took hold of his bloodied shirt as Jorik gasped, his eyes rolling before he finally lay still. I looked away, only to find myself staring instead into the dull, lifeless, eyes of Reesha. I crawled to the edge of the dais, dimly aware of shouting at the far end of the Great Hall. It was Haarl's voice, raising the alarm, calling for help that was already far too late in coming. I staggered to my feet as Haarl burst into the room, followed by Djuri and half a dozen other warriors. Sandar Tindirson was the last to enter, the young leader of Lake Tull skidding to a halt as he surveyed the scene of horror before him.

"No," Haarl gasped, drawing his sword but finding he had no one to fight. "Sandar, we're too late."

"Seize him," Sandar shouted, his handsome features distorted with rage as he pointed at me. "Seize the kinslayer. It was him I saw open the postern gate tonight. He's betrayed us all and delivered us into the hands of the Vorund Clan."

Head swimming, I could barely believe what Sandar was saying. I raised my hands, showing them to be empty, as I struggled to find the words to counter Sandar's lies. Only then did I realise they were stained red with my brother's blood. Djuri's fist slammed into my face before I got the chance to speak. I hit the floor with Jorik's final words ringing in my ears. *"Did you lead Blackeyes here tonight?"* Had my brother died believing that? There was no way I could ever know or put it right. As I slipped into blackness, it came as a welcome relief.

CHAPTER 25

I couldn't say how long I'd been lying on the cold, damp stone floor. Gauging from the chill and my aching muscles, it must have been several hours. I put a shaking hand up to my face, unable to make it out in the darkness, lightly running my fingers over my split mouth. At least I'd kept all my teeth. Why was I here? In answer the memories came flooding back as a jumble of images and sounds, like a waterfall swollen by the spring rains, battering and crushing me under their weight. Fresh tears ran down my face and I called out for someone to come and free me. The dungeons lay deep in the bowels of Ulfkell's Keep and beneath that great mass of stone no sound could penetrate, my cries going unanswered. Eventually I drifted into an uneasy and fitful sleep.

I awoke to the sound of voices and faint orange light filtering through a small barred window set in the door to my cell. Stiffly I sat up, straining to hear what was being said.

"... no *you* listen, boy. Tyrfingr be damned, he has a *right* to know the case against him." Etta, I was sure of it. Then another voice spoke in reply, lower and muffled, so I was unable to make out the words. I certainly caught Etta's sharp answer.

"Last I heard, Haarl, you weren't a coward, so don't let Blackeyes of all people tell you what to do. If your friendship with Rothgar counted for anything at all, let me speak to the lad before he's brought to the hall."

This time I heard Haarl's voice clearly. "Etta, you may be town elder but that don't give you the right to defy Blackeyes, not for the likes of him. Brunn told us to follow orders till the clan moot, or we'll have a blood bath on our hands."

I heard a swish and a sharp crack followed by a yelp from Haarl. I was no stranger to Etta's stick and couldn't help the painful smile spreading over my bruised face as she showed Haarl no quarter.

"Idiot. You really are all muscle and no brains, aren't you? We've already had a blood bath and, might I remind you, it was on your watch. By the clan moot it will be *too late*. It's probably too late anyway but I'll be damned if I don't try to do something. Now, are you going to stand aside or do I have to beat you to death?" Haarl muttered something inaudible and a moment later there was a rattle in the lock and the door swung open, filling the cell with dull orange light from a torch burning in a bracket on the opposite wall.

"I'll have to lock you in, Etta," Haarl muttered apologetically. Etta tutted as she made her slow way down to where I was sitting. The door slammed shut behind her and the room was dark once more, with just the faint light from the window set in the door illuminating Etta's craggy features.

"Etta, you know I'm innocent. You must believe me and get me out of here. It was Tyrfingr who killed Jorik and Sandar's the traitor. He lied to Djuri and Haarl ..." Etta held up her hand and silenced the flow of words.

"Rothgar, I know you're telling the truth but what I think matters little. There're some things you need to understand before your trial by the clan moot. Tyrfingr Blackeyes holds Reavesburg and his men have Ulfkell's Keep too. Someone killed the guards down on the docks and when Blackeyes' ships landed, they opened the main gates for his men. There were also traitors within the keep itself, opening the postern gate to allow Blackeyes and his warriors inside. Too many of our own were dead drunk after the feast, with too few left on guard to realise we were under attack until it was too late."

My breath caught in my chest and my head swam. I thought Tyrfingr's attack was one of assassination. This was even worse. We were occupied, and Ulfkell's Keep had been taken by our enemies for this first time in the century it had stood as the holdfast of the Reavesburg Clan.

"Sandar Tindirson," I said through gritted teeth. "He must have been the one. He voted against me at the clan moot when Gautarr was seeking power ... Could they both be in league with Adalrikr?" I shook my head, trying to clear the rushing noise as blood pounded through my veins.

Etta's gnarled hand took mine and gave it a bony squeeze. "Slow down. You're racing ahead and not thinking about what you're saying. I can't believe Gautarr would betray us to the clan he's spent his whole life fighting. As for Sandar, his vote against you in the clan moot last year proves nothing, unless you count Hrodi and Lundvarr as conspirators too. Sandar swears he saw you open the postern gate and ran to find Djuri when he saw Tyrfingr Blackeyes lead his men into the keep. Djuri himself has said he spoke to you in the corridor in the dead of night just minutes before your brother was killed, and there's another witness too. Ottama, Sigurd's serving girl, says she saw you heading towards the gate as she finished her duties and was heading off to bed.

"Sandar has played things well. Two witnesses from separate clans saw you in the vicinity of the postern gate, adding weight to his testimony. And they found you relatively unscathed in the Great Hall, with blood on your hands and the others all dead around you."

"And people believe that means I killed my brother?" I asked in despair. "They think I single-handedly managed to defeat Finnvidor and my old weapons master, as well as Jorik and that I murdered his wife and son?"

"Their story is that you were not acting alone, instead leading the killers to the Great Hall. You were captured afterwards when you were knocked unconscious during the fight, whilst the others fled."

My mind went back to the cold way Tyrfingr had killed my family and friends. "They made me watch," I whispered, glad the darkness hid my tears. "Blackeyes killed them one by one and I could do nothing, except watch. Now thanks to Sandar my head will adorn the walls of the keep and everyone will believe I'm a kinslayer." I pressed my hands to my temples, trying to blot out the pounding in my head that grew worse with each passing minute.

Etta took a shaking breath, though her voice remained strong. "Rothgar, I'm sorry but there's so little time. We need to counter Sandar as a witness, so I need you to think. Is there anyone who can vouch for you and speak in your defence? What were you doing in that part of the keep so late at night? I have my own ideas, though I'd rather hear the truth from you."

"I was with Desta," I whispered, confirming the crone's suspicions. "But you can't draw her into this, Etta, please. If people discovered the truth about us then anything could happen to her."

I knew instinctively Desta's testimony wouldn't help me; the word of a serving girl would carry little weight against that of the leader of the folk of Lake Tull. Djuri and Ottama had seen me *after* I left her chambers in any event, so Sandar could still argue it was me who had betrayed my clan. Even worse, people might believe Desta was involved in last night's events herself. In the darkness Etta tutted once more as she squatted beside me, sucking her gums in thought.

"I understand," she muttered at length in a low voice. "I'll see she's safe. Make sure you say nothing about her when you're in front of Tyrfingr Blackeyes. He has ... ways of finding out the truth. May the Creator preserve us. Gods, Rothgar, you need to be strong now." Etta had always seemed such an indomitable spirit, unbowed or cowed by anyone. It was the first time I'd heard her sound afraid, and the change sent a shiver running down my spine.

"The people who know what happened in the Great Hall are dead," I said. "There's no one else who can speak on my behalf, but people know me. I must have some friends at the clan moot who won't be swayed by Sandar's lies."

Etta placed her hand on my shoulder. "I'm sorry –

Tyrfingr himself sits on Reave's Chair and both Johan and Gautarr are gone. As the Vorund Clan swarmed into the town and the alert was finally sounded, some of our clansmen took up arms against them. Johan and some of his followers from Kalamar managed to fight their way down to the docks and regain two of their longships. One was torched before they reached the open sea whilst the other escaped.

"Bandor?" I asked.

"There's no sign of him or his mother. If Dinuvillan favoured them that night, they were on the longship that slipped through Blackeyes' fleet. There's no word of Rugga, either. If they'd been captured or killed, I suspect we would have heard about it, so with no ill-tidings we must hope for the best." The thought that Bandor and his family had escaped gave me some comfort, even if it robbed me of one ally at the clan moot. I wondered if Johan would be able to make it safely back to Kalamar and, if he did, what would he find? Would Petr Hamarrson, Johan's second, even now be standing on the walls of Kalamar Castle staring at a fleet of Vorund ships landing warriors on the shore?

"And what of Gautarr? You said he also escaped."

"Indeed. That part of Blackeyes' plan unravelled on the night. I've no doubt Gautarr Falrufson was the other great prize Blackeyes intended to seize, putting an end to the man who had defied him for so many years. But of course Gautarr was not in Ulfkell's Keep or even Reavesburg, camping with his followers some way from the wall. As Reavesburg fell, Gautarr struck camp and made for the docks, taking the Vorund Clan's warriors there unawares. His men fought their way back to their ships and all three were launched and managed to escape. It was that battle which drew away the men holding the gate as they went to the aid of their friends, which in turn allowed Johan and his men to gain the docks themselves. When he learned that four Reavesburg longships had broken free and eluded his fleet, Tyrfingr was furious. Galin, the warrior in charge of guarding the main gate, is now short of a hand for abandoning his post."

The thought that Gautarr had once again thwarted Tyrfingr gave me some comfort. I hoped for Bandor's sake Freydja had made it safely onto one of the three longships. Slowly, I brought my breathing under control, closing my eyes and trying to relax. The pounding in my head eased, leaving a dull ache in its wake, as I tried to put together the pieces. Etta was right, Gautarr was many things but he would never side with the Vorund Clan. Had Sandar acted alone? Ottama was another witness who spoke against me and she was in Sigurd's service. Did that mean the Norlhast Clan had some part to play in this treacherous business? Had Karas played me and my brother false all along? Etta was sceptical when I told her of my suspicions.

"I just can't believe Karas Greystorm would have married Nuna if he knew what was about to befall her brother. The Norlhast Clan have nothing to gain from this disaster. The loss of Jorik places them in a far weaker position, with their chief and his jarl now a prisoner of Blackeyes. They were relying on the alliance with Jorik to improve their fortunes. Instead, the Norlhast clansmen were all captured either asleep or so drunk they didn't even realise they were under attack. Karas or Sigurd would never have suffered such a humiliating capitulation if they were part of this scheme, I'm sure of it."

"And me? What could I possibly have to gain?"

"The problem is Sandar lacks an obvious motive to lie about what he saw. What does *he* gain from Tyrfingr's occupation of his lands? So people begin to look for reasons where none exist. Some remember how you fought against Gautarr last year. Had you won, you would have been chief in your own right."

"I was fighting for Jorik and the honour of my household," I countered. "I would have stepped aside once Jorik returned to Ulfkell's Keep. Any fool knows that."

"Yet some say you had designs on being clan chief yourself, as evidenced by rejecting the clan moot's decision to elect Gautarr and demanding trial by combat. At that point you believed Jorik to be dead. People remember that Adalrikr was well-loved by all, until one day he turned and murdered his entire family. Parallels are being drawn, and Tyrfingr fuels these rumours with his own lies, convincing more and more people that you were his agent, including young Haarl outside the doors of this cell." Etta's unwelcome words fuelled my rage and the drum began beating in my head once more, pain coursing through me.

"No, Etta, this is madness. What man would do such things to become chief when it would mean delivering himself and his clan into the hands of his enemies at the same time?"

"Tyrfingr has already told the clan elders you believed he would only wield the knife to dispose of your more powerful brother and his heir. As Jorik's brother, you would be his natural successor and once in power you could seek a truce with the Vorund Clan. It's now being said you never supported Jorik's headlong rush into war, believing it could never be won. So, Tyrfingr played upon your fears, offering you a chance to be rid of your brother and become chief in his place."

"I brokered the alliance that made war against Vorund possible, forcing Tyrfingr to act against us," I argued.

"Remember your people are confused and afraid. Their chief, his wife and his heir are all slain, his jarls dead or missing, and they are occupied by their hated foes. They are looking for someone to blame for their defeat and Tyrfingr has carefully manipulated them so that person is you. He has told them that he in turn betrayed you, using the opportunity to strike a blow to bring down both clans in a single night."

I hung my head, unable to comprehend how such lies could be believed by my own people. Etta sensed the fight leave me, my anger guttering out, swallowed by despair.

"I told you before that you have to be strong. They'll summon you to the Great Hall shortly and I didn't want you to learn everything from Tyrfingr's lips; I've denied him that pleasure, at least. Now, I'm afraid I have to leave, my boy –"

"Leave?" I snarled. "I thought you were coming to *help* me. There are some elders on the clan moot that will listen to you. Hrodi and ... and Lundvarr –"

"Are both cowards and will do what Tyrfingr Blackeyes tells them. I'm sorry, I only came here to try and prepare you for what's to come. You'll find no justice at the clan moot. Once sentence has been passed on you, Tyrfingr will want to do away with me as well, after he has tried to prise out my secrets. I'm so sorry, Rothgar – I had such high hopes for you and look where all my scheming has brought us." Etta sounded old and broken but I felt only bile and hatred rising up inside me as she struggled to stand upright, stick scraping on the damp stone floor.

"Go," I spat. "If you're so desperate to save your life and leave me here at Tyrfingr's mercy then, please, just go now. My clan has abandoned me, so why should you be any different?"

Etta stared at me, a black outline against the dim glow from the window in the cell door. "I've not abandoned you. I've done all I can. I'm sorry."

Etta turned and walked slowly back to the door, rapping on the thick wood with her stick. It swung open and without a backwards glance she shuffled into the corridor. Haarl slammed the door shut and I heard the key turn in the lock, followed by a scraping sound as he lifted the torch from its bracket. As their steps receded the light faded in the window, leaving me alone in the darkness once more.

CHAPTER 26

The Great Hall was as much a part of my home and childhood as my chambers in the North Tower. I had chased my brother and our friends around the feasting table when we were boys, fought duels with wooden swords before the hearth, watched my father rule our people from Reave's Chair. On dark winter nights we had gathered to listen to Darri's songs and stories, as he brought our history to life. The Great Hall I remembered had always been noisy and crammed with people, never more so than on the day of Nuna's wedding. Now it was dark and silent, the only light radiating from two small braziers set on the dais. Shackled hand to foot, my stumbling steps echoed on the stone floor, accompanied by those of the guards, six men of the Vorund Clan. It was a long walk from the cells and I found it hard to believe there was no sign of the violent struggle that took the lives of my family and friends in this very room.

The man who ordered their murder sat upright on the chair so recently occupied by my brother. In front of him wooden benches were set out in the traditional semi-circular arrangement of a clan moot. This time the arrangement fanned out from the central platform, reflecting that this was a trial rather than a debate. Considering the importance of the meeting, I was surprised it was so sparsely attended. I spied Lundvarr, Hrodi and Sandar on their usual benches. I thought they were alone until I was closer and saw perhaps a dozen or more warriors, sporting the Vorund sigil of the bear on their shields. The men stood silently in the shadows in a loose half-circle just behind the representatives on the clan moot. Each one wore chainmail and stood guard with swords or axes drawn, leaving no one in any doubt that dissent in Tyrfingr's court would not be tolerated. Two more warriors flanked Tyrfingr himself, and I noticed one of those men was short of his left hand, the stump bandaged in bloody linen and his arm supported in a sling. A sheen of sweat was gleaming redly on his forehead.

On the remaining benches the usual places reserved for the houses of Romsdahl and Kalamar were occupied instead by Karas, who was attended by Nuna and Sigurd, and Brunn Fourwinds, the bluff warrior of Ulfkell's Keep and staunch friend of my father. Though not yet turned forty he seemed older, and it was clear from his bruised and bloodied face he'd not readily accepted Vorund's rule. Perhaps I had one friend left at the clan moot after all as my escort forced me to my knees before Tyrfingr. His mocking smile enraged me and I fought to keep my emotions in check. Nuna's eyes were red and raw from weeping, her face taut with shock and grief. This was the hall where my family had ruled since the time of my great-grandfather. I appealed silently to their spirits now, praying that somehow they would ensure justice would be served this day.

"A traitor kneels before us," Tyrfingr began solemnly, his soft voice carrying easily across the silent room. "Yet he has paved the way for great things in the Laskan lands. By rights, all of you should thank him, for you owe him your lives."

"How, *exactly*, do you arrive at that conclusion?" Sigurd asked. Of all the men present before me, only Sigurd appeared unbowed by the events that had befallen us. Blackeyes smiled, obviously enjoying answering the question.

"Adalrikr has declared himself king of Laskar, so now all of the seven clans must bend the knee to his rule or face his wrath. Rothgar here was wise enough to understand that, even combined, the strength of the Norlhast and Reavesburg Clans would never be enough to defeat him. Jorik was bent on leading all of you down a path that would have resulted in your destruction. His actions have spared you all from that fate –"

"A lie," I shouted. "I would never help –" My protest was cut short as a mailed fist from one of my six guards struck me on the side of the head. Since I was chained I was unable to keep my balance and sprawled on the floor, my vision blurred. Dimly I heard Tyrfingr laughing as someone dragged me back onto my knees.

"Do not speak unless you are given leave. Though I confess you're right; I did lie. You sought to rule your clan and broker peace with Vorund, failing to understand the way of the clans is over. King Adalrikr will never tolerate rivals, only loyal subjects, and you had already proved you could never be trusted. So, yes, I allowed you to believe I would raise you to become the new Reavesburg chief, when I had no intention of making good on such a promise. It was a lie, one I told for the good of the realm. By delivering Ulfkell's Keep into my hands, in a stroke war has been averted. How many lives have been lost? Less than two hundred, and it would have been far fewer still if Jorik had not stinted on his duties as the host of the wedding, and left his most powerful jarl skulking in tents outside Reavesburg. Just think; if we had instead been forced to defeat you in the field, how many more young men would have left their homes never to return to their parents, their wives or their children? If you could save thousands of lives with a simple lie, would you not do the same? Jorik may have been honest but the man was a brute, his heart set on the glory of war, with no thought to what it would cost and where it would lead."

"Your honeyed words do little to mask the truth," Sigurd observed. "Whatever part Rothgar might have played, you don't even try to deny you and your men wielded the blades that killed Jorik, his innocent wife and child and two of the Reavesburg Clan's greatest warriors."

Brunn nodded in agreement at Sigurd's words. "Aye. By what rights do you dare sit on Reave's Chair? That was no honourable way to kill a man. And to butcher his child ..." Brunn struggled to compose himself as Tyrfingr regarded him with his black, fathomless eyes. "You speak to us as if you've earned the title in a trial by combat. Well, I'll never accept it and the people of Reavesburg won't either."

"They may not, of course," answered Tyrfingr. "They may be as brave and defiant as you, Brunn Fourwinds, in which case you will die together. I do not want more bloodshed but openly denying the right of your king to rule is treason, for which there can be only one penalty."

Karas shook his head angrily at Tyrfingr's words. "Damn it. A man calling himself a king doesn't make him one. Our clans have laws as to who has the right to lead us. We don't recognise Adalrikr as anything other than a murderer, who killed his own kin to rise to power. A less worthy king I cannot imagine."

"Our clans have warred against each other for the last one hundred and fifty years," Tyrfingr countered. "Did the Romsdahl Clan really ask to be united with Reavesburg? I think not. Sigborn Reaveson may be credited with peacefully negotiating that alliance. However, in truth it was settled with the threat of war and slaughter hanging in the air. Did the people of Kalamar have any choice when Hroar Helstromson seized their lands, wresting them from the control of Norlhast? The seat of Johan Jokellsward's house has been stolen from your own people, Karas Greystorm; surely you have not forgotten that? This has always been the way of things. If Laskar could be united these old rivalries become unnecessary. One land serving one king – is such a prospect so appalling?"

Karas' face darkened. "With Adalrikr on the throne? My clan will never accept the rule of a man who has sent countless ships against our shores, killing, raping or enslaving our people and raiding our crops and stores. Do you think all that can be *forgotten* if Adalrikr styles himself our king?"

"You were prepared to set old scores aside to join forces with your enemies, the Reavesburg Clan. In case you have forgotten, you married one of them two days ago. I'm sorry,

Karas Greystorm, you speak as if this is a matter in which you have a choice. You can accept your fight is unwinnable and earn some concessions from your king or you can defy him. Adalrikr will crush you as easily as I took Ulfkell's Keep. Make no mistake, even now our ships have set sail over the Redfars Sea, making for Riltbalt, Norlhast, Kalamar and Romsdahl. By the end of this year, Adalrikr will drive the Northern Plainsmen off into the Ice Fields and control the entire coast. The other clans will soon heed his call for loyalty when they understand the power their rightful king wields. Ultimately, that is all that is necessary. Power and the right to rule belongs to the strong and those bold enough to seize it. Even Jorik Kolfinnarson understood that much."

"Nonsense," Sigurd barked. "No clan has the strength to wage war on such a scale. Do you think mere words can frighten us into submission? Your plan to take Ulfkell's Keep was cunning, I'll grant you, but this is mere bluster. I came here today to hear the case against Rothgar, not listen to your threats."

"You will know the truth of what I say soon enough. Adalrikr has ruled wisely for the last seven years, building his strength and his fleets. The ships I speak of are real, as are the warriors sailing them, and when they break upon your shores you will regret your hasty words unless your chief is wiser and chooses to accept Adalrikr's offer here and now. Without your new-found allies do you still have the stomach for the fight? What will it be, Greystorm?"

Karas stared at Tyrfingr with revulsion and I could see he was holding his tongue as he pondered on Blackeyes' words. He rested his hand on Sigurd's arm as his jarl made to speak again, shaking his head in resignation. "Peace, Sigurd. The duty of a clan's chief is to make decisions for the good of his people. The Norlhast Clan cannot hope to prevail alone against Adalrikr – our chance to strike has passed, whether we like it or not. So, Tyrfingr, if I seek peace with your king, what are his terms?"

Blackeyes smiled. "You would rule in his name as the jarl of Norlhast, retaining your keep and lands. Furthermore, once Kalamar falls into our hands, as it surely will, all the lands held by Johan Jokellsward will be returned to your people. Consider this a reward for swiftly bending the knee to your new king." Sigurd looked as if he had taken a mortal blow. Karas' reaction was more measured. He stood and walked to the foot of the dais, before bowing his head and sinking to one knee before Tyrfingr.

"I do this for the good of my clan, Blackeyes, understand that. On behalf of the Norlhast Clan I, Karas Greystorm, clan chief swear fealty to King Adalrikr. Henceforth I recognise his laws and his rule in Norlhast."

"A wise decision," Tyrfingr acknowledged with a self-satisfied air. He took up a quill resting on a small table to his right and signed his name with a flourish at the bottom of a short document, before rolling the parchment up tightly. He gestured impatiently to one of the warriors by his side, who took some sealing wax and melted it above the brazier, in order to seal the scroll. Tyrfingr took the parchment back and impressed the black seal with his ring. "By the powers vested in me by King Adalrikr as his jarl of Reavesburg, you are named jarl of Norlhast. You shall rule that region in his name and by his authority. Galin, escort Karas and his lovely young bride from the hall and ensure they set sail for Norlhast with this decree. Without it, Greystorm's tenure as jarl will be short-lived when he meets our ships at the mouth of the River Taur."

The one-handed warrior stepped forward, clearly still in pain from his wound and Karas, Sigurd and Nuna rose and followed him, four other warriors from the hall falling into step just behind. As they walked away, Nuna turned and looked back at me just for a moment, her face stricken. Was she grieving for her lost brother, sister-in-law and nephew, the fall of Reavesburg or did she really believe I had betrayed us all? As their footsteps receded I realised I might never know the answer.

"And what of you, Brunn Fourwinds?" asked Tyrfingr quietly. "What do the elders of the Reavesburg Clan say to their king's offer? Adalrikr was concerned your own lands did not grow too large, so no new territory will be ceded to you, and Kalamar will no longer be yours to rule. However, the Northern Plainsmen have much wealth from their trade with the Berian merchants and the mages of Mirtan. Join us in crushing them in Adalrikr's name and you may take as much plunder and thralls back to Reavesburg as your ships can carry."

"I've raided the plains myself many times, with Kolfinnar and Finnvidor at my side," said Brunn. "You offer us nothing more than the spoils of war, which we could take for ourselves anyway. Your king insults us."

"Your late chief plotted against your rightful king," Tyrfingr replied dangerously. "These terms let you all keep your lives, a gesture that is more than generous, in the circumstances."

Brunn stood up suddenly, reaching for a blade he no longer carried. In a moment he was surrounded by Tyrfingr's guards. "A life as a thrall is no life at all," he growled, despite the sword inches from his neck. "Karas Greystorm may have fallen on his knees but I'll never do the same. The Reavesburg Clan will fight you to a man, rather than serve that dog."

"Is that so? Sandar Tindirson, you speak as the elder of Lake Tull for your people. Will you fight and watch your folk slain, women raped and homes burned?" Sandar looked right at me before he spoke. The able young man who had been so well-regarded by my father – the man whose lies bound me in chains.

"The people of Lake Tull will bow to Adalrikr as our king. We're farmers and fishermen, not warriors and I'll not send my people to the slaughter for the sake of your pride, Brunn. You'd do well to listen to Tyrfingr."

Lundvarr wrung his hands nervously, sweat beading on his forehead, as the attention of the clan moot turned to him.

He stuttered as he struggled to find his words. "Noln has suffered ... In the past ... Well, I mean to say, you may now be called our jarl yet just last year ..." Lundvarr swallowed as he gathered his courage. "Blackeyes, you yourself led the last attack that breached our walls. If I were to pledge the support of Noln, can you guarantee our town would be safe?"

"Adalrikr will bring wealth to all his followers if its people are loyal and pay their taxes," Tyrfingr replied. "The merchant port of Noln is important to him. If you feel this arrangement is unacceptable, I shall return and reduce the town you represent to dust and ashes." Lundvarr looked for a moment as if he might be sick. He bowed his head and nodded mutely.

Hrodi Whitebeard pointed a shaking, bony, spotted hand at Tyrfingr. "When I was young ..."

"This isn't going to be a long tale, is it?" Tyrfingr remarked, his words unheeded as Hrodi continued.

"When I was young, I could swing an axe as well as any warrior, fighting alongside Falruf and his sons in my time. Age has robbed me of my strength and sight. Now my hands shake so much my grandson has to scribe for me. I've been in battle and I know what it's like to be victorious as well as taste defeat. We're beaten here, Brunn. I wish it were otherwise but we've lost and the sooner people realise the truth of it, the fewer people will die. So, like Karas said, for the good of the folk of Olt, yes, I'll bow to King Adalrikr, if he'll spare our lives. I can do nothing more Brunn, and neither can you."

"Don't presume to speak for me, coward," Brunn spat. Old Hrodi looked away, his gnarled hands gripped tight about his stick. Tyrfingr ignored Brunn's outburst, signing and sealing more decrees, which were passed to the three elders of the clan. Finally he looked over at Brunn, still standing defiantly amid the knot of warriors watching him.

"Put him on his knees and hold him," he ordered, rising from his seat and drawing the ugly short sword at his side. Brunn's eyes went wide as he was forced down.

"No," I shouted as Tyrfingr swung the blade. Blood splattered over his men and across the dais, black in the dim light.

"The king's justice," he murmured, wiping the weapon and sheathing it before taking his place once more. I stared at Tyrfingr in horror. The Great Hall had never been a place for executions in all the time Ulfkell's Keep had stood as our holdfast. Lundvarr turned to one side and vomited noisily onto the floor, whilst Hrodi shook worse than ever. Only Sandar maintained his composure, his eyes glittering in the red light of the brazier.

"Mount the head next to the others above the gate," Blackeyes ordered as four of his men removed Brunn's body from the hall. "It will serve as a warning to others. Now, Rothgar, you have waited patiently for your trial. It will be a swift one, I promise."

"If you're hearing my case then I'm sure you're right," I retorted, more boldly than I felt.

"All I mean is the clan moot has already heard the evidence of your guilt. Admittedly, one of the judges has just died at my hand, although that doesn't prevent us from proceeding. Sandar told everyone how you opened the postern gate to allow us access to the keep. Two other witnesses from separate clans also place you there shortly before the alarm was sounded. I have explained how I used you for my own ends. Now, you have your opportunity to plead your case before your people or to confess your crimes."

"By all the gods, Rothgar, confess and have done with this, please," begged Lundvarr, his voice shaking.

"Confess?" I hurled the word at Tyrfingr. "You sit there having murdered my family in this very hall and expect me to admit to your crimes? I'll gladly tell the clan moot what really took place here that night, but you'll never get me to confess."

"I thought you might say that," Blackeyes answered, rising once more from Reave's Chair. This time his sword remained sheathed as he walked to the nearest brazier and began stirring the red hot coals with an iron poker. "You're as stubborn and stupid as your brother. However, once I've asked my questions, I think your elders here will know the truth." It was only then that I understood why the Great Hall was lit by braziers. By the end of the clan moot Sandar, Hrodi and Lundvarr had heard my full and sobbing confession.

CHAPTER 27

The rusted iron crows cage still bore the foul odour of its previous late occupant; an outlaw condemned to death by my brother for murder and rape if I recalled correctly. Every gust of wind stirred the cage, making it rock lazily back and forth, the rough iron rubbing at my naked, torn and tortured flesh. The confines of the cage offered me no respite, forcing me to stand upright, until my trembling muscles finally gave way, leaving me in an undignified slouch, resting awkwardly against the bars. In spring the nights were still cold this far north. After Tyrfingr's men had forced me, screaming, into the cage in the dead of night following my trial, the cool breeze had initially offered some respite from the pain of my burns. The relief was only fleeting, however, with the chill soon causing me to shiver, each movement sending another wave of pain washing over me. Exhausted, I eventually drifted into an uneasy half-sleep.

I awoke as dawn crept across the black sky, slowly filling it with red and green as the sun rose above the horizon. A crow landed on one of the bars, its claws scrabbling against the metal as it sought to find purchase. I looked into its dark eyes as it regarded me with interest, no doubt drawn to the sight of the weeping red wounds that covered my entire body. I bared my teeth in a snarl and the startled bird took flight, perhaps surprised to find I was still alive. Moments later, having recovered from the shock, the crow returned, staking its claim before more of its fellows became aware of the prospective meal Blackeyes had hung outside the main gate.

The crow was not the only visitor, as the guards opened the gate at dawn to admit tradesmen, merchants and travellers into Reavesburg. Their faces were confused and anxious as they found themselves greeted by warriors of the Vorund Clan, with six heads mounted on spikes clearly visible from the walls above the gate. News of the disaster had still to reach most of the small folk, and many soon forgot their business entirely as a growing knot of people gathered to gawk at me. As word spread of who it was hanging there, the crowd began to swell, their reactions a mixture of anger, disbelief and horror.

"Tyrfingr Blackeyes himself rules from Ulfkell's Keep. That's what the guards told me ..."

"Gods protect us. That's Jorik's head up there, with his wife and son ..."

"... betrayed his own brother, that's what I heard. Confessed it all before the elders and when they passed sentence he grabbed a sword and killed Brunn Fourwinds, cold and cruel as you like ..." The speaker had an annoying, nasal voice, though I couldn't make him out in the crowd.

"Are you *that* stupid?" argued one woman. "Think Tyrfingr would mount Brunn's head on the wall if that's what actually happened?"

"Argue all you like. That's what I've been told by men from Lake Tull, who heard it from their elder, Sandar Tindirson, and he was at the clan moot. That's more than you can say, woman."

I closed my eyes, trying to ignore their ignorant chatter. I had more immediate concerns as my black feathered companion was joined by two more crows. The first, emboldened by my lack of resistance, cawed and took a speculative peck through the bars at one of my wounds. I thrashed in the cage, driving him off for a moment. I fell back, exhausted, and after a moment the three crows returned. I heard a woman gasp in the crowd below.

"Mercy. He's still alive."

"Not for long," said the nasal voiced man, the one so convinced of my guilt. "That one's not bound for Navan's

Halls. There will be no room for him at the feast before the time of judgement, not for a kinslayer and a traitor." An angry murmur of assent rippled through the growing throng, whilst others tried to shout them down. There was another distant sound too, growing closer – booted feet marching towards the gate. A column of armoured men and riders was approaching, Tyrfingr Blackeyes at their head, mounted on a powerful destrier. The crowd shrank back in fear and, as they parted to allow his passage, I saw that in addition to the Vorund warriors Karas Greystorm and his men were also in attendance.

"Look carefully, Greystorm," said Tyrfingr. "This fate awaits those who prove to be disloyal to their king." Karas raised his haggard, careworn face and our eyes met. Nuna clung weeping to his arm, her hair dishevelled, with Sigurd supporting her on the other side to prevent my sister from falling. While Katla was also in attendance there was no sign of Amma, and I wondered what had happened to Nuna and Reesha's long-serving maid.

"I've done what I've done to protect your sister," Karas told me in a low voice. "I promise she'll be safe with me at Norlhast Keep. I'm sorry, Rothgar, truly."

He bowed his head and I watched as the Norlhast Clan solemnly filed out through the gate, heading to the docks and their ships, so that they could catch the morning tide. With them went the smaller delegations from Lake Tull, Olt and Noln. Lundvarr practically ran from Reavesburg, his eyes never straying near me, as he fled for the safety of his home. Sandar, however, took the time to pause and look up at me before he left. I wanted to call him a traitor and a liar, the true betrayer of his clan but my strength was spent. The young man seemed to find the wretched sight of me amusing as he turned, shared some joke with his attractive wife and their companions, and rode through the gate without a care in the world.

Tyrfingr sat there in his saddle for a time, drawing obvious satisfaction from my plight. "No words of regret,

Rothgar?" he mocked. "Those crows look hungry to me, so if you have anything you wish to say to your people, I'd get on and say it before they've torn out your eyes and tongue."

My hatred finally roused enough energy to shout back at the man. "You know the clan moot was a sham. I'm innocent," I roared to the crowd. Although some nodded in agreement I was dismayed to see others shaking their heads, already convinced by the lies they had heard.

"Feed him to the crows," shouted one.

"Aye, let him rot. You sold us to Adalrikr."

"Don't say that, you fool," shouted another man. "Can't you see this is all Tyrfingr's doing? Are you going to believe his lies?"

At that remark one of the Vorund warriors moved in, cuffing the speaker and knocking him to the ground. In moments the crowd erupted in violence, fists flying, curses being hurled. In the chaos some people fled, whilst others began throwing dirt and stones at the Vorund Clan. Another group tossed anything that came to hand in my direction. Most of the stones bounced off the bars of the cage, scattering the crows, a few finding their target. Fruit and vegetables intended for the market were also flung in my direction, leaving me splattered and dirty. Eventually the man who spoke in my defence was dragged away, unconscious, whilst the remainder of the crowd were driven back when Blackeyes' warriors drew their weapons and formed a ring around their leader. Tyrfingr looked on dispassionately as the hubbub finally died down, people sullenly melting away back to their homes and families.

I sank a little lower in the cage. Beaten and defeated, I realised I had to know why this fate had been reserved for me. "Why not Jorik?" I asked wearily. "He plotted your downfall, yet you granted him the mercy of a swift death. You did the same with Brunn. Why leave me here to linger?"

"You deserve this fate as the betrayer of your own clan..."

"A lie," I retorted.

Tyrfingr continued as if I hadn't spoken. "Your brother was never a traitor, and if you could ask him I think you'll find that watching his wife and son die was torment enough for any man. However, I'll admit I always wanted revenge against you."

"Revenge?" I was perplexed by that answer.

"You were a sixteen-year-old boy when you fought against me at Noln. I lost more than two score of my men and a ship as well. Do you think King Adalrikr is forgiving when he receives such news? I assure you, he is not, and I paid dearly for that defeat; now it's your turn to suffer. We'll see how long you last up there, watching the remains of your brother and his family rot above the gates." Most of Tyrfingr's warriors fell into line behind him as he turned and rode back towards Ulfkell's Keep. His remaining men took up their position at the gates and the crows, five of them now, settled once more on the bars, their unblinking black eyes watching me.

The crowd was gone, although a steady stream of men, women and children wended their way through the gates as the morning passed, with their wagons and carts full of wares bound for the town. I earned many curious faces and a few choice remarks, some of these visitors not even recognising who I was. I shuddered painfully at the noise of flapping wings around my cage, as my friends, the crows, gathered in greater numbers than ever. Flies had also begun to buzz around me in the increasing warmth of the sun, their tiny feet tickling as they landed to inspect my sores. Gods, I had been proud of my victory on the sands of Noln and this was my reward – Tyrfingr's vengeance would see me eaten alive, unless I died of thirst or exposure first. I closed my eyes, willing myself away from this, all the while knowing it was futile. The sound of sobbing drifted up to me as my cage swayed gently in the light wind. I looked down and saw Desta standing below me, Haarl at her side.

No, I thought. *No, Desta, go back to Ulfkell's Keep. I*

didn't say a word about you to Tyrfingr, even when the brands were burning into my flesh. Don't linger here and undo all that by standing vigil. I looked away.

"There, you've seen him now, Desta," said Haarl. "Won't do you no good to linger here, though." *Haarl's right, Desta, I thought to myself. Please, listen to him.* The sobbing continued, low and quiet, and I knew the guards at the gate were listening.

"Go," I shouted, my cry sending the crows wheeling about the cage, although this time they settled again before I even finished speaking. "Haven't you seen enough? Or are you going to stand there all day to watch me die?" Desta looked aghast at me as I drove the point home. "I don't want you here, Haarl. If our friendship meant anything at all then don't come back here again, and take the serving wench with you. Her bawling is the last thing I need to hear."

Haarl shifted uncomfortably, chewing his lip. "Come on, Desta," he muttered. "He's right. You don't want to see this." He slid his arm around her shoulders and gently led her back towards Ulfkell's Keep. I felt desolate as the pair walked away, Desta's tear-stained face looking back more than once until she rounded a corner and disappeared from view. I felt some relief, as well as degree of guilt I couldn't say goodbye in the way I wanted. Still, all too soon none of that would matter.

As the day wore on the guards would occasionally call up scornfully, mocking me crudely in order to pass the time. Such was my discomfort I hardly heard their words. My throat was raw and my mouth parched. No one offered me anything to drink and as the sun climbed higher, my thirst became worse, whilst the sun's rays slowly burned my exposed flesh as it followed its lazy arc through a bright blue spring sky. I closed my eyes, all sounds dimming and becoming more distant except for one.

Peck. Peck peck. There was an angry caw as two crows briefly fought to find the best vantage point to probe with their beaks through the bars. Peck peck. Each time they returned for a morsel of flesh I felt a sharp stabbing pain. After a while that dulled too. I shook the cage and tried to move away from the birds. It was futile, since a crows cage is aptly named, its design too constricting for me to be able to defend myself. I took perverse pleasure in the fact that the open wounds on my body were a more attractive delicacy than my eyes and face, which Tyrfingr had deliberately left unharmed during my torture. He wanted no one to be in any doubt who hung outside the gates of Reavesburg.

Peck. Caw, caw. The flapping of wings announced more arrivals seeking the best perch on the bars and I hardly cared. When pain is all you can feel, the thought that soon it will all be over has its attractions. Navan would greet me soon enough, and I would be re-united with my brother. As I thought of Jorik, I recalled his last words. *"Did you really lead Blackeyes here tonight to kill my wife ... and murder my child?"* Darri told me Navan hands over every soul to the Creator for judgement at the end of time. What would Jorik say to me when we met in the afterlife? My own brother had questioned whether I betrayed him with his dying words. My hatred burned hot once more and I thrashed in the cage, driving the crows away for a moment's respite.

Who was the real traitor? Sandar had lied to the clan moot but what advantage did he gain from placing Tyrfingr Blackeyes on Reave's Chair? Reavesburg had always defended Lake Tull's people since before Ulfkell's Keep was built, so why would Sandar turn traitor now? I found it hard to believe he was acting alone. Was the game more complex than I knew? Gautarr had resorted to treachery once already during my brother's rule, sending his own men against Jorik's ships. Was Etta right to believe Gautarr would never treat with the Vorund Clan? Gautarr's opportunity as a potential chief might have passed after his duel with Jorik. However, his son, Ragnar, was also ambitious.

Then there was Karas, now my brother-in-law. Greystorm had kept his seat at Norlhast Keep and with the offer of Kalamar's return his lands had actually increased. Had Norlhast's chief played both sides, pretending he was Jorik's ally, whilst secretly dealing with our foe to avoid a war he didn't believe he could win? After all, it was Sigurd's serving woman who had testified against me. Had my sister married the real traitor, a man I thought of as a friend? *Nuna, what will happen to you? You wanted to be the lady of Norlhast Keep. Will you also bear the sons of a man who conspired to murder your family?*

What did any of it really matter? I was done and my time grew short as darkness crept across the sky. It became colder and I felt the world around me melting away as the crows continued their squabbles. I was beyond feeling anything now, the pain dimming with my vision. As I closed my eyes, my last thought was of Desta.

CHAPTER 28

Agonising pain lanced up my back and I woke with a shout. Half-awake I gasped in fear, feeling as I did my dry lips crack, my body ingeniously finding a way to increase my torment one further notch. I tried to rise but the effort was too much and my head fell back with a thump against some sort of solid surface. I tried to keep still, although for some reason my body was swaying from side to side, each tiny movement causing me further discomfort.

"Damn it. If he cries out like that again they'll hear us back in Ulfkell's Keep." The voice was unfamiliar, the tone urgent rather than panicking. It was dark and I was unable to make out much of my surroundings. I was lying on something hard and felt so very cold, despite being huddled up under thick blankets.

"Rothgar. Can you hear me? It's Etta, lad. You're safe with us but you need to keep quiet." *Etta?* I sought to place the name, my fogged mind refusing to clear. She sounded like an old woman. Peering up from under the blankets all I could make out was a black shape above me, silhouetted against the stars in the night sky. Behind her I could dimly make out the twisted fingers of tree branches, slowly moving past as my body tortuously rocked one way then the other. I realised I was lying on a cart, trundling slowly down the road.

Now I concentrated I could hear the soft *thud thud* of the horses' hooves and the rumble of the cart wheels, as the animal pulled us along. Moments later the first speaker, a younger man, called out "Halt there, girl. That's it. Steady now, halt." The cart came to a stop with a gentle jolt that still wracked by body with pain. I gritted my teeth as a groan escaped my lips.

"What are you stopping for, Ekkill? We need to be away."

"Not with him in this condition. We can barely travel at walking pace and Blackeyes' men will be after us at first light, if not before. We need to reach those horses and quickly – and even if we do get there he's in no fit state to ride one."

"What did you think you'd find?" Etta's voice cracked like a whip. "He's been tortured and hung from a crows cage."

"And better for him and us if the crows had finished the job they'd started," reasoned the man. "I did what you asked. I freed him from that infernal cage. I thought you wanted to give him a decent burial so his soul could rest in peace. I never thought to find him in there *alive.* Even so, this lad's as good as dead – Blackeyes saw to that before he even hung him from the gates. Nothing either of us can do about it now, other than do him the kindness of a quick, clean death."

"Please," I tried to say, the word coming out as a wheeze. As I lay there listening while they debated my fate, I realised I preferred Ekkill's argument. Anything would be better than the pain and a chill was creeping through my flesh, deep into my bones. I shivered, another mistake, one over which I had no control, and I writhed in agony once more.

I must have shouted out again, although I had no recollection of doing so, for Ekkill leaned in close, whispering "Make another noise, boy, and I'll make sure it's your last. I've no quarrel with you, son, but I've a mighty desire to stay alive and no wish to end my days on account of you. Honestly, it would be a mercy. Do you want that? Do you want me to show you mercy?"

"You forget yourself, Ekkill. I give the orders and you're paid to obey them," Etta snapped.

"You don't pay me enough to die on account of his hollering bringing a score of Vorund's warriors down on us in the dead of night."

I felt rather than saw Ekkill clamber over the cart, his shadow moving above me next to Etta's. There was the unmistakable sound of steel being drawn and I caught a glimpse of his knife in the moonlight. I felt no fear; Ekkill was right, it would be a mercy to end this torment. Etta hissed as she too saw the blade and there was a sharp slap of flesh on flesh as she caught the man's wrist in her bony grip. Of course, *Etta*. Counsellor to the Reavesburg chief, except there was no chief any more. Now the old crone was interfering in my life once again, or at least what was left of it.

"Put that away, or a score of Blackeyes' men will be the least of your concerns, I can assure you." Etta's voice was strong and full of menace and Ekkill recoiled from her. When he spoke, he sounded sulky and fearful of the frail old woman.

"Alright. Alright, I hear you but you must see we can't carry on like this."

"No," Etta conceded. "We can't. Bring me that pouch over there. It contains the powdered remains of gildcrest mushrooms, so take care not to spill any."

"You want to *poison* him? A blade would be cleaner."

"No, I don't want to poison him. Mixed with shadow root it can be used to place a man into what some refer to as the dreamless sleep. It may buy us the time we need to reach Joldir."

"If he ever wakes up," Ekkill objected. "You're gambling with his life. Get the dosage wrong ..."

"Just help me prepare this and do it quickly, while he's still able to drink it." Etta barked.

I lay there whilst the pair of them moved out of sight, whispering together. I was unconcerned whether they successfully managed to prepare this particular concoction. If I had understood correctly, it would let me escape my broken body, one way or the other. When I felt a hand under my neck lift me upright, I tried not to protest and sipped weakly at the cup of brackish water, swallowing the mixture as quickly as I could. As the first mouthful hit the back of my throat I wanted to gag, taking a deep breath as I somehow kept the stuff down.

"Good." Etta said. "You should feel better soon. This

will take the edge off the pain, and you'll want to sleep in just a moment. Don't fight it." Etta was right, the pain was already dulling and I felt a wave of dizziness wash over me. The stars seemed to waver and swirl before my eyes, leaving green, red and blue trails of light in their wake. Etta and Ekkill continued to discuss how best to manage my rescue, though I hardly cared. My eyelids felt so heavy I was powerless to prevent them closing, so I only caught fragments of their conversation as I became lost in a whirlpool of colours.

"... then tie him to the saddle ... As long as ..."

"... you'll kill him – one way or the other ..."

"I thought that was your plan anyway. Now do as I say ..."

**

The singing was beautiful, its soothing cadence bringing me out of the depths of my nightmares. I was too frightened to think back upon what I had seen there and held onto the song instead, although the words slipped through my fingers. Finally the music ended, and I felt soft hands brush my damp hair away from my face, their touch gentle and cool against the burning heat of my skin.

"It calms him," said a voice – the voice of a young woman. "He has such terrible dreams and singing seems to help. I told you he could hear us."

"Perhaps," mused another stranger, this one a man. "Only time will tell."

I opened my eyes and found I was lying on a bed in a darkened room. My skin felt as if it was on fire, my limbs too weak and heavy to move. Slowly my eyes focussed on a figure standing at the end of my bed, a tall man – his short brown hair peppered with grey – who was in turn regarding me carefully.

"Where am I?" I croaked, my throat raw and scratchy from thirst. The man peered down at me and laughed, whilst the sound of fluttering wings filled the room, black feathers swallowing the light as they swirled about me. I screamed and tried to put up my hands only to discover that I was tied to the bed. The tall man peered closer at me with eyes black as coal, his mouth now replaced by the sharp beak of a crow. He cawed and plunged his beak down towards my face. I closed my eyes, screaming all the while, until my mind fled into the darkness once more.

***

Nereth stalked me down the shadowy corridors of Ulfkell's Keep, her beguiling voice softly calling my name. I knew it was a trap, so I took to the secret passageways I used as a boy. They were less easy to navigate as a grown man, and soon my clothes were dirty and torn as I squeezed deeper and deeper into the network of gloomy tunnels.

"Rothgar." Nereth's voice was little more than a whisper, yet I could have sworn I felt her breath on my neck. I spun around, eyes straining to pierce the darkness, finding I was alone. I reached down to my belt, cursing as I discovered there was no sword hanging by my side, no dagger in its sheath. Defenceless, I knew I had to hide, so I pressed further on, wending my way ever downwards into the complex that ran under the dungeons of the keep. Perhaps only Etta knew these tunnels better than I did, and I felt safe as I retraced my familiar boyhood steps. The lower levels were my own special haunt and not even Bram and Bandor had been this far down with me. Moving more confidently now, I took a left turn I knew would bring me to a small winding stair leading into the North Tower. My heart missed a beat as I almost ran headlong into a blank stone wall, running with damp. I cursed as I realised I had miscounted the turnings and somewhere nearby I thought I heard laughter. Feeling sick with fear, I turned and began to backtrack. After only a dozen yards another solid wall blocked the route I had taken just moments before. Now the corridor resounded with Nereth's mocking laughter, the very air vibrating as the shadows coalesced, weaving themselves together into the shape of a woman. I stumbled backwards in mounting horror as Nereth took form, feeling the unyielding stonework behind me of a wall I knew should not even be there. *It's only a dream, just a nightmare,* I assured myself as Nereth walked slowly towards me.

"No Rothgar, for both of us this is real. Now, tell me, where have you been hiding? Tyrfingr Blackeyes is anxious to know what's become of you." Nereth's pale hand reached out and a finger traced the outline of my face. Slowly she ran her touch down my body, following the line of the scar on my chest. I cried out in pain and fear, as I watched Nereth's beautiful face light up in triumph. "All too easy; I confess to being a little disappointed."

Without warning there was a deafening crash and the roof of the tunnel collapsed with a roar, huge pieces of stonework smashing into the ground all around me. Nereth recoiled with a cry of fear before vanishing under the great weight of rock. Dust filled the far end of the corridor where I sat crouched in terror, awaiting a fatal blow from the falling masonry. After a few moments, when the ringing in my ears had ceased, I realised all was still. Slowly I stood up in the cramped space, glancing hopelessly at the jumble of stone barring my path. I laughed grimly – even if I was able to shift the debris I would only uncover another dead end. The laughter died in my throat when I heard the sound of stone shifting and saw a faint trickle of earth as the pile of rock began to move.

"Don't just stand there," barked a voice next me. I spun around to confront the tall man once more, his face still disfigured by the crow's beak. I shrank back, shaking my head as one of the larger pieces of stone at the top of the rock pile became dislodged and rolled past my feet. The crow man was standing suspended in emptiness just beyond a hole in the wall of the corridor. "Step through and I can close this doorway so she can never follow you."

Although I wanted to believe him I was unable to tear my eyes away from that razor-sharp beak. I dimly heard fluttering wings, claws scratching on metal and the angry cawing of the crows squabbling over the choicest morsels of my flesh. The man reached out his hand, inches away from me in the tight confines of what remained of the passageway. There was a grinding sound as another, larger, piece of rock was shoved out of the way and bounced down onto the floor. A bloodied slender hand, covered in dirt, clawed at the air with broken fingers.

"It would be unwise to let her see me," the crow man said. "Come now or I must leave you to her."

I can't say what made me trust him at that moment. I seized his hand and he pulled me through the doorway, which snapped shut, plunging us both into impenetrable darkness. I felt the crow man's arms wrapping themselves around me as we began to plummet through black space, the wind rushing past my face. Somewhere far below, I thought I heard singing.

CHAPTER 29

The crow took flight from the branches of a long-dead tree in the sacred grove, catching the wind as it turned this way and that, rising on the unseen currents of air. Down below lay the fortress of Ulfkell's Keep, cut by men long ago from the dark stone, rocks piled high, one upon the other. The crow headed towards the keep, drawing closer until it wheeled about the tall North Tower, descending in a wide spiral before alighting in the courtyard outside the Great Hall. Inside there was the sound of singing and laughter and the crow hopped forwards, ungainly on its clawed feet, though still fast enough to scurry through the main doors and disappear inside unseen.

The Great Hall was packed with men, its air thick with the smell of their sweat and their sour, beer-tainted breath. There was something else in the air too, a faint smell the crow knew well, coiling through that darkened space amid the more pleasant scents of baked bread, roasted meats and spiced fruits. There was fear here, fear and blood. The crow flew up into the rafters of the hall, looking down on the scores of men lining the long tables. Watching over them, sitting casually in an old wooden chair, sat a dark-haired man, flanked by guards. Another man was kneeling before him, bloodied and beaten, hands tied tightly behind his back. He was tall and strong – a warrior of the Reavesburg Clan. And he was afraid.

***

Djuri looked up into Tyrfingr's dark eyes, wanting to face his enemy like a man. It was hard to show defiance to your foes after they'd spent a week beating you senseless, day and night. One of Djuri's eyes was swollen and bruised, forcing it closed. He had bitten his tongue at one point, making his words clumsy and painful when he tried to form them on his broken lips. The only parts of his body that didn't hurt were his hands; numb and lifeless from the ropes binding his wrists tightly together.

Things had been altogether different when Djuri was raiding the shores of Vorund last year, fighting alongside his chief, Jorik, and great warriors such as Finnvidor Einarrson, Johan Jokellsward and Brunn Fourwinds. All dead or fled now. Djuri was fearless when he fought in those battles – he had never felt more alive than in those exhilarating moments, as Jorik led his men ashore. Having your enemy in your own home, though, that was something else. And he'd been on guard duty when it happened ...

A sharp crack to the back of his head left him seeing stars as he pitched over onto his face, to guffaws from those assembled in the hall. Tyrfingr had been speaking to him and Djuri hadn't heard the question.

"How hard did you beat him, Galin?" Tyrfingr asked the warrior to his right, a broad red-bearded young man with his left arm in a sling. Djuri had heard of Galin in the days following the fall of Reavesburg. Blackeyes' second-in-command, who'd lost a hand as punishment for allowing Johan's ships to escape on the night of the wedding. It was hard to live with failure, something Djuri understood all too well. He was sure it fuelled Galin's treatment of him down in the dungeons.

"He's a big bastard," Galin answered. "They always think they're the ones who can take it, tough it out with you. They're always wrong. It just took a while with this one."

"Indeed." Tyrfingr rose from his chair and walked down the steps of the dais to stand in front of Djuri, who had been hauled back onto his knees by the two guards on either side of him. Up close Djuri could see his misshapen reflection in those dark, wholly black eyes. It was said Blackeyes consorted with witches and demons, those who had heeded Adalrikr's call to arms and flocked to his banner. Djuri could believe it, staring into that unwholesome, pale face.

"Yet he claims to know nothing concerning Rothgar's disappearance, despite being broken by you in the dungeons?"

"He claims to have spent all night in one of the wharfside taverns," Galin replied warily. "Several of our own men saw him drink himself into a stupor that night. He didn't rouse himself until midday."

Tyrfingr Blackeyes regarded Galin for a time before speaking. "A fact you only decided to check *after* spending a week beating him?"

Galin shrugged. "What does it matter? Leaving someone like this living free in Reavesburg is dangerous. He should have been executed, along with the others ..." The one-handed warrior's words trailed off as he saw Blackeyes' expression.

"Is that what you imagine a conqueror does?" A hush had fallen over the Great Hall. Djuri's breathing sounded loud in his chest as he listened. "We could have put everyone in Reavesburg to death, of course. Massacred the merchant port of Noln and sailed upriver to burn out the farmers and fishermen of Lake Tull. You can only take the possessions from a dead man once. You speak as a raider, Galin. Your king requires you to make these people his subjects, not his slaves. Loyal subjects pay their taxes, year on year, which swells your kings' coffers and brings us more power. What would you do? Gather together a flock of sheep and a few trinkets and baubles and sail back with them to Vorund Fastness? Do you think Adalrikr would be satisfied with such offerings? He requires us to build his kingdom in the north, and that starts here in Reavesburg."

Tyrfingr smiled and looked down at Djuri with those dark, fathomless eyes. "My terms to Jorik were fair. He rejected them and his arrogance brought all this to pass. Now his brief time as chief is over; Reave's Chair has passed to me as Adalrikr's jarl. You will find me more forgiving than my reputation, but do not forget that to defy me is to defy your king. And your king is not a forgiving man. I spilled blood in this hall, the blood of traitors. Your king merely demands loyalty from his subjects. What are you, Djuri? A loyal subject, or a traitor to your king?"

Death was the honourable course for a warrior, the course Djuri's friend Brunn had chosen. Djuri swallowed, remembering the stories of Brunn Fourwinds' defiance at Rothgar's trial, the true story Haarl had brought to him from the spyholes of Ulfkell's Keep, where the young man had watched events unfold. Haarl, who had already bent the knee to serve in Blackeyes' household. That lad was brighter than people thought. Folk spoke fondly of Brunn's memory, but what had his defiance at the clan moot earned him other than a pointless death?

Djuri licked his dry lips. He felt so tired. Most of his friends had cast him aside, blaming him for not preventing Jorik's murder that night. After all, they kept telling him, he had been on watch. People wanted someone to blame for their ills and Djuri and Haarl had been easy targets. Djuri could understand their anger, he supposed, which had left him drinking from the cheapest barrels down in the worst taverns before his arrest. Despite turning their backs on him those same people still scraped and bowed every time Tyrfingr and his men walked the streets of Reavesburg.

"And if I was ... If I was to become a loyal subject, what then?" The words were easier to say than Djuri expected.

Tyrfingr smiled without warmth. "I'm sure we can find a use for you. Is that what we have before us? A loyal subject of King Adalrikr?"

Djuri nodded wearily, hardly hearing the laughter and catcalls in the hall.

"A wise decision, Djuri. Very wise." Tyrfingr clapped his hands. "Servants. Bring us more food and drink. Let us have music and songs for my men."

Djuri was lifted onto his feet before the crowd, where he stood unsteadily, trying to take in what had just happened. He winced in pain as his bonds were cut and blood flowed back into his hands. Darri was ushered inside, limping down the hall, along with a number of scared-looking players. Behind came the serving women, carrying trays laden with meats, bread and ale for the men. Djuri recognised Desta, her face drawn and pale, as she approached Tyrfingr himself. She set the food before him, with just a tremble of her hands betraying her nerves. Before she could withdraw Blackeyes' hand closed around hers, drawing her closer.

"Tell me, pretty one, what's your name?"

***

I was awake, tears running down my face. My hands were clenched, gripping so tightly to my blankets it took real effort to force them to relax. My dream about Djuri had been incredibly vivid, the memory remaining so fresh and sharp I had to keep telling myself over and over it was only a dream. I lay there for a long time and the room gradually became brighter with the first light of dawn. The fever had passed and I was no longer tied to the bed. Since I felt so weak it hardly mattered, lacking the strength to even lift my hand to my face. Instead I slowly turned my head towards the brightening source of light, a half-shuttered window that allowed pale yellow sunlight to fill half the room, tiny motes of dust drifting lazily in its beams. The cold air smelled fresh and I could hear something outside. *Grunt, swish, clunk. Grunt, swish, clunk.* The three sounds repeated over and over and it took me a while to realise someone was splitting logs. A goat bleated from further off, provoking a series of belligerent retorts from its fellows.

I was so tired my body refused to obey my commands when I tried to move; I had never felt so frail and ill. I occupied myself by looking closer at the room I was in. The wooden floors were covered here and there with Oomrhani rugs that might once have passed for finery, although they had obviously seen many long years of hard use. The wooden walls were bare, save for a small fireplace set into one of them, whilst there was a single window and a closed door on the opposite wall. A table had been set against another wall, with three assorted chairs around it, whilst near my bed was a smaller table with a white ceramic bowl placed on top, a white cloth neatly folded next to it. I became aware of another smell too, one competing with the fresh air flowing in from the half-open window. It was the smell of disease, of a wound gone foul. It clung to the bedclothes in which I was wrapped, and fear washed over me. Bile rose in my throat and I coughed, spluttering and choking on the burning taste. Unable to so much as turn on my side, I was forced to spit down my chin, struggling to draw breath. Panicking, I finally found the strength to roll over in the bed, thrashing to free myself from the constricting blankets. The bowl next to me went flying, smashing into pieces as I retched up the watery contents of my stomach onto the wooden floor, mixed in with specks of dark blood. At that moment the door flew open with a crash.

"Joldir. Joldir, come quickly, he's awake." I felt hands around my shoulders, pulling me further over onto my side. I began to choke once more, truly afraid now. Was this how my life was going to end, choking on my own vomit? My arms flailed weakly as stronger ones held them tight and I retched once more onto the floor. I heard someone else come running into the room and felt their hands roll me back onto the damp mattress. My body shook and I became aware of how much everything hurt as I greedily gulped in air. Sweat broke out on my brow.

"Lie still, it's alright. You're safe with us but you *must* lie still. They hurt you terribly and you need to take your time to recover." It was a young woman who spoke, her voice familiar.

"How ... bad?" I gasped. "The smell ... Please ... I've fought in battles ... I know what can happen."

"Lie still." A man spoke this time. I looked up and saw the tall man once more. As I watched, his kindly face grew longer and turned black, until he opened his beak and cawed loudly. I screamed hoarsely and tried to fend him off. He was too strong for me, his open maw glistening redly, as he bent down and pecked the flesh from my face.

CHAPTER 30

When I next awoke it was dark, the room cool and lit only by the dying light of the fire, whilst a woman sang softly, her fingers plucking delicately at the strings of a lyre. It took me a moment to realise I knew the song – the tale of Sigborn Reaveson and his journey to the Fire Isle, where he earned the name Dragonslayer. It had been one of my favourites as a young boy in Ulfkell's Keep, and Darri had indulged my requests often enough that I knew the words off by heart. A smile broke across my face, until the memories of my former home and what had transpired there wiped it away. I let out a sigh and the singing stopped.

"Rothgar?"

My voice was hoarse from long disuse. "You play beautifully. For a moment I thought I was ... back home ..." I tried to sit up and to my surprise I found I could, although my arms shook with the effort. The woman leaned towards me and helped me ease myself into a comfortable position. In the dim light I could make out little other than her long hair, which brushed against my bare chest. The sensation was odd, my flesh feeling tight and numb. "You know my name," I remarked.

"Yes. Etta brought you with her from Reavesburg. This is a safe place and you can remain here for as long as you wish." Her voice sounded as lovely when she spoke as when she was singing, her tone rich and cultured. I thought back to those nightmares and knew then who it was that called to me in those dark times.

"I heard you. I heard you when you sang to me, when I was dreaming and felt lost in my nightmares. You brought me back."

"Joldir is the one you should thank, as well as Etta and Ekkill who brought you to us. Everyone thought you were going to die, except Joldir. He said you were strong and he was right, even when the fever had you in its grip all those weeks. And then you had such terrible nightmares, and the only thing that seemed to soothe you were the songs." She laughed, the pleasant sound rippling throughout the room. "My fingers are quite sore; I don't think I've ever had such a demanding audience, requesting a performance morning, noon and night."

"Did you say you've seen Etta? Is she here?"

"Nearby. You'll see her soon, when you're ready." So she'd done it. I had to admit I was impressed and could only admire the tenacity of the old woman, to somehow contrive a way to evade Tyrfingr Blackeyes and bring me here.

"I'm sorry," I said, throat dry as I coughed. "I don't know your name, even though you seem to have been at my bedside … did you say for *weeks*?"

"You've been badly hurt. I won't lie to you, Blackeyes has done … No, I'm sorry, all that can wait. My name's Arissa. I'm glad you're finally back with us. Etta's been frantic with worry; she'll be so happy to hear you've broken the fever and finally woken up." Despite Arissa's cheerful tone memories of a darkened room began to fill my mind, the pale faces of Sandar, Lundvarr and Hrodi looking on in horror, as Tyrfingr Blackeyes' red hot iron scored its way slowly over my flesh, time and again, long after I had confessed my part in my brother's murder. I gingerly ran a trembling hand across my chest. Much of my body was bandaged and where there was flesh open to the air I could only feel rough scabs and thick fresh scars beneath my fingers. My shoulder stretched painfully tight at the same time and Arissa moved swiftly, gently placing my arm back down beside me.

"Gods. What have they done to me?" I half-sobbed, pain rushing at me from every extremity, clamouring for attention.

"Help me, please."

"Shush. There is no one better skilled in the healing arts than Joldir, I promise you. You'll be strong and well again, in time." I took hold of Arissa's hand and held it tightly, fighting back the memories threatening to overwhelm me. Instead I recalled Arissa's singing and imagined myself curled up in Desta's arms, safe in my chambers in the North Tower, back in a time that now seemed to belong to another age altogether.

***

The crow flew north, which made me angry because I'd only caught a glimpse of Desta in my dreams so far. Ulfkell's Keep was far away to the south, retreating with each beat of the bird's wings. Somewhere, far off, I thought I could hear singing before the sound slowly faded away.

Nuna sat at table in Norlhast Keep, her food untouched, hands knotted together to stop biting her fingernails, a bad habit Katla was forever scolding her over. She was alone apart from her husband, Karas, who sat opposite. Her *husband*, the word still took some getting used to. Yet Karas Greystorm was her only family now, after ... that night. Her hands clenched more tightly, knuckles standing out stark white against the rich blue of her dress. Karas reached across the table and placed one of his thin hands over hers, giving them a gentle squeeze.

"You must eat, my love." The words were tender and kind. Karas had been nothing else since they left Ulfkell's Keep and set sail for her new home. It didn't help her feel any closer to him.

There was a knock at the door, which echoed loudly around the near-empty hall in which they were dining. Without waiting for the keep's servants, Styrman and Ottama, the doors were pushed open and Valdimarr, Adalrikr's emissary in Norlhast, entered the room, flanked by a dozen guards. Sigurd stepped from the shadows, hand on the hilt of his sword, and interposed himself between Valdimarr and Karas. Valdimarr was a short round man in his middle years. He had thick dark hair that was balding on top, so the torchlight reflected off the sweat beading on his head. Evidently Valdimarr had arrived in something of a hurry.

"My lord." Valdimarr uttered those two small words with such obvious contempt Nuna wanted nothing more than to stab him. From the look on Sigurd's face, Nuna guessed he felt the same way.

"We are dining, Valdimarr," Karas said evenly. "Can this wait?"

"I regret to say it is a matter of some urgency, requiring the jarl of Norlhast to dispense the king's justice." Valdimarr's voice had an oily, obsequious tone that made Nuna grind her teeth.

"As I said, can't this wait until after we have eaten?"

"No, my lord, it cannot. Some men have been arrested this evening, caught fomenting discontent and denying King Adalrikr's right to rule Norlhast."

Karas frowned. "What men? What evidence has been brought against them and who is their accuser?"

Valdimarr smiled indulgently, as if talking to a child. "They are no men of consequence. Whalers, I understand, who were a little the worse for wear after spending the night drinking. However, in my experience drink merely loosens the tongue, causing people to say what they *really* think, when their guard is lowered. Such talk cannot be tolerated."

Nuna felt Karas' hand tighten around hers. "Indeed. Well, the hour is growing late. Have them brought here tomorrow and I will hear from these men and consider the case against them."

"Ah." Valdimarr cleared his throat, allowing the pause that followed to stretch on interminably before continuing. "This matter is best dealt with now, my lord. Three of my own guards heard the men say things concerning the king that, frankly, cannot go unpunished."

"They said our king was a murderer and unfit to rule," supplied one of the warriors behind Valdimarr, who nodded his encouragement. "Then they began talking about it being the time for Norlhast to rise up, and drive the Vorund Clan from their lands. They also said that the jarl of Norlhast was a weakling, one who had failed his people time and again. They went as far as to say that, when the time came, his head would adorn a spike on Norlhast Keep, alongside the king's emissary."

"You see the extent of their treason," gushed Valdimarr. "They slight both you and our king. And they go further, speaking directly against him and plotting an uprising, no less. The evidence is damning and there can be only one sentence for such a crime. One sentence that must, of course, be passed by you as the jarl of Norlhast."

"I see. How many stand accused?" Karas asked, his voice quiet.

"Six in all. I have not yet interrogated their families at this stage. However, I tend to find such thinking breeds all too easily within the confines of the family. Perhaps this plot extends further than these six men. I could, of course, conduct investigations and discover the truth. Their siblings, wives and children might all be implicated, in which case I would recommend they too suffer the harshest punishment. I would suggest it is important to set an example to the rest of the people. If you wish to hear the matter tomorrow that would allow me to arrest the families of these traitors. They could be put to the question tonight and, by morning, you would be a position to pass sentence on *all* of them."

Karas sat there, staring at Valdimarr, who smiled back at him. Nuna's hands were aching with the force of her husband's grip. "Hang them," Karas told Valdimarr. "Hang the six whalers your men heard commit these crimes. There's no need to bring their wider families into this matter."

"A matter most excellently handled, my lord, showing both admirable mercy and restraint. I will attend to these malcontents within the hour. Do enjoy the rest of your evening meal." With that Valdimarr gave the barest hint of a bow before turning to leave the hall.

You did not fight them then. You do not fight them now. You left my brother in a cage to die and walked out through the gates without a backwards glance, bringing me here, to live like this. Nuna drew her hands away from Karas, more sharply than she intended, catching the white cloth on the table and sending her plate crashing to the floor. Red wine spilled from her goblet, staining the cloth. Ottama was there in moments, clearing away the mess. Nuna didn't wait for her to finish, rising and running off to her chambers, ignoring Karas' calls as she shouldered her way past Valdimarr.

***

The hour was late when there was a knock at her door. Katla answered it, and Nuna could hear the voice of her guard, Brosa, outside before Kalfr was ushered into her room. The stocky warrior smiled at her and, pleased to see him again, she felt her anger begin to melt away. Rothgar had spoken well of Kalfr Albriktson, and Nuna wasn't going to forget that this was a man who had helped her brother and stood by him.

"You've got the servants gossiping again, my lady," Kalfr grinned, creasing the thin scar on his face.

"I've had the lecture from Albrikt already, Kalfr. I don't need to hear it from you too."

Kalfr sighed and lowered himself into a chair by the window, gesturing for Nuna to join him. "My father was giving you good advice. You need to consider how all this appears to Valdimarr."

Nuna folded her arms and set her face stubbornly. "Why do I care what that odious man thinks?"

"You should care about *anything* that displeases Valdimarr, since he's Adalrikr's creature. People will expect you to be grieving for your family in the weeks after Tyrfingr Blackeyes' victory. Even so, you need to have a care, my lady. That display this evening was poorly judged. Valdimarr will regard it as defiance against his rule –"

"You forget yourself," Nuna interjected. "My husband is the jarl of Norlhast."

Kalfr sat forward and jabbed his finger at Nuna. "Your husband's no more a jarl than my four-year-old son, Varinn. Don't pretend you don't know that. You're a bright girl, Nuna. It's time you started acting like the lady of Norlhast Keep, for all our sakes."

Tears welled up in Nuna's eyes. "He ordered his own people to be sent to the gallows," she whispered.

"The way I heard it from Sigurd, he saved their families from the same fate. Karas had no choice. Do you really want Valdimarr in sole charge here in Norlhast? He's dangerous – cruel and all too fond of killing on a whim. At least this way, Karas can temper his actions. How do you think it looks if Karas can't control his own young, headstrong bride and prevent her from openly defying Valdimarr's decrees?" Kalfr sat back in his chair, looking tired as he rubbed his temples. "You must see how this plays perfectly into Valdimarr's hands and gives him the excuse he needs to be rid of you, and perhaps even Karas himself. Please, tell me you can see that."

Nuna nodded. "I know," she conceded. "I know. But I can't forget …" The tears were falling freely now. "Kalfr … I lost my brothers, my sister-in-law, my nephew … And the things they said about Rothgar at the end … how they executed him as a traitor."

Kalfr sighed. "I knew Rothgar well and I don't believe one word of that tale, and neither should you. Remember, Karas could do nothing to prevent any of this. Everyone who could fled that night – Gautarr Falrufson, Johan Jokellsward. They're good, brave men. Renowned warriors of Reavesburg, and the best they could do that night was flee for their lives. Karas' actions saved yours. Do you honestly think it was *easy* for him to bend the knee to Blackeyes? That this life is what he wants? This isn't about what we want, Nuna, it's about our survival."

Nuna knotted her fingers together, steadying her breathing and bringing her emotions under control. She thought back on her behaviour with a pang of regret. She knew this already, of course, but Kalfr's words had woken her from the madness and anger that wove itself through her grief.

She stood, clasping Kalfr's large rough hands in her own. "You're as good a man as Rothgar said, Kalfr Albriktson. You serve the lady of Norlhast Keep more loyally than she deserves."

The scene grew dark as a growing shadow fell across the room. Rothgar no longer saw events through his sister's eyes as the Crow Man took shape, unseen by Nuna, Kalfr or Katla.

"It's unwise for you to be here," the Crow Man told me. "Unwise and dangerous. It's time for you to come away."

I was powerless to resist and the world dissolved before my eyes, fading away as I was drawn into a deep, dreamless sleep.

CHAPTER 31

When Joldir opened the door to my small room I started awake with a painful jolt, noting with relief that at least the man no longer wore the crow's beak I'd seen in my fevered imaginations. Joldir's face had an honest and friendly look and I suppose he would be thought of by some as handsome: he certainly looked much better than I did. He was a relatively young man, perhaps in his middle thirties, though when he spoke he sounded older. That morning Joldir calmly explained how close I'd come to death, and how far I still had to go on the road to recovery.

"It's important your wounds are given air, so they do not fester under your bandages. We should be able to remove the last of them in a few days. Until then I would urge you to leave them alone. Drink plenty of water, mixed with a little wine and a small preparation of my own and this should, if Ilanasa is willing, prevent a further poisoning of your blood."

I nodded, too afraid to want to see what lay beneath the bandages, if this was worse than the injuries I'd seen so far. "Where am I?" I asked instead.

"You're in my home, in Lindos – a place I built with my own hands," Joldir told me with a self-satisfied air. "You're my guest, at least until you're well enough to think about where you might want to make your own home."

"Lindos … I think I've have heard the name but I couldn't say where it is," I admitted. I was sure Etta had mentioned the place when she was tutoring me, and imagined her shaking her head in despair at her inattentive pupil.

"It's one of the lost cities of the north, from before the Fallen Age," Joldir explained. "Little remains of it now. When you're stronger perhaps I can show you some of the ruins. We're up in a valley lying in the eastern spur of the Baros Mountains, not far from Olt – Hrodi Whitebeard's stronghold. Generally, I spend my time up here in peace, except when the local people seek me out to heal their ailments."

"Etta brought me all this way to you?"

"She's a remarkable woman. When you're well enough you may go to her cabin – and not before," Joldir answered with a smile. Before I could ponder on things further, there was a loud knock on my door and Joldir called for the visitor to enter.

A broad-shouldered man squeezed his way through the doorway. Despite the loose-fitting shirt he was obviously well-muscled and used to physical work. He looked in the prime of his life, perhaps just into his late twenties, his dark-haired head perched on a thick neck. His bushy black eyebrows rose in surprise as he looked long and hard at me.

"Lad's awake, then?"

"Yes, he is. Rothgar, this is Thengill. He helps me on my smallholding, tending the animals and tilling the land."

I nodded by way of greeting, wondering exactly how many people knew I was here. If Joldir thought I was convinced Thengill was just a farmhand then he took me for a fool. After growing up in Ulfkell's Keep watching Finnvidor and Olfridor drilling the chief's men, I knew a warrior when I saw one.

The big man seemed to read my thoughts. "No need to look so worried, son. Think you're the first person to come here seeking help who'd rather keep it quiet? Your secret's safe with me, and Joldir pays me good coin to make sure no one else comes nosing round trying to sniff it out."

Joldir smiled. "Thengill can be trusted. We all can, that's why Etta brought you here. Now, Thengill, did you come to pay a visit on our guest or was there something you wanted to tell me?"

"There's folks on the road to Olt, heading this way. Looks like it might be Birna and a couple of the townsfolk come to trade for supplies," Thengill explained.

"I'll go speak to her," Joldir rose from my bedside. "You'll be sick of hearing these words but rest as much as you can. In a few days, when you've eaten more and can keep it down, we need to get you out of that bed. Before that, though, we have other more pressing concerns to discuss."

I stared up at Joldir, my mind blank for a moment. "Such as? Do you require payment?" I flushed as I wondered where I could find the coin to pay this man. The appearance of his bodyguard took on a more sinister aspect.

"Payment?" Joldir appeared momentarily confused. "No. No, of course not. All that has been attended to by Etta. I'm talking about your gift – the Sight."

***

After learning the truth my first thought was to find my way back to Desta. It no longer mattered this was impossible for me in my physical state. Now I understood this was not merely the comfort of encountering someone I loved and missed fondly in a dream. I knew what I had experienced through the Sight was real, and the pull to explore the possibilities it offered was irresistible.

Earlier that day, after he had attended to business with his visitors, Joldir sat by my bedside and patiently explained things. "Etta was right, of course, as she so often is. When she's wrong she's spectacularly wrong. However, on balance, when Etta says a thing is so only a fool would argue with her."

I was unsure how I felt about that revelation. "Etta already knows about all this?"

"She suspected, after you confided to her about your dreams of Nereth whilst you were wounded in Norlhast. It was one of the reasons she brought you to me, because she was afraid if you had the gift Nereth could use it against you to determine your location, or worse still kill you. Those with the Sight make effective assassins, as well as formidable spies. When Nereth went over to Adalrikr and recruited her coven they became valuable servants for him. They kept certain weak rulers, like Karas Greystorm, in power whilst removing Adalrikr's more powerful enemies without his armies ever leaving Vorund Fastness … I'm sorry, this will make little sense if I start half-way through. We need to approach this from the very beginning."

"Go on," I said, my mind still reeling.

"In the Age of Glory the avatars worked great magic with the Creator to forge Amuran, and when they walked amongst the mortal races they shared the gift of magic with them. In the civil war that engulfed Valistria after the War of the Avatars was over, our original culture vanished almost entirely. The conflict gave birth to new nations seeking order amongst the chaos, including the Laskan tribes. In the Fallen Age the magical arts were all but forgotten, not helped by the fact that their practice became a matter of suspicion and fear for people."

I nodded, remembering all this from Darri's stories and Etta's tutoring of me back in Ulfkell's Keep. "So this is a lost magical skill, is that what you mean?"

"The more commonly known gift these days is the one possessed by the seers, or shaman as you call them here; those who are blessed, or as some would say cursed, with the ability to transport their mind across the Void to communicate with the banished avatars. The Sight is a variant of this ability, one that existed before the fall, which enables a person to link their mind with others, if they have a certain amount of talent in that area themselves. You possess the Sight, which was why Nereth was able to attack you when your mind was vulnerable."

"I only ever wanted to be a warrior, like my father," I said slowly, trying to let Joldir's words sink in.

"That attitude is why eventually the Laskan clans will be dominated by their neighbours, be it Mirtan, Beria or Lagash," Joldir replied. "Even the Northern Plainsmen understand there are deeper mysteries than the simple teachings and laws of Reave would have you believe. The clansmen turned their back on magic when they settled in Laskar, seeking to return to purer ways. In doing so I fear they have condemned those who followed them and settled here to a life of servitude."

"You're forgetting Adalrikr."

"Yes, times have changed. Adalrikr understands the value of magic and Nereth is one of his most formidable agents. It was a grave mistake when Sigurd Albriktson stayed his hand that day, when he had her in his power."

"And you also possess the Sight? Is that how you came to me in my dream and protected me from Nereth?"

When Joldir nodded I knew what I wanted. With my broken body I might never again lead men into battle, while this was something I could do for the cause against Adalrikr.

"Nuna," I said after a time, as the pieces began to fall into place. "I saw her. In Norlhast Keep. If I can share such things with my sister does that mean she's also able to use the Sight?"

"It's not uncommon for the gift to run in families," Joldir told me. "Her yearning for her lost family draws you towards her, although she's completely unaware of your presence, as far as I can tell."

"Can you teach me how to use this ... gift?"

"The Sight cannot be taught in the way you learn a language or train in the use of a weapon. The skill is more intuitive, more of an art and much depends on a person's natural ability. But yes, I will teach you what I know. In fact, it's essential that you learn if you hope to protect yourself from Nereth. She's also skilled in such arts and she can use them to harm you. This is why you must never use the Sight without me – at least not until you're ready."

Joldir had been reluctant to take things further that day. Finally relenting in the face of my persistence, he showed me what he called 'The Path' and, as easily as walking through a door, I found myself free of my body and far away in Ulfkell's Keep. I walked the streets of Reavesburg, on unsteady feet rendered clumsy by too much drink. I realised Joldir had been a presence in all my dreams involving the Sight, there in the background watching over me – guiding me and protecting me where necessary.

***

Djuri staggered and almost fell. He reached out and steadied himself, leaning against the tavern wall. The gloomy road swayed beneath his feet. He took a shuddering breath, squinting as he saw some figures approaching.

"Look who it is."

"Djuri Turncloak, Blackeyes' new lapdog. Looking like he's had a few. What's the matter? Conscience bothering you?" His accuser was a small man, black stubble covering a long chin.

One of them had reached him now. As Djuri struggled to stand upright he was shoved over, leaving him sprawled in the mud.

"No one should bend the knee, traitor." A kick landed hard in his ribs, forcing the air from his body. "You were one of Jorik's warriors. Now he's dead and you turn your back on his memory?"

"Coward," shouted the leader, Long Chin. Blows rained down on Djuri, one after another, although the drink deadened the pain. A kick caught him on the jaw and his head exploded with light. There was blood in his mouth and a red mist clouded his vision, his assailants swimming before his eyes. The pain faded further – a dull presence, somewhere far away.

Djuri caught the next kick, seizing the man's ankle and twisting, sending him crashing to the ground with a cry. He shrugged off a punch to the side of his head, rolling with the blow as he found his feet. The big man rose, towering above the three remaining townsfolk.

"What did you want me to do?" Djuri snarled through teeth red with his own blood. Long Chin looked up at him, open-mouthed, and took a hesitant step backwards. Djuri seized him with both hands, clamping them around his neck and lifting him from his feet. "What did you expect?"

Djuri flung the man away with a roar, slamming him into the wooden walls with a reverberating crash. His companions turned and ran, one of them tripping over his own feet as he did so, pitching over so that he fell face first to the ground. His friends hauled him away as Djuri turned back to the ringleader lying sprawled in a heap by the tavern.

"Call *me* a coward?" Djuri hit Long Chin hard in the mouth, felt the man's jaw break. He hit him again, shearing his knuckles on his teeth, though he felt no pain. "Don't. See. You. Stepping. Forward." The blows hit hard, one after the other. "Don't. See. You. Rising up. Don't. See. You. Challenging Blackeyes." Djuri breathed through his nose, looking down at the red mess that had once been the man's face. He was sitting on Long Chin's chest, though he had no recollection of pinning him to the ground.

He raised his fist again, listening to the whistle of Long Chin's breath through his broken nose and mouth. The pain from his bloodied knuckles began to lance through his hand. "I'm no coward." Djuri took a deep breath, turned and spat blood, letting his arms drop. The red mist was fading, the scene coming into sharper focus.

Djuri rose on shaking legs. Long Chin was moaning softly on the ground. Djuri took a step away, then turned back. "I'm no coward ... Just ... Just being a practical man. I'm not putting my head on the block ... Not for you. Not for Jorik. I loved him but he's dead now – and me adding my corpse to the pile won't change a damn thing. If you want to live ... you need to move on."

With Joldir's help, I forced myself to look away. I didn't want to see this. I knew I would never find Desta among the drinking dens and taverns of Reavesburg. I needed to find an opening – someone with a modicum of ability within Ulfkell's Keep enabling me to link with them, using the Sight. As I sought out Desta I drifted further away from the keep.

I was in a house, reeking of smoked fish, down by the riverside outside Reavesburg. I could feel an old man's stiff fingers, busy mending his nets. Then the view dissolved and I was riding with the crow once more, wheeling north. Drawn inexorably towards Norlhast and Nuna.

A shadow fell across the crow, which banked sharply as something fell towards it from the sky. Wings blocked out the sun momentarily as the falcon attacked from a long stoop, talons outstretched. The crow evaded its hunter, jinking one way then the other ...

"No."

I drew a sharp intake of breath, wincing at the pain in my chest as I did so. I was back in my bed in Joldir's house, sweat pouring from my body. I heard footsteps and the door to my room opened.

"What's happened?" Arissa's face was anxious as she looked at the pair of us. "I heard someone shouting."

"This was a mistake," said Joldir, breathing hard as he rose from the chair next to my bed. "It's too soon and that was too close."

"This happens anyway, whenever I'm asleep," I pointed out, rattled and disorientated.

Joldir looked at me seriously. "I can guard your dreams. Just promise you won't purposefully seek out anyone using the Sight. Not until you're stronger. Those ways are always watched by Nereth and it's clear she's still looking for you."

CHAPTER 32

I lay awake in my bed into the small hours of the morning, unable to shake the image of the falcon from my mind. When sleep finally came it was fitful and although I was untroubled by any further experiences of the Sight I awoke feeling unrested.

Arissa brought me some soup for my breakfast in the morning, along with news that Etta wanted to see me. Etta was still recovering from the long journey from Reavesburg, so Thengill carried me down to the small cottage where she was living, which lay a short distance from Joldir's home.

"Rothgar," Etta said as Thengill carefully laid me in a chair by the fire. "I can't tell you how good it is to see you. Arissa, would you be so good as to brew some tea for me and the lad? I still have my stash of leaves from Samarakand that I've been saving for a special occasion." She reached into her cloak and drew out a small, brown leather bag with a flourish.

"Joldir has worked wonders, truly. You look ..." She groped unsuccessfully for the right words.

"Not dead? Myshall's bane, Etta ..." I fought to keep the bitterness from overwhelming me. Seeing Etta was stirring all sorts of emotions and I was unsure which of them would break loose next. I took a breath to steady myself. "It's been hard, Etta. I'm sorry not to sound more grateful. You saved my life, after all."

Etta's eyes were damp with tears and for a while she said nothing. Arissa returned with a pot of tea and two cups, setting them down carefully on the table next to Etta before leaving the two of us alone. Etta smiled and began to busy herself with the teapot, pouring out two cups and handed one to me before picking up her own, blowing on its steaming contents. I struggled to hold the cup steady and, seeing my discomfort, Etta rescued me, setting my tea down on the table.

When she finally spoke, her voice was little more than a whisper. "I'm so sorry; I didn't want any of this to happen. Nothing went according to plan."

"So, what happened that night, in Reavesburg? How did you manage to bring me here?"

Etta grimaced as she recounted the night's events. "When I left you in that cell I didn't want you to have any hope. I was afraid Blackeyes would sense there was something amiss and maybe change his plans for you at the last minute. However, I always intended to try and free you. I'm the one responsible for what happened at Nuna's wedding and I was determined to try and thwart Blackeyes' plans, for your sake and the sake of your late brother. So I took to the secret tunnels in the keep and found my way outside to one of my agents, a man called Ekkill.

"I'd asked him to frequent the taverns in Reavesburg, listening for what folk thought of the alliance between Norlhast and Reavesburg, how firm their resolve was to fight Adalrikr and stop his rise to power. I was also interested to know if there were any rumours about Gautarr's intentions. I considered him to be the most unpredictable element of my plan and I needed to know if he still posed a threat to Jorik. Anyway, none of that mattered after Tyrfingr Blackeyes struck and took Ulfkell's Keep that night."

"So it was Ekkill who freed me?"

"I knew from using the spyholes in the keep that Tyrfingr would want to punish you publicly. That gave us the opportunity when darkness fell, so Ekkill stole up, dealt with the guards on duty and we freed you before slipping out through the gates on a stolen cart. From there it was a short journey to a roadside inn where I always stable fast horses. We had to tie you onto yours and to be honest, I never thought you'd make it here alive. We rode as hard as we dared but I'd never seen wounds like yours on a living man. I thought at worst you might have been beaten, as they did when they captured Brunn Fourwinds. Had I realised what Tyrfingr intended to do ..." Etta paused for a moment before continuing. "Well, I might have risked a daytime rescue, whilst you were still in the cells. That mistake was made and there's no undoing it. After that there was only one person in Laskar I knew who possessed the skill to even attempt to try and heal you. We made our way to Lindos and Joldir, against his better judgement I'm sure, took you in and let me stay nearby, whilst I waited for news. I've sent Ekkill to scout the land, trying to gauge how strong Blackeyes' hold is in Reavesburg and where he is resisted. I'm expecting his return soon."

"And Desta? What about her?"

"She's safest where she is, in Ulfkell's Keep. I'm sorry, I know you care for the girl but there was no time to devise a plan to bring her as well. It was risky to try and free you and I didn't want to push our luck any further that night. Haarl will look after her, I'm sure." At Etta's words the realisation struck me that I would have married Desta, no matter what Jorik said. None of that mattered any more.

Etta seemed to read my thoughts. "I'm sorry, I did what I thought was best. I did what I knew had to be done, acting before Adalrikr became even stronger; although it was still too late in the end."

"Why?" I asked. "Why do you fear Adalrikr so much? He's the strongest clan chief now, yet power has always ebbed and flowed between the clans since Reave's time. Why did you set us so determinedly on the path to war?"

Etta pursed her lips. "The reports of my spies have convinced me he must be stopped, otherwise there will be no end to this. Adalrikr is a bloodstain, spreading over the land. Do you think he will stop once Laskar is under his heel? Adalrikr covets the riches of Beria and the knowledge of Mirtan and he plans to use his northern army to deliver both to him."

The old woman slouched in her chair. She slowly blew on her tea once again, taking another sip, watching me thoughtfully all the while. When my tea had cooled a little she helped me to take a mouthful. The infusion both warmed me and calmed my fraying nerves; Etta knew a good tea merchant. I drank again, wondering if I might develop a taste for this southern delicacy. We sat in gloomy silence for a while, sipping our tea until I found a way to phrase the question that had been on my mind since my conversation with Joldir.

"Joldir told me I have some … ability. A magical skill he called the Sight. He says you knew about this, and it's one of the reasons you brought me here."

"Ah. I was wondering when we'd come to this."

"There's more," I continued. "Nereth has the same skill and she's used it to attack me. Once after I was injured in the fight with the coven at Norlhast and again since I've been here."

Etta set down her cup and looked at me. "Nereth is skilled in the black arts, trained by Serena herself in the Chapters of Seroch. When you came to me and told me your story, I knew I was right. Some people's minds are vulnerable to those who possess the Sight and someone with Nereth's skills, trained and honed by the Mages of Mirtan, is able to exploit that to their advantage."

I drank my tea with clumsy hands, trying to order my thoughts. I was tired and, if I was being honest, a little afraid. Afraid for me, and afraid for those close to me as well. Everything had changed.

"You're in the safest place," Etta told me. "One of the reasons why Joldir is in my employ is his gift of the Sight. I spotted his talent when he was young and sent him to study in Mirtan, where he also excelled in Seroch's medical school. He's been invaluable to me since his return." The old woman leaned forwards, an eager expression on her face. "Joldir has told me you have some power. Tell me, what is it like? Where have you been?"

It felt odd at first, explaining such matters to Etta, and I still half-expected all of this to be some fevered dream. For her part, Etta seemed pleased with the information she gleaned from me, especially when I recounted the events in Norlhast Keep.

"So, Nuna also possesses some measure of the Sight," Etta observed with relish.

Suddenly I felt both tired and angry at the old woman. "What does it matter? You can continue to gather your secrets and scheme and plot all you want. The alliance is over – Karas has taken his men home with him and Norlhast is occupied. Jorik's army is scattered and our stronghold is in the hands of our enemies."

With great care Etta set her own cup down on the table. "What Tyrfingr did to you and your family; I think about little else every day. It's the first thought I have when I wake, and my last when I lie down to sleep. Those crimes will not go unpunished, I swear it."

"I know," I said, placing my weak hand on her bony arm. Privately, though, I wondered how a cripple and a woman who had seen a hundred winters would bring down Adalrikr Asmarrson and his allies, no matter how much cause they had to hate him.

***

After such a long convalescence my body had become a skeletal frame. What flesh remained was criss-crossed with thick scars and deep furrows where Blackeyes had done his work, so nothing moved quite as it had before; the ugly patchwork of my skin drawn tight in places, the muscles underneath wasted away. My joints were stiff with long disuse, protesting even under the now insubstantial weight of my body, whilst my legs shook with the effort of keeping me upright. When Joldir removed the last of the bandages, I wept at the utter ruin of my body. Thin and pinched, with dark rings under my eyes and a patchy unkempt beard, I hardly recognised the man who peered back at me from the polished metal mirror I demanded Joldir bring. At least my face had been spared Blackeyes' red hot iron. Even so, here and there I could see small red marks on my cheeks, which I realised were the still healing wounds from where the crows had been pecking at my face. At some point I had lost one of my front teeth as well, although I had no memory of how that had happened. Looking into those strangers' eyes with despair and horror, I tried to consider myself fortunate the crows hadn't pecked them out, leaving me blind as well as a cripple.

"You're still very ill," Joldir explained. "In time your body will recover, though I fear that you will never be ... quite the man you were before." I knew Joldir was right; the warrior Desta had loved, who had ridden into battle and fought Gautarr Falrufson in single combat, he was gone forever. What of the man who remained? Could I really live out the rest of my days like this? Although I might have been in the depths of despair, Joldir possessed an iron will, determined to see me survive.

"You can't stay in this room," he told me. "Each day you will get up from this bed and each day you will walk a little further, eat and drink a little more. You need to feel the sun on your face again."

Yet that first day all I could manage was to allow Joldir to wash, shave and dress me in some ill-fitting loose clothes before I had to lie down on my bed again. The following day Arissa and Joldir helped me to stagger from my bed to the door and down the corridor into the main room of Joldir's house. I sat in one of his chairs by the fire while Arissa helped prepare some breakfast for me, reflecting that other than my visit to Etta's house this was the furthest I had travelled in weeks. For a time my life was measured in small victories, hard-won from my weak and treacherous body. Such as the first time I was able to dress unaided or the occasion when I managed to eat more of my broth than was spilled from the spoon by my shaking hand. I marked all these achievements with a degree of grim satisfaction, the days long and dull. I would eagerly look forward to our evening meal, which I shared with Arissa and Joldir, after which we would talk late into the night.

With their plain peasant's garb and the simple well-worn furnishings of their home, any casual observer would have thought Joldir and Arissa unremarkable common folk, making a living from their homestead as many did in Laskar. However, Joldir was a well-educated man, so the topics of our conversation in the evening always ranged far and wide. His knowledge of the healing arts certainly extended far beyond the counterfeit hedge magic of many professed healers. Visitors from Olt arrived on occasion, seeking his advice and preparations. Although Joldir kept me out of their sight, from what I could tell they paid him well in goods or coin.

Thengill was an occasional guest at Joldir's. More often than not he kept himself to himself and the two men did not appear particularly close. He seemed to have nothing in common with Joldir, although he obviously respected him, and I struggled to understand what kept Thengill working up here in the mountains. Joldir gave little away, merely saying he needed a strong back for the heavy farm work, though this hardly convinced me.

Arissa was pretty and slim with long auburn hair and striking bright green eyes, which sparkled whenever she laughed. She was younger than I first thought, just two years older than me and a year away from turning twenty. At Ulfkell's Keep I had heard many celebrated bards perform for my father and brother in the Great Hall. Despite their reputation few – with the exception perhaps of Darri – played and sang so well as Arissa. I had taken her to be Joldir's daughter or perhaps even his young wife, until he assured me with a wry smile that she was neither.

"Just a friend," he explained one night as we sat talking beside his fire. "Though these days I tend to think of her as my daughter, in all but name."

"How did you come to be here?" I asked, curious to know

more.

"My parents performed with a travelling troupe of players. Let's just say that my father wasn't a particularly kind man. One day I realised I'd had enough and ... I left ..." Arissa's voice trailed off, leaving her story incomplete, and she fidgeted with the hem of her dress. I knew of a few women who travelled with players and bards, in fact I had watched some of them play in the Great Hall. It was still a rare profession for a woman to take up, unless they were born into that life.

I flushed, realising I'd touched on a painful subject. "I'm sorry to hear that. Did you learn to play and sing as part of the troupe?"

"Yes – the one real gift my father gave to me, though I hardly think of my old family nowadays. My future is here, and Joldir has taught me much about his own arts in medicine. It's what I want to do with my life now."

"Both noble gifts in their own way," I observed. "Your voice is truly remarkable. It's a shame so few get to hear it." Arissa flushed with pleasure and Joldir looked at her proudly.

"A gift to me as well," he said with a smile. "Etta has this habit of bringing me waifs and strays to shelter every now and again since I settled here ten years ago; you're just the latest one. Some go the next day, others ... well, Arissa chose to make her home with me."

"I see," I said slowly. A chill ran up my spine as a further thought began to dawn on me. "And I'm placing you all in danger by being here – Blackeyes will be looking for me and Etta too."

"I took you in as a sick man needing my help; that's all that matters. Etta knows I've never been one to turn someone away if they're in need, even if it means harbouring a fugitive. I've no love of Adalrikr Asmarrson and his cronies. In this way I can play my small part in resisting them, helping you get stronger and develop your new skills."

"Joldir, is this wise?" We both glanced at Arissa as she looked at us defiantly. "Well? Every time Rothgar uses this

... this magic he's at risk from Nereth, isn't he? You told me yourself Nereth is becoming better at sensing you. That's what happened the other night, isn't it?"

"Leaving Rothgar ignorant of his gift merely makes him vulnerable to attack," Joldir told her. "This is for the best and I'm taking care of myself."

"And he knows the risks?"

"I do," I told her. "There are those with the Sight that have been driven mad by what they've seen. Some find their minds drift away from their bodies, diffusing and vanishing on the wind, never to return. Others are drawn to particular people, becoming obsessed with their lives, unable to leave them alone. Joldir has told me that two minds can even become fused, unable to live apart or exist independently. Despite these dangers I must learn to control this side of me, Arissa, otherwise I'll have no say in my fate. Nereth is already stalking my dreams ..." I shuddered at the thought and the conversation died.

Arissa rose and began gathering up the remains of our evening meal. "I'm sorry. I didn't mean to upset you. I worry for you both, that's all."

Joldir smiled at her. "You worry too much. I know what I'm doing."

Arissa pursed her lips, unconvinced, saying nothing more on the matter.

CHAPTER 33

That night I felt unsettled. Sleep refused to come and I put it down to Arissa's fretting. My dreams had been untroubled by the Sight for several days now but tonight there was something there – like a faint insistent knock at the door. I closed my eyes and turned over awkwardly in bed, drawing the covers tightly over me, trying to ignore the feeling.

***

The River Jelt follows the Northern Baros Mountains for over one hundred miles before flowing into the great icy Lake Tull. Despite the long winters, the land surrounding the river is rich and fertile, whilst the year-long supply of fish from the lake helps to keep bellies full whenever the crop yield is poor. Leif's father was at great pains to explain all of this as they headed inland, away from the smoking wreckage of their former home. He said they would have a good life on the south western shore of Lake Tull. Tullen was a large settlement and by all accounts well-defended. However, Leif listened only distractedly to his father's words, whilst his mother said nothing at all on their journey north. She just sat there, staring straight ahead as the wayn bounced along the rutted track, jostling them and their meagre possessions. Leif felt sure her thoughts didn't stray far from the day when a score of raiders from the Vorund Clan attacked their village, six days ago. That was all Leif thought about; the anger twisting in his gut during the day, whilst unwelcome memories haunted his fitful dreams at night.

Leif and his parents only escaped with their lives because they were out working in the fields furthest from Brindling when the warriors struck. When the first cries of alarm drifted across to them, his father had dragged all three of them down amongst the stalks of the barley field. When Leif glanced at his father, he saw nothing except fear in his eyes.

"Dad. What're you gonna do? Are you gonna fight them?" His question brought his father's hand down hard on the back of his head, pushing his face down into the muddy earth. Leif's eyes watered as he bit his lip to avoid shouting out.

"Shut your mouth, boy! You lie there and don't move a muscle if you know what's good for you. If they find us, they'll kill us. Understand?" Leif nodded, heart hammering, as he watched events unfold with mounting horror.

The Vorund Clan's fighters rode horses, cutting down the workers in the fields on the other side of Brindling as they charged. Shrill cries of alarm drifted to Leif across the valley, only to be silenced as the warriors whooped and laughed, cutting folk down one by one as they desperately tried to run, toying with some of them for a time, until they were weeping with fear or else begging for mercy. The black bear was emblazoned on their shields, sun glinting off their armour, swords and spears. As the last of the field workers was brought down, jerking wildly as a spear was thrust into his back, the raiders formed up into a wedge and headed straight for the village itself.

"How'd they get this far inland?" his father whispered, shaking his head, his eyes wide with fear. "Where'd they get horses? We can't outrun horses." Leif watched as his mother gripped his father's arm.

"Anders, Halma's down there with Gisla. We got to go to them –"

"Damn it, woman. Stay low and shut up, or we're all done for."

"She's nine, Anders. And Gisla just a baby, please – ah!" Leif dug his fingers deep into the soil, tears streaming down his cheeks, as his father struck his mother hard across the face. The warriors had reached the village now, breaking up into groups. Some had dismounted and began battering down the doors of the first houses. Leif heard screams and shouts and glanced at his own home, untouched so far. He saw Halma's frightened face at the window for a moment before the shutters were closed.

"Quiet I said. Oh ... Oh gods, Lina, I'm sorry. I didn't mean to hit you that hard. I'm so sorry, Lina, but there's nothing we can do for them. Just don't look, my love. Turn away. Come on Halma, *run* girl. You can't stay in there. *Run*."

Leif's mother's soft, quiet sobs were muffled as she hid her face while Leif was unable to tear his eyes away. He saw old Hamarr dragged from his home by two men. They were laughing as they stabbed him, smoke curling from the windows of the kindly man's wooden house, backlit by the orange glow of the flames within. A young woman was screaming for help in a nearby house. Oli stood his ground in the centre of the village, hunting bow drawn back. He loosed an arrow at one of the attackers, which thudded into his shield. Moments later a mounted raider charged Oli from the left, bearing down on the huntsman too quickly for him to draw another arrow from his quiver. Oli's head snapped backwards as the warrior's sword struck, and he fell to the ground in a shower of blood. Several houses were already engulfed in flames when the raiders reached Leif's home, the place where he had been born six years ago and lived all his life. He heard Halma screaming as a man began to kick down the door, little Gisla wailing thinly in the background. Without thinking he rose and began to run towards his sisters. He had taken perhaps half a dozen strides when the full weight of his father struck him from behind, knocking the breath from his body and driving him back down into the earth.

"Dad. Please, we need to help Halma ..." Leif gasped as his father firmly pressed his face into the mud. It was a strength born of fear and terror and a desperate desire to stay alive. Finally, Leif understood that whatever was happening inside his house, his father would do nothing to try and stop it.

"Son, I'm so sorry but I can't lose you too. There's nothing I can do to help your sisters. We need to hide, lie low and keep quiet, or they'll kill us too. You, me and your mother. Do you understand? Can I trust you to keep quiet?" Gradually, the pressure on Leif's back relaxed and he nodded silently.

From far away Halma was calling for help, the smell of smoke thick in the air as Leif numbly allowed himself to be pulled away by his father. His sister's cries had ceased by the time they reached the edge of the field and slipped through the hedge. Together they ran towards the woods nearby and remained there, crouched down fearfully in the hollow of a tree until night fell, finding no sleep even after the tortured cries of their family, friends and neighbours had long been silenced. Leif watched as Brindling was bathed in the dancing light of the fires while acrid, choking smoke blew through the woods. There was something else too on the wind, and Leif gagged as he realised it was the smell of roasting flesh. Leif would never forget that smell of charred wood and burning meat, which clung to him for days afterwards.

In the days that followed, Leif imagined himself taking vengeance on the evil men from Vorund. Yet as they rode in the rickety old wayn they had managed to salvage, pulled by Hamarr's faithful pony who had somehow escaped the carnage, his father talked of nothing other than returning to farming as soon as possible, talk that made Leif's blood boil. His father was a coward, who'd done nothing whilst his sisters had been murdered. Even now Leif could hear the laughter of Vorund's warriors as they wreaked havoc and death, whereas it was as if his father had forgotten everything. As for his mother, it was hard to tell if she heard anything at all.

Leif was jolted from his thoughts when he saw a small cluster of lights nestled on the banks of Lake Tull. It was dark and the lake was smooth as glass, the moon reflected brightly upon the black waters. Hamarr's pony followed the track with sure-footed steps, perhaps sensing their journey was nearly at an end. Leif's father was anxious as this was the first time they had dared travel at night. They pushed on regardless, the landscape a ghostly grey colour in the light of the moon that was bright enough for them to find their way. And all the time the lights of the town grew closer and brighter as they drew nearer to safety.

Tullen was smaller than Leif had expected. Earlier that day, they had passed several farms and homesteads along the road, all of them silent and abandoned, their fields growing wild and choked with weeds. They passed yet another of these now with its door wide open, swinging softly to and fro in the light breeze. Inside there was only darkness. Leif's father shook his head, whilst his mother stared straight down the road.

"Have the raiders come here too, Dad?" Leif asked quietly.

"No, Son. These farms have all been empty for a long time. Reckon there's a chance we could take one of these on, bring some of the fields back into use. Still early enough to sow some crops, eh Lina?" Leif's mother said nothing, acting as if her husband hadn't spoken at all.

"There's no wall."

"What's that?"

"There's no wall," Leif repeated. "There's nothing to defend us, if the raiders come again. I don't know, Dad, Tullen looks small. You think we're at the right place?"

"Road north only goes one place, and that's Tullen. Been a few years, mind, since I last came this way. Seems like they've fallen on hard times."

They rode on in silence into Tullen itself, the town still and quiet, most of the wooden houses dark and cold with no signs of life. In the centre of the town was a long hall, a low murmur emanating from within; the first sounds of people Leif had heard other than his father since they'd set out five days earlier. His father snapped the reins and steered their wayn towards the building, drawing it up by the door. After tying Hamarr's pony to a post outside he helped Leif's mother clamber down from the wayn, whilst Leif jumped lightly onto the road. He heard laughter within the long hall and realised how unfamiliar it was since the torching of his home. He felt his father's hand on his shoulder.

"Stay close, Leif, and don't say anything unless I tell you to. No knowing what these people will be like with us."

His father took a breath to steady himself and pushed open the door to the long hall, bathing the three of them in the warm orange light of a fire pit running the length of the room. Leif could see several figures sitting around the pit, eating and drinking. A large cooking pot was set over the fire, the delicious smell of lamb stew making Leif's mouth water. At the sight of the three strangers at the doorway the talk and laughter died away in an instant. The man nearest the door, a big burly fellow with a thick black beard, rose to his feet. He folded his arms and stared at Leif's family suspiciously.

"Strangers," came a soft voice from the far end of the hall. "The hour is late for visitors to Tullen. What are your names and what's your business here?"

Leif glanced at the speaker, a young man with long blond hair sitting at the head of the fire pit. It was the seat traditionally reserved for the town elder, although this man seemed far too young to hold such a position. The rear of the long hall behind him was partitioned off by an expensive black velvet curtain.

Leif's father cleared his throat before speaking. "Name's Anders, I'm a farmer from Brindling. This here's my wife, Lina, and my son, Leif. We were hit by raiders from the Vorund Clan six days ago. Brindling's been razed to the ground and the three of us are the only ones who made it out alive. Lost my two girls ... They ... I should have gone to them ..." Leif felt his father shaking, his hand clasped tightly on his shoulder and it took him a moment to realise he was crying.

"Vandill, make some room at the fireside and let these people sit down," said a young woman to the right of the man at the head of the fire. The big man, the one who had stood when they arrived, gestured for them to take his place and other members of the townsfolk rose to fetch them food and drink. The woman who had spoken served Leif herself, a smile on her pretty face. Leif cupped his hands around the wooden bowl, warming them and breathing in the rich smell of the stew.

His stomach rumbled loudly and the woman laughed. "You look like you need that. Eat up and you'll feel better, I promise."

"I'm sorry to hear of your loss," the young man was saying to his father. Leif's mother sat next to him, still saying nothing, spooning the stew into her mouth as she stared blankly into the glowing fire.

"Never heard of raiders coming this far inland," his father answered, having recovered his composure. "They were mounted and well-armed – we never stood a chance against them."

"He doesn't know," Vandill said, his voice a deep bass rumble.

Leif watched as his father glanced up and down the row of faces at the fireside, looking worried. "Doesn't know what?" he asked. "What's happened?"

The blond man answered his father's question, face grim. "Reavesburg has fallen to the Vorund Clan, Anders. Jorik Kolfinnarson was betrayed by his own brother on the night of his sister's wedding to Karas Greystorm of Norlhast three weeks ago. Jorik is dead, and his jarls either fled or were slain. Tyrfingr Blackeyes now sits on Reave's Chair in Ulfkell's Keep and rules Jorik's former lands in the name of Adalrikr Asmarrson, who now styles himself as the king of Laskar." Despite the warmth of the fire, Leif felt a chill creeping up his spine.

"Fallen? No – there must be some mistake ..." His father's voice sounded weak as he trailed off and set aside his meal, hands shaking.

"I'm sorry, these are no false rumours. I was there as a wedding guest and saw everything with my own eyes. Reavesburg is ruled by the Vorund Clan, as are the Norlhast Clan. Karas Greystorm was the first to bend the knee before Blackeyes rather than resist him. Tyrfingr has sent out riders throughout the land, bringing the news of the fall of Jorik and the rule of their new king, as well as demanding tribute. It seems some have exceeded their orders, choosing instead to prey on the weak and vulnerable in order to seize plunder for themselves. These are dark times for us all."

"We can offer them shelter and our protection," added the woman who had given Leif his food. "These poor folk must stay with us, Sandar. They shouldn't be out on the road, not with the land full of Vorund's warriors. It's a miracle they reached us here safely."

Tullen's elder nodded in agreement. "Of course, I'll not see them turned away, unless they desire otherwise. Anders, I'll be honest with you. Tullen's fortunes have been waning of late. A fever has struck a number of times in recent years, taking many of the townsfolk in its passing; you'll have seen some of their former homes as you travelled along the road. Others left more recently with the news of Jorik's fall, hoping to find a passage through to Vittag or Helsburg on the other side of the mountains. I fear few of them will survive that journey. Those people you see gathered in the long hall tonight are the ones who chose to stay here and continue our way of life in Tullen. You and your family could join us, if you want to. You said you were a farmer, so if you wish you could take on one of the abandoned homesteads and help us raise a good crop to see us through winter."

Leif counted the men and woman round the fire; perhaps two dozen of them and all young at that – it was no wonder their town elder had seen so few years. There were even fewer folk here in Tullen than there had been in Brindling, and that hardly made him feel safe. It seemed to him the townsfolk heading towards the mountains were the ones with the better idea. In contrast his father's face brightened at the elder's offer.

"You're too kind ... You hear that, Lina? We can take on one of the farms and go back to how things used to be. Make a new life here with these kind folk."

Leif's mother was unmoved by his father's obvious excitement and relief, never meeting his eye as she finished her stew by wiping a heel of bread in the bottom of her bowl. Leif's father looked at her uncertainly for a moment, unsure what to do in the face of her lack of enthusiasm. He turned his attention back to the elder again. "Please don't take offence, she's not been coping well since ... It's not that we're not grateful. Thank you ... I'm sorry, I didn't catch your name before."

"My apologies. I forgot my manners entirely when I heard your dire news. My name is Sandar Tindirson and this is my wife, Ginna. I'm the town elder for Tullen and speak on behalf of the people of Lake Tull at the Reavesburg clan moot. You're most welcome to our community, though I wish the circumstances of your arrival were more favourable."

"Thank you, Sandar. I don't know how we can ever repay you for this."

"New company and extra hands to help with the work at harvest time will be repayment enough. You can all make a fresh start here, Anders, and put the awful events at Brindling behind you." There was a general murmur of assent at Sandar's words and Vandill came forward and engulfed his father's hand in both of his. Ginna smiled and wrapped her arm around her husband, nestling in against his chest.

Leif looked down into his bowl and stirred the contents with his spoon, the food's savour lost. All anyone ever spoke of was forgetting what had happened and moving on. Sandar was just as much a coward as everyone else who accepted that the Vorund Clan could murder whoever they liked and did nothing about it. He set his unfinished meal aside, sick to his stomach as anger coursed through him. Looking up, he found himself meeting Ginna's smiling gaze, her eyes sparkling red in the light of the fire.

CHAPTER 34

Joldir's home was built traditionally, with a coursework of stone as the foundation and timber walls rising up towards a steeply-pitched thatched roof. His house was large, extending to three sides of a square, with a wall of piled stones comprising the fourth side enclosing a courtyard, within which an intricate mosaic had been set. This was laid out in precisely cut smooth polished cobbles, each about as big as my fist. The design comprised a dragon and chimera in battle, their sinewy bodies locked in complex swirls of black and red, set against a white background. The whole picture could only really be properly appreciated if you were a bird on the wing. I was becoming more closely acquainted with the mosaic at a far more intimate level. Thengill's guffaws made me burn with shame so intensely I almost forgot the pain in my side from where I had fallen. As Arissa rebuked him the thought of a woman standing up for me only made my humiliation feel all the more complete.

"How, *exactly*, is that helping, Thengill? Hasn't Joldir given you some work to do?"

"Aye, and I'll have finished my chores and be sitting by my hearth this evening smoking my pipe, and he still won't have made it across the courtyard," Thengill told her, his bare thick hairy arms dangling loosely over the top of the wooden gate set into the wall. With a chuckle and a shake of his head he hoisted the next sack from the back of the cart as if is weighed nothing, slung it casually over his shoulder and headed into the barn, still chortling to himself.

Cursing under my breath, I felt with weak hands for my crutch and gathered my strength to stand on my feet. I was sick to death of the four bare walls of my small room in Joldir's house. I wanted to see the mountains and the ruins of Lindos. I wanted to see the fields and the road wending its way slowly down the valley towards Olt. I wanted these things so badly I was willing to let Arissa put her arm around my shoulders and help steady me as I took a few tottering steps, heart pounding with the effort, lungs burning. After the dimness of my room, the morning sun was painfully bright, almost blinding me, so that all I could see was the gate, inching closer with each shuffling step.

I crossed the courtyard with grim determination until the gate was only a few feet away, Joldir watching my progress from the threshold. I stretched out my arm and almost fell into the gate, my breathing laboured. I clung to it like a drowning man clings to driftwood.

Arissa rubbed my shoulders gently. "You made it, Rothgar. Well done." She spoke to me like a child taking his first tottering steps; I suppose in a way I was. As my breathing became less ragged, Thengill returned to the cart to fetch another sack.

"Didn't believe you'd make it," he remarked. "Looks like you've more fire in your belly than I thought. Only pity is now you've got to make it all the way back."

I glanced at him ruefully, despising the mocking look the man gave me as he carried the last sack from the cart and disappeared into the barn once more. I was a cripple in his eyes, a destitute beggar who didn't even own the clothes on his back. A man earned his place in Laskan society and the respect he was due. What was my place going to be now?

"Rothgar." The familiar voice made me start and I looked up to see Etta, her stick tapping the ground lightly with every step as she walked up the road. I was dismayed to see the ancient crone's slow gait now outpaced my own. As I watched her approach, Joldir joined us and Arissa placed a steadying arm around my shoulders.

"Joldir. Arissa." Etta's gapped-toothed smile was

friendly enough and Joldir inclined his head towards her politely. "You both have my thanks, from the bottom of my heart." Etta reached out one of her gnarled hands towards mine. "How are you, boy?"

Even smiling was too much effort. "I've been better."

At that moment Thengill emerged from the barn. "Etta," he called out. "Any word on when Ekkill might be back this way?"

"I've not had a message from him since he left and I doubt I will before he returns." She turned to me with a conspiratorial look. "Ekkill's still away scouting out the Reavesburg territory for me, finding out what Blackeyes is up to and how Jorik's surviving jarls are faring." She said this as if I would be pleased to see the man again. I could only remember a whispering shadow, counselling Etta to slit my throat and I wasn't keen to renew his acquaintance, even if I did owe him my life.

"When you're well enough, and not before, it would be good if you would pay me another visit," Etta continued. With a nod to the four of us, she turned back down the road.

"You can always come and see me too, Arissa," Thengill said with a leer, a big grin on his wide, black-stubbled face. "If you can tear yourself away from the cripple for half an hour, perhaps you can sing *me* a song at my house. I don't see why the boy needs to have all your attention – that's no life for a fine young woman like you."

"That's enough, Thengill," said Joldir.

Arissa's temper flared at once. "I thought you preferred the company of Joldir's sheep and goats."

"We'll see," Thengill replied, still grinning. "The boy and his grandma won't be here forever, lass, and then it'll just be the three of us alone up here once more. My company might seem all the more appealing then."

"Come on," Arissa snapped, marching me far more quickly than I would have preferred back towards Joldir's house.

***

Despite my exhaustion I resumed my lessons in the Sight with Joldir before first light the following morning. I still burned with shame from Thengill's mocking laughter, the warrior only seeing a cripple. I knew if I could master my new ability that would make all the difference.

I had told Joldir about Leif. It had been strange to find myself drawn into Sandar Tindirson's world, and I wondered why I'd seen those events. This morning I was determined to steer a true course, and asked Joldir if he could use the Sight to find Desta. Joldir explained that whilst he might be able to I would be unable to join him.

"At the moment you lead and draw on my strength, whilst I help anchor both of us in the Real," he told me. "When you learn control you can play my role. For now, when we do this you must be the one to find the Path."

Frustrated, I focused everything I had, taking the time to be still, truly still. After a while I began to discover a world that would otherwise have escaped my notice altogether. Early morning, pre-dawn, the world was dark. As I drank in the stillness I became aware of so much more. Farm animals stirred and I could sense the wings of bats as they flitted from the roof of the barn out into the dark sky, seeking out the last of their prey before sunrise. I could hear a faint fluttering, barely audible, as a moth beat itself against the glass of the lamp in my room in a futile effort to reach the flame within.

I drew further into the stillness, purposefully clearing my mind of the jumble of thoughts, fears and memories that would otherwise intrude. I became acutely aware of my body, my breathing slow, steady and deep. My heart beat with its regular rhythm, in time with each breath, sending blood flowing through my veins. I could hear the creak made by my joints after each subtle movement of my body. My muscles ached from the previous day's exertions whilst my skin still felt tight in places, some parts left numb and unfeeling from my treatment at the hands of Tyrfingr Blackeyes ...

I withdrew from that unpleasant memory, closing my mind and willing myself further into the very centre of the stillness. I relaxed and, as Joldir instructed me, tried to find the place where my waking and sleeping mind met. I tried without grasping, allowing the stillness to take me there as I retreated further into myself.

***

The first light of dawn stole across the sky, dark clouds emerging from the blackness in which they had been hidden. Nuna watched as it caught the white sails of the distant fishing boats that had been out all night, returning with their catch in time for the market at Norlhast.

The light revealed the keep too, allowing Nuna to see the heads of the six whalers her husband had executed adorning the white stone wall above the gates. Whilst she had forgiven Karas for passing sentence on them, something still made her look out from the window of her chamber every morning at the grisly sight.

"You're up early, my lady." Nuna started at Ottama's voice. She had not heard her enter. She turned to find the young maid busy lighting candles above her fireplace.

"Katla is still unwell?"

Ottama nodded. "I'm afraid she's still indisposed, my lady, though I am sure she will recover soon. Sigurd asked me to attend to you this morning, if it pleases you."

Nuna smiled and allowed Ottama to help her dress, noting how deftly her fingers laced up her gown. After Ottama brushed and artfully arranged her golden hair, Nuna smiled as she looked at her reflection in the mirror.

"That look's lovely," she remarked, pleased at how bashful Ottama appeared at being paid such a compliment. "You have obviously waited upon a woman before."

"I've been in service at Norlhast Keep since I was a girl, my lady. I attended Thora, Karas's second wife, and her two daughters until the blood plague took them. Afterwards Sigurd was good enough to take me as his maid and allow me to remain here at the keep."

"Well, I'm pleased Sigurd had the foresight to retain your services, Ottama," Nuna said, still admiring her hair. "I believe Katla might have a few things to learn from you."

Ottama shifted awkwardly, not meeting Nuna's gaze in the mirror. Nuna found herself looking at the servant girl more closely. She was a slim, small breasted woman, her face plain and unremarkable, her brown hair tied back in a tight bun. Nuna could barely recall exchanging two words with her until now, which was remiss of her as the lady of the keep.

Nuna turned to look at her directly. "I'm sure Sigurd can spare you some of the time, if I ask him nicely. I was always attended by two maids, Katla and Amma, in Ulfkell's Keep ... until ..." Nuna's words faltered as the memory caught her unawares. For a moment she could hear Amma's screaming all over again.

"I know my lady. I was there ... that night." Ottama seemed to shrink before her eyes as she slowly began backing away. It was only then Nuna remembered Sigurd's serving girl had been among those who'd testified against her brother.

Gods, she's terrified of me, Nuna thought. She took a deep breath and placed her hands together on her lap, hiding their tremble. "I remember. You have nothing to fear from me, Ottama, you understand, don't you?"

Ottama's brown eyes were wide. "I didn't know what they would do to your brother, my lady. Tyrfingr Blackeyes spoke to me himself and ... and I was so scared of him. I only ever told him the truth, my lady. I *did* see your brother that night, although I never said he let the Vorund Clan into the keep, my lady – I swear it."

"I believe you," Nuna told her. "You only told them what you saw that evening – what else could you have done? Many people have much worse to feel ashamed of following the events that surrounded the fall of my household. Your part in this was small, Ottama, and I bear no grudge against you. My brothers' fates were sealed by Tyrfingr Blackeyes and no one else can claim responsibility for that crime.

"Now, I am the lady of Norlhast Keep and, as such, it is my command that we shall speak no more of this. Instead, you will attend my chambers again tomorrow morning and instruct Katla *exactly* how to arrange my hair in this fashion. I shall speak to Sigurd personally concerning the matter."

"Yes, my lady," Ottama answered, a shy smile curling at the corner of her lips. Nuna reached out and took Ottama's hands in her own, squeezing them gently. It was time to build bridges and look to the future. It was what the lady of Norlhast Keep should do.

CHAPTER 35

Leif shuddered despite the warm night, throwing off his blanket and sitting up in bed, rubbing his face wearily with clammy hands. The door to his room opened, and he heard his mother's soft footfalls as she walked towards him.

"Mother?" he whispered. There was no answer; there never was since she'd lost her voice. Leif sensed her loving presence near him as she seated herself on the edge of the bed, drawing him close, hugging him tight. He returned the hug, feeling safe and warm in her arms. In the next room he could hear his father snoring softly, the comforting low rumble filling the silence. After a few moments Leif noticed his mother was trembling and it dawned on him she was crying. He put up his hand and stroked her cheek, wiping away the tears noiselessly falling from her face.

"It'll be alright," he told her. "We're safe here, aren't we? Safe in Tullen. Dad says so." He felt rather than saw his mother nod, squeezing him tighter still. Then she rose, stroked his hair and smoothed the covers of his bed.

Leif pretended to snuggle down as she closed the door and returned to his snoring father, a knot twisting in his stomach. When he heard the door to her room shut he sat up once more, hugging his knees to his chest. Leif tried to believe his father's words – he wanted to believe them so badly. Yet every time he dreamed he saw Halma, calling to him for help. His feet were leaden, rooted to the spot with fear. Far off, Gisla was crying in her cot and that was when he'd awoken with the shout that drew his mother.

Determined not to cry and disturb her again, Leif got up and padded barefoot over to the shutters. He opened one side of them, careful to choose the one with the well-oiled hinges his father had repaired last week. The summer night air was cooler than his stuffy bedroom, pleasant on his face and Leif rested his elbows on the window sill and looked out over Tullen, the town dark and quiet, its long hall silent at this late hour. He caught the tang of wood and fish from the smokehouses down on the lakeside, carried on the breeze. It should have reminded him of home, but Tullen wasn't home, no matter how many times his father said it was. There was nothing left of his old home now. They hadn't even stopped long enough to bury the bodies of his sisters, the thought a dead weight on Leif's chest.

How could his father forget? Leif's hands clenched into fists as he asked himself the same familiar questions, his nails digging painfully into his palms. His father worked hard in the fields, particularly in the early days, when they were trying to establish their new farm, returning home and dropping exhausted into his chair by the fire while Mother prepared their evening meal. Leif had to admit that when he had a job to do, such as helping his father with sowing, tending to their smallholding or feeding the cow or their chickens, he felt better. Sandar had let them stay in a large well-appointed farmhouse on the edge of the town, making them a gift of the cow himself. Vandill called round later that day, one big fist clutching a wicker cage containing six chickens, the other a sack full of seeds. Everyone in Tullen went out of their way to welcome them, with Vandill helping his father with the ploughing and sowing that spring. A few times Leif had gone with his father to the long hall, to share food and drink with Sandar and his friends. Tullen's inn had been closed for over a year and the two smaller taverns had been shut for even longer, so the long hall served as the communal hub of the town and folk gathered there almost every night to eat, drink, tell stories, play music, dance and sing late into the night. Leif's father joined in such revelry enthusiastically; first once a week, then later twice or three times. Now his father spent most nights there, although his mother never came, only leaving the house to tend the animals. Before Brindling burned, Leif would have given anything to stay up late in the village tavern, listening to Hamarr's stories and Oli's jokes. Now he could take little pleasure in such things, even when Ginna and Sandar tried to be kind to him. For all their friendliness and gaiety, Tullen seemed a lifeless place beyond the sounds and fires of the long hall. Leif was the only child in the whole town, if Tullen could really be called that, the young folk of their new community either taken by the fever or else long departed for safer refuges further inland or over the Baros Mountains.

The night was clear, the stars shining brightly, and the room began to feel cold. Shivering, Leif reached up to close the shutter, pausing as he watched a patch of stars disappear behind the black shape of a fast-moving cloud. He still struggled to read the weather in this part of Laskar, Vandill telling him the lake shaped the winds and rain, occasionally causing the town to be shrouded in mist all day. As Leif looked on, the blackness spread out further across the night sky, more stars winking out of sight, disappearing faster and faster. Without warning, the darkness enveloped the whole sky, swallowing the moonlit roofs of the town and pressing right up to the window.

Leif was unable to see or breathe and panic gripped him. His throat closed tight; he could neither call out for help nor draw breath. He fell backwards, terrified, his head striking one corner of the bed as he crashed onto the floorboards. Stars filled his vision for a moment and then there was nothing.

***

When first Joldir told me I was living in the ruins of Lindos, my imagination conjured an image of decaying splendour; ancient castles, imposing statues, grand palaces, broad avenues and vaulting bridges clinging to the mountainside long after its citizens died in the War of the Avatars. Once I was well enough to make my own way about the farm I found the truth to be underwhelming, much to Joldir's amusement.

"It was over two hundred years ago. Lindos was razed to the ground in the War. What little was left was taken for building material by the first people who came to settle here afterwards." A black goat stared at me and bleated loudly, is if mocking my romantic notions. "I'm afraid this is all there is," said Joldir, gesturing at the assorted collection of a dozen or so small cottages and houses that lined the road. Most of these had long ago fallen into disrepair, roofs sagging or in some cases missing altogether. Only the largest house showed signs of occupation, as this was where Thengill had made his home. Further down the road, a thin trickle of smoke rose from a tired-looking cottage Etta had claimed, marking my destination this morning.

I looked about me, searching for some sign of old Lindos. I saw the remains of one broken blackened tower thrusting up from the forest at the head of the valley beyond Joldir's fields. Behind the valley rose the northern range of the Baros Mountains, their monstrous bulk seeming to fade towards their base in the faint morning haze, so that they hovered impossibly in the sky. Turning the other way, there was only the rutted muddy road leading to Olt at the foot of the mountain, whilst Lindos Valley itself claimed a commanding view over the plains of western Reavesburg. The summer air was cool but pleasant and fresh.

"What happened to the settlers?" I asked.

"Birna told me they died in a particularly harsh winter, some forty years ago. Until I came, no one sought to reclaim this land, thinking it twice cursed ... Steady," Joldir caught my arm as my ankle turned on a rut in the road. Pain shot through my shoulder and into my back at the jolt. I gasped, grateful I would still arrive at Etta's house in clean clothes with my dignity intact. Joldir looked at me with concern. "Are you sure you're up to this? We could leave this visit for another day, if you're not strong enough."

"I'm fine," I snapped back, more angrily than I intended.

"You're the one who keeps telling me to push myself each day."

Joldir laid a placating hand on my shoulder and I paid close attention to the road, until we arrived at Etta's front door. Joldir knocked smartly and her unmistakeable voice called us to come inside.

The cottage consisted of two rooms, a dusty and unkempt living-room with a bedroom leading off from this. The ancient shutters were closed, the cracks between the wood allowing in just a small fraction of light, casting the place in shadow. There were cobwebs everywhere and a distinct smell of mould, the air tasting stale on my tongue. Etta was crouched on a stool by the fire, tending a boiling kettle, steam rising from the spout.

"Rothgar," she said by way of greeting as we entered. "I can't tell you how good it is to see you standing there. Joldir, my thanks for bringing him to me and for all you've done besides. Will you stay for some tea?"

"Why not?" replied Joldir, helping me to sit down in a rather rickety old chair before taking a seat himself. Etta busied herself crushing the dark leaves into a small metal pot, before pouring the hot water from the kettle on top of them.

"I love what you've done with the place," I remarked. Etta cackled at the joke as she placed the lid on the pot. I'd begun to develop a taste for tea myself and I wondered what Jorik would have said, if he could have seen me now. There had been a time when all I would have craved was some cold ale from the cellars of the old keep.

"What news?" Etta asked Joldir when she had finished. "I saw you and Thengill took the cart down to Olt yesterday."

"Birna told me Kalamar and Romsdahl both remain under siege by Adalrikr's forces. Sinarr, known as The Cold One, leads Vorund's forces against Kalamar whilst Joarr the Hammer is fighting Gautarr's men at Romsdahl. Olt is only occupied by a small garrison of warriors, led by Hrodmarr Hroarson. Hrodi Whitebeard has offered them no resistance and in return his town remains open to trade."

"Old Hrodi was always shrewd enough to sense which way the wind is blowing." Etta turned to me. "And what *other* news is there?"

I licked my lips, trying to order my thoughts. What I saw with the Sight was somehow incredibly personal and intimate. Speaking of those things with Etta felt like I was breaking a confidence. Perhaps in a way I was, holding nothing back as I recounted the most recent events I had seen, concerning the lives of Nuna and Leif. Desta, however, remained frustratingly elusive.

Etta sat quietly as she listened to my tale, her hands clasped around her stick. "So clear and well-ordered. This one sees far and deep – he can truly read a person. I swear, Joldir, he shows as much promise as you did, if not more. Tell me, are the ways still guarded?"

"Nereth watches the Path when we reach out towards Norlhast," Joldir told her. "If news has reached her of Rothgar's escape it's logical she would pay close attention to his sister, although there's been no sign of her in the last few weeks."

"Nuna is the key to events in Norlhast. We need to find a way to bring them back into this fight and go to the aid of Johan's household in Kalamar. Can she be reached?"

Joldir shook his head. "Whilst her mind is open to the Sight, so far I don't believe she has sensed me or Rothgar."

Etta pursed her lips, deep in thought. "What of this boy, Leif? What do you make of him?"

"Again, he's gifted," Joldir replied. "He could be useful to us if we could bring him here. There are no occupying forces at Tullen, so it might be possible ... However, after Rothgar's vision last night I'm concerned we may face something else in Tullen."

"Perhaps," Etta mused. "Sandar lied to condemn Rothgar, making him a traitor to his clan. Perhaps you're right ... Perhaps he's something more."

"What do you mean?" I asked. Joldir and Etta both exchanged a glance before Etta replied.

"There are many sides to the gift of the Sight. Some use it as you and Joldir have done, reaching out to those with a measure of the skill to see the world through their eyes. It can be a powerful weapon as well – remember how Nereth first ensnared you in the world she created to mirror Reavesburg, borrowing from your own memories? There are others who lose themselves, setting aside their bodies forever and living as wandering spirits. When they enter a person's mind they do so for one purpose; to supplant their soul and destroy them utterly."

"Skin thieves and shadow spirits," Joldir added. "Although their true name is the durath. A corruption of a noble gift Morvanos exploited as he plotted to overthrow those avatars loyal to the Creator. Imagine how dangerous such a creature would be, able to take the form of someone without those closest to them even being aware of what had happened."

I thought on their words as Etta served us our tea. "Is that what Leif saw last night? One of these 'shadow spirits'?"

Etta shrugged. "It's possible. There's a reason you and Leif have sought out one another, Rothgar. It all ties back to Sandar Tindirson, I feel sure of it."

"I should go there, with Thengill," Joldir said. "Leif could be valuable to us and he's an ideal age to be trained. If what you suspect is true, he's in danger if he's left where he is and Sandar will need dealing with."

"Not until Ekkill has returned. If a skin thief has taken Sandar, and it would make sense to possess the person with greatest influence, it would be better if the three of you faced him together."

"What about me?" Joldir and Etta looked surprised at my question. "Sandar's testimony condemned me. He should answer to me for his crimes."

"You're in no condition to undertake such a journey," Etta told me. "Not yet, at any rate. And this will take ... special skills and preparation. It's something Joldir, Thengill and Ekkill have been trained to deal with." I folded my arms, annoyed as I knew Etta was right. I couldn't walk down the road unaided – the journey to Tullen was unthinkable.

"Still no word from Ekkill?" asked Joldir.

"Not yet. If something had happened I would know. For now we wait and discover all we can about events in Tullen and Norlhast. Your place is here, Rothgar, to help us learn all we can so, when the time does come to strike, we will be ready."

CHAPTER 36

In the days that followed every attempt to find Leif using the Sight met with failure, leaving us wondering about the boy's fate. My mind was still trying to absorb Etta's revelation that there were those with the Sight who had forsaken their physical form forever. I thought at first these spirits were wandering freely across Amuran. Joldir corrected that notion as we sat together in Etta's house by the fire one evening, talking long into the night.

"Someone who has taken the path of the durath cannot survive for long in the physical realm, the realm of the Real. They require a host to live in this world, one who they must consume utterly. For a durath who fails to take possession of someone's spirit is destroyed in that struggle."

"Then why would they take that risk?" I asked.

"Because of the rewards. To be durath is to be immortal, for their possessed bodies do not age. Moreover, even if you kill the host a durath's spirit is free to find another. The oldest and most powerful of the durath are skilled in overcoming their victims and have taken many forms over the years."

"And all this comes from the power of the Sight?"

Etta nodded. "Morvanos discovered how to sunder spirit from flesh in this way. He called those who were willing to join him to a place of darkness and brought forth the first of the durath, naming them the Sundered Souls. Then he sent them out to take possession of their new bodies, replacing people of influence and power with his own agents. When the War of the Avatars began the durath sowed discord and confusion, turning allies upon each other and allowing Morvanos' forces to gain the upper hand in the early days of the war. They remain loyal to him even now, two centuries later, despite his banishment beyond the Void."

"And they can't be killed?"

Etta shook her head. "Not by normal means, unless they fail to successfully destroy the soul of their new host. However, when Vellandir's avatars learned the nature of this particular foe they discovered a way to defeat them. Garradon forged weapons etched with runes of power, creating a blade that cuts through both soul and flesh. Such knowledge is only known to a few in these days. It's why I paid for Joldir's tuition by the Mages of Mirtan in Seroch, so he could learn the art and bring those skills back with him to Laskar."

I shuddered. "Is that what's stalking me through my dreams? Is that what Nereth is?"

"No," Joldir answered. "Nereth simply possesses the Sight, she's not one of the durath. Nereth was a fellow pupil with me in the Chapters of Seroch. For a time she was in my charge, until I completed my studies and returned here."

I stared into the flames as they danced about the glowing logs in the heart of the fire. My mind was slow, almost unwilling to accept and believe what I was being told. The Sight had been described as a gift, yet now I was beginning to understand it brought both danger and temptations. A log snapped, sending a shower of sparks into the chimney as I realised something else.

"Nereth joined Adalrikr because he's powerful. Adalrikr, the loving fourth son of Asmarr, who suddenly rose up against his father and took his titles, killing his three brothers ... After he became one of the durath."

"You've guessed the truth," Etta said softly. "Now you know who I've been fighting all these years. The young man who was once Adalrikr is long dead. The shadow that consumed him is old, one of the first who eagerly heeded Morvanos' call and sundered soul from flesh. The durath set aside their birth names when they embraced this path. Morvanos named him Baltus, First of the Sundered and made him one of his generals, second in power only to the great warrior Kumil himself. Amongst the durath he became known as Vashtas, which means Flayer of Souls in the Lagashan language. I have been hunting this one for years, gathering the tools and the people I needed to destroy him, tracking him down and unmasking each of his disguises. Always he has eluded me. Now he is King Adalrikr, a king bent on raising his army to bring the whole of the north under his heel."

I felt a coldness seeping through me, starting in my stomach. I swallowed, my throat tight. "And to destroy Adalrikr you forged your alliance with Norlhast and pitted our clans against him. You sacrificed the lives of my family ... and you destroyed my future."

Etta's lined face was a mass of spider web shadows in the darkness of the room. "Yes, I know. Are you asking if I would do it all again, if it meant I could bring an end to him, once and for all? It's a question I've asked myself ever since the night of your sister's wedding. All I can say is Adalrikr represents a great evil, one that has to be destroyed."

"Why does it fall to you to bring him down?"

Etta was silent for so long I thought she had ignored my question. "He took from me the one person I ever loved, long ago. Isn't that reason enough?" She met my gaze for a moment. "We've all made sacrifices. All of us."

***

I wrestled with my thoughts after I returned home with Joldir, trying to make sense of everything I'd learned. Etta had always been the spymaster of the Reavesburg Clan, so why was I surprised she made use of those around her to ensure the success of her schemes? The answer, of course, lay in the fact that, until now, I'd always thought she was loyal to the Reavesburg Clan. Now I saw something different. Had my clan been manipulated all along as she pursued her own personal vendetta?

More than ever I missed Desta. It was foolish to follow the Path whilst I was angry and tired, without Joldir at my side to steady my course. Tonight, though, I wanted something private, something just for me alone.

***

Djuri must have been strong in the Sight, for the pull of his mind was the most powerful in Ulfkell's Keep as he stood guard on one of the towers, wrapped in his cloak against the coastal wind. It was strange; I had grown up with Djuri and known him all my life. However, it was only now that I understood him. There was anger and bitterness, wrapped up with remorse, a terrible sense of regret and shame that left an empty hole deep inside his spirit. Perhaps Brunn Fourwinds had been the wiser man in refusing to bow to Adalrikr.

I left Djuri up on the battlements and followed the faint sense of a presence nearby, seeking it out slowly and carefully. The cat flexed its claws and purred. She knew I was there, an odd sensation for me; I was used to being a silent witness to events around me. Yet the animal welcomed me, as if I were one of her own kind, and perhaps that was truer than I realised. Our minds touched, curious. We were one.

The cat rose from the ragged blanket she used for her bed at the foot of the stairs and set off with purpose. She found the door easily enough. I had last stood there months ago, a different man. The cat sniffed, drawing in the scents. She purred, appreciating the pleasant memories that came flooding into our minds together. Experimentally, she nosed at the door and gave it a soft shove. Unlatched, it swung open and the cat darted through the gap on soft, silent paws.

Desta was there, in her nightgown, brushing her hair before going to bed. Candles cast her chamber with a dim glow and by their light I could see she was not alone. Haarl was on the bed, half-wrapped in the covers as he sat watching her, a vacant smile on his face. It took all my self-control not to leap, hissing, onto the bed and claw my friend's eyes out. Instead I blinked once, slowly, before slinking into the shadows of the room to hide.

"Are you *ever* coming to bed?" Haarl asked, a plaintive

note to his voice.

Desta smiled as she continued brushing. "What's the hurry? If you want to go to sleep you don't have to wait for me."

"Sleep's the last thing I was thinking of right now," Haarl told her, patting the side of the bed. Desta arched an eyebrow as she continued with her strokes, smiling again as she did so. Her long dark hair fell about her shoulders in a way that was achingly familiar.

"I see," she teased. She set down the brush, blew out all but one of the candles and walked towards the bed. "What could you have in mind, Haarl?"

"Only what every newlywed has on their mind, my love."

"Really?" Desta laughed. "I think that's just you, but I'll indulge you all the same." Desta slipped under the covers and wrapped her arms around Haarl as she kissed him. "After all, there'll be precious little time for this next year, when there's three of us." Desta turned and blew out the candle by the bed, plunging the room into darkness.

I realised my mistake, thinking I could return to Ulfkell's Keep and everything would be the same. I'd come here seeking comfort, as if that were Desta's only purpose in life. It was a painful lesson to learn the truth especially as, despite the dark, I could still see and hear all too well. The cat darted for the gap in the doorway and slipped back out into the corridor. Together we padded through the darkness of the keep until we had left the sounds emanating from Desta and Haarl's room far behind.

The cat dropped lightly back into her bed, mewling softly as she shared my bitterness. It was an odd sort of comfort and it was harder than I expected to disentangle our minds from each another. For a moment I thought about slipping away from my crippled body, seeking out a simpler life, far away from Lindos. Only for a moment ...

***

I opened my eyes and heard urgent knocking on my door.

"Rothgar." Joldir's voice, sounding concerned as he opened the door and strode inside.

"It's alright –" I began before Joldir cut across me.

"Where have you been? I felt you go and I couldn't find you. I told you *never* to use the Sight without me – something you should be even more wary of now you understand the dangers ..." He paused as he looked more closely at me, his eyes narrowed. "What's happened?"

"She didn't wait." I sat up in bed, an empty feeling in my chest. "I thought she would wait for me. It's all I've been holding onto ... after ..." Tears flowed down my cheeks and I had no more words. Joldir sat on the bed next to me and gently put his arm around my shoulders, drawing me close as I wept.

CHAPTER 37

As the summer days shortened, the talk around Joldir's table each night turned to bringing in the harvest, stabling the livestock and setting enough food aside to see us through the winter. Though I was stronger I was a poor excuse for a farmhand. Still, I insisted I helped where I could around the farm, feeling this went at least some way towards repaying Joldir and Arissa. I also had another motivation; sleeping well after any physical work, which always left my dreams free from the Sight.

Thengill had scythed his way through the barley field during the day, leaving me to bundle the crop into sheaves and stack them, ready for threshing by Joldir and Arissa back in the barn. Now as the shadows began to lengthen, Thengill joined me in bundling the sheaves, making three to each one I fashioned. A variety of insects flew around and I irritably waved them away from my face, my shirt soaked with sweat, body burning and aching, hands cut and sore from tying the stalks together as Thengill had shown me. My fingers seemed to have a mind of their own, stubbornly refusing to obey my commands, as they fumbled over my latest knot. I tried twice more without success, cursing and swearing, before feeling a hand on my shoulder. I glanced up into the bright sunshine to see Thengill, stripped to the waist, looking down at me. He was not so much well-built as a solid slab of muscle, sporting the various scars, both large and small, that are the hallmark of the warrior's profession. Tattooed across his chest was the black bear of the Vorund Clan, a mark I knew was reserved only for their most respected warriors. Thengill's dark brown eyes regarded me carefully, and I tried to work out if this was meant to be a challenge of some kind. If so, it was likely to be a short one, as I had just been bested by a sheaf of barley.

"You're lucky Lindos is so remote," I said at last. "A tattoo like that could get a man hung in Olt, even if Tyrfingr Blackeyes calls himself jarl of Reavesburg. What were you, one of Adalrikr's jarls or bodyguards?"

"I served Asmarr," Thengill answered. "Right now, I'm hot and I don't see anyone else about, do you? Don't see the need for the pair of us to tread so carefully round each other, not if you're sticking around for the winter. My little secret's nothing compared to yours, after all."

"If you were Asmarr's guard I imagine there's little love lost between you and Adalrikr. Did you know him well, at Vorund Fastness?"

Thengill refused to meet my gaze, instead tying the barley sheaf together with well-practised hands. "I thought I did. Come on, we'll soon start losing the light."

***

Returning from the fields along the road to Lindos as the sun set I was dripping with sweat. Exhausted, I sat down outside Etta's cottage, breathing heavily as Thengill looked on anxiously. He must have gone to fetch help because the next thing I knew Arissa was looking down on me. When she spoke her lips moved but the sound of her voice was distant and muffled. My surroundings shimmered, as if I were underwater. There was a blinding flash followed by pain, like a nail being hammered into my skull, and I arched my back in agony, screaming.

Nuna caught her finger on her needle and cried out, causing Katla and Ottama to look up from their embroidery. Nuna watched as a red bead of blood formed on the tip of her still smarting finger. She sucked it as she rose from her seat.

"Did you hear that?" she asked her maids, who looked at each other blankly.

"My lady, I heard nothing," Katla told her.

"I heard someone screaming … At least, I thought I did."

Nuna walked to the window, looking out over Norlhast in the fading light. "I hope Valdimarr isn't torturing some poor soul."

"Don't worry yourself, my lady." Ottama rose and closed the shutters. "I'm sure it's nothing. Sometimes the seabirds' cries can sound like those of men, especially when the noise is carried here on the wind. Anyway, it's getting late and it's long past time for us to help you get ready to retire for the night."

Nuna allowed her maids to prepare her bed and help her undress, still shaking her head from time to time. She'd heard something, she was sure of it. Left alone in her room in the dark she felt restless and worried.

***

"I knew it. I just *knew* it. Out all day with Thengill, working in the fields without so much as a break and now look at him." Arissa's distant voice sounded furious. "Why didn't you do something, Joldir, so he didn't feel obligated to go in the first place? If either of you had the brains you were born with, you would've realised he should never have been out there ..."

The tirade continued as Joldir leaned over and looked more closely at me, pressing his hand gently onto my brow. The cool touch was both relief and agony in equal measure, although I was unable to move or speak. Etta's door swung open and she hobbled outside her cottage.

"What's happened?" she demanded, walking over to my side. "Is he awake?"

"I'm not sure if he sees us or if he's far away, lost with the Sight," Joldir replied. "He's had some kind of seizure, which is preventing me from joining him."

Etta sagged at the news, leaning on her stick. "Preventing you from protecting him – or us for that matter. There's no doubt, then? This must be connected to the ... work you've been doing with him?"

"Perhaps we pushed him too far too soon, combined with his labours in the fields this month and his weak condition. And he took the news about this girl hard, the one he had back in Ulfkell's Keep. That kind of thing can make a

307

difference."

Arissa's voice wavered. "Are you saying we might lose him, after everything he's been through?"

"No," Etta replied. "This one is strong. Can you hear me, Rothgar? We've come too far together for you to give up now, my boy."

I wanted to answer, to tell them I was awake and could hear them. For some reason, though, the words would not come. Thengill and Joldir carried me back to my bed. I tried to hold on to their voices but instead I slipped slowly away. Far away.

***

Djuri slouched in the saddle, trying to relieve the ache in his back and buttocks. He'd never been a keen rider and his journey with Bjorr over the past week had taken in the various villages and hamlets that still remained occupied between Reavesburg and Noln. Taxes were due and as a key trading port Noln, his destination before returning home, was expected to contribute generously.

He glanced back, looking at the column of men riding behind him, a mixture of warriors from both Vorund and Reavesburg. Riding by the side of the carts Haarl caught his eye and gave him a brief nod. There was Ulf nearby, head down and hood up, shield slung over his back. Blackeyes paid good coin to anyone willing to wear the banner of the bear, regardless of clan. The men of Vorund still outnumbered them three to one, however. Blackeyes was generous to those willing to turn their cloak, not foolish.

The heavily armed group rounded the bend in the road and Noln came into view, spread out before them at the bottom of a gentle incline. The tide was in and Djuri saw two ships in the harbour, both flying the banners of the bear. Vorund warships. Djuri frowned, wondering what this signified and Bjorr, a grim warrior in Galin Ironfist's company and the man in command of this venture, gave his horse the spurs and led them forward at a swift trot.

They rode into Noln unopposed and wound their way through the main square and the town's streets down into the docks. Djuri saw Lundvarr, the town elder, deep in conversation with a knot of well-armed men. He looked nervous as usual.

Bjorr swung down from his saddle and strode forward, calling out a greeting to the men on the dockside. The eldest of them, a grey-haired grizzled man with piercing blue eyes, turned and broke into a broad smile as the two men embraced.

"Bjorr. Well met, old friend. What brings you to this flea-ridden excuse for a town?" Lundvarr, upset at the slight, wisely said nothing, shrinking back from the pair of warriors.

Bjorr waved a hand in the direction of his company. "Collecting the king's taxes, Randall. Tyrfingr's got us scouring all the towns and villages on the coast. It's surprising what people have hidden away when you ask them … persuasively. That's the word. *Persuasively*. Now it's Noln's turn to generously contribute to his coffers."

Randall laughed and turned to Lundvarr, beckoning him forwards. "You hear that, Lundvarr? Today you can serve your king twice in one day. Provisions for my ships and coin for Bjorr's men here. That should put you in good standing with your new liege, wouldn't you say?"

"Of … of course … Of course," Lundvarr stammered, looking positively horrified at the prospect. His eyes met Djuri's, not holding his gaze for long.

Djuri hoped Lundvarr didn't recognise him. However, he quickly realised the man had greater worries than which members of the Reavesburg Clan had turned their cloak. The normally bustling port of Noln was deserted apart from Randall's two warships. There were no Reavesburg ships, nor any sign of the merchant vessels that were normally such frequent visitors. With the fall of Ulfkell's Keep trade in Noln had died. Despite the poverty of Lundvarr's situation the list of demands from Randall and Bjorr was extensive. Noln's town elder bowed and scraped before hurrying off to make the necessary arrangements. Djuri swallowed and looked away, glad on this occasion it hadn't come to violence. Noln still had supplies at the moment – by winter Djuri guessed they would be spread thin.

"What brings you this way?" Bjorr was asking Randall, looking up at the two powerful warships, the sigil of the bear displayed proudly on their sails. "I thought you were up north with Sinarr, laying siege to Kalamar." Randall's men laughed and Djuri felt uneasy. He turned to Haarl, where the young man was hunched in his saddle, staring straight down at the ground.

"You've not heard the news, have you?" Randall clapped a hand on Bjorr's shoulder. "How long have you been on the road? We're sailing south, lad, bound for Romsdahl and that bastard Gautarr Falrufson. Siege is over and Kalamar's a burnt-out ruin – Sinarr saw to that in the end. Now he's taking his forces south to join with Joarr the Hammer and break Romsdahl before winter. Could do with you and your crew with me for that one, Bjorr, if Tyrfingr will let you go."

Bjorr shook his head. "Can't see Blackeyes or Galin Ironfist being happy if I don't show up with the king's taxes, tempting as it sounds to take the fight to Falrufson."

"Ironfist is it now?" Randall asked. "Heard Galin was short of a hand after letting Johan Jokellsward slip the net at Ulfkell's Keep. Took my lads here to finish the job, you can tell him that." Boisterous cheers went up at that remark from a few of Randall's men, although Bjorr's crew remained silent. "Anyhow, reckon there's time for a drink or two and to exchange a few stories before the tide's right. You coming?"

Bjorr nodded to Djuri. "Stay here with Ulf and Haarl. See to it the supplies are loaded onto the ships and Lundvarr pays us what he owes." He set off with Randall and the rest of his men before turning back. "If I find it's short, even by a single silver crown, I'll know the reason why, won't I?"

Haarl spoke up. "It'll be right, Bjorr, you can count on that."

"Right, course I can. After all, we're the king's loyal subjects now, aren't we?"

CHAPTER 38

Leif drew his covers tightly around him as he lay in his bed. His father sat perched by his side, hand on his shoulder, murmuring comforting words that meant nothing.

"Another nightmare, Son? It's alright. Just a dream, nothing more than that."

"Dad. I really want us to leave Tullen. I don't like it here."

His father sighed in that familiar way, and Leif despaired he would ever be able to make him listen. "There's no going back to Brindling, Leif. We've a life here now, and plenty can't say that in these times. Tullen's folk have been good to us, helped put us back on our feet. Autumn's here and we'll be harvesting the rest of the crops soon. You can lend me a hand, like you did last year."

"Anders." Leif shuddered at his mother's voice. "Vandill's here. He says Sandar's asking to see you."

Leif's father sounded annoyed at the interruption. "At this time of night? What does he want, Lina?"

She appeared at the doorway, lamplight behind her shining through her thin nightgown, revealing her curves. Despite the hour, her dark hair was artfully arranged, as if she were on her way out to some party, which was not so far from the truth. Leif's parents now spent most evenings down at the long hall and had only just returned tonight.

"How should I know? He says it's important and won't wait till morning. I'm sure it won't take long, and I can look after the boy while you're gone."

Leif reached out, clasping his father's hand tightly. "Dad. *Please*, don't go."

His father hugged him before rising to leave. "Man like Tindirson asks you to pay him a visit, that's not something to be ignored, Leif. I'll be back soon and your mother's here." He hugged her warmly before leaving the room. A few minutes later Leif heard the door open and close and the sound of his father's footsteps receding down the street. Lina sat down next to him, saying nothing, her hands contentedly holding her stomach. Leif ignored her, trying without success to get comfortable.

"You might as well give up your little campaign," she told him. "Your father has everything he wants here. Next summer, when the baby is born, our family will be complete. You're not going to spoil that, are you?" She took hold of Leif's ear, twisting it sharply and making him cry out. Furious with himself, he bit his lip, stifling the sob he felt rising in his chest, and she fixed him with a fierce gaze. "No, of course you're not."

"No," Leif whispered.

"No, what?" she hissed.

Leif took a shuddering breath as he held back his tears. "No, *Mother*."

"That's better. *Much* better." Lina carefully smoothed out his covers and straightened Leif's hair, soft hands caressing his forehead. "What are we going to do with you, child? You're such a worry to me these days. You look so ... wan and sickly. I thought children were meant to be so full of life."

Leif tried to shrink away from her as she peered at him in the darkness, still absently stroking his head. "Anders is happy now. Don't you see that? Things couldn't have gone on the way they were, with all your mother's moping, never saying a word to anyone. That was no life for either of them, was it? Now Anders has his darling Lina back, only *better* than before. Now he has a woman who wants to please him and build their new life together, here in Tullen. And he has you, Leif, his only son. There's power in that, you know. Power, running through your blood."

Leif breathed a sigh of relief as she took her hand away and left him alone in the darkness, unable to bear being near her since that summer night when everything changed. He waited a long time for his father to return from the long hall, eventually falling into an uneasy sleep, granting some respite from the daily fear holding him in its grip.

***

The shadows in Leif's room lengthened, shifted and twisted. A doorway appeared, light spilling through, driving away the shadows as the image of the sleeping boy faded. I walked towards the doorway, into the light, leaving Tullen behind me.

I found myself standing in a grassed courtyard underneath an overcast sky, the clouds dark and heavy. In the centre an old yew tree grew, gnarled roots rippling through the otherwise immaculate lawn. Nereth stood before me dressed, as ever, in black. Her cloak was trimmed with white fur, held together at her throat by a silver clasp that shone brightly despite the absence of the sun. Her eyes looked straight into mine.

"The cloisters of my Chapter, in Seroch." Nereth laid a delicate hand on the old yew tree. "I spent many happy years here before I journeyed north. Sometimes I wish I could return, to a time when things were so much simpler."

"This isn't real?" I asked.

Nereth smiled and walked towards me, arms held out before her. I was unable to resist as her hands took mine. Soft and warm, their touch gentle. A small voice in my head urged me to flee as I stood there. "No, Rothgar, this is something else. A world of my devising, a place where I can feel safe and remember other times. And now, here you are, calling upon me uninvited, after I spent so much time and energy trying to find you."

Remember the voice told me and, as the memories came flooding back, I released Nereth's hands. "You've followed me before, in the secret tunnels of Ulfkell's Keep. You appeared as a falcon as well. You tried to kill me."

Nereth slowly walked around me and still I was unable to move, as rooted to the spot as the yew tree. "Something awoke in you that day in Karas Greystorm's hall – when my sisters were taken from me. When they were *murdered*, murdered by you and your friend Halfhand. You called us witches then – now you know we had more in common than you imagined." Her hand brushed my shoulder before moving to caress my cheek, her red lips inches from my face. "I wanted you dead, I don't deny it. Your powerful protector prevented me seizing the moment. Tell me, who is he?"

Her breath was warm against my throat and I tried to turn away, tried to forget Joldir ever existed. I brought Desta to mind, remembering carefree times before the wedding of my sister.

"Very good." Nereth's voice was barely more than a whisper. "Very good. That takes both skill and training. You know how to walk the Path and you're strong enough to close your mind to those with the Sight. Even so, it's only a matter of time before you tell me what I want to know. So, *tell me*, who has been schooling you?"

I recalled sitting before Olfridor in the training circle with Bram and Bandor, the three of us just ten years of age. I remembered my pride in how I acquitted myself that day, as my father looked on. A small frown creased Nereth's forehead as she stared into my eyes. I looked deeper.

The fire in the long hall cast a warm glow over its occupants. Sandar stood before a small crowd, his arms outstretched. Before him knelt a man, hands tied behind his back – Anders, Leif's father, a look of confusion and terror on his face. Sandar looked on as Ginna moved forwards, her arms around Anders, comforting him. Slowly Sandar turned towards the tall curtain that divided the long hall in half, reached out –

Nereth took a step back from me, startled. Her slap to my face left my head ringing as I staggered and almost fell in the courtyard. "How ... How *dare* you."

What *had* I … we, just seen? Nereth was looking at me in shock at the ease with which I'd drawn her down the Path before she'd wrenched us back here. Now the air shimmered and there was a distant peal of thunder. I glimpsed movement to my left and turned to see a figure walking in the shadows behind the stone columns at the edges of the cloister. Nereth saw it too.

"Who are you? What are you doing here?" Although her voice was defiant I could see the surprise on her face. Despite her challenge the figure ignored her, continuing to circle the cloister, remaining half-hidden in the shadows.

Nereth took a step forwards and as her attention switched to the mysterious intruder I found myself free from her influence. I slowly backed away, searching as I did so for some means of escape. The figure emerged onto the grass and I saw the Crow Man, shimmering as if seen through a summer heat haze. For a second time thunder sounded and this time it was quickly followed by the patter of rain, the cool heavy drops falling onto my clothes and skin. Nereth fumbled with her cloak, drawing up her hood just before the shower turned into deluge as the storm broke. In moments I was soaked.

The Crow Man's eyes were black orbs, dark and unreadable. His beak clacked as he spoke, each word clear and distinct. "You have something of mine, Nereth. It's time to return it."

Nereth looked back at me and my step faltered for a moment, before I regained control once more. The rain continued to fall, washing away the colours and causing the edges of the cloister to fade from sight. The Crow Man continued to advance and, as he drew nearer, it appeared as if the whole world was reduced down to the three of us standing before the twisted shape of the yew, itself little more than a dark shadow.

"He came here unbidden, as did you." Nereth peered at the Crow Man from beneath her hood. "But you're not a stranger, are you? I know you, I can feel it. Who is it – who hides behind that disguise?"

"I doubt you would recognise me, Nereth, after all this time. I remember you, when you were little more than a young girl. Why did you choose to serve Adalrikr? You know what he is and his ambitions; nowhere will be safe from him, not even the cloisters of your old Chapter. Is this what you fight for, to see your childhood haunts reduced to nothing, only living on in your fading memory?"

The Crow Man was near now. I had circled round, away from Nereth, almost within touching distance of him. Nereth watched us both intently as the rain pelted down, puddles forming on the perfect green lawn.

"I know only this," she told us. "That there will be a reckoning amongst those who stood against him. The north is poised to fall to King Adalrikr and that will only be the beginning. The First of the Sundered has returned to Amuran and we must heed his call or die. All those who have the gift of the Sight and understand its true purpose know what is to come. Your tutor has surely told you this, Rothgar? Or am I mistaken?"

"I know enough to know which side I should be fighting on," I replied. The Crow Man took a final step as I spoke, taking a firm grasp of my forearm.

"We must leave," he told me and I nodded, feeling the world begin to tip beneath my feet and slide away.

Nereth was powerless to prevent us escaping, vanishing into the driving rain that fell all around me from every direction and none. Her voice was little more than a whisper as we fled. "You took my sisters from me, Rothgar. I promise that, when the time comes, you'll watch as I take yours."

CHAPTER 39

My eyes opened, peering into the gloom. I was back in my room in Joldir's house. Head spinning I eased myself up in bed, nightshirt soaked with sweat, arms trembling with effort. Someone was sitting in the chair next to me and there were running steps, heading towards my chamber. Moments later the door flew open and Arissa appeared, carrying a small oil lamp.

"Joldir, I heard someone shouting. Is everything ..." Her voice trailed off as she saw me watching her. Joldir rose unsteadily from the chair next to my bed and waved her forward.

"Everything's well, Arissa. Rothgar has returned to us ... eventually." Joldir drew in a shaking breath and reached out to support my back as he sat down again at the edge of my bed.

"Nuna," I whispered, my voice hoarse from long disuse.

Arissa ventured forwards slowly, setting her lamp down on the small table. "It's Arissa," she told me. "You're in Lindos now, with me and Joldir. Etta's been so worried. If it weren't so late I'd run and tell her the news now."

"No. Nuna's in danger. I saw Nereth, and she threatened her." What I had seen so clearly with the Sight now seemed distant and fogged, my head throbbing. "She told me the Sundered have returned. And I've heard about the siege of Kalamar. Kalamar has fallen to the Vorund Clan."

Joldir gently eased me back into bed. "We know about Kalamar. You've been ill for six weeks and the news reached Olt more than a fortnight ago. Are you telling me you saw this with the Sight?"

I shook my head, regretting it instantly as I winced in

pain. "No, not exactly. Not Kalamar itself. I was down at the dockside in Noln, where I heard a man called Randall, one of Adalrikr's men, telling everyone the news."

"It's no idle boast. I'm sorry, I know you had friends there. The reports we've received have been scant and there's been no word of the fate of Johan or his family."

My eyes were already feeling heavy and I found myself sinking back into the bed. I gripped Joldir's arm with the last of my strength, fending off sleep for as long as I could. "You came for me. I'm not sure I would have escaped from Nereth a third time if you hadn't been there. Thank you."

"I intend to keep a closer eye on you from now on. Now rest, all this can wait until the morning."

I wanted to tell him to check on Nuna and make sure she was safe. Even as the thought formed in my mind I was already drifting into a deep, dreamless sleep.

**

The following morning I sat outside in a comfortable rocking chair, wrapped in a thick woollen blanket, watching the sun slowly climb above Mount Lindos. It was markedly lower in the sky than the last time I had seen it; autumn was nearly done and soon winter would be upon us. I pulled the blanket more tightly around me and watched as Etta opened the latch of her door before lowering herself onto a low stool opposite me with an audible crack of her knees.

"It should be you sitting on this stool, at your age," she muttered tartly.

"You forget I've had a near-death experience. I'm barely strong enough to sit in this rocker."

Etta raised an eyebrow. "Every day for me is a near-death experience. You're obviously feeling better to cheek me like that. You gave us all a scare, I can tell you."

"I'm sorry."

"I'm the one who should be saying that. I pushed you too hard."

I paused to reflect. "I'm not sure it's that simple. If Joldir hadn't schooled me and helped me develop the Sight I'm not sure I would have been strong enough to face Nereth."

"Joldir told me he helped you escape from her."

"I was able to resist Nereth before he appeared – more than that, I pulled her down the Path until she stopped me. And we saw something ... strange. Something to do with Sandar Tindirson and his followers in Tullen."

Etta folded her hands together under her chin, resting her elbows on her knees. "Tell me."

I recounted everything the Sight had shown me since I fell ill. This morning my mind felt fresh, enabling me to give Etta an orderly account of my visions and what I'd learned. Etta supplied her own information from time to time, corroborating some of the events I'd seen with reports that had reached Olt in recent weeks. When I woke this morning the first thing I remembered were Randall's words, their meaning too awful to contemplate. It felt like a hammer had struck my heart; Kalamar had fallen to Adalrikr's men. I couldn't be sure if Johan and Bandor had actually escaped Nuna's wedding alive. Even if they had managed to return home, it seemed it was for nothing.

Etta was unable to offer me any comfort. "A large refugee camp has sprung up around Olt," she told me. "The weather is turning and some of Tyrfingr's men have been somewhat over-zealous in collecting his taxes and enforcing his rules. Numerous smaller settlements have been attacked and destroyed, leaving people homeless. Others have left seeking shelter in the larger towns and cities of Reavesburg or else beyond our borders. Many of those heading south brought tidings of the fall of Kalamar, so it seems beyond doubt the tale you heard was true. What also worries me is there's been no word from Ekkill since I sent him scouting. I fear he became embroiled in whatever took place at Johan's stronghold. He's been gone far too long."

Or perhaps he abandoned you the first chance he got, I thought to myself. Instead I said "What of Gautarr and his men? Is Romsdahl still defying Adalrikr's claim to be king of the north?"

"For the time being," Etta sighed. "By now Sinarr's forces will have joined Joarr's men in laying siege to Gautarr's fortress. There will be no breaking the army that surrounds him, at least not without outside aid. Romsdahl's walls are thick but it remains to be seen whether Gautarr has set enough supplies aside to see him through the coming winter. Joarr and Sinarr can simply starve him out, as long as they're patient."

I rocked back and forth, remembering Johan and Damona's hospitality when I visited Kalamar Castle on my way to treat with Karas Greystorm. I thought of Bandor and everything we had shared growing up together under the protection of my father. It all seemed so long ago.

"I need Joldir to help me, today if possible," I told Etta. "Nereth threatened Nuna before she lost her hold on me. I need to know she's safe and I have to try and warn her she's in danger."

Etta leaned forward and placed one hand on my knee. "Has it occurred to you Nereth has set a trap for you? That she *wants* you to seek out your sister, whilst she lies in wait?"

"Yes, which is why I want Joldir's help. I'll be safer with him than if I go on my own. I can't sit here and do nothing, Etta, surely you must see that?"

Etta looked at me intently. "There are times when you remind me so clearly of Kolfinnar. People always compared him with Jorik, yet you have many of your father's ways. Brave and bold and a man who knew his mind, as any good clan chief must. I always thought you were better suited to the title than your brother. Would that you had been the eldest son, Rothgar, perhaps things might have turned out differently."

"They are as they are," I replied. "I must do this. Do you understand?"

"Of course. And Joldir will be with you, I'll see to that."

***

The Hall of Norlhast Keep was packed and noisy. Nuna

set next to her husband, attended by her maids, Katla and Ottama. Albrikt, long-time advisor to his clan, stood nearby and Nuna thought he looked older, his face more lined, beard greyer. Albrikt leaned forwards and whispered into Karas' ear and the Norlhast clan chief nodded, although Nuna had to immediately correct herself, for Karas Greystorm was now the jarl of Norlhast, Adalrikr Asmarrson's vassal. After all, no chief would have tolerated being summoned to attend a meeting in his own hall.

Nuna felt more comfortable when she saw Sigurd and Kalfr amongst Norlhast's warriors, all gathered to protect Greystorm. Brosa was there too, the young warrior whom Karas had appointed as her personal bodyguard. He smiled at her as their eyes met and she felt calmer, more at peace, until the doors of the hall were pushed open with a booming crash.

Styrman belatedly began to announce Valdimarr's entrance before being roughly shoved aside by one of the Vorund Clan's warriors. Nuna saw there were two dozen of them, perhaps more, flanking Valdimarr on either side as he strode down the length of the hall. As ever, the little man was sweating under the weight of his chainmail. That was how Nuna had taken to thinking of him – *the little man*. It was a small, petty revenge of the kind she thought Kalfr would approve. It was her private rebellion against the authority of the creature who now controlled all the affairs of Norlhast, in her husband's name, of course.

"My lord." Valdimarr gave Karas his usual, perfunctory bow, which amounted to little more than a brief nod.

Karas stood and walked down to meet his visitor, his own warriors parting before him as he did so. "Valdimarr. The request for an audience was an urgent one, so I trust you have tidings of some import that you wish to discuss. We are all anxious to hear what you have to say."

Valdimarr smiled and reached inside his fine velvet cloak. Nuna saw Kalfr and Sigurd move closer to Karas, the two brothers either side of him, watching for any sign of treachery.

However, all that emerged from Valdimarr's cloak was a small package, wrapped in a dirty brown cloth. Nuna found she had been holding her breath and exhaled slowly. She knew the absence of something as obvious as a blade didn't mean there was no threat. Such direct action was hardly Valdimarr's style.

Valdimarr slowly unwrapped the package with exaggerated care and a hush descended on the crowd of onlookers. As he pulled the corners of the cloth away Nuna had to stand up to see what it contained, and even then she was unsure what she was looking at. A long, dark object lay nestled in Valdimarr's hand. He smiled as he held it towards Karas.

"The king of the north is as good as his word, to those loyal to him." When Karas didn't move to take the proffered object Valdimarr stepped closer. "Why do you look so suspicious, Karas? I'm offering you a gift – more than that, in fact. This is a symbol of your inheritance, a birthright of your people."

Karas held out his hand and Valdimarr dropped the object into his palm with a solid thump. It took Nuna a moment to register that it was a key, rust-spotted and blackened. She watched Karas run his fingers over it, saw them come away sooty and dark.

"What is this?" Karas asked.

"The key to Kalamar Castle, or what's left of it. Petr Hamarrson's resistance to King Adalrikr is at an end. Sinarr sent one of his ships north to Norlhast to bring news of the latest defeat of the Reavesburg Clan and to pass this on."

Karas turned the key over in his hand, inspecting it carefully. A few of the men accompanying Valdimarr began to smirk, glancing at each other as if sharing some private joke. "This has been burned. What has happened to the people there?"

"Kalamar has been burned to the ground, its walls smashed and brought down, my lord." There was more laughter at this statement, Valdimarr's men no longer bothering to try and hide their mirth. Brosa looked angry, only holding back from saying something at a shake of the head from Sigurd.

Albrikt's face was one of pure outrage. His jaw worked and he opened his mouth a number of times before he was able to put his words together. "Burned to the ground? Valdimarr, surely you know Kalamar Castle was built by our clan. Our dispute with Johan Jokellsward and his forebears centred on its return to our people. Without it, why, those lands are worthless and, worse still, undefended from raiders."

Valdimarr appeared to be enjoying himself. "Do I need to remind you the clans are no more? There is only one kingdom now, the kingdom of Adalrikr. Did Tyrfingr Blackeyes not promise to Karas Greystorm in Ulfkell's Keep that the *lands* of Kalamar would be returned to him, honouring his place as the jarl of Norlhast in King Adalrikr's service?"

"Well, yes –"

"And if it pleases your king to leave Kalamar Castle as a ruin, as a reminder to the people in the north of his realm of the fate of those who resist him, is that something you would wish to object to, Albrikt?"

"No, we do not," interjected Karas. "As you say, Valdimarr, a bargain was struck."

***

There were angry mutterings amongst the Norlhast warriors after Valdimarr and his men left the hall. Sigurd silenced them with a glare as Karas sat down heavily in his chair, the key still clutched in his hand.

"They mock us," said Brosa. "We have fought for generations to regain that castle. Destroying it and then going through this sham of returning the key only proves how little they really think of us."

"Adalrikr was never going to allow us to possess a second stronghold in the north," Karas answered. "This wasn't about honouring any arrangement with his allies. He's showing his strength over us. Now the only resistance

Adalrikr faces on the western coast of the Redfars Sea is in Romsdahl."

Sigurd approached Karas and leaned in close to him. "We would do well to retire to your chambers, my lord. There are too many prying eyes and ears to discuss this matter here."

Karas nodded and rose from his seat, Nuna at his side. The blackened iron key fell to the floor with a dull thud as they left the Great Hall. As she reached the door, held open for her deferentially by Styrman, Nuna felt a breath of wind, like tender fingers, brush her cheek. Her hands absently stroked her skin and she glanced back once, peering beyond the crowd of warriors that surrounded her and her husband. In the corner of the Great Hall she thought she saw two figures standing in the shadows.

Ottama laid a hand on Nuna's shoulder. "My lady?" Her maid was peering in the same direction, frowning. "Is something the matter?"

Nuna blinked and the space was empty. She shivered and turned away. "No, it was nothing. Nothing at all."

CHAPTER 40

Etta and Joldir were adamant I restricted any further use of the Sight until I was stronger. Understanding the wisdom of their advice didn't stop it being difficult to set such things aside – after all, without the Sight, what was left for me?

"I listened to you when you said you wanted to be sure Nuna was safe," said Joldir. "Now it's your turn to listen to me. This draft will dull your senses and ensure you dream deeply and safely, untouched by the Sight until you're fully recovered. I can't watch you day and night."

I took the proffered bottle with little enthusiasm. Nuna had sensed both of us in the hall at Norlhast, I was sure of it, although I hadn't been able to establish a strong enough connection to warn her she was in danger. In truth, though, what would I have said to her even if we had been able to speak? I had no idea where Nereth was and Nuna didn't even know I was alive, let alone that I had the gift of the Sight. For now, it seemed there was nothing more I could do.

"Dulls the senses?" I asked.

Joldir put a gentle hand on my shoulder. "The effects are not long-lasting, I promise. Just for a few weeks, until you're well again. I learned of this when I studied in Seroch at the School of Medicine, where it was first used to treat those unable to control their abilities as seers. Used properly, it's just as effective in inhibiting the Sight. It is called ataraxia and I can assure you it's safe. I've used it myself, on occasion."

I pursed my lips and drank the mixture in one draught. It was not as unpleasant as I expected, with a hint of cinnamon. I sat back in a chair outside Joldir's house, huddled in my blanket. The northerly wind brought banks of dark clouds scudding across the sky, heavy with rain. I saw Thengill emerge from the barn and look in my direction. He paused for a moment, before unlatching the gate and crossing the courtyard.

"Rothgar," he called out, striding towards me. I nodded in greeting as Thengill approached. He stood before me for a moment, scratching his head before thrusting out his hand. I reached out and watched as my thin hand was engulfed in his huge calloused paw.

"Good to see you … on the mend, I mean." Thengill released his grip and scratched his head again. "I didn't mean to work you so hard. Didn't think, really. Arissa gave me a fierce scolding, let me tell you … Anyways, the thing is, I'm sorry about what happened. Really sorry."

I smiled, amused at the thought of the young girl taking the warrior to task on my behalf. "It's fine, Thengill. I was taken ill, that's all. I should have known when to stop working."

"Right. Well, that's that, then. No need to talk about it again, I suppose?"

"You're back early from the market," Joldir observed, trying to help Thengill move onto a subject where he was more comfortable.

Thengill scowled. "It's not been the best of mornings. Had to show those refugees clogging up the road my axe to get their thieving hands off our goods. Reckon it's only a matter of time before things get ugly down there – they're fast running out of food and Birna told me there's some that's sick too. Might as well have let them have the harvest, though. No sooner did I get the cart inside Olt's gates than Whitebeard's men were there. They took everything – every damn sack of barley on the cart. Made out I was lucky they didn't pay a visit to Lindos for 'overdue taxes', as they delicately put it."

Joldir sighed, looking resigned at Thengill's news. "There was nothing you could have done. We've enough set by for winter, which is all that really matters."

Thengill was unconvinced. "You don't get such a good harvest every year. There might be a time when you wish you had the coin in your pocket stolen from us today."

"There's nothing that can be done about it now. I'd rather be short of a few barley sacks and some coin than worrying about the Vorund Clan paying a visit to this valley."

"It's going to happen, sooner or later," muttered Thengill. "You and I both know I'm right. If it isn't Blackeyes then those folks left homeless by his raiders will start getting restless. When they do they'd best not find Rothgar Kolfinnarson sat on a chair in your courtyard, there for all the world to see."

I grimaced, doubting even Desta would recognise me. That bitter thought lacked its usual sharp edge this morning. Instead a warm glow filled me from within, suffused with the soft scent of cinnamon. There seemed little point worrying about such things when they were beyond my control, as I sat and watched the dark clouds gather above us.

**

Joldir's ataraxia potion had the effect of causing one day to merge with the next. This was because Joldir had to increase my dosage after it became clear the Sight was still intruding on my sleep. As I rested in bed or dozed from my spot in the courtyard I watched deft needlework creating beautiful pictures, saw through tired eyes reading dusty tomes by flickering candlelight, felt stiff old fingers repairing netting after another long night on the boat.

Joldir was unimpressed at my resistance to ataraxia and ordered me to drink his potion twice rather than once a day. This had the desired effect, blocking off those fleeting fragments of other people's lives. Yet with the Sight gone it felt like I'd lost another part of myself. I needed my strength back, so I set myself the goal of eating everything Arissa put in front of me and took as much exercise as I could. I bitterly remembered my first days in Lindos, the humiliation of falling on my face in front of Thengill in Joldir's courtyard. This time, however, it was Thengill who leant me his arm as I found my feet once again. I wondered if he still felt guilty for triggering my illness until one day I saw Arissa watching us approvingly from Joldir's doorway.

"Something amusing you?" Thengill asked, eyes narrowed.

I quickly wiped the smile from my face as Arissa hurriedly resumed her sweeping. "No, nothing at all – just catching my breath. Do you think we could make it round the courtyard one more time?"

"Aye, lad. Why not?"

***

I was exhausted when I fell into bed that evening, in a pleasant way. Though my body ached I felt my strength returning; my belly was full of Arissa's delicious stew and who would have thought Thengill would have been such an effective nursemaid? While the nights were growing colder I was warm enough wrapped up in the thick woollen blankets Joldir had supplied. I turned onto my side, making myself comfortable, and closed my eyes.

There was the curtain in the long hall in Tullen. Sandar stood before me, a smile playing on his handsome young face. He reached out and took hold of the thick cloth with one hand.

"Do you want to know what lies behind the curtain, boy?"

I nodded and watched as Sandar stepped to one side, drawing it back as he did do. There was a loud cawing as a thousand black beaks opened and the crows burst forth from behind the curtain in a vortex of beating wings and discordant noise. With a cry I fell back, shielding my face with my arms.

It was silent and dark in the cellar. Slowly, Leif uncurled his stiff and sore body and rose to his feet, rubbing his eyes. It was the same dream he experienced every night since his father had … gone. Every time was as frightening as the first. He wondered if he had called out in his sleep, because he could hear footfalls on the stairs, growing louder and nearer. He backed away from the solid oak door, cowering down into the corner of the room. He heard the sharp scrape of metal on metal as one of the two bolts was opened on the other side of the door.

Leif turned to me and my heart lurched as I found myself standing in the same room as him. He looked at me, meeting my gaze and I knew the boy could see me as clearly as I could see him.

"It's you," he said simply. "I knew someone would hear me, sooner or later." The second bolt slid free and his face spasmed with fear. "Please, you have to help me."

I glanced at the door, feeling a sense of dread as it began to swing open. There was no other way out of the cellar.

Leif took my hand in his. "She's coming –"

My eyes flew open. My room was dark and I was cold. It took me a moment to realise where I was and that I had thrown my blankets onto the floor. I eased myself up and sat on the edge of the bed, running my hands through my hair, breathing deeply. Something had happened to Leif's parents, leaving him in real trouble, so he had reached to me, called to me for help. I tried to find him again but the Path was hidden, fogged and distant as a result of the cinnamon draught. Leif might have been strong enough to draw me to him for a moment but I was unable to retrace my steps and find the boy. I padded across the soft Oomrhani rug to the other side of the room, guided by memory in the pitch blackness. My fingers carefully sought out the small bottle on the shelf and I caught a waft of the familiar spices as I removed the cork and took a sip. Afterwards as I lay there, wrapped up tightly in my blankets, I knew that out there somewhere Leif was being punished. For a long while I was unable to shake the image of the boy's frightened face from my mind. Anders would never have left his boy locked up in a cellar and I'd already seen the disturbing change in Lina. There was something evil at work in Tullen and Leif needed help. He needed *my* help – and I was in no position to give it.

CHAPTER 41

As the weeks passed my strength slowly returned and Joldir thought the threat of another seizure had passed, though none of us really knew the exact cause of my illness. I was still tired and lacked the stamina to play a full part in the work on the farm, although I was determined to help where I could. As I stepped outside into the still dark courtyard I noticed it had started snowing lightly once more, white flakes drifting lazily through the air. I knew when this latest flurry stopped, Joldir would be outside, sweeping the square clear once more. Beyond his gates the snow lay thicker and I took care not to slip as I followed the compacted icy paths worn between the farm buildings. The cold bit into me and I closed my eyes as the wind whipped up the drifts and drove a battering white cloud of tiny ice shards into my face. I pulled my cloak tighter and made for the milking-shed where I knew Arissa would already be hard at work. The snowstorms she'd predicted had finally come during the past week and we'd been forced to bring Joldir's goats and sheep in from the fields to shelter from the weather. Joldir and Thengill had selected some of the livestock for slaughter to provide us with meat through the winter months. The rest now lived inside two large sheds, the sheep occupying one with the goats residing in the milking-shed. The cart horse lived in the barn, with our stores of hay and barley oats for the animals. Thengill would already be clearing out the sheep's shed before bringing them their fresh feed. The cold had seeped into my bones by the time I closed the door of the shed firmly behind me, and I had to spend a little time warming my hands before starting milking. Last week Ella had made her displeasure clear when I had reached for her udders with frozen fingers, an incident which left Arissa doubled over with laughter. She looked up as I entered the building with an amused grin.

"You're learning," she observed as I blew into my cupped hands, never breaking the rhythm as she milked her own goat into the pail at her feet. Ella looked up at me and bleated, giving the distinct impression she was unimpressed I was milking her this morning. I made doubly sure my hands were warm before I took my seat.

"Has it started snowing again?" Arissa asked, glancing at my shoulders, which were dusted in a light covering of snowflakes.

I nodded as I set to work. "A little. I don't think Thengill will be able to make another trip to Olt safely now, not until there's a thaw." Three days ago Thengill had explored the road and announced it was virtually impassable. The recent falls would have made it even more difficult if not impossible to get through, so the five of us were now isolated up in the mountain valley. Things would be bad in the refugee camp down in Olt, even if the snowfall was lighter at the foot of the mountain. Arissa and I talked of small matters and inconsequential things to pass the time; which animals seemed to be faring well, how the stores were holding up and so forth. Thengill had spotted signs of rats in the granary yesterday, and Joldir had placed a number of mysterious wooden contraptions about the place in an effort to catch them. Arissa and I agreed it would have made more sense for Joldir to buy a cat.

Once the goats were milked and the animals fed I had some time to myself whilst this weather persisted. Thengill had muttered something yesterday about mending a fence at one of the outlying fields, both of us silently acknowledging I would be of little use. I watched him walk up the path, a dark lumbering figure against the bright white snow, as I made my regular daily call on Etta's cottage. I knew she'd heard the crunch of my boots as I approached, for she bade me enter before I even knocked on the door. I pushed it open, enjoying the welcome warmth radiating from her fire.

"Shut the door, lad," Etta ordered, as I stepped across the threshold. "It's cold enough, and I didn't put these logs on the fire to warm the sky." I smiled at the rebuke, hiding the fact I was worried about her now winter had Lindos firmly in its grip. If she had the strength to grumble and grouse I knew all was well, at least for today.

"You look better," Etta told me. "Now the body is healing, what of the mind?"

I shook my head. "I haven't touched the cinnamon draught in over a week and I still don't feel ... myself. It's hard to explain." I shrugged. "I had a window into the world around me and, without it, I feel trapped and useless."

"Give it time. Joldir said he's never had to give someone such a heavy dose to inhibit the Sight. Your gift will return."

"What if it doesn't?"

Etta scowled and waved a dismissive hand. "I don't believe that, not for a moment. Listen to me, when they broke your body they awoke the true strength that lay within your mind. You were saved for a *purpose*, I know it. And this boy, Leif, he has a part to play in matters as well. When the Sight returns to you, then you'll be able to unlock this mystery."

"And what about Leif? If you're right we need to find a way to help him before it's too late."

Etta looked exasperated for a moment as I began our familiar argument before her expression softened. "This again? Rothgar, we're trapped up here until the snows thaw – there's nothing we can do for Leif until then."

"Joldir offered to go earlier this summer with Thengill, before Leif was imprisoned. You stopped them, saying they should wait for Ekkill."

"A sound decision at the time," Etta said. "If the durath have a presence in Tullen they shouldn't be under-estimated. You don't know Ekkill as well as I do – we need him for what we might have to face there."

"If Ekkill's so important to our cause then where is he?" I

replied sharply. "We don't even know if he's still alive."

Etta crossed her arms and fixed me with her fierce one-eyed stare. "He's alive, I'm sure of it. Anyway, if I'd sent Joldir and Thengill to Tullen there's a good chance they would have been away when you fell ill. Have you thought about that? Were it not for Joldir's care you might not be sitting here now, drinking my tea, insulting my judgement and arguing with everything I say. I'm sorry, Rothgar, we must deal with this when the time is right. For now, we can only wait."

I sighed and decided to draw the conversation away from such a difficult subject. "And you, Etta, how are you doing now winter is setting in?"

"Between you and Arissa fussing over me it's a wonder I get any peace at all. Though I confess, Arissa bakes the best bread in all of Reavesburg." As she said this I caught the smell of a fresh loaf hanging in the air.

"Arissa's offered to play for us tonight," I said, already regretting our argument. "Joldir says now we're in the dark and cold of winter it would be good to lift our spirits. I wondered if you wanted to join us?" Etta looked at me with her one good eye, considering the offer.

"The paths are icy and treacherous. Tempting as some company sounds, I'd rather not spoil the night for everyone by breaking my hip and dying the next morning."

"Who says that would spoil the evening?" I quipped.

Etta grimaced. "Very funny. Pass on my thanks to Arissa and tell her I'll be listening at the window. Her voice can still provide me with a little company, even if I'm not with you in person." I hesitated, wondering whether to suggest we came to Etta's home instead. I was wary of making her feel under any obligation to feed and entertain us, so I kept the thought to myself. Etta didn't press the matter.

"I'll pass on your apologies. You'll be missed."

*＊＊

When I curled up in my bed under my blankets that evening, there was a pleasant warm glow inside me. Joldir had prepared a tasty mutton stew, which Thengill, Arissa and I all enjoyed as we gathered round his table, washing it down with cold ale from Olt. Then Arissa had brought out her lyre and sang to us, the first time I'd heard her since I had lain on my sick bed, feverish and half-delirious. Sometimes they were unfamiliar songs, half-remembered from that time. On other occasions, I recalled the same ballads being performed by Darri in Ulfkell's Keep – songs that my father, Jorik, Bandor and Olfridor used to sing along to on dark winter nights. Hearing them interpreted through a woman's voice gave them a new feel and shape. On some occasions we joined in together, on others Arissa captivated us as she performed solo. Thengill seemed to be lost to all around him in such moments, having eyes only for Arissa.

When Thengill eventually left for his own cottage at the end of the night and I retired to my room I had to admit the air had lost some of its chill. It took me a little while as I lay in my bed to realise the world of Ulfkell's Keep – brought to mind by Arissa's songs – felt distant, belonging to another time. Here I was able to enjoy the company of people who cared for me, something many people in Reavesburg were unable to say. In Lindos, it dawned on me for the first time, I'd found a new home.

CHAPTER 42

As the winter days shortened I found myself both rising and returning home with the darkness, each day having little to distinguish itself from the next, other than the reassurance my strength was finally returning. However, my efforts to regain the Sight proved fruitless, the Path remaining elusive. Joldir continued to be encouraging, telling me that my abilities would return in time, although I sensed some doubt, a slight wavering in his gaze whenever we spoke. I couldn't help wonder if my increased doses of ataraxia might have had a permanent effect. I became increasingly disheartened as mid-winter came and went and a new year began with little real progress to show for my efforts.

Arissa touched me when she presented me with a small gift to mark the first day of the 210th year. It was only a trifle, a small honey-scented candle Joldir purchased on her behalf on one of his trips to the market. Still, I made sure it was placed prominently in a holder on the table in my room, so she would see it. Arissa was careful to present Thengill with a token as well, though when he met my gaze I knew he resented the attention Arissa had shown me. Etta lived by the fireplace in her cottage now, Joldir and Thengill helping move her bed into the living-room. Despite my worries she proved as tough as ever, surprising all of us with her fortitude.

Outside the snows fell again, heavy and thick this time, the drifts cutting us off from Olt and all the rest of Amuran. My last winter in Ulfkell's Keep had felt isolated. This was different; we might as well have been the only five people in the world.

***

The black column of smoke stood out stark against the opalescent snow-bearing clouds that morning. Even without this clear sign, there was the faint hint of smoke in the air. The five of us stood gathered outside Etta's gate, staring upwards with anxious faces. Thengill was the first to break the silence.

"We need to set a watch on the road. No knowing what kind of trouble is going to head our way now."

Arissa's green eyes were wide with worry. "Why now? Is it the camp that's burning or the town?"

"I doubt it's Olt that's afire," Thengill replied. "Hrodi's been loyal to Blackeyes and his men these past few months. I'll bet anything it's smoke from the camp outside the gates. The only thing that surprises me is it's taken this long." Arissa stared at him in horror, though we all knew the truth of Thengill's words.

"I doubt anyone would be foolish enough to try and take the road up into the mountains," muttered Etta, wrapped in the folds of her thick cloak.

"Desperate people will try anything," countered Joldir. "After all, they've nothing to lose. Rothgar, I think it would be prudent for you to watch the road for us this morning." I nodded, pleased to have a role to play. Joldir turned to Thengill. "My friend, I trust your axes are sharp. You have the next hour to make ready. I want you guarding Lindos with Rothgar by then."

***

Standing next to Thengill I felt distinctly inadequate. The Vorund warrior was dressed in immaculate well-oiled chainmail, wrapped in a dark woollen cloak against the bitter wind. Hanging either side of his belt, Thengill's exquisitely decorated axes had a honed sheen to them, their edges keen and sharp. I pulled my own cloak more tightly about my body, grimly aware I only carried a small knife, more useful for coring apples than drawing blood. I comforted myself that two eyes were of more value than one, though it was hard to remain alert after three uneventful days, crouching in the bitter cold. To make matters worse, it was snowing again, making it harder to see anything further down the valley.

"Joldir's probably being over-cautious," I remarked, my breath forming a white cloud between us. Thengill looked at me, his dark eyes shining with purpose and excitement. How long had it been since he'd come here as Joldir's guard? Well over a year. No wonder he looked at me now as if I were the village idiot, daring to question his purpose.

"You think? Well, be sure to run and tell Joldir that. I'll stay here, so if they do come they'll have to get past me. I'm not afraid of taking off a few frostbitten fingers to keep the fruits of my hard-earned labour safe."

"And Arissa too?" I asked.

Thengill frowned, his face taking on a dangerous aspect. "What about her?"

"It's obvious you like the girl, Thengill. Have you done anything about it except make your usual crude jokes? You'll get nowhere unless you woo her properly."

Thengill looked confused at my remark. "I'm not sure I _"

"What's that?" I interrupted, waving at him to be quiet. The wind was sending the falling snow whirling this way and that, making movement difficult to see. I peered down the snow-choked valley, Thengill leaning forward close to me, our conversation forgotten. A moment later the falling snow blew clear, revealing a number of dark shapes making their way slowly up the valley towards us.

"That's well spotted," Thengill acknowledged. "How many, do you reckon?" I paused, for the snow had closed around the figures again, hiding them from sight. We waited there for several nerve-wracking minutes, our occasional glimpses of the group never long enough to see them properly. What did become clear was that the group was large, moving slowly and with purpose towards Lindos.

"What do you think? Fifteen, maybe a full score of them?" Thengill sounded calm, certainly calmer than I was feeling.

"I'd say more again. I'll go tell the others we have guests. They won't be here for some time yet." Thengill nodded as I left, his face intent.

***

Arissa's voice was pleading. I knew Etta well enough to know it was obvious she was wasting her time. "Etta, please. Come inside, where it's safe. They'll be here soon."

Etta, standing just outside Joldir's gates, smiled. "Maybe the sight of me will frighten them off, my dear. Don't you worry, I can look after myself. It's a young woman like you that should be taking more care for her safety."

Arissa looked ready to argue until Joldir placed a placating hand on her arm. "We don't have time to stand here arguing. Go inside the house and bolt the door. Please, hurry and do as I say."

Arissa reluctantly obeyed, closing the door of Joldir's house against the snowstorm. I wondered if we would be best following her example; we were ill-prepared to meet this kind of threat. Only Thengill was properly equipped and ready for a fight, although Joldir casually held a six-foot quarterstaff by his side, giving the impression he knew how to use it. Then there was me with my knife and Etta with her wits. Together the four of us stood in front of the gates, waiting in the falling snow.

I blew into my hands, clapping them together to get the blood flowing. I could hardly feel my fingers, despite the thick gloves I was wearing, and doubted I could hold my knife properly if it came to combat. The endless waiting began to sap my strength and resolve, and I shook the snow from my shoulders before wrapping my cloak around me even more tightly in an effort to stay warm. It was then I heard a voice, distant and indistinct; snow muffled words carried to us on the wind.

"Did you hear that?" The others turned to me, shaking their heads. We stood there in silence, straining to catch any sound. One of Joldir's goats bleated from the nearby shed and Thengill turned to me, eyebrows raised. "It wasn't a goat," I hissed. Thengill opened his mouth to make some retort when the wind turned and the voices carried to us once more.

"... not abandoned like the others ..."

"I told you ..."

"Quiet." The last speaker spoke with an unmistakable tone of command. The chattering died down instantly. I screwed my eyes up, trying to peer through the swirling snow, unable to make anything out.

"Don't sound much like homeless folk coming to us for succour, does it?" observed Thengill in a whisper. I knew what he meant; there were precious few men living in the refugee camp and all the speakers had been young men. Had the Vorund Clan finally found us and, if so, were they after our supplies or had they come for me? It was difficult to imagine anyone being foolish enough to mount a raid in this weather. I took off my glove, gripping the cold handle of my knife as I drew it from my belt.

Joldir saw the motion. "Put that away. We don't know who we're dealing with yet. I'd rather resolve this peacefully if we can, even if we're outnumbered."

"I wouldn't let your hand stray too far, all the same," added Thengill.

"Good advice, if you weren't already outflanked." The voice came to my left, and I whirled around to find a bearded longbowman standing less than fifteen feet from us by the courtyard wall, an arrow knocked and aimed directly at my chest. He broke into a smile at my astonished face. "Isn't that right, Gunnar?"

I sensed more movement and turned to see another, older grey-bearded man standing to our right. He was also armed with a bow, as were two more figures behind him. Thengill swore, making no move towards his axe. I also slowly raised my hands away from my knife, noting the first speaker was also accompanied by a second bowman.

"What's that, Ulfarr?" called out the grey-bearded archer. "You asking me to put an arrow through the big ugly one?"

"What? No. No, I'm bloody well not. Not unless he does anything stupid, that is."

"Eh? Was that a yes or a no?"

"You've got to be joking," muttered Thengill, glowering at the older man. My heart was pounding in my chest as one of the other bowmen stepped towards Gunnar and said something to him.

"Aye, right then, Olaf. Just watch yourself, big man; target your size and at this range, it'd take some effort to miss, I reckon."

Joldir turned and addressed himself to the younger man who appeared to be the leader of this band. "My name's Joldir and this is my farm. What gives you the right come up here so heavily armed and threaten us in this way?"

Ulfarr smiled again, keeping his bow trained on me. "You're a fine one to talk with that hulking brute at your side. If he's a farmer then I'm a milkmaid. If I wanted you dead, you'd be lying there stuck through with arrows already. It isn't a good idea to expect a friendly welcome wherever you go, not now Blackeyes is jarl of Reavesburg." He spat sourly into the snow and I felt myself relax, just a little.

"No friend of Blackeyes, then," said Etta. "The question is, are you any friend of ours?"

"Dinuvillan be praised. Etta, you're alive." The voice was so familiar I could scarcely believe my ears. A figure appeared, emerging ghostlike from the swirling snow. Even wrapped up in his cloak and furs I would have recognised that gaunt visage anywhere, as Johan Jokellsward stepped forwards, arms held out wide to show us he meant no harm.

CHAPTER 43

Jokellsward's men gathered together in the barn that night to shelter from the weather, their numbers too great for Joldir to be able to accommodate them anywhere else at such short notice. Johan had some hardened fighters with him. I recognised Petr Hamarrson and Rugga, standing alongside a weary-looking Bandor. However, the group also comprised a number of women and children, including Damona, Johan's wife. Twenty-nine of them in total, a combination of survivors from the fall of Kalamar and a handful of men who'd escaped with Johan on the night of my sister's wedding. Pleased as I was to learn Johan and Bandor were alive, their arrival posed us problems. Our visitors had brought blankets and bedding but their stocks of food were low and it was obvious a prolonged stay would soon exhaust our supplies. The barn offered shelter from the snow and a cookfire had been lit in the centre of the building, enough to keep people reasonably warm. I spent some time helping Joldir and Arissa, who were busy finding spaces for people to bed down for the night. In the dimly lit barn no one recognised me. I looked about unsuccessfully for Bandor among the crowd, wondering whether I should speak to him.

I started as a hand gripped my arm and I glanced down to see Etta standing beside me. "Come with me, we need to go somewhere more private to talk." I let her steer me out of the barn and we made our way over to her cottage, feet sinking knee deep into freshly-fallen snow. She pushed the door open and I felt the welcome warmth of her fire on my face as I followed. Inside Johan, Bandor and another man I didn't recognise were waiting for us.

Bandor stood, looking at me uncertainly. "Rothgar?"

I smiled and crossed the room to embrace him. "It's good to see you. When we heard Kalamar had fallen ... well, we all feared the worst." I stepped back and took in just how thin and tired he looked.

"So, it's true; you're alive." I'd expected a warmer response as Bandor stared at me like a stranger.

"I told you, didn't I?" said the third man, who wore studded leather armour, with a sword hanging at his side. His voice was familiar, though I was unable to place him. He looked to be the wrong side of forty, still trim and fit, with a slight frame and dark curly hair, silvered at the temples.

"You did," Johan replied, an edge to his voice. "But ..."

As words failed him I began to understand, seeing myself as they were seeing me for the first time. Still the same face, though thinner and more haggard, I was now slightly stooped, the easier to carry the scarred flesh and twisted muscles on my back. My walk was slow, weak legs trembling even now from the bitter cold, whilst the breath wheezed in my chest, a remnant of the infection last summer. Bandor was looking at the thin, skeletal hands that clasped his own with a mixture of pity and horror on his face. I was a mere shadow of the young warrior they remembered from Ulfkell's Keep. Never had I been more keenly aware of what Tyrfingr Blackeyes had taken from me.

"He looks a damn sight better than the last time I saw him," remarked the other man. "He was more corpse than Rothgar Kolfinnarson. Listen, Rothgar, what I said that night ... You should have seen yourself. If you'd been in my position, knowing Blackeyes' men would soon be after you ... Believe me, you'd have thought the same thing. I honestly believed letting you go would be doing you a kindness. Maybe I was right." I remembered a shadow looming over me in the cart as we fled the keep. *'Better for him and us if the crows had finished the job they'd started.'*

"From Ekkill, that counts as an apology," observed Etta

tartly. "All that's in the past now."

"Agreed," I said, a little shakily. "What's done is done and, in the end, Ekkill, I owe you my life. You have my thanks. I seem to owe a debt to so many people these days, yourself included."

Ekkill bowed his head, a smirk playing on his lips. "I'll be sure to remind you of that, should the occasion arise."

"I'm sorry, Rothgar." Johan had recovered his composure. "I didn't recognise you when we first met; I just assumed you were one of the farmer's men. You seem to have learned the art of blending in with your surroundings."

"So well your men almost stuck him full of arrows." Etta's reprimand was sharp.

Johan was in no mood for the lecture. "It wouldn't be the first trap we've walked into since Sinarr drove us into the wilderness. I didn't know if I could trust Ekkill. Only a fool wouldn't have scouted out the land, and Ulfarr's proved himself a good man."

Ekkill scowled. "So you say. Pity Old Gunnar's so deaf every time you issue an order he hears a different one." I saw Bandor glance nervously between Ekkill and his father. Johan ignored the jibe.

"There are few of us left," he explained to me and Etta. "We've lost more than we've gained these past months, even with picking up who we could on the road. Gods, where to begin? So much has happened since Ulfkell's Keep fell."

The five of us talked late into the night as the fire burned low. Johan explained how he and Rugga managed to escape on the night of the wedding with a score of men, as well as Bandor and Damona. Sailing north, they successfully evaded pursuit by heading far out into the Redfars Sea, eventually landing in darkness near Kalamar several days later.

"By then the castle was already under siege by Sinarr's men, with Petr leading the resistance. We were too few to change the tide of the battle, so we did what little we could; picking off scouts, harrying their supply lines and then retreating into the hills. It was then that your man, Ekkill, found us. We thought he was Sinarr's spy at first, until he proved he knew enough to convince me he was one of yours. That's when I first learned you were still alive and there was a chance Rothgar was too. Lindos was many miles south, whilst my people were still trapped by the siege with Petr and those few left with him to defend the walls of the castle. As the weeks passed I watched, powerless, as Sinarr began to try and starve out everyone else trapped inside." Johan paused, staring into the dwindling fire. He rose and tossed another log into the hearth, which crackled as flames jumped up around it.

"Sinarr the Cold One," muttered Etta. "Word is he's now travelled south to lend his men to the siege against Gautarr in Romsdahl."

"Then Falrufson's days are numbered. Sinarr worked dark magic with fire, blasting a great breach in the castle walls with lightning and smoke."

"They call it fire powder in Samarakand," Ekkill supplied, drawing a dark look from Johan.

"Whatever it's called, the result was the same; Kalamar Castle fell. I was forced to watch as they breached the walls and burned the castle to the ground. Sinarr's men poured through the breach and set light to the castle. They didn't even try to hold it as an outpost of Adalrikr's new kingdom."

"Karas Greystorm swore fealty to Adalrikr after Jorik's death," Etta explained. "Tyrfingr rewarded him with the return of Kalamar and its surrounding lands, whilst ensuring it was a worthless gift as punishment for his part in Jorik's alliance."

Johan nodded, his bitterness all too evident. "I'd heard the rumours Greystorm turned his coat, for all the good it did him. The man has no honour – I told Jorik it was a mistake to trust him. I told you," he continued, rounding on Etta. "I told you, and you wouldn't listen."

"He did it for Nuna's sake." My voice was quiet, my words stilling the room. "He swore fealty to save his life and hers. You should remember the man you're talking about is my brother-in-law."

"And you'd do well to remember you're no longer the brother of the chief –"

"Father. Please." Bandor's interruption brought Johan up short. He drew a breath and looked at me more kindly, more like the man I remembered.

"I'm sorry, Rothgar. When you've lost your own daughter and grandchild and then seen your home destroyed, well, it's hard to sympathise with anyone choosing to ally themselves to this so-called king of the north, whatever their motives might be. These long months on the road, they've been very hard."

"We've all lost someone," I agreed. "I've seen Petr amongst the men with you, so some of your people obviously managed to escape."

"I'm afraid all the people of Kalamar now reside in that barn. That was the one moment when I felt like my presence up north made any real difference. As the castle burned, I could see people fleeing Kalamar. Petr had the same idea as us to use the surrounding hill country as his refuge. When the castle was lost Sinarr's warriors became undisciplined in their race to seize the spoils, giving Petr the chance to lead a small group of warriors and their families through a gap in the siege lines. There were soon Vorund warriors hard on their tail but as luck would have it Petr led his party straight towards our own hideout, giving us a chance to aid their escape. I lost six of my men that day, though not one of those pursuing Petr returned from the hills." Johan smiled, an expression that took years off him. "I'll never forget seeing Rugga reunited with Ingirith and his children. A rare moment of happiness, and all too brief, as Sinarr knew some people had reached safety in the hills and killed his men. He sent more of them after us, so we turned south and did what we'd been doing ever since landing at Kalamar; striking them where we could and then melting away when they came after us."

Johan paused, looking thoughtful. "I can't say there was much of a plan to any of it. I thought at first that there would be others like us, still fighting for the clan, who we could join forces with. Turned out most folk either bent the knee or chose to seek refuge over the mountains. We struck back where we could, even gaining a name for ourselves in some parts as the Company of Shadows. Perhaps that gave some folk a measure of hope at first. In the end, it was a matter of trying to keep everyone alive as winter came on and making for Lindos. I thought if anyone might know what to do, Etta, it would be you. We were doing alright until winter closed in on us. During those last few days I wasn't sure we were going to make it here at all. It took us three days to climb through the drifts in this valley. I lost two people to the cold just yesterday." That last comment was met with silence, just the fresh log crackling in the fire, flames now dancing and casting flickering light across Johan's craggy features. I was gladder than I could say to see him again. However, he was changed.

"Hard times and bitter news," Etta said at last. "I'm sorry for your loss, yet perhaps the snows are now your friend. These latest drifts will have cut the valley off for good since you began to make your way up here and will have covered your tracks. There's sanctuary here for you and your people, although I suspect it will be short rations for everyone to see us through winter. I'm afraid that's the only plan I have, Johan – for now at least."

"What about tidings from closer to home?" I asked. "We saw smoke rising three days ago near Olt. There's a camp outside the town comprising the landless and dispossessed, forced from their homes by the Vorund Clan. Did you pass that way?"

A shadow passed across Johan's face. "My scouts came upon the aftermath. It looks like Blackeyes' men destroyed the camp you describe during the night. When we arrived early that morning it was all over, though the fires were still burning fiercely. There were bodies, hundreds of them, piled high nearby in a great mound, already half covered by fresh falling snow. We didn't linger long."

"Hard to say why the camp was attacked," Bandor told us. "I doubt they had much. It may be there was disease and the folk of Olt were afraid it would spread to them, or perhaps those outside got desperate and tried to get inside the town. Who can say? Result was the same; more misery and death under King Adalrikr's rule."

"So, that's our story, or the bare bones of it at least," said Johan. "What about yours? What did happen in Ulfkell's Keep that night, and how did you both manage to escape?"

As Etta and I began to tell our tale I realised it was the first time I'd talked about those things to anyone. I spoke haltingly of the murder of Jorik and his family, Finnvidor and Olfridor in the Great Hall and the travesty of the clan moot that convicted me of their murder, following my tortured confession. Johan said nothing as he listened, his brows furrowed, jaw clenched tight.

Etta then took over the tale, recounting how she and Ekkill liberated me from the crows cage and made their desperate flight away from Reavesburg. Events in Lindos had moved at a different pace to Johan's adventures, so the story of my illness and recovery under Joldir's care took little time. The only thing Etta and I didn't mention, as if by some unspoken pact, was my discovery of the Sight. Perhaps that was wise, at least until my gift returned.

As we finished Johan sat back, running his hands through his hair and looking thoughtful. "Adalrikr planned this campaign carefully, probably placing his agents within the clan over some years. Lundvarr was always going to be easily swayed and Old Hrodi Whitebeard's a realist – you don't get to his age without being shrewd. It's Sandar's part in this which interests me. His lies to the clan moot helped to seal Rothgar's fate and, even if he wasn't in the Great Hall when the attack took place, I'd be prepared to wager he had some part in letting Blackeyes into the keep that night."

I thought on Johan's words. Was that why I had been dreaming about Leif, because he was close to Sandar? My sleeping mind trying to unlock mysteries my waking mind had chosen to ignore?

Etta kept her own counsel as she replied. "We may never know the truth as to what happened that night. There'll be time this winter to see if between us we can make the pieces of the puzzle fit. Right now, the three of you must be exhausted. Take advantage of the fact you don't need to set a guard and get some rest."

"That's good advice," Johan admitted as he stood and made for the door. "It's good to see you again Etta, and you Rothgar."

"We'll speak tomorrow," added Bandor, patting my shoulder. "There's a lot more to tell you about the deeds of Johan's Company of Shadows."

"I'll hold you to that promise," I told him as they went out into the night. Ekkill, however, made no similar move to leave. I wondered if I was expected to allow them some privacy and began to take my leave. Etta hushed me and made me sit back down again.

"I've business with Rothgar, Ekkill, so if there's something you want to tell me you'd better get on with it."

"This has got to be worth silver, if not gold," he told her, nonchalantly lounging back in his chair.

"Your orders were to bring me tidings of Kalamar, and that was over six months ago."

"I did more than that; I brought Kalamar, or what's left of it, back to you."

"Unannounced, at winter time, stretching our supplies to the very limit. Had you forewarned us I would have stopped Joldir taking half of his crops off to market. Much of that was seized by the Vorund garrison anyway. We could have fed our allies, rather than our foes."

Ekkill looked amused. "There's an obvious answer to that dilemma, isn't there? Anyway, I've brought back valuable information and Johan can be useful to you – people will rally round him and follow him into battle."

Etta scowled, unconvinced. "A mere score of warriors will not be enough to drive Tyrfingr Blackeyes from these shores."

"Are your purse strings really tied so tightly you'll take issue with me on this?" Ekkill laughed, shaking his head at Etta's stubbornness. "This 'mere score' includes Rugga the Rock, Petr Hamarrson and Johan himself. His son, Bandor, is as skilful with a blade as any I've seen and he's made a name for himself these past few months. Svan and Brandr are in his company and Ulfarr's crew are pretty handy in a fight too. More importantly, Johan Jokellsward is a man born to lead. There's been some raiding inland, true enough, with many people losing their homes and livelihoods. Even so, Blackeyes' occupation has been relatively bloodless; there are still people in the clan lands ready and able to fight. They'll rise to the call, if Johan gives it."

The fire was dying down again now, leaving Etta's lined face shrouded in darkness, just the red embers gleaming in her eyes. She gave a low throaty chuckle, rose stiffly from her seat and went into another room, returning a few minutes later with a small bag.

"You're smooth-tongued as ever, Ekkill. Here, there's silver for your efforts. If Johan raises his army, I'll see it's turned into gold."

Ekkill weighed the bag in his hand, bouncing it up and down. "A fair deal, I suppose, although I don't think silver will be of much use to me trapped up here."

"You'll find ways to spend it, I'm sure," Etta told him. Ekkill smiled in return, took his leave, and left the two of us alone together.

Etta let out a long sigh. "Mark my words, it doesn't do to let a man like that get any kind of advantage over you. He needs frequent reminders I'm the one in charge."

"Who is he?" I asked, curiosity getting the better of me.

"My first apprentice. Ekkill was an orphan boy I took under my wing many years ago. He's been like a son to me, though perhaps I schooled him too well. He's not a son I would necessarily trust. You should take care around him."

"I'll be sure to remember. Anyway, you asked me to speak with you. What did you want?"

"To know what you think."

I paused for a moment, collecting my thoughts. "Johan's arrival has changed everything. Ekkill's right, if Johan and his band stand up and defy Adalrikr's rule, I think others will follow."

The old woman smiled at me. "It's good to hear you talk this way. The time has come to choose the path that leads to your future. Do you think you're ready?"

CHAPTER 44

Everything had changed and the person who felt it most was Joldir. I should have foreseen what would happen the moment Johan first emerged from the snow; perhaps Joldir did. After all, Johan was head of the House of Kalamar and served as jarl to both my father and brother. In his eyes Joldir was just a farmer and the time had come for him to prove his loyalty to our clan. In the days that followed, it was Johan giving the orders as to how affairs were to be managed in Lindos, with Joldir rarely consulted until after the event. In a day his small kingdom was taken over by Johan Jokellsward, who considered it his right rather than a privilege.

Johan, Damona and Bandor took up residence in Joldir's fine house, with Joldir himself consigned to living in his workshop, so he could at least still carry on his trade. Arissa remained there to wait on Johan's family, fortunate to keep her own room. Thengill was *persuaded* to move out of his large house to accommodate Rugga, his wife, Ingirith, and their young son and daughter. By now, word had got round that I was Rothgar Kolfinnarson, leaving me in a strange position. Too badly maimed still to be regarded as a warrior in Laskan society I remained of high birth, being both the son and brother of the last two clan chiefs. There was no longer room for me in Joldir's house, so I was asked to share my new cottage with Thengill.

"Don't think I asked for this," the big man grumbled as he angrily dumped the last of his possessions on the floor. "It was a choice between living with you or Etta."

Living arrangements were important because having adequate shelter was everything. With twenty-nine additional people living in the valley, this became Johan's main concern, as we all prepared to winter together in Lindos. Initially, many people lived in the barn while Johan put us to work repairing the other abandoned cottages in the valley. It was a difficult season to carry out the necessary repairs to make those in the best condition weather-proof. A small barracks was established for some of the men. Svan and Brandr, two warriors from Kalamar, men that were clearly close to Johan and who had come here with their wives, were given the opportunity to establish their own homes. Meanwhile Petr earned a lot of respect by bunking down with his fellow warriors without complaint. There was also Gylla and Sefa, two young unmarried women from the group of survivors from Kalamar. They lodged with Etta, an arrangement I doubted any of them approved of.

I knew from what Bandor had told me that Ulfarr and his men were cut from a different cloth to the rest of Johan's warriors. Ulfarr's crew had been bandits and robbers, scratching a living in the Kalamar hill country, when they came across Johan's company after the fall of Kalamar. Johan was sorely in need of more fighting men and offered the eight of them a pardon in return for their blades. Not everyone thought well of the idea, particularly Rugga.

Those eight were now down to five. Ulfarr, Skari and Myr were all skilful warriors born and bred in the north. Then there was 'Sir' Patrick Wild, who claimed to be a fallen Berian knight. He must have fallen quite some way to be plying his trade as a robber in Laskar and no one really gave his story much credence. There was no doubt he was Berian, his accent gave that much away, although he was fluent enough in the northern tongue. As for the knightly part, there was precious little in evidence aside from his affectation for chivalry around the womenfolk, which they seemed to enjoy, whilst the men considered it to be a foolish way to behave. He wore a dented breastplate that, at a stretch, might once have comprised part of a larger suit of armour, and carried a battered triangular shield in the Berian style, though any sigil had long since been worn away, just a few flecks of green paint remaining on the faded wood. The only thing he carried that remained in immaculate condition was his sword, which he polished and sharpened every day. This was clearly an expensive weapon, and Arissa told me it was the reason many of the womenfolk believed in his tale.

He was certainly the most approachable and courteous person in Ulfarr's band, always giving me respect whenever we shared a word. He was also the only one who showed any real kindness to its fifth member, a young blond man called Olaf, who looked about as at home in this company as a worm eyed by a flock of hungry birds. Olaf seemed to play a role both as a servant and scout to Ulfarr and his men, armed only with a short bow and hunting knife. Skari bullied him mercilessly, which probably explained why he had a habit of never meeting your eye when addressed.

Johan put a good number of his company to work felling trees at the head of the valley to provide the additional fuel our new community needed. Joldir and Thengill helped with a different task, slaughtering the first of the sheep and goats. Joldir's flocks would keep our new community fed through the winter, and although we started with the weakest animals, we all knew none would be left by the spring. I helped with preparing the dead animals, the steaming pile of offal and uncured skins I left lying in the snow as vital to our survival as everything else.

"You look tired," Joldir observed after I had finished my bloody work one morning.

I cleaned my hands in the snow, breathing hard. "I'd rather be useful than watch everyone else do the work."

Joldir nodded, rolling his shoulders. "Willing hands are always welcome around here. Brandr and Maeva's cottage has taken a lot of work to make it weather-proof. The wood could have done with being more seasoned but their new roof should see them through this winter at least."

For a time the pair of us worked in silence alongside Thengill, placing the meat in the underground cold store ready for the women to salt or dry it. When Thengill left to begin curing the hides I noticed Etta approaching us through the snow.

"Has Johan asked you to speak to me, Etta, or is the slaughter of my livestock something else that's beneath his notice?" Joldir did not try to hide his bitterness.

Etta looked tiny, even wrapped up in layers of black cloth against the biting wind. "Johan understands you're making a sacrifice. The problem of providing everyone with adequate shelter has been solved. Now we need to discuss how to feed seven times the people you made provision for until the spring thaw."

Joldir looked out across the valley, a frown creasing his forehead. "Johan's expecting me to give up the farm. No seed for the coming year's crop and the slaughter of my livestock to feed Jokellsward's men. It'll leave me with nothing."

"That's not entirely true. Your work as Olt's healer remains profitable and you've always been frugal, Joldir, so I'm sure you would have the means to restock down in Olt come the spring. I don't need to remind you it was me who set you up here in Lindos. A sizeable favour and now it's time for you to return it. Johan has the right to demand all this anyway, as jarl, so I'm only discussing this with you out of courtesy."

"A score of warriors commands a lot of loyalty, it seems," Joldir sighed. "The extra fires in the valley will have been seen down in Olt by Blackeyes' men. They'll know there's more folk living up here, and when it thaws they'll send a patrol to investigate. Lindos won't be safe for any of us come the spring."

"Perhaps," Etta mused. "I've thought about this; the women and children who've come here could say they were driven this way, following the destruction of the camp at Olt. Livestock perish in winters such as these, stores can be lost. It wouldn't be such a stretch for you to tell that tale and begin again, if you chose to remain here."

"And if the Vorund Clan chooses to move us on?"

"Then you would have made the wrong decision."

Joldir shook his head. "Such a story won't explain the presence of twenty well-armed men in the valley if they're spotted when they leave, nor do I suppose these families will be parted voluntarily when Johan leads his company out of Lindos. Do you think Dalla will willingly leave Svan, or Ingirith abandon Rugga? Anyone remaining here will be risking their lives." He looked meaningfully in my direction. "No, the moment Ekkill led Johan into this valley I knew my time here was over. It's over for all of us."

"Johan's a good man," I told Joldir. "I've known him for years and in that time he's always given wise counsel, as well as proving himself in battle."

Joldir's smile had little warmth. "Let's pray he can raise his promised army. For now, as far as Tyrfingr Blackeyes is concerned, Johan is a landless outlaw, his Company of Shadows and their supporters a band of criminals who'll face the noose if they're caught."

"Which is why he needs our help," said Etta.

Joldir looked long and hard at Etta. "What other choice do any of us really have?"

**

That evening I ate with Johan's family and his warriors in Joldir's home. Arissa served us roasted chickens, goat stew and freshly-baked bread, and Joldir was also in attendance, favoured with a seat near Johan himself. It was a noisy gathering, Rugga's loud voice booming out over proceedings, Ingirith holding onto his arm, whilst their two small children, Egill and Kitta played nearby. Petr Hamarrson looked relaxed, drinking with restraint, dark eyes watching over proceedings, his hand resting lightly on the hilt of his ancient sword. It was clear Johan trusted this young man with a great deal of responsibility. Whilst Rugga's huge build and fearsome reputation drew most men's attention, I had noticed it was

Petr who organised the company and had given most of the orders since their arrival. An older warrior I didn't know, called Varinn, also joined us, his lined and scarred face telling its own story. I knew he had escaped from Kalamar with Petr and he was clearly good friends with Rugga, sharing many a joke with him whilst Petr looked on quietly.

I found myself sitting next to Damona and Bandor. Close up, I had been shocked to see how loosely Damona's clothes hung from her once full and attractive figure. She was still a beautiful woman, even at forty, though with more grey in her long blonde hair than I remembered. It was her eyes and the lines around them that betrayed the privations and sleepless nights of her long journey.

"Rothgar," she purred. "Despite everything we've endured, the gods are good it seems. When Ekkill said you were alive I could scarcely believe it was true, not until I saw you with my own eyes." She laid a hand adorned with rings that sparkled in the lamplight on my arm. "That evil man ... Wasting my daughter's life ..."

"Mother, please. Not here." Bandor placed a consoling hand on her shoulder.

"I've often wondered, after I first heard she'd died that night." She glanced up at Johan who was busy talking to Joldir and Varinn. "I begged Johan to turn back, did you know that? He was determined to fight his way out and reach the docks, with Reesha still in the keep. My daughter and grandson, and he left them behind."

"Mother," Bandor spoke more forcefully this time. "We've talked about this. There was nothing we could have done. You know what happened to Finnvidor and the others. If we'd gone back, none of us would have escaped."

"You don't know that," snapped Damona, rounding on him and causing a hush to fall around the table. "We left them there – left my daughter there to die, and now ... here you all are eating, drinking and joking as if nothing's wrong." Tears welled in her eyes and her hand gripped mine painfully, nails digging into the flesh of my forearm.

"Oh, Damona," Ingirith cried, rushing to her side and wrapping her arms tightly around her. Johan stood, rooted to the spot, struggling to find any words of comfort for his wife, and I wondered how many times this argument had played itself out since the night of Nuna's ill-fated wedding.

"Seems it's the way of things these days," muttered Varinn finally. "War's a bloody business and it don't have much regard for fairness. Places people in situations where there aren't a whole lot of great choices to pick from. Ask Eykr here, who lost his wife and son the day we fled Kalamar. Ask Dalla why it was her brother died from the cold, just days before the rest of us reached safety and Joldir kindly gave us shelter. We all know death's only a step away in these times, so if you see us laugh and joke, my lady, please don't think it means we've forgotten those we've left behind. It's the warrior's way to take his ease as and when he can, and no disrespect's meant by that."

"I'm not a warrior and neither was my daughter," Damona replied through gritted teeth, ignoring Ingirith's shushing. "She was a young woman and a mother and yet ..."

"I was there," I said quietly. Damona turned and looked at me, as if seeing me clearly for the first time. "From when the attack began until the time Reesha died, it was mere moments. Even if you'd tried to reach the Great Hall you would never have gotten there in time, I can say that much for certain. If you'd turned back from the docks, Blackeyes would have killed you as well."

Johan finally found his voice. "Thank you, Rothgar. It's a small relief to know that for sure. Tyrfingr Blackeyes' crimes won't go unpunished – I'll have my vengeance on him and his clan." There were nods of approval from Petr, Rugga and Varinn at those words. Next to me Damona's voice was barely a whisper.

"Your vengeance won't bring back my Reesha or Kolfinnar." She waved Ingirith away and people returned to their meals, a sombre mood descending upon our gathering. Joldir suggested Arissa play something, helping to lift the deadening silence.

"I'm sorry," Bandor whispered to me over the music. "She hasn't been herself since that day."

"Who has?"

Bandor dipped some of his bread into his wooden bowl, soaking it in the remains of his stew. "Who'd have believed things would turn out this way? We've all thought long and hard about what took place that night; what each of us did, the decisions we made. Until we met Ekkill all we'd heard was that Blackeyes had you executed, along with your brother and all the others. I'd never have dreamt he'd do what he did." Bandor paused and swallowed. "Crippling you."

"It came as something of a surprise to me as well." The jest fell flat and a shudder passed up my spine, setting loose all manner of twinges and aches along the way. "Blackeyes wanted his revenge for his defeat at Noln. What's done is done. You couldn't have stopped this happening to me any more than you could have saved your sister or Jorik. We shouldn't feel guilty about the parts we played – those who're really responsible aren't in this room."

Bandor nodded. "I'll pay them back. For what they've done to you and for Reesha, Jorik, my nephew and everyone else who died in Ulfkell's Keep and Kalamar." His fist clamped tight around his mug, knuckles white.

"And I'll be there by your side, just like the battle of Noln," I added. "It's good to have you here." Bandor looked at me strangely, and it took me a moment to realise how ridiculous I must have sounded. He flushed as he tried to find the right words to save what was left of my pride.

"Well, I know what you mean but ... Well, it can never be like it was before, can it? You'll never fight again, not now Blackeyes has robbed us of your sword arm, though I can see Etta has plans for you. You've always had a quick mind and Father's going to need advisors, when he finally drives

Adalrikr's from our lands. There'll be a place for you at his side."

"What, as the crippled advisor of Johan Jokellsward, clan chief of Reavesburg?" I snapped. "My family's ruled the Reavesburg clan for over sixty years, with yours swearing fealty to us. What gives you the right to hand out favours to me, like I should be grateful?" I was on my feet, cold fury in the pit of my stomach, as Bandor looked at me aghast. "Tyrfingr took everything from me and I'm due my vengeance, every bit as much as you are. Who are you to tell me to stay at home with the women and children, while you ride out to take all the glory with your damned Company of Shadows?"

Bandor paled. "Rothgar, I'm sorry. I didn't mean any offence."

"No lad, you just spoke the truth," rumbled Rugga, his great hand resting on my shoulder. "Johan here is still one of Jorik's jarls and there's some say he's the rightful chief of Reavesburg too. No one's going to follow a cripple in a time of war, especially one who's spent the past few months hiding as a farmhand, whilst we've been fighting for the honour of our clan. Don't be too quick to take offence when someone offers you something out of friendship." He folded his massive arms across his chest, daring me to challenge him.

"Cripple," shouted his little daughter Kitta before Ingirith could intervene and clap a hand on her mouth. Although Rugga chuckled, Johan looked less amused.

"You've spoken your mind, Rothgar. I can forgive you for that, after what you've been through but Rugga's right. Marl's line is extinguished and while you're the last remnant of that great dynasty you've no following and no realistic claim to be chief. People would rather vote for Hrodi at the moot. If we see this through and free our lands, then there's only two people with a strong claim to be chief. Gautarr Falrufson, who's no friend of yours, and me. Support me, and there's a chance we can prevent Falrufson taking power. I loved your father and brother and I followed them willingly, even if I didn't always agree with them. The gods know I love you too, so don't ever again show me or my family such disrespect that you make me doubt your loyalty. You'll get your vengeance when I get mine. Now, do I have your support or do you want to ask my men which of us they'd rather follow?"

***

I stood in the courtyard, cold air stinging my cheeks. My breath frosted the air, lit by the moon. A clear night and it was already a freezing one, although some people were still about, despite the late hour. I could see Sefa outside the barn with her arms wrapped around Ekkill's neck, giggling and laughing as he tried to undress her. She led him slowly around the back of the building, out of my sight. Inside the barn I could hear Ulfarr's deep tones, arguing over the outcome of a card game with his crew.

The door of Joldir's house opened and I turned, expecting to see Arissa or perhaps Bandor coming out to speak to me. Instead it was Joldir who approached, his face grim.

"That was poorly handled, Rothgar. What were you thinking?"

What indeed? "That my time was done, and I'd been cheated of my chance for revenge, whilst Bandor sat there looking down on me – *pitying* me." My anger had long since given way to shame at my outburst, and I rested myself on the courtyard wall, pretending to ignore the sounds of Sefa and Ekkill's unashamed behaviour. "I'm not proud of what I said. It's just hard, seeing Bandor, knowing he's regarded as a skilful warrior whilst I'm considered less than a man. There was a time when he followed me into battle."

Joldir leant on the wall next to me. "You're right. Whilst I saved you, you're no longer the man you were before. I did what I could when you were brought to me. Was I wrong to do that?"

"No. None of this is your fault. You only tried to help me."

"That Johan is prepared to include you in his council

shows the regard he still has for you, whether or not you can still wield a sword. You and I both know our time here in Lindos is coming to an end. He's offering you a place at his side, so if it's vengeance you want, this is the moment."

"I swore my oath, you heard me." It was hard to wipe the image of Rugga smirking as I'd offered myself to Johan's service. "And you? What will you do when the time comes for Johan to leave?"

"I'll move out with him. Lindos is no longer safe and Johan will need a physician. Arissa and I have discussed this, and we've agreed we will travel with him together. She can assist me and in all conscience, I could hardly leave her behind. In any case, Etta has been most insistent I lend whatever help I can to Johan's cause."

"What hold does she have over you?" I asked.

"She's opposed to Adalrikr, and that's all that matters. I've had a long time to reflect on things, up here in Lindos. I'm not going to live out my life regretting not seizing the opportunity to join the fight and, if Dinuvillan is on my side, help to drive the knife into Adalrikr's heart."

"There's steel in you I've never seen before."

"I'm a realist. This is still going to be a dangerous business, but it's probably my last chance to take revenge for the friends Adalrikr took from me, all those years ago before I came to live here."

I wondered whether to press Joldir for more details, deciding against it when I saw the dark expression on his face. "Then our fates are bound together," I said instead. "Two fools on an errand that will probably lead us straight to Navan's Halls."

Joldir said nothing further as we stood together in the icy darkness, watching the stars glinting in the night sky.

CHAPTER 45

It was raining, just as it had been for the last four days after leaving Lindos Valley. With the coming of spring the snows had melted at the foot of the mountains, turning the roads and every small track into a river of mud, fed by the rain and further swelled by melt water from the hills. Shivering, I pulled my sodden cloak around my shoulders and was seized by yet another fit of coughing. Joldir pushed a waterskin towards me and I tried to drink, hands shaking so much I spilled most of the liquid down my chin. I hawked and spat, ignoring the stares of my companions, aware their patience was wearing thin.

"Thought you were meant to be a physician," muttered Skari One Eye, the second in Ulfarr's crew and a man who was as ill-favoured as his name suggested. He wore a patch over his missing left eye that did little to hide the ugly scar running down his face.

"He needs rest," Joldir replied, his voice calm. "There's only so much I can do."

"What he *needed* was to stay with Varinn and our supplies, out of our way. This is no place for the princeling."

"That's enough." Johan sat unmoving on the other side of our camp, face hidden under his cloak, dark with the rain. "He's here and, this far out, he's not going back. Anyone want to take issue with that?"

Skari looked as if he very much wanted to take issue until he looked at Ulfarr, who was shaking his head. Myr the Silent looked at me darkly saying nothing, in keeping with his name. He had lost his tongue as punishment at the hands of one of Reavesburg's jarls and had been an outlaw ever since, until he fell in with Ulfarr and his men. Our camp lapsed into a miserable silence, broken only by my occasional cough. A fire might have lifted our spirits and helped with my fever but we couldn't take the risk.

"You need to eat and drink something," Joldir told me quietly. I took the offered strip of dried meat and began chewing without enthusiasm, although it did give me some respite from my coughing. I had insisted on coming, supported by Bandor, though I now suspected it was against his better judgement.

"A few handpicked men," Johan had explained to his company assembled in Joldir's barn, when winter first began to relax its grip. "I'll go with Petr, Rugga, Ham and Kimbi. We'll leave Lindos the moment the thaw begins, strike out for Tullen and see what this traitor, Sandar, has to say for himself."

"And if the Vorund Clan sends its own men into Lindos whilst you're gone?" asked Maeva, Brandr's nervous wife.

"No one will be left behind," explained Joldir. He was now a regular advisor to Johan, a move bearing the hallmarks of Etta's handiwork. As for the old woman, she occupied a corner of the barn where Johan had called this meeting, bringing together his company and its followers.

Johan glanced at Petr, who began to deal with the practicalities. "Joldir's right, we're leaving Lindos come the spring. An advance group will make its way to Tullen, scout out their defences and see if we can find a way to reach Sandar. The rest will follow behind at a slower pace, bringing the supplies."

"It's not without risk, dividing your men like that," Varinn observed. The older warrior was a cautious man, which probably explained his advanced years. "If we're caught out in the open, well, it'll be all the harder to defend the women and children."

"Staying in Lindos is even more dangerous," Joldir said. "The Vorund Clan's bound to send a patrol up the valley as soon as they can. I'd rather not be trapped up here when they come."

Petr nodded. "Those following behind will look little different to many that'll be on the road with the spring, seeking out new opportunities now the roads have become passable again. You'll just be one more caravan on the move. With the womenfolk and children, plus all that baggage, you'll stand out a lot less than a group of well-armed warriors."

"So, who's going to be leading the way?" asked Ulfarr, his men gathered around him in a tight knot.

Petr regarded them levelly, the young man unbowed by their stares. "Your crew will be joining us in the advance party, along with Thengill and Ekkill."

"What a surprise," muttered Skari to Ulfarr in a stage whisper that carried to every corner of the barn.

"Varinn will take command of those following on behind," Petr continued, ignoring the remark. "We'll meet up again once we've handled our business in Tullen. You're to make your way to Falsten, where Sigolf Admundson is the elder, and, if all goes well, we'll re-join you there afterwards."

Several conversations broke out at once. I saw Brandr trying to comfort Maeva, who looked unimpressed they would soon be leaving their new home. Arissa looked worried and Thengill reached out, putting a big arm around her shoulders. Old Gunnar was asking anyone who would listen for them to explain the plan to him, since he had only heard about half of it first time round. Johan's voice boomed out, cutting through the chatter and silencing everyone.

"I've done hiding. I've sure as hell done with running as well. The way I see it, it's time for us to pay back those who've sided with our enemies and betrayed their clan. From what we know Sandar's always been a spy for the Vorund Clan, aiding them in the fall of Ulfkell's Keep. I'd like to make an example of him and show Blackeyes what's coming his way too."

"Well said," roared Rugga. "I'm with you, Johan. We all are!"

Johan smiled, bringing warmth to his gaunt features. "I know I can always count on you, my friend. The way I see it, we've all got a choice. We can accept that Blackeyes is Adalrikr's jarl in Ulfkell's Keep and bend the knee, or we can start to fight back, rally others to our cause and muster the men we need to drive this so-called king of Laskar from our land. That doesn't happen unless there's folk willing to make a stand."

Skari shook his head and spat sourly on the floor. "Well, at least you ain't stupid enough to start your fight in Olt; Hrodmarr's garrison outnumbers us at least five to one. But what's to say Sandar doesn't have similar numbers on his side when we get to Tullen? Could turn out your mighty stand starts with us running for our lives from Sandar's boys, with our tail well and truly between our legs."

Rugga's face darkened and he took a step towards Skari. Myr interposed himself between them, face impassive, hand resting loosely on the hilt of his sword. He would have been an imposing sight to most yet Rugga dwarfed Ulfarr's man, looking down at him with a sneer.

Petr raised his hand. "Enough, Rugga, it's a fair question and the honest answer is we don't know. What we do know is Olt's beyond our reach. There's no guarantee Hrodi will side with us, and without his support we don't have the numbers to take his keep. Tullen's smaller and with Reavesburg at the head of the river it's never needed to build its own defences. It's of less strategic importance, so there's a good chance Blackeyes won't have bothered to station any men there. The westerling men are farmers, not fighters, so when we turn up demanding justice there's a good chance they'll be too afraid to stand against us."

"There's a lot of *ifs* in this plan of yours, no disrespect, Hamarrson," Ulfarr said, arms folded. "We roll in there anything could happen. You think the folk of Tullen will just hand over Tindirson? He's still their town elder and he speaks for the western folk in the clan moot."

"A man can find a hundred reasons not to do a thing," interjected Johan. "It's the doing that's hard. I've led you this far and now I need you to follow me again and help me take a stand. Those who do will be well rewarded, that much I can promise."

"You can only be well rewarded if you're not dead," remarked Skari with a scowl, although he'd lost the argument. The barn was filled with men who'd followed Johan their entire lives, serving from boyhood in his household and fighting alongside him. They were men who had lost everything at the hands of their enemies and they were ready for revenge. A shout went up, led by Rugga, and even Old Gunnar now seemed ready to re-join the fight.

As the gathering began to break up I approached Johan, who was talking to Etta, my mind made up.

"I want to go with you," I blurted out.

Johan pursed his lips, obviously seeking some polite way to discourage the idea. "I thought you might say that. It's going to be a hard and dangerous journey on foot. Are you sure that's wise? You're still recovering."

"I wouldn't be recovering from anything without Sandar having a hand in the betrayal of his clan. I deserve my chance of revenge, surely you see that?" Johan looked ready to argue further before Etta interrupted him.

"Perhaps it would be useful to have Rothgar there. After all, you're going to be accusing Sandar of some serious crimes. It would look better if his main accuser was present, giving evidence first hand."

Johan paused, looking unconvinced. "After all your efforts to save him, I'm surprised to hear you of all people speak in favour of this idea."

"If it were Bandor, would you deny him the chance?" persisted Etta. "He deserves that much, after all he has suffered. There're risks whether he stays with me in the caravan or goes with you. The time for choosing the safest path is long gone, so let him play his part in this."

Johan sighed in resignation and turned back to me. "Are you sure about this?" I nodded, glad in some ways I wasn't being given the chance to change my mind. "I can't guarantee his safety, Etta, you know that."

"Send Joldir with him and have Thengill act as his guard. A good healer might well prove invaluable and Thengill's easily as strong as two men, and handy to have in a fight. They can help Rothgar on the journey if necessary."

"As you wish." Johan turned back to me. "You've earned the right to seek recompense for what you've suffered. I'll do my best to give you that chance."

I nodded. "Thank you – I won't let you down, I promise."

He looked down at me, his face no longer smiling, and there was steel in that craggy visage that made me wonder how well I really knew my father's old friend. "I hope not, Rothgar. I hope not."

***

Olaf's worried face swam into view. "Is he alright?"

"Just help me to get him up, please." Joldir's voice, sounding tired.

I laughed, though it quickly turned into a gurgling cough that seemed to last forever, my breath rattling deep inside my lungs. "I won't let you down, Johan … I'll not let you down …"

"What the hell's he going on about now?" Skari, not bothering to disguise his displeasure that I was still alive.

"This is ridiculous." Ulfarr's voice, more measured and calm. "Johan should never have brought him. He'll be dead before we ever re-join the caravan."

"We have to press on to Tullen," retorted Joldir. "He deserves that much."

Skari grunted. "Don't ask me to help. Olaf can do it if he's so concerned."

Joldir and Olaf each took one of my arms and supported me, as we continued the slow trek towards Lake Tull. I felt dizzy and sick, although my fever began to lift somewhat.

"He's not so bad, Skari, once you get to know him," Olaf was saying.

Joldir sounded surprised. "Really? I'm not sure I'd want to."

Olaf laughed. "There's not many would have let *me* join up. I was in trouble when we met. Went to Kalamar seeking a better life than herding sheep and found myself on the run. Wasn't my fault, that fight. It was him, taunting me and pushing. He went down with just one punch, hit his head on the cobbles and that was it."

"Life has its unexpected turns," Joldir tactfully observed.

"That's true. Ulfarr found me crapping myself on my own in the hills, hiding out there from Kalamar's guard."

"And Skari opened his arms wide and welcomed you in, did he?"

"Hah. One Eye's like that with everyone, hadn't you noticed? I've shown him I can pull my weight. And now, here we are, serving Johan Jokellsward, a proper jarl of the Reavesburg Clan. My brothers wouldn't believe it if they saw me today."

"My brother accused me ... of having a hand in murdering him," I muttered, willing myself to take another step. Olaf was strong, holding almost all my weight.

"What did he say?"

"Never mind. Let's just get to camp tonight."

As I struggled towards Tullen with the aid of Joldir and Olaf I recalled my last meeting with Etta, sitting in her cottage late at night, the day before our departure from Lindos. I hoped she was faring better than I was.

"Remember our suspicions, Rothgar. If I'm right and there's a skin thief hiding in Tullen, dark forces are at work. You've seen first-hand the power of magic, so if you're still determined to go on this journey promise me you'll be careful."

I nodded, feeling some trepidation now we were about to leave. "Of course. This is just something I've got to do, you understand? For me and Leif too."

"I wouldn't have argued your case if I didn't believe you

needed to be there, and it gave me the perfect excuse to place Joldir and Thengill with Johan. Leif reached out to you for a reason, giving us an insight into what we might face there and if I'm right, they'll know what to do."

"I'm still not sure," I began, wondering how to broach the subject that had been troubling me since Johan announced his intentions to set out for Tullen.

"You think we should tell Johan our suspicions," Etta guessed.

"It feels wrong to hold this back from him."

Etta grimaced. "Johan Jokellsward's no lover of the magical arts. To warn him we would need to explain that you and Joldir have the Sight – a gift you're not even able to use at the moment. He's old-fashioned, so using magic to aid his cause isn't something he'll accept easily."

"Is it our place to make such decisions, when we're talking about the man who might be the next Reavesburg clan chief?" I persisted.

Etta gave a throaty chuckle. "Hmm. Do you really think I shared *everything* I knew with your father, or Jorik for that matter? Knowledge is power and part of the skill of wielding it is knowing who it should be shared with and when. Suppose we're wrong and Sandar is nothing more than a weak, treacherous man. If we confide our suspicions in Johan, we've revealed our hand and will only succeed in looking foolish, perhaps even mad if we're wrong.

"No, trust me in this. Johan needs to see such things for himself and learn there is only one way for them to be defeated. That's why you must stay close to Joldir, Thengill and Ekkill. Their weapons bear runes of power that will banish the durath forever."

Unconvinced, I agreed to Etta's plan. I owed the woman my life and didn't want to part from her on bad terms. Her journey to Falsten would pose its own dangers. As I stood in the doorway I clasped her thin bony hands in mine.

"Travel safely, Etta. Varinn seems a good man. I'm sure

he'll see you safely to Falsten and I'll meet you there soon enough."

"Aye, lad, that you will. That you will."

CHAPTER 46

I must have drifted off to sleep, because the next thing I knew
Bandor was sitting next to me. Another dreamless night, free
from any visions – there was no sign of my gift returning, even
though I'd not touched a drop of ataraxia for months. I began
to doubt the Sight would ever trouble me again. The thought
left me feeling angry and useless, so to distract myself I
glanced around the camp. It must have been our seventh night
on the road, if my count was right. I knew I was delaying our
progress; we should have been in Tullen two days ago. Guilt-
ridden, I wearily asked Bandor how far we had left to travel.

"We're here," he replied, patting me on my leg. "Ekkill's
gone down to scout things out with Thengill and Olaf. They'll
be back soon, and in the morning we can make our move."

"Then Sandar had better watch out – I'm here to wreak
my doom upon him."

Bandor gave a bitter laugh and handed me a wineskin.
I drank a little, coughing and wiping my mouth with the back
of my hand. Though it felt like my fever was lifting, there was
a rattle deep in my chest that wasn't a good sign. I coughed
again and Bandor turned towards me, looking concerned.

"Leave it," I hissed. "I've made it this far. I've got
another day in me, maybe even two."

"Don't joke about such things."

"Why not? Be honest, they must be taking bets on
whether I'm going to make it." Bandor flushed. "Well? Come
on, what are they saying?"

"What does it matter? You're here now and we'll make it
to Falsten afterwards."

"Stand to make a profit if I do?"

Bandor grinned. "A tidy sum as it happens. Skari's going to lose a fair amount if you live through the night and reach Tullen."

"Forget Sandar, then. Once I set foot in Tullen, I'll know I've achieved something."

Bandor laughed. I heard the sound of footsteps and Sir Patrick, who must have been on watch, walked into the camp, leading Ekkill, Thengill and Olaf in his wake. Bandor stood and the other men including Johan looked up expectantly, eager for news.

"Well?" Johan asked.

Ekkill spoke up. "Tullen's undefended and, as far as we can tell, virtually deserted. There's a few homes in the centre of the town that show some signs of occupation, and a fire burning in the long hall. Otherwise we only passed empty farmhouses. No sign of guards."

Rugga smiled, rubbing his hands together. "This will be easier than I thought. Sandar's people have obviously abandoned him."

"Perhaps. It looks like some of the farmsteads have been left to run wild for years."

Johan frowned. "That doesn't sound right. Tullen has always been the most prosperous of the western towns after Olt, hence Sandar's place on the clan moot."

"Perhaps they didn't want to lose their influence," I said. From their startled glances the fact that I was alive came as a surprise to many of Johan's men. "Stands to reason if Tullen fell on hard times Sandar would still want to maintain his rights and vote."

Thengill shook his head. "It don't feel right to me. Wouldn't surprise me if this Sandar's long gone, especially if rumours of his part in Ulfkell's Keep's fall have been circulating. Reckon we could be wasting our time."

There were some groans amongst the men before Johan silenced them. "By the morning we'll know. Now, everyone get some rest; we'll be going to pay Sandar a visit at first light."

The men bustled about, those not on watch shaking out blankets and wrapping themselves up in their cloaks. Joldir and Thengill came over to join me and Bandor.

"Feeling better?" Joldir asked, pressing his cold hand against my forehead. "I gave you something for the fever, not that you knew much about it."

"His cough is still bad," Bandor told him, ignoring my glare of disapproval.

Joldir pursed his lips. "You've an infection in your lungs, left over from your illness last year. You need time and rest to recover."

"Neither of which he'll get, whilst he's marching with us," Bandor muttered.

"I feel better, really. If I could just shake this damn cough."

"If we can keep the fever at bay, I'll be happy. Here, chew this." Joldir passed me some dried and rather unappetising-looking brown leaves. "They're more effective as a tea. Since Johan's banned any fires you'll just have to get the benefit this way instead." I took the proffered leaves and put them in my mouth. They had a sickly, bitter taste, and as I coughed and bit down on them I realised it was familiar.

"How long have I been taking this?"

"Three days now. The fact you even have to ask shows how far gone you've been."

"All the medicine Joldir's given you won't be much use if you get a blade in the guts," Thengill remarked. "Etta wants you kept safe, so when we go down into Tullen you stick close to me and Ekkill. If things turn … unpleasant, I need to know where you are."

I fingered the long dagger Bandor had given me before we left Lindos. The unspoken fact I was no longer strong enough to wield a sword hurt my pride. "I can look after myself, thanks."

Thengill shrugged. "We'll see tomorrow, I guess."

***

Johan's men moved silently with one purpose in the half-light of dawn, warm breath frosting the air. No one spoke, each man already knowing his part. The archers fanned out left and right to ensure no one flanked us, whilst Johan led the rest of his men on foot towards Tullen. I followed, hand on the hilt of my dagger, my own breathing laboured as it rattled thickly in my chest.

Thengill walked next to me, wary eyes scanning the empty farm buildings as we continued our approach towards Tullen without incident. Johan led his small force, Rugga to his left and Petr at his right, Bandor and Kimbi close behind. Nearby a cockerel crowed, making Sir Patrick start. Skari sniggered at his alarm.

"Sir Patrick Wild quails before the chicken of Tullen," he hissed. "You're a real loss to the Berian knighthood, aren't you?" A few stifled, nervous laughs rose up and just as quickly died on the lips of Johan's men. It didn't matter how often they'd done this; there were always nerves before a fight.

"That's enough," Petr said curtly, cutting off Patrick before he could retort.

"I don't like the look of this," muttered Joldir nearby, his knuckles white where he held his quarterstaff. "Where is everyone?"

As our scouts had reported, Tullen appeared virtually deserted. There were no gates and no guards, allowing us to enter unopposed. As we walked up the main road a couple of chickens pecked the ground nearby – the only signs of life. I could see Ulfarr and Olaf skirting around some of the buildings to our right, checking no one was lying in wait for us. On our other flank Ekkill and Ham did the same, moving swiftly and silently. I should have felt safer knowing they were there but a tight knot formed in my stomach, twisting my guts. It clenched even tighter as we reached the doors of the long hall.

Skari hawked and spat into the dust at his feet, rolling his neck one way then the other, holding his hammer firmly in his hand. Johan turned to Ekkill, a questioning look on his face. Ekkill shrugged and shook his head, before taking up position nearby, his bow ready. I saw Ulfarr gently push open the door of a nearby house and slip into the darkness within.

The door to the long hall swung open, the red light of a fire glowing inside. An attractive young woman walked out onto the threshold, smiling warmly. If I had any doubts about the truth of the Sight she banished them there and then, for this woman walked straight out from my dreams concerning Leif. Ginna Sandarswyfe stood before us.

"Visitors," she said. "You've travelled a long road to reach Tullen. Please, put down your weapons and come inside. You'll find a warm welcome awaits you."

The appearance of a young woman rather than a horde of screaming warriors unsettled some of the men; whatever else they'd been expecting, this wasn't it. Rugga frowned and glanced at Bandor, who started to lower his sword. My heart was hammering in my chest all the same, and I noticed that Skari, Patrick and Myr were also ill at ease, each starting to fan out from the main group, giving themselves space, weapons ready.

Johan stepped forward. "We've not come here for your hospitality. We're here for Sandar Tindirson."

"And you've found his wife. I am Ginna, and you, sir, who are you?"

"Johan Jokellsward, Jarl of Kalamar. Where is Sandar?" Ginna chose not to answer, walking slowly towards Johan, a hypnotic swing in her hips drawing the eyes of several of the men. I felt Thengill tense beside me and I realised my hands were shaking, sweat running down my back. I turned to see Olaf staring about wildly, his bow unready and forgotten in his hand. Joldir was standing next to me, leaning heavily on his staff. His eyes met mine for a moment.

"Do you feel it?" he whispered through gritted teeth, as Ginna reached Johan – far too close. Only then did Petr and Rugga react, each stepping forward to block her path. She looked at each of them in turn, a playful glint in her eye.

"No closer, my lady," said Rugga hoarsely.

"This is close enough to gain the measure of the man. So, you're Johan? No longer the jarl of Kalamar, I think, much as you would like to cling to that old title. Kalamar is a pile of weed strewn rubble, blackened stones and bleached bones. You're nothing more than an outlaw now, leading your ragged band of thieves and murderers."

"That's enough," barked Petr. "Shut your mouth. How dare you talk to your jarl in this way."

Ginna only smiled, reaching out and stroking Petr's stubbled jaw with her hand. "My husband is a great lord, whilst your master is nothing. What is it you call yourselves? The Company of Shadows? A shadow cannot exist without the light. What will you do when you are devoured by the darkness?"

Johan looked levelly at Ginna, apparently unruffled. "I didn't come here to suffer your riddles and insults. Where's your husband?"

"Johan." Sandar stood at the doorway, flanked by several men including one large stocky bearded man I recognised as Vandill. Sandar regarded us all much like a king might look down upon his subjects, long sleek blond hair framing handsome features. I should have felt anger at the sight of the man who betrayed me and whose lies condemned me for murder. Instead, the cold fingers of fear crept up my spine and I wanted to crawl away and hide from him, from all of them.

"Why are you here, Johan?" Sandar's words were honeyed and warm, seemingly unconcerned at the sudden appearance of an armed band in his home.

"To bring a traitor to justice. You betrayed your clan, siding with Tyrfingr Blackeyes and aiding him in his capture of Ulfkell's Keep."

"And on what evidence do you dare accuse me of such crimes?"

"On my word. On the word of Rothgar Kolfinnarson." Somehow I found the strength to push myself in front of Thengill, mastering the urge to cower away from the young man.

Sandar looked at me, a faint smile playing on his face. Ginna entwined herself around him in a strange, possessive gesture that made me feel sick. In the shadows of the long hall more figures began to emerge, including Anders, Leif's father. He was wearing fine woollen garments rather than his normal farming clothes, clean shaven with his black hair brushed neatly back. The sight of him made me want to weep, though I couldn't say why.

"What's left of him, anyway," mocked Vandill, raising a ripple of laughter amongst the folk of Tullen.

Sandar raised an eyebrow at my appearance. "Rothgar, this is an unexpected surprise. I'd heard of your incredible escape from Ulfkell's Keep. Tyrfingr Blackeyes has men out searching for you. I wonder what he'd give to know who's been sheltering you all this time? Seeing your condition, I think the price on your head might be about to drop."

"Don't trust this one," whispered Ginna into his ear, though her words still carried. "He's powerful in the Sight. The gift lies dormant, his strength building, like waters behind a dam. Soon it will break."

Sandar nodded. "Who is that with you, Rothgar? Is it Joldir, Etta's pet? Our leader devoured your master and sent you running for the hills. You show rare courage coming here to face us once more."

I glanced at Joldir, who stood there, sweat beading on his forehead, eyes blinking furiously as he tried to keep them clear. "So it's true. I hoped she was wrong when Etta told me her suspicions."

"Etta has meddled in our affairs long enough. When this is done, we'll pay the old crone a visit and settle this once and for all."

"You're in no position to make threats," interjected

Johan with a frown. "We're here to demand justice for our clan."

I nodded, keen to try and wrest the initiative back from Sandar. "You lied before the clan moot, supporting the claim of a pretender to Reave's Chair. You aided in the betrayal and fall of your own clan chief and handed people who thought you were their friend over to our age-old enemies. I was there when Tyrfingr murdered my family and I know you had a hand in their deaths. Someone has to pay for all the blood that flowed freely in our lands since that night in the Great Hall."

Sandar laughed and looked straight at me, his clear blue eyes boring deep into my soul. It took all my strength not to turn and flee. "I should deny it. I should make the … effort Adalrikr expects. I find it so … difficult. I am loyal to my king, of course, but the flesh … He never warned me; it's so intoxicating, so hard to resist the pleasures of the flesh after all this time."

Johan's mouth dropped open. "Is that a confession?"

Skari turned to Myr, a wicked grin on his scarred face. "That's a pity, I was looking forward to torturing the pretty boy." Myr stood there, the hardened warrior still as stone, eyes watchful and sword drawn.

All the folk of Tullen were laughing now, a jarring, evil, twisted sound. Sandar looked as if he was enjoying himself. "What if it is, Jokellsward? If I confess my sins to a worm, what does it matter? What threat does it pose to me? You are all just flesh, warm, living *flesh*. You have come to us like a gift from the gods, and a gift should never be spurned."

Joldir placed his hand on my shoulder. "Get back. Get back behind me now." Thengill stepped in front of me and I felt strong arms pushing me away, and then the world tipped over on its side.

CHAPTER 47

Leif cowered under his bed, ashamed at his fear while unable to do anything about it. He heard the footsteps on the stairs and tried to still his breathing, fighting back regrets and sobbing tears that threatened to overwhelm him. He should have run away, should have persuaded his father to come with him whilst he still could. All too late now. His parents were gone, leaving him all alone and imprisoned, for reasons he still didn't fully understand.

Another step, someone trying to move quietly but that stair had always creaked. Leif bit back another sob and waited, tense and still as he heard the bolts slide back on the cellar door. He watched as a pair of black-booted feet crossed the floor towards him and, despite himself, Leif cried out in alarm as a figure suddenly crouched down and a black-bearded face came into view.

"Don't be afraid, son, I'm not looking to hurt you. Name's Ulfarr, what's yours?" He broke into a grin, which suddenly fixed on his face as Leif's mother hit him hard over the head. Ulfarr grunted, tried to rise as a second blow crashed into his skull, blood running down into his eyes. He managed to half-stand, bloody face hidden from Leif's view, before Lina sent the man flying back through the doorway and into the wall with such a noise Leif thought the whole house was about to collapse.

He recoiled, pressing himself up hard against the wall, as her face appeared under the bed. "Stay there, little boy. I'll be back for you." He watched her bare feet recede from the room, as silently as they had come, and this time, when the sobs rose up in his chest, Leif could do nothing to contain them.

***

My face was lying in the mud. I struggled to work out why I was no longer inside, hiding under my bed, while the sounds of shouting, fighting, people dying filled my ears. Strong hands seized my collar, hauling me onto my feet.

"I knew this was a mistake," growled Thengill. "Now, move."

I was dragged across the road, ducking instinctively as someone made to grab me, stumbling over a body lying on the ground, before crashing into the side of a house. Thengill released me, stepping forwards and drawing both axes. Somewhere I could hear a child sobbing.

Dizzy and shaken it took me a moment to absorb the scene before me. Johan and his men were in a tight circle, surrounded by the townsfolk on all sides. It should have been an easy fight for his warriors, as the men and women of Tullen were unarmed and unarmoured. Yet they moved faster than I could have believed, dodging axe, hammer and blade effortlessly, laughing all the while. A hideous sound, like fingernails scraping along the inside of my skull. Even as I watched, Ginna caught hold of Kimbi, one of Johan's swordsmen, as he lost his footing, separating him from the circle as she threw him easily over her shoulder. Kimbi fell with a shout, blade spinning away, and in moments the townsfolk were upon him, pinning him to the ground, biting, gouging, tearing and ripping at his armour, clothes and flesh. His screams mingled with their laughter as they tore him to pieces before our eyes.

"No." Petr broke from the circle, swinging his famed ancient sword left and right, which glowed with an odd, blue light, futilely trying to drive them off. They scattered from the bloody corpse, scrabbling away on all fours like rats. Vandill was among them and stood up, his teeth glistening redly.

"Petr, get back here," roared Johan – too late because the townsfolk were back, interposing themselves between Petr and the small circle of eight men. There was no sign of Joldir or Ekkill and I realised with a jolt that I had fallen over Olaf earlier, now lying face down with blood pooling around his mangled body. Sandar's people made no move to attack Johan, instead intent on keeping Petr separated. A few seemed to notice me and Thengill for the first time, their eyes bright and eager, stark white on red gore-spattered faces.

Vandill leapt forward without warning, forcing Petr to stagger backwards as he tried to push the bigger man away with his shield. Vandill caught hold of the rim, tearing it from Petr's arm and sending him sprawling in the mud. Rugga took half a step forward before being driven back into the circle by a flurry of blows from the crowd of townsfolk, snarling as he swung his hammer, connecting with nothing more than the air. Vandill didn't even look in his direction, taking the shield and driving it down towards Petr's throat, as he lay prone. The young warrior twisted away, struggling to untangle his sword from his heavy travel cloak as they became wrapped together. Vandill slammed the shield into Petr's ribs with a sharp crack, leaving him gasping on the ground.

"I thought Kalamar's finest warrior would be more of a challenge," mocked Vandill. He raised the shield high above his head, and then grunted as a white feathered arrow buried itself in the middle of his chest.

I spun round to see Ekkill perched on one of the roof tops, bow in hand, already drawing back another arrow. "I'd kill him now if I were you, Petr."

Hamarrson needed no second invitation, driving two foot of steel through Vandill's body as he rose from the ground. The big man took a tottering step as Petr pulled out the blade, the shield falling with a dull clang to the floor. Tullen's townsfolk took a communal intake of breath, releasing it as one in a long hiss of disapproval. Vandill's head wobbled as he stared shakily at the arrow protruding from his chest, while Petr was looking in disbelief at his sword; still as clean as if he had just finished polishing it. Ekkill loosed another arrow, only for Ginna to snatch it from the air with no more concern than as if she was swatting a fly, her eyes never straying from Vandill. The big bearded man turned to her, a grimace on his face and he coughed, dust spewing from his mouth. In that moment something seemed to give, and Vandill crumbled before my eyes, his body dissolving in trickles of fine sand. They ran from his head, the fingers gripping at Ekkill's arrow falling away into dust and, as the wind caught him, the trickle became a river, pouring to the ground and leaving Petr staring down open-mouthed at a mound of white powdery sand.

Ginna screamed and I heard Sandar shouting, ordering the attack to resume. Two men who had broken away from the main group hurtled towards me, running on all fours, bounding over any obstacles in their path, agile as cats. Thengill stood in their way and suddenly I was aware of someone else at my side, half-seen through the corner of my eye. I turned with a start, knife drawn, finding there was no one there. Turning back to my attackers, I saw the air shimmer between them and Joldir stepped out of nowhere directly into their path, swinging his staff. It was no longer plain wood but jet black, six feet of polished ebony with glowing blue runes running its length. The first man was almost upon him and found himself unable to stop as he was impaled on the end of the staff, vanishing in a billow of white sand with a despairing cry. His companion checked his stride in surprise, allowing Thengill time to bury the head of his axe into the man's face. He sank to his knees, dust rather than blood pouring from the wound. Thengill's second swing took his head clean from his shoulders and the man's body disintegrated.

"Johan. Petr. To me," Joldir shouted. I saw another of Ekkill's arrows strike home through the neck on one woman, turning her to dust in an instant. It cleared enough of a path for Johan and his companions to sprint to our side, Bandor barging his way through, knocking one man over with his shield, as Ekkill's arrows forced the crowd to scatter for cover. Together we formed a semi-circle, blades held ready, backs to the wall of the house, Ekkill on the roof above.

Thengill turned to look at Joldir, a shocked look on his face. "*All* of them? Is that even possible?"

Johan rounded on the man. "What are you talking about? What devilry is this?"

"Devil is the word," growled Thengill. "This is an evil place and these are evil foes. You've never fought their like before."

"Sandar and his people have been consumed by dark forces," Joldir explained. "Shadow spirits who first entered our world when Morvanos began his war for Amuran."

Furious, Johan gripped Joldir's shoulder. "You've seen this before? Are you saying you *expected* this? And you let us walk into here without any sort of warning?"

Joldir grimaced. "Would you have believed me if I'd told you first?"

"Well, we certainly believe you now," answered Johan, his eyes darting around as he watched the buildings for signs of our attackers. The townsfolk had melted away, hiding from Ekkill's deadly arrows. I could hear him scrambling about on the roof.

"Ekkill. Get down from there," shouted Thengill. A moment later I heard the sound of bowstrings and four or five arrows flews from the surrounding buildings. I heard Ekkill give a cry, followed by a loud crash and then there was silence.

"We can't stay here," Sir Patrick said, crouching behind his shield. "Get back. Get inside the house." We all scrambled through the doorway, as arrows began to rain down on us from all sides. Patrick and Rugga held their shields high in an effort to give us shelter as we squeezed inside.

"Shut the door," Johan ordered and Rugga and Ham set their shoulders to it as more arrows thudded into the wood. One found its way through the gap as the door closed, taking Ham through the throat. He crashed back into Petr's arms, thrashing about madly, red hands trying uselessly to staunch the bleeding as he slid noisily to the floor.

Nearby Skari was tending to Myr, who had taken an arrow straight through the thigh. Myr's face was contorted with pain as Skari broke the arrow and drew out both parts with a well-practised hand. Rugga stacked furniture up against the door and Bandor and Patrick pulled the downstairs shutters closed. In the other corner of the room Ham grew still and Petr gently laid him out on the floor. Joldir walked over to him.

"Let me see your sword." Petr stood and drew it from his scabbard; a fine piece of steel, shining bright in the gloom of the shuttered house. A couple of the men gasped, as they saw the blue glowing runes etched into the blade, six of them, five bright and one dim. We crowded round to peer closer and I was amazed at the fine detail in the etchings, chimera and dragon, locked in combat. I glanced over at Joldir's staff, which bore perhaps fifty or more of the same markings.

Joldir smiled. "The gods are not so cruel, it seems. Ekkill has keen eyes. How old is this blade?"

Petr frowned, baffled. "It was handed down to my father, Hamarr, by my grandfather and his father before him. It's an old sword yet it never loses its edge and it's light as a willow stick. It's a famous runeblade and a family heirloom, although I've never seen it ... light up like this."

Joldir took the weapon, holding it out straight in front of him. "The runes only glow if a shadow spirit is nearby. An old blade indeed, from the War of the Avatars. Only a weapon bearing the Mark of Garradon can harm a shadow spirit and kill them. Any other weapon is ineffective."

"You're only telling us this *now*?" snapped Skari. "Don't you think it might've been a good idea to mention this *before* we all marched in here? So, what do we do? Are you, Petr and that big bastard, Thengill, going to take on Tullen single-handed with your fancy weapons while we stay safe in here?"

"I only suspected Sandar was one of them," Joldir replied in clipped tones. "Thengill, Ekkill and I could have handled him. I never expected the durath to have taken control of the whole town."

At that moment Ekkill appeared at the top of the stairs, knife in one hand, sword in the other. He looked a little battered and bruised, with a cut above one eyebrow.

"You alright?" I asked.

"More or less. Sandar's lot aren't the best archers I've ever seen, although I broke my damn bow, diving through that window."

"Ham's dead," Thengill said shortly. "You can take his."

"How many others did we lose?"

"Three – Ham, Kimbi and that lad Olaf, and Myr's taken an arrow through the leg. Could've been worse. How many arrows have you got left?"

"A round dozen," Ekkill answered, patting the quiver on his back. "Could maybe find some more outside, though I'd rather not test my luck out there right now."

"Wait, where's Ulfarr?" Sir Patrick asked. "Has anyone seen him?"

"I've an idea," I replied, walking towards the cellar door at the back of the house.

CHAPTER 48

I found Ulfarr lying unconscious at the foot of the cellar stairs, his breathing shallow. Stepping over him and leaving Thengill to tend to the man, I unlocked and pushed open the door to Leif's prison, which swung open quietly on well-oiled hinges. I walked across the dark room, over to the bed by the wall and gingerly bent down. Leif was still there, curled up into a tight ball, hands over his head.

"What have you found?" asked Thengill.

"A boy. I know him; it's Leif." I saw him stir a little at the mention of his name and I slowly reached out my hand. His head snapped up and he glared at me, teeth bared and expression fierce despite his tear-streaked face. I stayed still, arm outstretched, hand extended towards him, willing him to reach out and take it.

"The durath would never take one so young. We should get him out of there," Thengill told me.

"I know, just give me a minute. Leif, I know what's been happening since you came here." Leif stared back hard, his face suspicious.

There was shouting coming from upstairs. "Fire arrows." Ekkill's voice. "Looks like they've found a target they can actually hit."

"Come on," called Thengill, as he stooped and picked up Ulfarr and began heading up the stairs, before pausing to look back at me.

"I'll be right behind you." The big man nodded and moved off, shouting to the others to get ready to leave.

"Come on," I said to Leif. "It's not safe here. Come with me now. I've got men with me, warriors who can protect you. You ever heard of Johan Jokellsward and his company?" There were a series of thuds as more arrows landed and I could hear lots of banging and shouting upstairs. I wondered grimly if Johan was fighting to get out, or whether Sandar had lost patience and his shadows were trying to get inside. With agonising slowness Leif uncurled his body and slid out from under his bed, watching me all the time. I could smell smoke and knew the house was alight.

"We have to go," I told Leif.

Leif looked at me, seeing me properly for the first time. "You're the one who comes to me sometimes, in my dreams. You and the pretty lady. I used to be scared of your dreams about the crows, though I like you better than her. I don't trust her at all."

"Her?" I answered with a hoarse voice. There was no time for further discussion as I led the boy upstairs, where Rugga and Skari were taking it in turns with their hammers to batter down the wooden panels at the back of the house, which was rapidly starting to fill with smoke. I put my hand over my mouth as I started to choke, steering Leif towards the widening gap.

"Let's go," shouted Rugga, kicking the last of the boards out of the way and forcing his massive body through.

We followed as quickly as we could, Patrick and Bandor now carrying Ulfarr between them. The smoke from Leif's burning home actually worked in our favour, masking our escape, though it was only a matter of time before Sandar and Ginna found us again. We all took shelter behind a nearby house and Johan called Joldir over to him.

"We'll need to clear the archers in those houses if we're to reach the long hall. You say our normal weapons can't touch them, so what about fire? Can we burn them out?"

***

Dark figures approached us, silhouetted by roaring orange flames as the whole town of Tullen burned. Thick black smoke billowed into the sky and the heat was so intense it was like staring into the heart of a furnace. I hoped the wind didn't fan the flames in the direction of the barn, where we had left Ulfarr in the care of Leif. There was nothing to be gained from worrying about that now. Ekkill raised his borrowed bow, down to just four rune-engraved arrows as a friendly cry from the nearest figure confirmed it was Skari leading Sir Patrick and a limping Myr.

"What are you waiting for?" asked Skari as they joined us outside the doors of the long hall. He pulled a flask of oil from his pack and motioned to Patrick, who was holding a burning torch in his hand.

"No," cried Johan. "We came here for Sandar."

Skari looked unconvinced. "What's the difference between burning him to death like the others and a good hanging? Dead's dead and I'd sooner see this finished than stay here a moment longer."

Johan shook his head stubbornly. "I want him taken alive, to answer for his crimes."

"Won't be any choice to make if we carry on standing here," Thengill observed, staring up at the roofs of the nearest buildings, which were now well ablaze. Flames and sparks were shooting upwards, drawn by wind and it was only a matter of time before the thatch in the long hall caught fire too.

"Skari's right," added Joldir. "A shadow can't survive the burning of its host. If you capture Sandar, put him on trial, condemn him and put him to death, that's not enough. Even if you hang such a creature they can leave their host and seek another, slipping through your fingers."

"What if Petr here was to take off this monster's head?" countered Johan, gesturing to his second. "If we use a runeblade these durath die forever. Isn't that what you told me?"

"The strongest durath can leave their host before they meet such a fate. Set fire to the long hall and have done with it. Guard all the exits and let them burn; there'll be no escape from this for any of them then."

"No, not without knowing for certain that Sandar's inside. I'll not leave here with three dead men and nothing to show for it except doubts and ashes."

"Johan, Sandar wants you to come inside and face you on his terms. He underestimated us – don't make the same mistake."

Johan shook his head and motioned to Ekkill and Petr. "Guard these doors and make sure no one enters or leaves, do you understand?"

"Four arrows and one remaining rune on Petr's blade may not be enough," Ekkill pointed out.

"Then shout loud enough and we'll come to you. The rest of you, follow me."

The long hall was dark and refreshingly cool as the doors closed behind us, allowing some respite from the searing heat and choking smoke of the burning town. As my eyes adjusted to the gloom, I saw the main hall was empty. The only light emanated from the long fire running the length of the hall, that and the unnatural ghostly blue glow of Joldir's staff. Thengill brought up the rear, most of the dozen or so runes still glowing bright blue on both axes he carried. The hall brightened as Sir Patrick and Bandor began lighting more torches, passing them out to the rest of the company. Their flickering orange glow revealed a thick black velvet curtain, embroidered in silver and gold thread, dividing the main hall from the living quarters comprising the final third of the building.

High, girlish laughter rang out, making me start as it swirled around us, coming from all directions and none. I spun around, knife drawn only to find myself confronting empty space. I heard Sir Patrick mutter a prayer as our torches guttered for a moment, as if caught by a gust of wind none of us could feel.

"Joldir of Lindos. A new name seems to have given you fresh courage." Sandar's voice; calm and measured. It was as if he was next to me, whispering the words in my ear.

"Most of your brethren are dead, Sandar, and you'll soon be joining them," Joldir called out. "You've poisoned and destroyed the innocent people of this town. Now it's time for you to pay for those crimes."

"Spare me a moral lecture, please. After all, you're the one who's been harbouring an exile from the Vorund Clan in your home. I wonder how many friends and relatives of your company he's killed in his time?"

Thengill merely gave an apologetic shrug, ignoring the surprised expressions of his companions. "What's done is done. I don't see how clan matters much here, leastways not when it comes to fighting creatures like you."

"That's true enough," agreed Skari. "You wanted to know if this bastard was inside, Johan. Well now you know, so let's burn this place to the ground and get our arses the hell out of here."

Johan was staring hard at the curtain. "Who are you? *What* are you? I was friends with your father. Did I ever know you at all, or were you already this dark shadow when Sandar was appointed elder for the people of Lake Tull?"

Laughter again, echoing around us. I felt Ginna run her hands through my hair and lashed out with my knife, finding nothing there. Sir Patrick's prayers grew louder, his hand shaking as he held up his flickering torch. Johan growled and snatched at the curtain, wrenching it down so it fell to the ground like a swathe of night.

I gasped as I saw that the walls behind were lined from floor to ceiling with skulls, piled high, one atop the other. Their sightless empty sockets stared out over some kind of crude stone altar, lit with flickering candles giving off a dull red glow. On top of the altar was an archway some four feet wide and six feet tall, constructed of smooth rounded black stones that rested upon each other so loosely it seemed as if the merest breath would send them tumbling to the floor.

Three figures stood in front of the altar. Sandar, blue

eyes bright, almost feverish as he watched us advance. Ginna laughing as if this had all been a fine joke, her pretty face distorted into an evil grimace. Anders stood to one side, his handsome face dispassionate and empty and a small part of me grieved for Leif, as I realised the man who had been his father was gone forever.

"You're brave, Johan, to come and face me here. You should have listened to Joldir."

Johan took another step forward, leading us on towards the altar. "What have you done? Who were these poor people?" My eyes ran up and down the walls, trying to count the skulls. Were there a hundred there? More?

Sandar smiled, making my skin crawl as I took another step nearer. "They were just flesh. Have you ever tasted the flesh of men, Johan? It makes you strong; first the thrill of the hunt, closing in on your prey. Then the kill, followed by the taste of warm, red meat."

"They're the people of Tullen," I whispered. "You pretended there was a fever, taking the villagers, as you killed them one by one." I shook my head, scarcely able to believe how Sandar could have avoided detection by those in the town.

"Folk of Tullen and those that travelled through these parts. There have been many on the road since Blackeyes took Reavesburg and Sinarr broke Kalamar. Rich pickings."

Skari had heard enough. "Right, so it's safe to say this bunch are completely mad. It doesn't mean we have to spend all day in polite conversation. Anything else you feel a pressing desire to know, Johan, or can we do what I said we should bloody well do all along and torch this place? Myr agrees with me, don't you Myr?" The big mute warrior nodded, lowering his torch towards the fallen curtain.

"No," answered Joldir. "First, we have to destroy the altar. We can't afford to leave that standing."

"You're welcome to try," Sandar replied with a smile, raising his upturned palms to his mouth and blowing on them.

We were battered by a hail of black shards, sharp as

broken glass. Half-blinded as I blinked to clear my eyes, I took a faltering step backwards, hand cold and sweaty as I gripped my knife and saw the dark shape of Anders coming towards me. Sir Patrick blocked his path and Anders struck him with an open-handed blow, sending him crashing into the fire pit. I held out my knife and torch, backing away until the wall pressed against my back, hemming me in as Anders bore down on me. There was an evil grin on his face, lit red from the fire and the altar candles. Without warning there was an arc of blue light and Anders' face exploded into dust, his body crumbling away before my eyes. Thengill charged on with a roar, racing to join the fight as Joldir and Sandar duelled, sword and staff clashing and I followed his lead, unsure what else to do.

Ginna was already on Sir Patrick, tearing at his face as he struggled to escape from the fire. Bandor swung his sword at her and she aimed a well-placed kick to his chest, sending him crashing into Rugga, leaving the two men in a sprawling heap on the floor. Myr's sword flashed past, although he was slowed by his wound and Ginna easily evaded him, dancing past Skari's hammer as she sprang towards Thengill, who was now fighting alongside Joldir as they pressed Sandar back.

Johan had rounded all of them and raised his two-handed sword high above his head, bringing it down with all his force on the stone archway. The blade rang with an ugly, clanging sound as the stones turned it away in a shower of sparks, unbalancing Johan and sending him down onto his knees. Ginna screamed, pouncing on him and dragging him to the floor.

There was no time to think as I stepped forward and plunged my knife into the small of her back, a quick, sharp thrust that met so little resistance I thought at first I'd only cut through cloth. The hot blood that ran over my hand showed otherwise as Ginna gave a high-pitched, inhuman scream. She rounded on me, taking me firmly in her grip and throwing me across the floor as if I weighed little more than a kitten. My back slammed into the base of the altar and I gasped, winded, fighting to draw breath like a landed fish. I tried feebly to push myself up from the ground as Ginna sprang towards me, a fierce hungry gleam in her eyes. Only then did I realised I'd lost both my knife and torch somewhere in this shadowy hall of bones.

At the last moment Ginna was forced to turn away from me as she evaded Bandor's sword once more. Skari and Rugga now pressed in on her too, working in unison and driving her back towards the wall. Finally Rugga's war hammer swept round and landed a solid blow to the side of Ginna's head. There was a dull crunch as she sank to her knees, blood running down her face, mouth open in surprise.

I took a shuddering breath, dimly aware of Sandar's shouts as he continued to hold off Joldir and Thengill. Blood poured from Ginna's wound, thick and black on her pale face. The air around her wavered as she took her dying breath and I blinked as something dark, like coiling smoke, poured out of her mouth. It flowed from Ginna's body as she slumped onto the ground, twisting and turning in the air, wrapping itself around Rugga as he took a step back in surprise. Skari saw it too.

"Rugga. Are you –" Rugga's shield slammed hard into Skari's face, snapping back his head and sending him crashing to the floor. Myr parried the next swing of Rugga's great hammer, face impassive as ever, as he blocked what would otherwise have been a killing blow. Bandor was watching the fight with wide eyes, unable to take in what had just happened. I could scarce believe it myself.

I finally managed to stand, bent double with the pain lancing through my back. There was a haze in the air now and I could smell smoke; glancing up, I saw the fire had finally reached the thatch in the roof of the long hall. Thengill was bearing down on Rugga as Myr fell back before the fearsome blows of his hammer. Sandar seemed unconcerned with the impending destruction of his home. His sword moved in a silver blur as Joldir now battled him on his own, his attacks lacking their earlier speed, leaving him on the defensive more and more often as their fight progressed.

Rugga turned away from an exhausted Myr just as Thengill brought down one of his axes in a savage cut. Rugga met the blow, easily turning it aside with his shield. A giggle escaped his lips, a shrill unnatural sound so out of character with the man I knew it set my teeth on edge.

"I was fond of that young girl's body. This one will serve. You'll all pay for breaking her, one by one."

The two great warriors moved slowly around each other, ignoring the pieces of burning thatch now steadily drifting down through the air around them. "Should've burned you when we had the chance," panted Thengill.

"It'll be your body I leave to burn, exile."

Thengill took that moment to kick out at the embers of the fire, sending a great shower of sparks into Rugga's face. The big warrior took a startled step backwards, swatting away ineffectively at the burning cinders with his heavy hammer. Thengill seized his chance, landing a blow with his axe on the hammer's shaft, shearing away half of Rugga's fingers and sending the weapon crashing to the ground. Thengill's next swing buried his axe deep in Rugga's throat, bringing him to his knees, maimed hand clutching at the wound. Then Rugga's startled face melted away as his body crumbled to dust. His huge shield fell with a clang to the floor, rolling to a stop at Thengill's feet.

"No!" Sandar's scream rent the air, a shrill, keening cry. He slashed at Joldir without restraint, the blows sending Joldir's staff spinning out of his hands. It landed with a clatter behind him, well out of reach. Johan and Bandor began to move towards Sandar as he raised his sword over Joldir, both of them too far away.

I heard rather than saw the arrow as it flew past. Sandar grunted, the long shaft protruding from his left eye. He swayed to one side, crashing into the altar, his sword scraping along the stonework. Sandar slid down on the ground, coming to rest in a sitting position, legs stretched out in front of him, back resting against the altar. He turned his head jerkily, fixing me with a one-eyed stare, a grimace on his face and his long blond hair dripping red on one side. There were no final words as the drops of blood turned into a pink sandy trickle and in moments the young man was no more than a pile of white ash, half covering his sword.

"Don't all rush to thank me," Ekkill said, calm as you like as he lowered his bow in the doorway. "You do know this place is on fire, don't you?"

CHAPTER 49

My cough had returned, each spasm sending stabbing pains deep into my lungs. I was paying the price for the journey to Tullen and breathing in the smoke from the burning town we left in our wake had made matters worse. I blew gently on my tea, hands wrapped around the cup for warmth, and took a sip as I sat in the corner of the inn at Falsten. Arissa returned with a blanket, which she draped around my shoulders with a smile.

"You look tired. Is there anything else I can get for you? Shall I ask the innkeeper to bring you some food?"

I shook my head, nauseated by the very thought of eating. Joldir's brackish herbs had given me an empty, unnatural strength to complete the weary journey from Tullen to re-join Varinn's caravan in Falsten, one that suppressed my appetite. Tea was the only thing I could face today.

"Arissa, would you be so good as to fetch me another cup?" asked Etta, stick tapping on the wooden floor as she approached our table. "Strong and black; you know the way I like it."

Arissa headed over to the kettle on the fire, pausing to lay a hand on Sir Patrick's shoulder as she passed Ulfarr and his crew. The Berian's scabbed and bruised face broke into a lopsided smile as she asked after him. Nearby Skari made some joke and they all laughed, Myr even going so far as to break into a thin smile. Sitting in a corner on the other side of the room, Ekkill was whispering into Gylla's ear. She turned to him, smiling, placed her arms around his neck and planted a kiss on his cheek. Etta pulled up her own chair on the other side of my table and slowly lowered herself into it, her old joints creaking in protest. I knew how she felt.

"Arissa's right, you need to eat. You look terrible."

"Thanks. I forgot how much I've missed your encouragement. How's Leif doing?"

"The same; quiet and withdrawn. It's hardly a surprise, when you think what he's been through." Etta sighed. "The main thing is he's safe now and in good hands with Joldir."

"He was reaching out to me, all this time." My voice broke without warning and I had to set my cup down with shaking hands. "If we'd gone to Tullen straight away his parents might still be alive; Leif might still have had a family and a chance to lead a normal life."

Etta looked hard at me, silent for some time. "Life's too short for such regrets. I think Ingirith may be able to offer Leif a new home with her children. It will give her something to focus on beside her grief at losing Rugga."

Arissa returned with two more cups of tea and joined us, her long auburn hair hanging in a long plait down her back, green eyes bright and full of life. As we chatted about inconsequential things in the relative safety of Falsten under Sigolf Admundson's protection, I knew I should have felt happier – or at least relieved at having survived what took place in Tullen. Now, it seemed as if Falsten was part of another world altogether; a world less predictable and intelligible than I had been led to believe.

Something had been coming through Sandar's archway before Joldir smashed it with his runestaff. There had been a shifting in the air within the darkness. A nameless presence gathering itself. I had seen the fear in Joldir's eyes as he took that swing, scattering the black stones in every direction, the blue light of his staff dimming as every rune was expended in the effort. I would never forget the terrible roar of anger as those stones had tumbled to the ground, a sound that plagued my dreams every night since.

Afterwards the survivors of Johan's company had sat on a hill outside Tullen, watching Sandar's town burn, thick black smoke leaving a dirty bruise across the clear blue sky. No one said a word as we nursed our wounds and watched the long hall consumed by the flames, the thatched roof eventually falling into the building with a great crash. Leif sat some way apart from the rest of us, keeping his own vigil. It was the second home he'd watched burn, though I knew he would have different regrets this time; regrets no seven-year-old boy should have.

Tullen burned fiercely as night fell and no one objected when Petr began to build a campfire. We huddled around in a tight circle, faces dark and troubled as we watched the dancing flames, each of us thinking of the four men no longer with us. Johan finally broke the silence, turning to look at Joldir, his face troubled.

"I've seen many terrible things in my time. Women raped and children murdered on raids, men I've grown up with and known from boys weeping and calling out for their mothers as they've lain there, dying from their wounds. I thought we were going to deal with a traitor today, hand out some justice and a measure of revenge for those Tyrfingr's killed. What I saw today ... Well, that was evil. There's no other word for it. Evil."

Ulfarr leaned forward. His head was bandaged and there was a dark bloodstain on the cloth. "The way I see it that was evil some of us were prepared to face and others weren't. Another member of my crew's lying dead down there, after we went in without so much as a warning as to what we were going to find." He spat into the fire, a scowl on his face.

Joldir looked tired and weary, shoulders hunched as he sat there wrapped in his cloak, warding off the cold of the night. "I'm sorry. What more can I say?"

"You can start by explaining what in hell's name is going on," snapped Skari. "You owe us all that much. What were they? What happened to those townsfolk? I've never seen a thing like that in all my life. Hope I never will again."

"They were consumed by the durath," Joldir looked around at their blank faces. "Skin thieves, shadow spirits;

creatures who can steal a man's body and consume his soul. You've heard the tales of the War of the Avatars and how Morvanos forged creatures in the shadows beneath the earth to swell the ranks of his armies. While Morvanos may be banished beyond the Void his servants live on and grow stronger."

"There's more," I added. "Adalrikr's one of them. Etta's known this all along, which is why she's been so determined to end his rule of the Vorund Clan."

Joldir nodded. "It's true. Adalrikr's been one of the durath for several years; a far more dangerous foe than Sandar."

"He can still be killed?" asked Johan. "A blade etched with one of these runes would put an end to him?"

"The durath are vulnerable in this world to certain magics, such as a runeblade," Joldir answered. "Adalrikr included."

Johan looked hard at Joldir. "Weapons you and your friends possess but we, aside from a stroke of good fortune in Petr's old sword, sorely lack. Did you make your staff and etch those runes into Thengill's axes?"

"I did."

"Good. Then you will make more, so my men are armed and ready to face these creatures of the night."

"What?" Skari spun round, the light from the fire revealing his battered face, a dark red line across his forehead where Rugga's shield had smashed into it. "Wasn't today close enough? We've just walked into a town full of those things and were lucky to make it out again alive. I say we offer up our thanks to Dinuvillan and clear out of here at first light."

No one spoke as Johan measured his words, taking his time. A log cracked in the fire, sending up a shower of sparks into the night. "You forget, Skari One Eye, that Ulfarr's crew follow me now. Nothing's changed. Adalrikr sent his ships to my stronghold, killed my people and destroyed my birth right. He murdered our chief and set a pretender, a man who's our sworn enemy, on his chair. I'm still jarl of Kalamar and I intend to join up with my men in Falsten and raise an army to drive these bastards from our shores. Now I've seen their true nature nothing's going to turn me aside from that path."

"Nothing's changed?" Skari looked incredulous. "Take a good look around, Johan. I'm not sure I agree."

Johan turned to Thengill. "What about you? What have you got to say?"

The big man shrugged. "I failed my chief when Asmarr was killed, the man I was sworn to protect. I've had plenty of time to think on that since. Plenty of time to prepare for a fight I've known is coming, so I don't intend to shy away from it now the moment's here. I'm with you, Jokellsward."

"The Company of Shadows is going to lead the fight to drive Tyrfingr Blackeyes from our lands," Petr agreed, eyes bright. "And these skin thieves will be put to the sword too." Sir Patrick and Bandor nodded at those words and somewhat to my surprise, Ulfarr did too.

Skari scowled, seeing which way the wind was blowing. "You're in this too?" he asked Myr. The big man turned his blank slab of a face to his friend and nodded once.

"Guess that settles it then, chief," Skari muttered. "I'm in. Let's face it; where else have I got to go?"

***

I shivered as I stood outside, a woollen blanket drawn tightly around my thin shoulders. There were the sounds of mirth from inside the inn. Men glad to have a roof over their heads, a bed to sleep in and food in their bellies. The simple relief found in being safe and warm, at least for now.

I glanced over to the hastily erected scaffold in the town square, just visible in the moonlight, where the bodies of ten men swung back and forth in the wind. Tyrfingr was unable to garrison every town as strongly as Olt and clearly hadn't expected Falsten to offer up much resistance. Varinn had made short work of the Vorund warriors, stealthily entering Falsten at night with his men, killing those on sentry duty and catching the rest asleep in the inn they had taken over as their headquarters. They surrendered and turned themselves over to him in the hope their lives would be spared.

For now, Falsten was safe and our latest refuge. Some of the younger men in the town had even joined up with Johan's brotherhood. The Company of Shadows was no more; a name everyone felt was too close to the real shadows we found ourselves fighting. People in Falsten took to saying that the eagle of the Reavesburg Clan was flying again, now Johan had liberated their homes and was leading the fight to regain our lands. The Brotherhood of the Eagle was born in that small village, calling on ties of loyalty as close as blood, ties as close as those between brothers. People cursed the name of traitors such as Sandar Tindirson, although only a few of us knew what had really taken place in Tullen. Part of me wished I could forget what I'd seen.

"Arissa told me I'd find you out here." Bandor approached me with a smile, now a confident young man in whom I saw more and more of his father each day. "Come back inside. You'll catch your death in this cold."

"In a minute. I need some air." More laughter drifted out from the common room and I shook my head. "How can they forget so quickly? I've dreamt about Tullen every night since we left."

"Remember what Varinn said back in Lindos, how people deal with things in their own way? Is it so wrong of them to relax and enjoy themselves while they still can? It won't take long for word to spread that Father's mustering his forces here, and sooner or later there'll be more fighting. There's no knowing when your days are over; I know that much from my time on the road."

Bandor was right, of course, and I wished I could set such things aside as easily. He put a hand on my shoulder. "Are you alright?"

"I'm not sure. You go back inside, I'll be along in a moment."

Bandor looked worried, though he did as I asked, patting me on the back before returning to the inn. I was briefly bathed in a square yellow patch of warm light and laughter washed over me as he opened the door. Then it was dark and cold once more. I looked up into the night sky, admiring the swath of blue and white stars adorning the heavens. I watched as they winked in and out of view as a scattering of dull grey clouds scudded past, driven by the wind.

"Not enjoying the festivities?" asked Thengill. I'd not heard him approach until he was standing beside me, face shrouded in shadow.

"Can't say I feel much in the mood for them," I admitted. "It's like the world has changed … I don't feel like I'm part of it anymore."

Thengill let out a long sigh. "I can understand that. I felt completely lost when Asmarr died. He was a great chief, a man I was willing to risk my life for. When the time came, I wasn't able to protect him from his own son, and that's just it because it wasn't Adalrikr who killed Asmarr and his brothers. Adalrikr would never have betrayed his own family; the lad loved his father, so I trusted him completely. Meant I wasn't ready when he struck and Vorund Fastness became a bloodbath. I've often thought since it would have been better if I'd died that night. Somehow I got away with a few of those still loyal to Asmarr. Adalrikr's men were hunting us down, so we fled into the Northern Plains and found ourselves scratching out some sort of living, hunting for game mostly, thieving sometimes. Stuff I'm not proud of."

"What happened? Lindos is a long way from the plains."

"After six years on the run we'd found some half-way lawful work, acting as paid guards for one of the nomad tribes for the past year. Adalrikr hadn't forgotten about us, it seems, because one night a score of his men hit our camp and they'd no mind to take any prisoners. Found myself fighting one of those skin thieves, after he took the body of my friend, Dragmall. Took me right back to Vorund Fastness, when you couldn't tell friend from foe. Knew even if I killed him that skin thief would rise up again, but what else could I do? I buried my axe in his head and watched a shadow spill from him, wrap itself around me and try to take my soul. Only it couldn't. It just broke when it touched me, shattering like glass. There I was; last man standing in the grasslands, everyone else I knew and trusted lying dead at my feet."

There was a lump in my throat as I felt his loss, mingled with the pain my own memories. "What did you do?"

"Took one of the horses, gathered some supplies and left. What else was there to do? Had half a mind to leave, maybe head to Beria and find work as a mercenary there. What I couldn't shake was how Adalrikr hadn't forgotten me, even after all those years. He'd sent men after me and my friends. When his shadow didn't come back to him I knew he wouldn't leave it there. Running and hiding hadn't worked out too well, so I figured I'd head back to Vorund and face him."

"On your own?"

"Didn't say it was the best plan I'd ever had. I didn't get far, just to one of the small fishing villages on the coast and that's where Ekkill found me. I'd half-drunk myself to death in some shabby tavern by then, so I was ready to tell anyone who'd listen what had happened to me. Thing is, Ekkill believed my outlandish tale. What's more, he offered to give me shelter and a refuge from those hunting me."

"He brought you to Joldir in Lindos?" I guessed. Thengill nodded. "In return for what?"

"Wondered that myself, after I arrived. The deal was I'd act as Joldir's guard should he need it, and make myself handy on the farm when he didn't. Took me a while to realise it was because I was useful. The skin thieves couldn't touch me for some reason. Joldir spent *months* carving those runes into my axes, turning me into a weapon he could turn against the durath. In return, when the time is right, I get to take my vengeance on that thing calling itself Adalrikr and fulfil my oath to Asmarr."

I kicked a small stone in front of me, watching it bounce away down the road. "Sounds like you know which side you're on and why."

"Took me a while to figure it out. Six years hiding in the plains, all the while my broken oath eating away inside me. I'm still alive for a reason, and that reason is to take Adalrikr's head off with my axe. I've been given the tools and in Johan a leader, one who's not going to stop until that black-hearted bastard and those following him are dead and buried. You're alive for a reason too. You understand that, don't you? Etta takes care of those useful to her, and you already proved your worth in Tullen."

And there it was, that guilty feeling as I thought back. I'd gone to Tullen because I wanted to fight Sandar and his followers, only to be reminded once more I was never going to be a warrior again. The crippled son of Kolfinnar Marlson, a mere shell of the great men that lineage represented. I shook my head. "I only played a small part, standing by as others fought for my clan. War is coming and this is your time now."

Thengill laughed, a deep booming sound I'd rarely heard before. "Is that what you really think? You're supposed to be the bright one. Couldn't see it myself at first, when you came to Lindos as a cripple who'd never earn his way in the world. Now I know you've some bones to you, the stuff a clan chief's made of. I saw you step in whilst others gawked and put your knife in Ginna. You probably saved Johan's life, though in all that confusion I don't suppose he remembers much about it. I've seen grown men run screaming from the durath when they understood what they were facing, whilst you stood your ground. And you possess the Sight, a rare gift, and one you probably would never have discovered if you were still wielding a sword. A warrior's life like mine is a short one. Reckon you've a chance to become one of Johan's closest advisors, where the real power sits. Well, you could if you had the sense to come inside out of the cold."

I paused on the threshold of the inn, placing a hand

on Thengill's shoulder. "One more question. Why does Etta want to bring Adalrikr down so badly? What is there between them?"

Thengill shrugged. "That's something you'll have to ask her. I've told you my story and it's for Etta to tell you hers."

Inside the inn people were drinking, shouting, telling jokes and in Ekkill's case entwining his arms around Gylla as they kissed. Thengill led me back to my table and ordered meat and drink.

"You look freezing. Where have you been?" asked Arissa, her face concerned.

"Just thinking," I replied. I looked at the people gathered around us; men and women, young and old, warriors and whores, exiles, reformed bandits, a fallen knight, the homeless, widows and widowers. It was hardly a band likely to strike fear into the hearts of our enemies, yet I felt a sense of pride as I took my place amongst them. After all, this was my family now. This was my brotherhood.

EPILOGUE

The rowing-boat moved slowly, travelling gently with the flow of the river and listing slightly to one side. Humli stood watching from the river wharf as the boat drew closer and tried to make up his mind whether it was occupied. There was a bundle of dark cloth piled up in the middle – could that be a person? If it were, the shape wasn't moving, which didn't bode well.

He licked his lips, wondering whether he really wanted to hook the boat, bring it over to the wooden wharf and peer inside. Life as a fisherman had been simple enough before Blackeyes killed the chief and half of Ulfkell's Keep's warriors. Humli didn't believe those ignorant folk who said the chief's brother betrayed their clan. It was a stupid plan if he had, getting hung up in that crows cage for his pains. Anyways, the result was the same; pain and misery for the Reavesburg Clan, and he'd seen a fair amount of misery on the River Jelt since then. Bodies. For days at a time last year bodies of men, women, children and animals had floated past, some little more than bloated grey lumps of reeking flesh. Later came the boats of refugees, not realising Ulfkell's Keep had fallen, or choosing not to believe the rumours were true. Dozens of boats and makeshift rafts had floated up the river each week for the first few months after the defeat, many containing people with nothing more than the clothes on their backs. All bore the same haunted, frightened look.

Humli had been the one to tell some of them the news that there was no safety in Reavesburg, with Tyrfingr Blackeyes sitting in Reave's Chair. Some turned away, seeking refuge elsewhere – wherever that was. Others chose to take their chances and moored their boats on the river wharf, gathered their meagre possessions together and grimly walked into Reavesburg. Humli wondered what sort of reception they would get. That winter his daughter had told him people were going hungry in the streets after Blackeyes' men took all the provisions and supplies; only handing it out to those who proved their loyalty.

The river refugees were a less frequent sight this spring, after that long, hard winter. Yet here was the little boat, drifting closer all the time. Humli took hold of the long pole and reached out, hooking the boat before it drifted past his reach. Gently he steered the boat to the wharf and tied her securely before reaching inside to pull back the pile of blankets.

He started as the bundle moved, a bare foot poking out, pale and white, veins blue with the cold. He pulled the blanket away and the smell of unwashed body engulfed him as he revealed a young woman lying at the bottom of the boat, curled up tight, her clothes ragged and torn. Humli clambered into the boat, placing his hand to her cheek. She was alive, stirring at his touch.

"Where am I?" she croaked, eyes fluttering. Her lips were cracked and dry, eyes encircled by dark rings.

"Reavesburg, lady," Humli explained. The woman was exhausted and in no condition to travel any further. Humli lifted her gently into his arms and clambered back onto the wooden dockside. As he did so he realised the woman was pregnant. Poor girl. Where was her husband? Humli didn't like to think on that, and instead began to carry the young woman towards his cottage.

"You'll be alright," he assured her. "My daughter works in Ulfkell's Keep and they have food there. I can send word and she'll know people who can help you."

"Thank you," the woman said in a rasping voice through her cracked lips. "You're a good man. I had to flee my town ..."

"Don't think about that now, lady. Let's get you somewhere safe, give you some food and water." The woman's head lolled back and Humli worried she'd lost consciousness. She wouldn't be the first refugee he'd seen die, though she would be the first to do so in his arms. He quickened his pace, trying to sound soothing as he spoke to her again. "My daughter's name is Desta. She's a good woman and kind. You just hang on, love, and she'll be able to help you."

"Lina," whispered the woman. "My name ... My name is Lina."

CHARACTER LIST

Where a character's name appears in square brackets they have already passed on to Navan's Halls at the start of Hall of Bones.

The Reavesburg Clan
The household of Kolfinnar Marlson, eighth Reavesburg clan chief, at his stronghold of Ulfkell's Keep in Reavesburg
Kolfinnar Marlson – eighth Reavesburg clan chief and father to Jorik, Rothgar and Nuna
[Alaine Kolfinnarswyfe] – Kolfinnar's late wife
> **Jorik Kolfinnarson** – Kolfinnar's eldest son, married to Reesha (Johan Jokellsward's daughter)
> **Reesha Jorikswyfe** – Johan Jokellsward's daughter and Jorik Kolfinnarson's wife
>> **Kolfinnar the Younger** – Jorik Kolfinnarson's son
> **Rothgar Kolfinnarson** – Kolfinnar's younger son
> **Nuna Kolfinnardottir** – Kolfinnar's daughter
Etta the Crone – Kolfinnar's chief counsellor
Finnvidor Einarrson – jarl of Ulfkell's Keep
Olfridor Halfhand – Kolfinnar's weapons master, brother of Gautarr and Egill Falrufson
Brunn Fourwinds – a warrior of Ulfkell's Keep. Bram's father and captain of Kolfinnar's warship, *Marl's Pride*.
> **Bram Brunnson** – childhood friend of Rothgar, son of Brunn Fourwinds
Haarl – childhood friend of Rothgar
Djuri – a warrior of Ulfkell's Keep
Ulf – a warrior of Ulfkell's Keep
Darri – Kolfinnar's bard
Humli – father of Desta, a fisherman on the River Jelt

Desta Humlidottir – a servant at Ulfkell's Keep and Rothgar's lover

Amma – Nuna's maid at Ulfkell's Keep

Katla – Nuna's maid at Ulfkell's Keep

Ekkill – one of Etta's agents

The household of Johan Jokellsward at his stronghold of Kalamar Castle on the northern border with Norlhast

Johan Jokellsward – jarl of Kolfinnar

Damona Johanswyfe – wife of Johan and Bandor and Reesha's mother

> **Reesha Jorikswyfe** – Johan Jokellsward's daughter, married to Jorik Kolfinnarson
>
> **Bandor Johanson** – son of Johan Jokellsward and Rothgar's best friend

Rugga, the Rock of Kalamar – a warrior of Kalamar

Ingirith Ruggaswyfe – wife of Rugga and confidante of Damona

> **Egill Ruggason** – son of Rugga and Ingirith
>
> **Kitta Ruggadottir** – daughter of Rugga and Ingirith

Kaun Quicksteel – a warrior of Kalamar, Johan's second

Petr Hamarrson – a warrior of Kalamar

[Jokell] – the adoptive father of Johan Jokellsward

Svan – a warrior of Kalamar, married to Dalla

Dalla Svanswyfe – wife of Svan

Brandr – a warrior of Kalamar, married to Maeva

Maeva Brandrswyfe – wife of Brandr

Eykr – a warrior of Kalamar

Gunnarr – a warrior of Kalamar, known as **Old Gunnarr**

Ham – a warrior of Kalamar

Kimbi – a warrior of Kalamar

Varinn – a warrior of Kalamar

Ulfarr – the leader of a band of outlaws, now a follower of Johan Jokellsward

Skari One Eye – the longest serving member of Ulfarr's crew and his second

Myr the Silent – one of Ulfarr's crew
Olaf – one of Ulfarr's crew
Sir Patrick Wild – one of Ulfarr's crew, a fallen Berian knight from Brighthorn Keep
Gylla – a destitute young woman
Sefa – a destitute young woman

The Household of Gautarr Falrufson at his stronghold of Romsdahl Castle on the southern border with Vorund
Gautarr Falrufson – jarl of Kolfinnar
Jora Gautarrswyfe – the wife of Gautarr Falrufson
    [Hroarr Gautarrson] – the late eldest son of Gautarr Falrufson, he drowned at sea during a storm
    [Svena Gautarrdottir] – the late daughter of Gautarr Falrufson, died of a pox in childhood
    Ragnar Gautarrson – younger son of Gautarr Falrufson and his sole surviving child
    Asta Ragnarswyfe – called **Asta the Fair**, the wife of Ragnar Gautarrson
        Hroarr Ragnarson – son of Ragnar Gautarrson
        Halla Ragnardottir – daughter of Ragnar Gautarrson
[Egill Falrufson] – the eldest brother of Gautarr Falrufson and the leader of the Romsdahl household until his death. Father of Throm and Freydja
[Tora Egillswyfe] – the wife of Egill Falrufson. After her death her children were fostered by Gautarr Falrufson
    Throm Egillson – Egill's son and Gautarr's nephew, raised by him since being orphaned
    Freydja Egilldottir – Egill's daughter and Gautarr's niece, raised by Gautarr since being orphaned
Audwin Strongshield – warrior of Romsdahl, Gautarr's second
Domarr the Oak – warrior of Romsdahl
Haki – warrior of Romsdahl
Igull – warrior of Romsdahl
[Falruf] – the father of Gautarr, Olfridor and Egill

Other Members of the Reavesburg Clan

Hrodi Myndillson also known as **Old Hrodi** or **Hrodi Whitebeard** – town elder of Olt

> **Radholf Hrodison** – eldest and only surviving son of Hrodi Myndillson

>> **Alfarr Radholfson** – eldest son of Radholf and grandson of Hrodi

Joldir – a reclusive farmer and healer living in Lindos, near Olt

Arissa – a former bard and adoptive daughter of Joldir in Lindos

Thengill – a former warrior, now working as a farmhand for Joldir in Lindos

Birna – healer at the town of Olt

Lundvarr – town elder of the merchant port of Noln

Sandar Tindirson – town elder of Tullen on the shores of Lake Tull

Ginna Sandarswyfe – wife of Sandar Tindirson

Vandill – a fisherman living at Lake Tull

Anders – a farmer from Brindling

Lina Anderswyfe – wife of Anders, a farmer from Brindling

> **Halma Andersdottir** – eldest daughter of Anders and Lina

> **Leif Andersson** – eldest son of Anders and Lina

> **Gisla Andersdottir** – youngest daughter of Anders and Lina

Hamarr – the elder of the village of Brindling

Oli – a huntsman living in the village of Brindling

Sigolf Admundson – elder of Falsten

Former Clan Chiefs of Reavesburg

[Reave] – first clan chief and founder of the Reavesburg Clan

[Sigborn Reaveson] – Reave's son and second clan chief, also known as **Sigborn Dragonslayer**

[Ulfkell Sigbornson] – Sigborn's son and third clan chief, the last of Reave's line

[Pengill Svennson] – fourth clan chief of Reavesburg

[Oli Pengillson] – fifth clan chief of Reavesburg

[Hroar Helstromson] – sixth clan chief of Reavesburg, Kolfinnar Marlson's grandfather

[Marl Hroarson] – Kolfinnar Marlson's father and seventh clan chief

The Vorund Clan

Adalrikr Asmarrson – clan chief of the Vorund Clan, Adalrikr took the title from his own father, Asmarr, after murdering him and his three elder brothers. Also known as **Adalrikr Kinslayer**

[Asmarr] – former clan chief of the Vorund Clan and Adalrikr's father

Tyrfingr Blackeyes – Adalrikr's jarl

Joarr the Hammer – Adalrikr's jarl

Sinarr the Cold One – Adalrikr's jarl

Galin Ironfist – a warrior of Vorund and Blackeyes' second

Bjorr – a warrior in Galin Ironfist's company

Randall – a warrior in Sinarr the Cold One's company

Hrodmarr Hroarson – a warrior of Vorund

Valdimarr – a noble in Adalrikr's service

[Dragmall] – a warrior in Asmarr's service

The Norlhast Clan

Karas Greystorm – Norlhast's clan chief

[Katrin Karaswyfe] – the late first wife of Karas Greystorm she died in childbirth, her son stillborn

[Thora Karaswyfe] – the late second wife of Karas Greystorm, she died of the blood plague

> [Gretta Karasdottir] – the late eldest daughter of Karas Greystorm, she died in childhood of the blood plague
>
> [Katrin Karasdottir] – the late youngest daughter of Karas Greystorm, she died in childhood of the blood plague

Sigurd Albriktson – jarl of Norlhast Keep

Kalfr Albriktson – younger brother of Sigurd and warrior of

the Norlhast Clan

Luta Kalfrswyfe – the wife of Kalfr Albriktson

>**Thyra** – Kalfr's eldest daughter

>**Tassi** – Kalfr's eldest son

>**Gilla** – Kalfr's youngest daughter

>**Varinn** – Kalfr's youngest son

The Coven – **Nereth**, **Lysa** and **Shula**, a trio of witches who have attended to Karas Greystorm since the death of his second wife, Thora

Albrikt the Wise – chief counsellor to Karas Greystorm until his place was taken by the coven. Father of Sigurd and Kalfr

Ottama – Sigurd's servant girl

Styrman – a servant at Norlhast Keep

Vrand – a warrior of the Norlhast Clan

Brosa – a warrior of the Norlhast Clan

[Bekan Bekansson] – the previous Norlhast clan chief, who was killed in single combat by Karas Greystorm

[Norl] – founder of the Norlhast Clan

The Helsburg Clan

Bothvatr Dalkrson – chief of the Helsburg Clan

The Vittag Clan

Ingioy the White Widow – chief of the Vittag Clan

Valka – daughter of Ingioy and one of her jarls

The Riltbalt Clan

Gunnsteinn Haddison – chief of the Riltbalt Clan

The Kingdom of Mirtan

Serena – Grand Mage of the Three Chapters and ruler of the neighbouring Kingdom of Mirtan

The Gods

The Creator – the god who, through his servants the avatars, created the world of Amuran

The Avatars

Altandu – avatar of light

Bruar – avatar of fire

Ceren – avatar of darkness

Culdaff – avatar of the air and winds

Dinas – avatar of time

Dinuvillan – avatar of good fortune

Garradon – avatar of defensive battle, the general of Vellandir's forces opposed to Morvanos

Ilanasa – avatar of healing

Lamornna – avatar of nature and creation

Meras – avatar of love

Morvanos – avatar of chaos, leader of the rebellion that began the War of the Avatars that led to the Fallen Age

Myshall – avatar of misfortune

Nanquido – avatar of the waters and the seas

Navan – avatar who guards the Halls of the Dead in the afterlife

Rannoch – avatar of the earth

Rathlin – avatar of death

Vellandir – avatar of law and justice, leader of the avatars who opposed Morvanos

ACKNOWLEDGEMENTS

Hall of Bones is a much better book thanks to my wife, Liz, eldest daughter, Emma, Laurence Keighley and Michael Gillett, who all generously gave up their time to read early drafts of the manuscript. Thank you all for your helpful advice and encouragement along the way, which provided the motivation for me to finish this novel.

I'd also like to thank my agent, John Jarrold, for his support and guidance. John's editorial input was incredibly helpful in honing my voice as an author and developing my craft and style. Hall of Bones was the novel I submitted to John that resulted in me becoming one of his clients. I've thoroughly enjoyed our creative working relationship and look forward to seeing where this will take us on future projects.

US artist Anne Hudson did a great job with the artwork for the book, combining this with Viking imagery from Ukrainian artist Arkadiy Ivanchenko. Anne's created a really striking cover that ties in perfectly with the story.

Finally, thank you to my readers. An author's biggest battle is making people aware their books exist in a crowded market, so if you have time to leave a review on Amazon or Goodreads that would be fantastic. They really do make a world of difference. You can also sign up for my newsletter via my website for writing updates and to get your hands on exclusive free short stories.

Twitter – @TimHardieAuthor

Facebook – Tim.Hardie.Author.Public
Website – www.timhardieauthor.co.uk

Made in the USA
Coppell, TX
20 November 2022

86737866R00246